THE
GLORY BOYS

The Glory Boys

Gerald Seymour

COLLINS
St James's Place, London

William Collins Sons & Co Ltd
London · Glasgow · Sydney · Auckland
Toronto · Johannesburg

First published 1976
© Gerald Seymour 1976

ISBN 0 00 222399/6

Set in Monotype Times
Made and Printed in Great Britain by
William Collins Sons & Co Ltd Glasgow

to Rosalind Wade

1

There was quiet in the car now, attention riveted on the twin headlights far behind in the darkness. The man in the back seat had swivelled round, wiped the condensation from the back window, and peered hard into the void of the retreating road. The passenger in the front had also twisted round in an attempt to follow the passage of the lights, while the driver scanned the tilted mirror to his front. The road was not straight, and on the sharp curves where the high hedges came close to the tarmac they would lose the lights, and then find them again as the course of their route levelled out.

For the three men the tension had begun some fifteen kilometres back. The driver had been the first to speak, but that was long after his companions had noted his continual and hurried glances up at his mirror. He had spoken in the slow, high-pitched dialect of the pure Palestinian Arab.

'It's been with us a long time, the car behind. I've surged three times, pushed the speed up seven or eight ks an hour. It doesn't affect him – he's just maintaining the same distance. By the big farm, near the wood, you remember, I slowed then. Right down, cut back by about twenty. He didn't close up.'

That was when they had started to take notice. Picked up the two powerful beams away in the distance, begun to sweat a little, allowed the nervous silence to take over.

The front passenger pulled the glove hatch open and rummaged for the plastic envelope containing the maps that had been supplied with the car. He felt in his pocket for his cigarette lighter, and then with the maps and the small flame he bent double, the papers down on the floor and the light shielded by his body. He ran quickly through the pages that showed in detailed and intricate pattern the road system of northern France. He hesitated on one of the maps, his finger tracing a line with difficulty in the flickering, shaking light.

'We're just past Béthune – that was the last town. Another two or three kilometres there's a turn-off to the left. Runs through some villages. Auchy . . . Estrées. It's difficult to see like this. It looks as though the road winds round the villages, a by-pass. It's a broken line on the map, not for lorries. We can get through that way, and still be in good time for the boat. We have the time?'

'There's time enough.' The man in the back spoke, his words carrying away from the other two as he continued to search the road behind. 'He's still there. I lost him a moment, but he's there again.'

The road was straight now. Clear and fast, high trees on either side, the headlamps swinging past the tall trunks and melting away into the night across the fields. There was an occasional lighted cottage or farmhouse, but that was all. Three in the morning, and with the soulless cold of the early hours settled deep on the countryside. The men in the car shivered, the fear they felt accentuating the chill. From the back came the request for the heater to go on, declined by the driver.

'We've just cleared the mist on the windows. I don't want it again. I want to be able to see from all the windows. I want to be able to see all the way round.'

As if to emphasize the point he wound down the window on his door, letting the bitter night air flood into the saloon. There was a howled protest as the wind and draught cut in from the space above the glass.

'Don't worry,' shouted the driver, lifting his voice above the noise. 'The turn-off is very soon now. He'll be gone then. Look for the signs and remember the names of those villages.' Optimism, the way they all wanted it.

The man beside him said, 'Auchy and Estrées, those are the two we want.'

They came too fast to the junction, and the driver had to break hard to avoid overshooting the narrow road that curved away to the right. The car protested fiercely as it was swung round, tyres indenting the gravel chips. The man in the back was flung across the wide seat. To steady himself he clung to the heavy grip-bag that shared the seat with him. When he looked again the twin lights had disappeared.

It was a winding, delaying road now. An uneven surface, pocked by the use of tractors and heavy farm machinery. Hay from the fields showed up high in the overhanging trees where it

8

had been whisked from the carts by the branches. The speed came down. The driver still returned to his mirror, but saw only darkness.

'We'll not know for a bit yet. The curves are too quick . . . he'd have to be right up our bottoms for us to know he was there. Right up.'

He laughed, and the others joined him. Too loud to maintain the pretence that they were still calm: the apprehension came through with the successive giggles. It had been a long drive, three days of it already gone, across hundreds of kilometres of Italian and French roads. So little distance left. Less than two hours to the ferry port, far less. And now the first crisis, the initial moment of the unexpected.

The minutes went by as the driver carefully threaded his way along the centre of the road. The man in the back allowed his eyes to wander, the compulsion of his vigil at the rear window waning.

'Can we have the window closed now? I'm frozen here. All right for you bastards, but here I'll die of cold.'

'Just a few more minutes. Till we're sure we will keep the air coming in and the windows clear. You should not feel it that hard. You said you spent your winters in the Jordan mountains, you will have known the cold then, the snow on the hills – '

'Not the Jordan mountains, the mountains of Palestine.'

The laughter spread through the car. The driver turned behind him, his face huge with the smile.

'Accepted. There was no snow, no mountains for it to fall upon in Haifa. Palestine Haifa. No cold there.'

'What can you know of Haifa? Too long ago when you left for you to have memories there.'

The driver said, 'No, I have a slight memory of it. I was four years when we left. There is a memory, though it is faint. One does not know how much is memory and how much is the image of what one has been told in the camps of the former life.'

'I have been to Haifa,' the front passenger interrupted. 'I went by lorry to work there on a site, a building project. They took us daily from Jenin. It must have been beautiful once. They were spreading concrete over the earth when we came. It was stop-gap work before I went to Beirut to study, just to fill in the time while I waited.'

They drove down a gentle incline into a tight-knit, snug village.

9

Big church, civic building, market across to the right, and a ribbon of houses. Few lights. A grey, hostile, closed hedgehog community, battened down for the night to repel strangers, no movement except for the long-legged dog that scurried from their path. They laughed again as they saw the animal race away into the shadows. This was a private place, offering no refuge to visitors. The road ran straight through, without hesitation. There was a bridge and then they were past the village and climbing again.

The driver was still smiling as he looked again into his mirror. Two bright circles of light, perfectly and symmetrically framed in the chrome fitting. He stared hard, watching their progress down the same hill they had travelled over on their way into the village. He said nothing, but flicked his head between the view in front and the mirror. The man in the back saw his movements and swung round heavily in his seat.

'It's still there,' he said. 'The bastard is still with us. Coming into the village now, perhaps three, four hundred metres behind us. Go faster, while he's dawdling through the village, get some distance between us.'

The car surged forward, the power of its engine pulling it over the road surface. There was no consideration now for the ruts and holes. The chassis jolted and bounced as the wheels undulated on the uneven tarmac, lurching where the deeper pits had been half-filled with stones. The driver was totally concentrating now, his hands far up on the wheel, feet alternating between brake and accelerator, body deep into the well of the seat. The new speed communicated his anxiety to his passengers.

'Get me a route mapped out,' he snapped, eyes not diverted from the front. 'We don't want to find ourselves boxed in in some miserable farmyard. I want all the options, and good notice before the turnings.'

The front passenger had the maps on the floor again, and was struggling with the lighter.

'I can't do it, not with the wind, and not with the banging. I can't see a thing, the scale is too small.'

'You can have the window up, but I can't slow it, not now. What's at the back?' He yelled the last question over his shoulder.

'He's there still. The lights were gone for a moment just as he was coming out of the village, but they're back again. You can see them yourself, now we're on the ridge and in the open.

Staying with us. As we've speeded so have they. Who do you think they could be? What bastards are they?'

Questioning, lack of decision.

That angered the driver. 'Don't waste yourself worrying over that sort of nonsense. Makes no difference who the bastards are. What matters now is that we know what road we are on and where it goes to. Shut up about everything else.'

Tortuously the man with the maps traced out a path. He had folded the sheets so that only that part of the region they traversed was visible. It made a small square. His eyes were very close to the paper, but it was some time before the flame of the lighter, stronger now the window had been wound up, permitted him to find the route they were taking. Every movement of the car jolted his finger from the lines he was tracing out for them. He was aware of the frustration building up inside the car as his colleagues waited for his information, but it was a network of country lanes and minor roads that they were asking him to ferret through. He took his time. Perhaps no opportunity to rectify a mistake: one alone would be disastrous. Let them wait till he was ready, and certain. When at last he was satisfied he drew an envelope from an inner pocket of his anorak coat and began to write. He had trouble with the spelling of the villages, the printing was so miniature, and several times he was obliged to look again and work slowly through the longer words. He flicked the lighter closed.

'It will be the last time we can manage it for such a long time. The flame has little more power. We are well, I think. We are on the road to Fauquembergues. First we must pass through Estrées, but it looks to be the same road. At Fauquembergues there are three roads that divide just beyond the village. We take the most northerly, the one to the right. After that, on to Liane and so to Samer. Boulogne must be signed there.'

'How far to Estrées?' said the driver.

'Two, three kilometres, perhaps. We go straight through. Then Fauquem . . .' His voice tailed away as once again he sought to read his scribblings in the half light of the dashboard illumination.

'You're sure, now? No doubts about the route?'

'None at all,' the passenger snapped back.

He felt irritated. We hardly know each other, he thought, we've been together for days now but have no personal contact. Had never met before the planning of the mission. Had only talked in the most general and superficial way; that was as it was intended. Each one dependent on the other, needing to trust totally in the skill and resolution of his colleagues, but without the deep-rooted certainty that comes from long-standing knowledge and companionship.

The driver swerved on a bend, nearly taking them off the made-up surface and on to the raised and heavily grassed verge. Preoccupation and anxiety bent him away from his principal role of driving the motor. Friction would follow, increased by the man who sat beside the driver, quiet and resentful at the lack of faith shown in him. In the back the third man gazed out through his window at the lights, held as if by elastic at the same unincreasing, undiminishing distance.

It was standard in these operations, the three men knew, that the attack team would come together only at the final stage, that they would have been drawn from different camps and different backgrounds. They were briefed to keep clear of questioning their comrades on personal histories. From involvement follows breakdown and collapse under interrogation. Know the code-name only, what more do you need to know? they had said. But without an understanding of each other the strains in adversity were that much greater, fuelling the apprehension inside the car.

The driver stamped his foot on the brake. On the speedometer the needle sagged back from beyond a hundred kilometres to below forty. Both his passengers hung on to their seats.

Straddled across the road was the solid, unyielding mass of a Friesian herd. Perhaps on their way to milking, perhaps being transferred from one field to another farther away, perhaps being collected for market, perhaps . . .

'Murdering hell, what in the whore's mother's name do we do with this?'

'Blast the horn. Get the old fool in the front to shift them.'

'The car behind, it's closing quickly.'

'Use the grass at the side of the road.'

'The bloody peasant with them, at the front . . .'

'Get on the grass, that's the only way round.'

'The car behind us, it's less than one hundred and fifty metres. It's slowing but still closing on us.'

Inside the car there was a babble of shouting. To the front the herd seemed unmoved. Sad and heavy eyes looked at the car,

12

then back to the black and white dog that snapped and yelped at the cows' hooves.

'Shut up! Shut up! Stop goddam-well talking,' yelled the driver.

He wrenched the car across on to the grass. Momentarily the wheels began to spin, then bit into the soft ground.

'Take it easily, slowly, or we'll be stuck.' More instructions for the driver. But he alone of the three was remaining cool, closing his mind to the shouting.

The car moved on, bumping over the loose earth that had been excavated from the ditch that ran beyond the grass and short of the field's hedge. The bumper nudged aside a cow, sending it butting its way amongst the safety of its fellow creatures. Huge, dark figures, snorting and scraping their bodies against the paintwork of the vehicle. Their smell crept into the sealed saloon, drawing twisted grimaces from the men inside.

'He's right on us. Not sixty metres away . . .' The shout from the back was cut off as the glare of the pursuing headlights illuminated the interior of the car. The passengers ducked down, only the driver remaining upright.

'All right. All right. We're nearly out now. He has to come through this crowd too.' Before he was clear of the herd he was changing up, running through the gears, weaving to avoid the leading animals before bursting back on to the open road. He caught only the briefest sight of the farmer, walking proud and straight at the head of his herd.

The car rushed forward. Ahead the road stretched into the emptiness beyond the reach of their lights. It was then the three men heard, all together, the first blast on the siren as the vehicle behind them attempted to untangle itself from the shuffling barricade. The piercing, sing-song wail of the amplified call drove through the windows and doors and roof of the car, filling it with noise, and they could see flashing among the confusion of the cows' backs and heads was the blue, rotating police lamp.

The man in the back pulled the grip towards him, slid back the fastener and plunged his hand in among the shirts and socks and underpants and books, before he fastened on the hardness of the Luger pistol. Some of the grip's contents spilled out on to the leather seat-work, snagging on the raised foresight of the gun as he pulled it from the case. The magazine was in position.

'There's your answer,' he said quietly. 'Now we know who we have running with us.'

There was no reply from the front. He cocked the gun.

From his office in police headquarters in St Omer, twenty-five kilometres to the north, the man who had been issuing orders for the last hour could plot exactly the position of the fleeing car. His size, not grotesque but huge, belied the efficiency of his work. The big wall map where an aide continually moved coloured pins demonstrated this. The position of the car, kept up-to-date by the constant radio calls from the pursuing police vehicle, was shown by a yellow marker; his own men, barely separated, by a red one. Stretched out ahead of the path of the three Arabs was a near-continuous line of blue pins, straddling the minor and principal roads that led to the coast and to the port of Boulogne.

He had not expected the car to turn off from the main coast road across which his major force was concentrated, but as a precaution he had placed single police cars, each manned by two officers, on all parallel B routes. It had been his intention that the car that held his interest would be unaware that it was under surveillance before it was stopped by any one of the sixteen blocks now in place. The use of the pursuit car's siren and lamp had changed that.

It had been a brutal day's work since the teletype message bearing the instructions from Paris had forewarned him of the need to set a major operation in readiness. By late afternoon, at a time when he would normally have been thinking of home and his supper, the fleet of black Citroëns had started to arrive in the discreet yard at the back of his headquarters. He had shaken several hands. Men from the Ministry, from the security services. There had been one who wore no tie, was dressed in creased jacket and slacks, and to whom everything was relayed. That one spoke his French adequately, but was not fluent, had a Central European accent and dangled a silver, six-pointed Star of David round his neck. He was treated with something close to deference.

The local man had been told little, informed of only a part of the background to the event, but had established, and forcibly, that if a car was negotiating his personal territory then it was preferable to have his own men on its tail.

'These lanes will swallow you up,' he'd said with the certainty of intimate knowledge. 'If you have no local experience, you will lose them, easy as a flea in a rug.'

The point had been accepted. One of the canniest of his drivers had taken over from the security services' surveillance that had shadowed the car across two-thirds of French territory. It had been going well, earning congratulations from the big men of the Paris counter-espionage division, until the angry and staccato bursts over the radio had warned of the intervention of the cows. But little, he had reflected, was lost. The men he hunted were still being shepherded into the fine mesh net that he had laid for them.

'When will they reach the blocking point, on their present route?' He spoke to his aide.

'Four to five minutes, Sir. Not longer. Just the far side of Fauquembergues, at the cross-roads. Where the petrol station and the café are.'

'Two men?'

'Two, Sir. Roben and Miniux. We're in touch with them. They are alerted and have been told they have only to hold the *fedayeen* a few minutes. The larger force is already heading toward the point.'

'Tell them to go carefully,' he said, adding as an aside – because he too was now consumed with concern – 'it was not intended only two should make the interception.'

It was the driver who spotted the red light in the centre of the road.

It was being waved slowly up and down, the international sign to halt. As he closed the distance the gendarme's fluorescent arm-band gleamed back at him above the brightness of the torch. He shouted to the others.

'There in the front. A police check. They're waving us down.'

It was the moment for one of the three to take control. The man in the back was the first to react, perhaps because it was he who clasped the only firearm in the car. Someone had to lead. There had been too much indecision in the previous few minutes, too many voices raised, his own among them. He leaned forward, head and shoulders pressing over the top of the front seat. His voice was shrill, but clear and commanding.

'Burst right past him. Don't hesitate, don't slow at all. Go to his left and speed faster as we go by. He'll be armed, so keep your bodies low as you can ... right down. Don't hesitate ... and when you get very close, put down the front lights, then on again.'

15

The car hurtled toward the lone policeman, bearing down on him at some twenty-seven metres a second. The driver could see the whiteness of his face above the dark of the uniform and rain cape, could see the shape of the torch, beam now agitated, and the movement of the illuminated arm wrestling with the webbing strap across the right shoulder. The driver could see the fear fill his face, the eyes grow large. His feet were rooted to the ground, rabbit-like, transfixed.

'Kill the lights!'

The command was barked from the back of the car, and the driver instinctively carried out the instruction. Too much initiative had been heaped on his shoulders before; now he was just able to obey, to react. Fifty metres in front of him the policeman disappeared into the blackness. Almost immediately came the next order.

'On again, the lights.'

The driver shrieked with horror. Ten paces beyond the front of the car was the policeman, directly in their path, his submachine-gun close to his right hip, pointed directly at the windscreen. He never fired.

The radiator of the car smashed into his upper thighs. His body jack-knifed into the air. The car recoiled from the impact, then shuddered again as the policeman clipped the roof before spiralling over the top of the car. The driver swerved across to the right, late and with effort, just avoiding the blue patrol car parked at an angle and filling half the road. The man beside him felt the nausea rising deep in his intestines and into the constricted pipe of his throat. The third man had closed his eyes just before the fragile, toy-like figure was brushed aside, trying to shut out the vision of the gaping, incredulous mouth of the policeman.

As Roben hit the road surface, shattering his vertebrae, and destroying what faint source of life was left to him, Miniux opened fire.

From the car they never saw the policeman who crouched back from the road and close to the ditch. At his shoulder was the steel framed butt of the squat MAT 49. There were thirty-two nine-millimetre rounds in the magazine, and he fired them all at the car, moving his finger from the trigger only when the hammering kick of the weapon subsided. The bullets ploughed their way first into the engine of the car, then worked their pattern back toward the interior. The first to die was the front passenger, four shells hitting him in the chest. The driver too was struck, feeling the pain spreading from his left arm and then into the torn wounds in his side. But the man behind, protected by the body-work and the seats of the car, survived the low velocity spray.

The car veered first to the left, then wove a way down the centre of the road as the driver fought to maintain a direction against the contradictions of the damaged steering system. His head went down once, but he jerked it upward, taking in again the contours of road, hedges and fields. A few more metres, perhaps, but not a journey. He was incapable of that, he knew. Strong enough only to get clear of the awfulness of the noise of the bullets, and the smell that they brought, and the terror that followed the collapse of the windscreen and the side windows.

He managed another three hundred metres down the road, then with great effort dragged his foot across to the brake. It took so much force to bring the car to a stop. Vermilion blood, his own blood, billowed and spilled across his knees, and ran to a pool on the rubber mat under his feet. That was death, he could recognize that. There was no way to staunch that life-flow. He looked at it, abstracted, the desire to rest supreme. The rear door opened and he saw a face at his window and then his own door gaping open. He felt himself sliding out, the rough earth coming to meet him. A hand arrested his fall and held him upright. A voice – familiar, but he could not put a name to it – was close to his ear.

'Dani, Dani, can you hear me? We have to run from here. Bouchi is dead, he has to be – he's so still. The siren is closing. But I can help you . . .'

The driver shook his head, very slowly, very deliberately.

'You go alone.' He paused, seeming to suck in air that his carved lungs could not accept. 'For Palestine, for a free Palestine. You'll remember that when you meet with him. Remember Palestine, and remember me, when you meet with the Mushroom Man.'

His eyes blinked. There was not enough strength to laugh any more, just enough to move the delicate, soft, brown eyelids, and he died.

The sirens came no closer. Must have stopped at the block, the survivor thought, as he reached inside the back of the car and pulled clear the grip. The Luger was now in his pocket. He ran to the back of the car, unscrewed the petrol tank guard, and thrust his hand into his trousers for a packet of cigarettes. He crumpled the carton, enough for it to fit comfortably into the petrol aperture. With his matches he lit the thickened paper, dropped it into the hole, and sprinted for the comfort of the darkness. He heard the explosion behind him, but didn't turn.

An official black car brought the Israeli secret service officer to the cross-roads. Roben still lay in the road, a policeman's coat draped over his face, and the car skirted him at crawling pace. Further up was the parked patrol car with a knot of uniformed men round it. They were feeding Miniux with brandy from a flask. A long way beyond that, difficult to see clearly, was the smoking skeleton of the burned-out vehicle.

'How many have we found here . . . of them?' The Israeli pointed down the road.

'We found the two men. They are still inside – unrecognizable, of course. There will be problems of identification. The car reached that far, the policeman who fired on it says after it stopped it caught fire. That could be expected: it took many bullets.'

The Israeli looked back at the detective who had spoken, then stared out into the short horizon that would soon be broken in the first pencil-line of dawn. He said, 'It's very strange. Just two of them. The information that we gave in Paris was that there were three travelling. Perhaps we have lost one. Mislaid him somewhere on the way.'

The young Arab's sole preoccupation was to put distance between himself and his pursuers. He had sprinted the first few hundred metres till the sodden fields and the churned mud of the farm animals had taken their toll of his strength. His feet sunk into the softened ground, causing him to heave and pull to withdraw them. Soon he had switched to a more gentle trot – not to safeguard his strength, but simply because he was not capable of

18

faster movement. He punched his way through thick hedges, tore his coat on a strand of wire, fell once when trying to keep up his momentum and clear a dried-out ditch. But all the time he kept on his way.

He reasoned that if he were fortunate there would be no search in daylight, and that the gendarmes would be satisfied with the debris of the car. They would poke about among the charred bodies, and find little justification in launching a manhunt for him. That was if he was lucky. If they were coming after him now it meant that the following car had spotted the three of them when the lights swept the inside the second before they ducked down to avoid the brightness and the recognition.

Or the one who had fired from the side of the road, the one they had never seen, what if he had seen them in silhouette as they sped past him? If he had counted three, then they would now be massing with their dogs, and their cordons, and their large scale maps. The bag that dragged him down with its weight – that would be his salvation. Here was the vital change of clothes, the travel documents, the mould back into society when he arrived at the ferry port.

Once, when he slipped past a darkened farmhouse, old, rectangular, and alien, there was barking, but otherwise his journey was a silent one. There would be no help for him in this wet and clammy countryside. He must keep going, however much the pain in his stomach, from the violent exertion without food, slowed him down. It would be difficult to move once the sun rose away behind him – where the car was, where Bouchi and Dani lay – but till then he must continue to run.

This was what the training had all been for. This was why they had urged and pummelled the recruits up the soft shale hills of Fatahland, why they had screamed and kicked them to the point beyond exhaustion, toed them into activity when they collapsed, and then, when they could move no more, left them to find their own slow path back to the tented camps. And the next morning it had been the same, and the next . . . and the next . . . They had gone on driving the young men till their stomach sinews had hardened, their lungs were cavernous, and their thigh muscles rippled and rolled in use. After that, and only then, they taught them weapon drills, the craft of being in open country. Then had come the sophistications of disguise and concealment.

When he had first arrived at his camp, he had been a raw,

attractive and intelligent young man, but they had spotted the bitterness, and turned his hatred of Israel into an obsession. It had not taken them long: seven weeks of the intensive course had been enough. The product was then ready for use. The determination sharpened, the viciousness honed: the mark of the killer. That was the role they had fashioned for Abdel-El-Famy. They were pleased with what they saw, and confident of success when they gave him his orders.

The man who now struggled and heaved his way over the fields of northern France, hugging the hedgerows for protection from the eyes of the country people who would soon be rising from their beds, was a very small pawn in the complex power-game of the Middle East. Individually he was insignificant, unexceptional. Under his given name he featured on none of the tens of thousands of personal files maintained by the Israeli and Western European intelligence services.

Back in Nablus, the sprawling valley town on the Israeli-occupied West Bank of the Jordan river, he had flung stones at the Israeli soldiers who every afternoon a little before one o'clock massed close to the school gates. There was nothing particular about that. All the High School children did it, all were at some stage caught in the pincer nets of sprinting Jewish soldiers, thwacked on the head and shoulders by the billy sticks, and taken off in lorries to the barbed-wire compound and left to cool their heels for a few hours. He'd been through the process, known that when the officer and the 'political adviser' came to interview them it was not the time for insolence. He'd bided his silence then, and been sent home – with an army boot in the seat of his jeans to help him on his way. Nobody filled in papers about boys like that; it would have tied up the bureaucracy for a lifetime.

But the regular afternoon rock-throwing, and the sprint back to the safety of the labyrinth of alleys and deep shops in the casbah, affected young people in a different way. Some grew beyond it, learned to control their dislike of the occupying force, and as age and responsibilities increased were able to co-exist with the new order. A few, a very few, were left scarred by the experience. Abdel-El-Famy was one of those, and tilted, half-consciously, away from passive acceptance. At eighteen he had left Nablus, had taken the bus that wound into the Jordan valley and crawled for fourteen hours across the Jordanian and Syrian plains before dropping down through the winding Lebanese hills to Beirut. There were always places in the Palestinian-orientated universities for those from the Occupied West Bank. Those who had lived under Israeli rule, and rejected it to come out, were traditionally lionized. He enrolled for a course in English studies, was a good student, but throughout was brushing against a quite new science, one that away in Nablus the military governor had effectively stamped out: the science of revolutionary politics.

Through the long, hot afternoons after classes, the students sat at the café on the Corniche disputing the road to the recovery of Palestine. Choking them from the exhausts were the huge Fords and Cadillacs that paraded the tourists and visitors through the city. A few hundred yards down the road was the looming bulk of the United States of America's Embassy complex, complete with heavily-armed personnel carriers manned by Lebanese troops. The open jeeps of the Squad 16 militia, with their angled, crimson berets and toy-like Armalite rifles, would cruise past the young people, eyeing them, letting them have no doubt that they were in a foreign country, without rights and without privileges. They were strangers; tolerated, but not welcomed. They could only afford the thin, upright bottles of Pepsi-Cola, which they had to drink with patience and restraint to make last. And while they sat and watched the affluence and arrogance of another country, they argued and bickered over the way to regain their own State. In the old days it had been clear that the answer lay in violence, and they had clubbed together their piastres to buy the papers – Arabic, French language and in English – that carried the long and detailed reports of the activities of Black September and the Popular Front for the Liberation of Palestine. Two bottles had lasted all day in the roadside café where they had settled with their papers and a transistor radio to hear the news of the assault on the Olympic Village in Germany. Fifth September, 1972: it had been a drawn-out and heroic day. They had worshipped the *fedayeen* who died on the airport apron at Furstenfeldbruck, reviled what they called the 'treachery' of the German police in ambushing them, rejoiced at the death of eleven Israeli sportsmen.

But out of the violence of Munich was born a respectability for the Palestinian cause; and the leaders, so the young people in the cafés said, were beginning to anticipate the leathered seats around the conference tables, the scent of the huge black official cars that would carry them there, were wanting to finger the

21

gold-cased pens that signed and initialled treaties. The arguments in the bright heat, with the sea shimmering up to the beach front, became more bitter, more divided. There were some who said any Palestinian State was better than nothing, however small, however much an exercise in diplomatic geometry, wherever the lines were drawn. There were others who saw only the complete return of their former lands as being sufficient, the argument of no compromise. This was the view of Abdel-El-Famy. He understood that the table-based arguments would only sap his resolve and desire for revenge. His presence at the cafés became less and less frequent, as he sought out the men untainted by weakness who were prepared to fight on regardless of any moves by the leadership of the Palestinian refugee community towards a half-peace.

He joined the Popular Front for the Liberation of Palestine General Command, a small but deadly organ in the so-called 'Rejection Front'. He became one of fifty-five young men, aged between seventeen and twenty-five, who had taken a solemn oath of initiation, who knew they would be sent on missions with little prospect of return or survival. It was as he had wanted it.

Just eight days ago he had been called forward from morning parade and instructed to present himself at the tent of the General Command's leader. There were three others inside when he opened the flap door, their faces all in shadow from the diffused light that passed through the grey canvas roofing. Apart from the man who directed the General Command's operations, the only figures he knew were those of 'Bouchi' and 'Dani' – new arrivals, placed with different training sections, and therefore virtual strangers. They were told they would be travelling to London, that their mission was regarded as of the utmost importance to the whole Arab movement. They were given a code-name, and an operational plan to work to, and a target to seek out. Abdel-El-Famy was no longer a penniless refugee, from a bare bungalow in the hill above the market place of Nablus. His existence had taken on a new purpose, and, like a stoat hungry for rabbit's blood, he was not to be easily deflected. His threat to the uneasy peace of the Middle East was enormous, and if he succeeded the reverberations of his action would be felt by millions throughout the Western world.

*

22

Famy lay high up among the bales in the roof of the barn. It was past eight, and he had been resting there for more than twenty minutes, yet still the breath came hard for him, and the sweat rolled in great rivers from the shiny, dank hair down across his face and on to his shoulders. He had stripped off his clothes, except his yellow underpants, and lay prone on the hard, irritating surface of the packed straw. He estimated he had travelled twenty-five kilometres. Four hours. One more such effort and he would be in Boulogne and ready for the ferry. He had decided it was better to arrive a day late in England by roughing it across country to the ferry port rather than risking all in the hope of finding a bus and a lift on the roads in the immediate aftermath of the interception. He would stay in the barn all day, emerging only as darkness fell again over the fields.

He heard children playing far away, high-pitched voices carrying to him, and when he moved to peer through a hole in the wooden planking he saw them, bright in their school clothes, and with their satchels on their backs, skipping and playing as they went away up the road. Harmless and unseeing, they offered no threat. And he began to rest, body splayed out on the bales. Once he was aroused from his sleep by a dog's sharp bark, and from the same vantage-point he watched the progress of a farmer across his land, with the dog far in front trailing a scent. Otherwise there was nothing to disturb the tranquillity he needed. In his sleep he was far away; in the hills above the town where he had been born, playing on the slopes and rolling stones down at the imperturbable goats, playing at football in the dusty school yard, working beside his father on Saturdays in their ramshackle garage.

Perhaps it was the evening coming on, as the sun dipped, and the warmth fled from the ageing timbers of his refuge, but his dream switched abruptly in mood from the happiness of his childhood to the day just after his fourteenth birthday when the big tanks had rumbled their way into the square at Nablus. He recalled the echoing machine-gun and rifle fire, the wail of the Red Crescent ambulances, and the fear on the faces that huddled in steel-shuttered doorways. It was the first time in his life he had seen terror on grown men's faces. He would not forget it. He was not asleep much longer, waking quickly but then finding himself confused and needing a minute to work out his situation, where he was, and why.

23

It was dark in the barn when he set off. It was difficult to walk at first, as the stiffness and damp of the previous night seemed to have locked the suppleness of his knees. It would be a hard trek again, but by dawn if he pushed himself once more he should be near to the boat, ready to dispose of the muddied, drenched clothes and to substitute the precious, clean garments he carried in his grip. With laundered clothes he could assume his final identity, and take on the name of Saleh Mohammed, Algerian passport Number 478625, born 22 August 1953 at Oran.

There is a restaurant, specializing in fish delicacies, that overlooks the sea at Sidon. It is roughly half-way between Beirut and the nest of tents far to the south where the General Command maintained its headquarters. Before the Palestinians took their war into Israel, and before the retaliatory air strikes and commando raids that inevitably followed, this was a place in which tourists delighted. But the package holiday-makers, the tour operators discovered, were not seeking any great excitement when they paid out their dollars and francs and marks. They were prepared to give the possible excitement of the war zone a very wide miss. Flights of Israeli Phantoms this far north were rare, but the sight-seers needed more convincing.

So the restaurant is near-deserted, and the square Crusader castle that stands just to the front of the white tablecloths no longer suffers the armies of stilletos and sandals. Out on the terrace is as comfortable and as discreet a place to discuss matters greatly confidential as any in the town.

The leader of the General Command seldom came to Beirut. His independent stand had won him many enemies inside the overall Palestinian movement, and his presence in the Lebanese capital would make him vulnerable to the attentions of the Israeli agents who at a few hours' notice could call in their country's assassination squads from the sea. He was high on their death list, perhaps given the ranking of Number Three after George Habash and Abou Iyyad. He had received a phone call on a secret unlisted number in the little village close to his tent camp in mid-morning urging him to make the rendezvous. The message was from a journalist who sympathized with the politics of the General Command and who was on the staff of one of Beirut's biggest dailies with its offices and printing works on the chic,

24

well-heeled Rue Hamra in the heart of the most fashionable part of the Lebanese capital.

As he picked the flesh from a small, bone-packed mullet the journalist passed to the intense-eyed man opposite him a piece of news-agency copy ripped from the teleprinter in his office that carried exclusively the reports of the Agence France Presse. He was aware of basic details in the organization's operations, and had realized the significance of the eight-line story. It was the first news the General Command had had of the progress of their unit since it had flown from Beirut to Athens, and they had started their overland journey to London.

'They are reliable, this Agency?' asked the General Command Leader, through a mouthful of fish.

'One has to believe them. They are taking just the main points from all French sources, but most of this story is taken direct from the Sureté statement. There would be little room for error. But the other agencies, Associated Press and UPI, are carrying much the same. In less detail it was carried on the Overseas Service of the BBC as well. The facts are not in dispute.'

'It speaks of road blocks. Road blocks stopping them. Of the car being machine gunned. Now at that time in the morning why are there road blocks, why have countryside police been issued with weapons of the size of sub-machine-guns? There is only one interpretation, I think you will agree. There is only one explanation for such precautions to be taken in circumstances such as these.'

The journalist nodded, and sipped at the water in the narrow-stemmed glass in front of him. He said quietly: 'It has to be the Israeli service. Our people have been compromised. The French would do nothing on their own. If our people were going right through France they would be allowed to do so. The Israelis have prodded the French, poked them into action. Did they have arms?' It was a bold question for him to ask; normally he would not be privy to such minute mission details.

The leader smiled. 'Not much, perhaps a pistol, not more than one. No grenades, no explosives, no rifles. They are further on down the road: to be collected. But that is not for your paper. Perhaps you could let it be known from "a high source in the men's movement" that they were not armed. But not identify the group. Yes?'

'There is no difficulty in that. "Two unarmed Palestinians gunned down by the French police" – that will make good reading.

25

Perhaps the Paris office of our paper can work up the involvement of the Israeli Secret Service, and the two can be married together.' The journalist began to take a quick note in his pocket-size pad of the form of words he would use.

The two men attacked their meal, pulling with their fingers at the larger bones, spitting out the smaller ones, and dousing their hands in the bowls provided. The terrace was quite empty, other than the two diners at this one table. When he had finished the commando leaned forward. There was no one within yards who could have overheard what he said, but old habits die hard.

'The reports speak of two men being found in the car. There could be no doubt of that one fact?'

'No doubt at all. That is common to all the stories.'

'And if they had captured a prisoner, a third man, would they have released that information?'

'Most likely,' the journalist replied. 'It is not the sort of thing they are going to hold secret. There is no reason for them to.'

Again the smile played around the mouth of the General Command's leader, dallied there a little, and then faded. He was not one given to conventional humour. One would not expect that from the man who was responsible for a morning's carnage at the bright modern Fiumincino Airport of Rome that left thirty-one dead, nor from the man who ordered his subordinates into the northern Israeli settlement of Kiryat Shmona, an operation that filled seventeen coffins. But irony amused him. And it would be ironic if the death of that man's colleagues were to enhance his own safety. It was no part of the journalist's role in the movement that he should be aware of such interests.

The leader said: 'I would be interested to hear if there are any further arrests, or sightings, or . . .' He let it tail away. He had said enough. The journalist waved his arm at a distant figure who hovered at the entrance to the kitchens, gestured a writing motion with his hands to signify that the meal was over and that he wished to accept the bill.

'Before you leave there is a message I want you to deliver. It is sensitive. I want it handed only to the man whose name I shall give you. It is in Beirut, and must reach him this afternoon.' The leader drew a sheaf of papers from inside his khaki combat jacket, revealing for a moment the polished, light-brown shoulder holster he wore through all his waking hours, and with a ball-point pen began to write. Had he looked the waiter who brought the

26

reckoning for the meal could not have seen what was being written, as the leader protected the message with his hands. The pen moved hurriedly and with bold strokes across the paper, the Arabic symbols firm and decisive.

While the bank notes were away being sorted out at the cash till he said: 'It must go straight away to the commercial secretary of the embassy that I have named on the folded paper. I will tell you what it says; you'll want to open it if I don't tell you, and I would rather not have it delivered as if it's been half-way through the *souk* in Baghdad.' He laughed, and the journalist shuffled in embarrassment, and muttered his protestations. 'No, I know you, you are all the same. It merely says that we go on as before, but at reduced strength. There; that tells you all or nothing. For you, my good friend, I think it tells you nothing. Nothing. And you should be happy that way.'

And he was away, striding between the tables inside the restaurant towards the car park where his Fiat waited. Once he raised his right arm above his shoulder, a final farewell to his luncheon informant. One of his bodyguards had stayed at the front door of the building, and he now fell in behind. Two more were sitting in the car. As the leader settled into his seat the driver engaged the gears, and they moved off.

'We have to be patient a while,' he said. 'Two of the men on the European operation have been intercepted. They are dead. There is no word of the third, nor of whether the French even know of his existence. If there were to be one who has survived, and could go on with the task, which one would we select?' He was speaking with the man who sat beside him, an older man whose judgment he trusted.

'Of those three?' the other paused for a moment's reflection. 'It would be the one we code-named "Saleh". Saleh Mohammed. The one that calls himself "Famy".'

'That is a good judgement. Pray to God it is that one who lives. They were all fine boys, but he was the best. The youngest, but still superior. It is a great problem that he faces, the one who has lived, if that is indeed the case.'

His companion stroked the sleek, steel darkness of the barrel of the Klashnikov rifle that lay across his lap, his eyes playing on the cars that flashed by them. The leader was talking softly, half to himself, and there were no interruptions.

'Much will depend on the people that he meets there. These

Irishmen, they represent an unknown factor, and one man on his own must be more dependent on them than we had planned. More is required now than a simple availability of weapons, explosives, transport and a safe house. The foreigners must provide a different dimension. They must become involved.'

He was silent. The other man said: 'Will they provide that?'

'It is imponderable,' said the leader. 'Probably, but I cannot say with certainty. In Tripoli they were friendly enough. They wanted to co-operate then – were anxious to buy weapons. They were making a gesture towards us then. That was the conception of the plan. They have killed many times in their own struggle, but always have been fearful of the scale of mission that we are prepared to stage. Perhaps their cause is only worth fighting for, not worth dying for. There were promises in Tripoli, endless promises. As I have said, we shall have to be patient.'

Again the smile.

After their swim the young man and the girl had taken their towels, draped them on the grass away from the pool and close to the high wooden fence that shut it off from the road and the car park, and sprawled down on them. It was hot that evening in London's south-west suburbs, and facilities were overstretched. But few wanted to be in the shade, far from the water, and so the couple found the privacy they searched for.

Five-and-a-quarter miles down the road were the main runways of Heathrow Airport, and every few seconds the couple's voices would be drowned, losing the competition with the Rolls Royce and Pratt and Whitney engines that surged overhead. But in between the cacophony there was time to talk, not of anything special, nothing heady, just the kind of things that were being endlessly repeated by other couples who shared the grass with them but were out of earshot.

She was seventeen-and-a-half, was called Norah, and punched a cash register in a supermarket from eight-thirty in the morning till five-fifteen in the afternoon. She lived at home, and thought the boy she had met beside the pool the previous evening quite the most interesting she had encountered in her limited experience. She wore last year's bikini, which had been right for Benidorm and the ten days of concentrated Spanish Mediterranean heat but now seemed tight and restricting, as if unable to cope with the developments of the previous twelve months. He seemed to like it, though; his eyes were seldom off it. Most of the time they lay on their backs, stretched out and relaxed, fingers touching, his short-cut nails searching out the lines of her wrist, the crannies between her fingers, the soft sensitive places on the underside of her knuckles. He'd kissed her last night, quietly and gently in the lane behind her house, after the cinema and the ditching of her friend. He'd held her loosely with none of the frantic endeavour she was used to from the series of boy-friends who took her for a coffee and a dance or a film and then believed it their right to maul and explore her afterward as due return for a pound's expenditure.

This one was different. No thigh pressed hard between her legs, no fumbling under her blouse, no hand trying to get inside her jeans. The boy had kissed her, long and easily, seemed to think that was what they both wanted, was right, had told her he'd see her tomorrow, same place. She'd come to the pool, and he'd been there, where he'd said he'd be, looked happy enough to see her again.

She had done most of the talking, last night and again this afternoon. He seemed to want that, didn't interrupt, looked interested. He said very little himself as she chattered about her holidays, her friends, her mother and father, her work, the prices in the shops, the television programmes she saw when she was at home, the films she went to on her nights out. He didn't reciprocate. Last night, in her bed at the back of the semi-detached house a mile-and-a-half away, she'd blamed herself for that. 'Course he didn't say anything, didn't give him much of a chance to get a word in,' she'd said to herself.

Soon the dew would be forming on the grass, and the coolness of the middle evening was beginning to embrace her bared shoulders. She shivered a little, and reached out for the jersey she had brought with her. She'd come equipped this time to be out late in the open air, uncertain what the next few hours would bring, but excited and expectant.

'I'll catch my death, dressed with nothing, like this,' she giggled, and turned toward the boy anticipating he would be smiling back at her. But he was sitting up now, his head arched back, neck taut, long fair hair pressed against his shoulder blades, eyes staring and intent on the huge obliterating frame of the Boeing 747 three thousand feet above them.

'You're late, big bird,' he said soundlessly against the roar of the aircraft. 'Don't be late next week, not for the plucking of the Mushroom Man.'

'What did you say?' she shouted, wriggling closer to him to hear his reply.

'Nothing, nothing. Just that they're flying late tonight.' Her ear was close to his mouth, and he spoke softly with his delicate Irish brogue, flavouring the words.

'What plane is that?' she said watching over his shoulder the vast airborne mass, almost beautiful with its white fuselage and the deep sky-blue livery line running its length, tail erect and crowned with the simple star on the pure background.

'That, my little girl, is a Boeing seven-four-seven, manufactured at Seattle, in the State of Washington, USA. It's valued at a little more than fifteen million pounds, and that one is flying in Israel's colour. El Al, and late again.'

He got up from the grass, and began to pull on his trousers over the dried-out swim suit. Before he draped his shirt over his shoulders she saw again the reddened disfigurement of the healed wound, in diameter little more than a pencil width, low to the left side of his chest. She had asked about it the day before, and been told of a stumble while carrying a pitch fork, on the farm, many years back.

'Are we doing anything tonight?' She mentioned it hesitantly, though she'd already told her mother she'd be out late, at her friend's home.

'I'm sorry,' he said, seeing her face fall open with the disappointment. 'I'm sorry, I really am, but I can't tonight. I have to meet a man . . .'

'About a dog' she said.

'No, it's real. I have to meet a man tonight. It's been planned a long time, and he's coming over from abroad to see me. Really. There's some business I have to do, take a few days. I'll see you then, again. Definitely. Definitely. Come on, I'll walk you down to the bus stop.'

She was near to tears when he left her, waiting for a red double-decker to take her back to an early night at home.

*

For two hours Ciaran McCoy stayed beside the train departure board at Waterloo Station, waiting for the man he was to meet to come forward and introduce himself. He had fulfilled all his instructions. Red tie, light raincoat over his right arm, Avis Rentacar sign displayed in his hand. Endless faces scurried past him, running to catch their trains, running away from them, all anxious not to stay a minute longer in the belly of the great terminus than was necessary. It was futile and frustrating. He'd been buffeted, pushed and shoved by those who saw him as an obstruction in their path, but never noticed, not acknowleged. Close to midnight, he walked across the now near-empty concourse to the battery of telephone booths and dialled the seven-figure number he had been given.

His call was answered by a switchboard deep behind the Edwardian façade that housed a North African embassy in a smart SW7 address overlooking the favoured Rotten Row and the spaces of Hyde Park. McCoy asked for an extension, was surprised when the operator did not demur that there would be no one there at this hour, and was further surprised when the phone was promptly answered. He couldn't remember the word he was supposed to give. Been waiting too long, too wrought up to remember it. Bloody foreign word, and he didn't know what it meant.

'It's McCoy here. Ciaran McCoy. I was told to call this number. Our friend hasn't shown.'

The voice at the other end was calm, reassuring, in perfect English. Unmindful of the lack of the code-word. There had been a delay. The situation was uncertain. The project might be called off, might not. Developments were awaited. He should telephone again tomorrow evening, but not so late. The voice wished him goodnight, and the call was terminated.

Five seconds after McCoy put the receiver back into its rest the tape recorder stopped rolling. It was standard procedure that all calls to that number were automatically monitored; and had been so ever since the extension number was obtained from a second officer of that embassy in exchange for Foreign Office silence about his drinking habits. The diplomat had done well from the bargain; the conservative Moslem government he represented in London would have looked badly upon his behaviour.

31

The tape would be one of scores of conversations recorded that night that would be replayed by short-hand typists working from the basement of a substantial building in Curzon Street, Mayfair, a bare mile from the embassy.

3

David Sokarev always carried the Mauser pistol in the glove compartment of his car. It rested there on top of the maps and the packet of boiled sweets that his wife had bought him as an aid to ending his smoking habit. On top of the gun and hiding it was the rag that he used to clean the overnight moisture from his windscreen. The pistol was loaded, but with the safety catch in force, and was used only twice a year, when he went on the shooting range east of Beersheba. Left to himself he would have placed it in a drawer and forgotten about it, but he had been ordered to possess a gun, and therefore it was easier simply to leave it in the car. If the occasion had arisen when he was obliged to fire in anger he would probably have missed. His chunky, iron-rimmed spectacles were a witness to his poor eyesight. The pistol was never disturbed, rejected like the boiled sweets, but, like them, of insufficient importance to have an issue made of it.

There had been a suggestion that his work made him too sensitive a man to be driving himself to work, and there had been talk that he should have a driver pick him up from his home, take him to the laboratory, and then late in the day bring him back to Beersheba. He had railed at that as preposterous, asked them whether there were so many able-bodied men without proper jobs to do that they could spare one for such sterile activity. He had won his case, and drove himself.

He was a careful and methodical man, and unlike so many of his fellow-countrymen drove slowly and with circumspection. It took him between forty-seven and fifty minutes from the time he left his flat on the third floor of the block till he presented his identity card at the gate at Dimona. Colleagues using the same

32

route would flash past him, hoot their horns and wave cheerfully at old 'Tortoise', as they had nicknamed him. It was a boring ride to have made most days a week, and most weeks a year for the last sixteen years, but his mind was seldom concerned with the other traffic. The problems of plutonium, sub-critical masses, fission, isotope separation, neutrons – they were what enveloped him, as the little car trudged its way back and forth the twenty-four miles across the Negev desert. He would read, too, as he drove, the book propped against the steering wheel. He was able, apparently, to take in the printed word while successfully avoiding the fast-moving hazards which shared his road; but few of his colleagues lightly accepted the offer of a lift.

When he had started to work at Dimona the project had been at the apex of Israel's secret list. He had not been able to tell any family friends where he went each day, nor the nature of his work. The buildings, tucked away among the sandhills and placed well back from the road, were described to the outside world as housing a textile factory, and no one who knew him could comprehend a link between David Sokarev and man-made fibres.

But the Bedouin who used to pass, listlessly urging their camels between the dunes, had taken the news of the cranes and bulldozers and cement-making apparatus across the border to the military governor of the Egyptian town of El Arish. The message had gone to Cairo of huge construction works deep in the Negev desert, of wire fences sprouting up, of armed troops patrolling. The concern in Cairo was passed to the American State Department in Washington. There, too, anxiety was expressed and the foolproof system of international espionage set in motion.

From a United States Air Force base in northern Iran a U2 plane had taken off with orders to fly over Dimona and photograph the new complex. The pilot had violated Israeli air space at an altitude of fractionally more than fifteen miles. At the IAF field which had specific responsibility for Dimona they could only watch the radar blip of the American reconnaissance aircraft and contain the frustration that it was beyond their own operational ceiling. It had been a brilliantly hot October day, back in 1960, when the photographs were taken. Sokarev had been working in his temporary, prefabricated wooden offices, awaiting the fulfilment of the Director's promise that he was high on the list for more suitable and permanent premises. He, like everyone else who pored over charts and diagrams and formulae, was unaware of the pictures being recorded in the upper stratosphere.

After the U2 landed in Turkey the rolls of film were rushed under conditions of great secrecy direct from the cameras in the plane's nose to another aircraft standing ready and fuelled to fly to Washington. They showed the little wooden hut where Sokarev worked – or at least its roof – but there was small interest in that compared with the bulky shape discernable a hundred yards away across the sand and surrounded by the lorries that were needed to bring up the materials. The men expert in interpreting altitude photography identified a medium-sized nuclear reactor, the integral plant necessary in the manufacture of the plutonium that is at the heart of an atomic explosion.

When Dimona was washed out into the open the news made slight adjustments to Sokarev's life. The degree of security that had wrapped round the very existence of the project was relaxed. The Israeli Government issued statements about the requirement for nuclear energy for peaceful uses, ranging from electricity power to the extended life of vegetables on shop counters. Sokarev was pleased. Fewer of his friends regarded him with such curiosity. Life became more normal.

In the halcyon days after the June victory of 1967, when the nation's defences seemed secure and the Arabs had taken a bloodied, broken nose, been pushed back far from the Israeli settlements, across the great buffer zones of Sinai, the Jordan valley, and the Golan Heights, then there was little to concern Sokarev about the pace of his work. He was at forty-one a young man for his job, on the up, regarded by his colleagues as brilliant and directing his energies toward what his project director blithely called the 'agro-nuclear complexes': the reclaiming of desert land through the use of thousands of millions of gallons of sea water, distilled through nuclear power. The project did not last.

The war of attrition across the Suez water-way exacted a toll both from human life and from the fragile Israeli economy. New tensions rose along the Egyptian and Syrian borders. And on the day in October 1973 when Sokarev and his family were at prayer, Yom Kippur Day, the Arab armies breached the great defensive lines that lay along the Canal and which bestrode the Golan. The peace was hard-won this time; none of the trumpeting of 1967 followed the cease-fire. Reports filtered through the foreign press of new, far-reaching Soviet rockets, sited on the plains

34

behind Damascus and protected by nests of anti-aircraft missiles, rockets that could reach any Israeli town, either with a conventional high-explosive war-head or armed with a localized nuclear device. To Sokarev and to many of his team it was clear the time had come to consider intensely, if perhaps belatedly, what was called in the common rooms round the world where men specialized in physics, the 'nuclear option'.

The days at Dimona started earlier, ended later. Sokarev and the team that was built round him wrestled with the problems of abbreviations in time and expenditure for the fashioning of the bomb. Extraction of uranium from the phosphate ores of the Negev was increased, as the plant gulped up more than twenty-five tons a year. Some of the ablest men in the Department were sent to the United States, and then to West Germany to study at the European nuclear centre. As a result the costly Jericho missile system was developed with a range of more than three hundred miles, the country's own and independent delivery weapon.

The politicians began to talk. 'The possibility of nuclear weapons moving into the Middle East theatre should not be eliminated,' said Moshe Dyan. Israel's President proudly announced that his country had assembled the knowledge and equipment to construct the bomb.

And from the reactor in the desert came the tiny quantities of plutonium 239, at little more than eight kilograms a year, in bulk the size of a fruit from the Beersheba orangeries, yet with the capability to create a twenty kiloton explosion. The bombs, equivalent in destructive capacity to those dropped more than thirty years earlier on Hiroshima and Nagasaki, could not be tested, but at least the stockpile was starting.

It had been a brutal twenty months for Sokarev, of fierce hours, interminable arguments over government money, that never extended to the budgetry minimum he maintained his department must have if research were to continue. He took his papers home at night, but increasingly they were covered with the columns of figures that represented the finances of the programme and were expressed in the currency of the inflated Israeli lira. He longed for the days when his working brain had been overwhelmed only by the horizontal characters of the equations he sought to set up and then disprove, and, if he could not find the flaw, then rejoice in the knowledge of perfection.

That he was tired showed. His face was greyer and had the

35

pallid yellowness that comes from perpetual artificial light, denial of sunlight, and the harassment of worry. His trousers fitted him poorly and had stretched, while his shirt bulged over his belly; the tennis that he had played twice a week, and which had been his principal form of enjoyment, was now denied him.

But the guard who stopped him that Thursday morning at the first of the security perimeter gates and who knew the personnel who came and went at the plant noted that the normally worn face of David Sokarev was a little brighter, a little livelier. As he looked into the scientist's window, waiting for the Polaroid identity card to be produced, he saw almost a spark of recognition in the other man's eyes. Generally there was no acknowledgement, but today there was an inclination of the head, near to a greeting.

'You're looking well today, Professor,' the guard said, as he handed the plastic-coated card back to the waiting hand.

'So I should be. Off out of here for a few days. My last day and then away for a bit.'

'Holidays?' the guard asked, before moving back to swing up the red and white painted 'Stop' barrier that blocked advance.

'Of a fashion. A few days in London, then on to New York, and perhaps San Francisco after that. The last isn't finalized. A few lectures, to meet old friends. Something of a holiday, yes.'

Twice more the car was stopped by grey-brown uniformed guards. Each time they swung their sub-machine-guns across their backs, and walked forward to check the card. All three men who spoke to the professor as he arrived that morning were to notice the fractional bounce that had lifted him.

'I'm late in,' he said to his secretary in the outer office. 'Was held up talking to the man on the gate.' She said nothing. It was one minute past eight o'clock.

'What have we today?'

'Mostly meetings. The Director wants to see you as well, preferably in the afternoon. Two sub-committees in the morning, so that will fit well. And there was a call a few minutes ago from the Foreign Ministry. They want to drive down from Jerusalem to see you, but they'd like us to fix a time for the afternoon, and call them back. I would suggest about four, after you've seen the Director.' She was a pretty girl, tall and straight-backed, and wearing an eye-riveting mini-skirt high up on her sun-browned thighs. Efficient as well, and the office was chaos every time she went for military service.

36

'What do they want in Jerusalem?' He was behind his desk now, scooping at the papers from his tray, and scattering them over the wooden surface.

'It was the security division from the Foreign Ministry. Protection Branch. They said they wanted to talk about your trip.'

It was closer to six in the evening, and many of the Dimona workers were already on their way home, before David Sokarev's desk was clear enough for him to feel able to abandon his work for the three weeks of his visit to Europe and North America. There were no more letters to sign, charts to check, scribblings to be made in the margin of reports. No more excuses to prevent him seeing the two men who waited in his outer office.

He saw they were both young when they came through the door. Fit and good-looking. They shook his hand. He neither apologized for keeping them so long nor did they seem to expect it. Joseph Mackowicz had come to talk, Gad Elkin to listen.

Mackowicz said, 'I am glad you could see us, Professor. We are both to be travelling with you throughout your journey. We will be very close to you at all times. It is best on these visits that we get to meet the people we accompany before we leave, rather than meeting at the airport, just seeing each other a few minutes before departure. I think you have little experience of being escorted on a visit abroad?'

'I have not been away for some years. It was a long time ago and then I travelled only with my secretary.' He saw Elkin smile from his chair. 'Not the one I have now, I can assure you. A rather more formidable lady. When I indented to take Anna to handle my correspondence, type my speeches, things like that, it was refused. Not enough money for her to go, I was told. I did not anticipate that if they could not scrape together the lira for Anna they would be able to send two gentlemen such as yourselves. I had resigned myself to travelling on my own.'

'Your typing will be taken care of; the embassies will find a girl for that.' Mackowicz did not react, was not one to rise to even the most gentle humour. 'We have the places that you will be visiting, and we will supervise your programme. What we want for the moment is a guarantee that you will afford us your co-operation, and take most seriously our advice.'

The professor looked hard at the young man, adjusted his

37

glasses, then pushed them back to the bridge of his nose.

'I would never knowingly not co-operate.'

'That, Professor, is excellent news. Not everybody in a position similar to yours is happy to have us in such proximity. Some talk of embarrassment for their foreign colleagues. I can assure you if there is embarrassment it will be a necessary cross to bear.'

'I had not given myself such importance,' said the professor slowly, a tinge of sadness in his voice. 'Nor had I realized that I might be at risk. It is not the sort of situation that one considers.'

Mackowicz said, 'We had not considered our athletes at Munich to be either politically important or at risk. We knew, we'd been told, that an Arab attack, from the Black September faction, would come at about that time somewhere in Europe, at some international gathering. No one put the sum together, and no guard was given to our people. They died defenceless, and it will not happen again. A single tennis player, or swimmer or runner, if they represent Israel, then they are protected. It was all laid down in the reorganization that followed Munich. Inevitably, so too, for a politician, a diplomat, or a scientist of your status.'

Anna carried in a tray with coffee. No milk, too expensive, sugar, coarse and with the granules over-large. The men stopped talking while she was in the room and handing out the mugs. The professor thanked her, said he would send a postcard, and see her on his return. She should go home, he told her. He could lock up. She waved, a small feminine gesture, at the door, closing it behind her.

'Gentlemen,' said Sokarev. 'I am only a scientist, perhaps only a technician. Not versed in the ways outside Dimona. I read the paper, not often, but I read it, and I listen to the wireless in the evening. Though I had not imagined it before I can accept the possibility of threat. But I would not take it as a great one, a small risk only. So I ask myself these questions. First: why did you come here tonight, a long journey – and we have discussed nothing of importance so far? Second, I say: why do we need two men to look after me? Why cannot this be done by our own people from the embassies when I get off the plane, or by the police forces of the countries that I visit?'

There was silence in the room. Sokarev continued to gaze at Mackowicz, waiting for the answer. He watched him light his cigarette, unhurried, patient with the ignorance. In the distance there was the noise of a car starting up. The other scientists would

38

be gone soon, and the cleaners would be on their rounds. Permeating the room came the semi-audible moan of a far-off electric generator. A fly played around the professor's nose till he swatted it away.

It was Elkin this time who spoke. 'It had been intended there would be just one of us. The situation changed, and we have to change with it. You are regarded by the Government as high-risk category. You have much specialized knowledge from your work here. You head an important team. All those things make you an important target, but then all those things we knew weeks ago when your itinerary was filed. Since that time there have been movements – information – that have suggested to us that your protection should be increased. Our work, in a way, can be considered perhaps as sensitive as yours. You would not wish me to say more.'

'You have said nothing,' retorted Sokarev.

'We have listening posts,' Mackowicz cut in. 'We have people who listen for us, and we have people who interpret what they hear. It's a difficult, drawn-out process, and many times we are wrong. Often there are several factors in the air at the same time; rarely do they come to land together. But from what we learn we try to form a shape, to anticipate their actions. This is what we are doing at the moment. The pattern is not yet whole in this instance, but it has a form, an outline.'

'Specifically, there is a threat to me?' There was puzzlement from Sokarev, his confidence about to drain.

'We cannot take it that far yet,' said Elkin. 'We know a squad from one of the Palestinian terror groups has been moving north across Europe. They were intercepted on our advice by the French authorities. At least two of them died. We believed from our informants that there were three. If so, one is not yet accounted for. They were on the road to Boulogne when they were blocked. It is reasonable to assume from that route that their destination was a cross-Channel ferry, and Britain. We have no political leaders, no military men in Britain in the next month. Only yourself, Professor.'

Sokarev was quiet, subdued and unhappy in the presence of these chilling young men, and growing resentful of the message they brought. The silence, long and perceptible, even to the point of shuffled feet, was broken by Mackowicz. 'You will not have read about this, nor will you need to repeat it. Six nights ago the

39

same group that has held our interest in Europe mounted a raid from their advance base in Lebanon across the fence towards Ramot Naftali, south of Kiryat Shmona. They were ambushed by an army patrol. There were five in all and we captured one. The rest we killed in the action. The IDF statement that evening announced that one of the terrorists had escaped, though he was in fact in our hands. Under interrogation he talked to us. They often do, you know. We gave him his life by barter. He would survive but he would take back with him a radio transmitter. He could give us further information about operations. That was the agreement we made. There were no messages, and he is dead. We have many eyes and ears in Fatahland, and yesterday we were told. He died not nicely, but in pain, and choking because his testicles were blocking his windpipe. You will see from what I say that information is not easy to come by, and when we do have access then we listen to what we are told.'

Sokarev felt he wanted to vomit. He rose up unsteadily from his chair and moved across the room. By the door he switched on the light, banishing the spreading shadows, flooding the office from the flourescent bar hung from the ceiling. Apart from a single photograph and from a chart that showed him which members of his team had booked their annual leave or were on extended sick leave the walls were bare. As he wanted his office – uncomplicated. The photograph showed his three children; two girls in army slacks and regulation V-necked navy blue sweaters, and between them his son, a head taller and in light, air-force summer khaki, with his pilot's wings on his chest. Home together for a 'shabbat' leave, and they'd be together again same opportunity tomorrow. They expected to fight, could comprehend the modern war fought crawling at belly-level beyond the frontiers of their country. But to Sokarev the dark and sinister images that the two security men had introduced to his office were hostile and alien.

'You are presumably going to tell me what this terrorist said under questioning?' He had stayed by the door.

Mackowicz and Elkin stood up. Mackowicz said, 'He told us they had been planning an attack in Europe. He did not know the location, he did not know the target. He knew only the code-word for the operation. Under extreme interrogation he gave it to us. The PFLP General Command are the terrorist grouping, and they have given to this operation the word "kima". It is an Arabic

word, of the Palestinian dialect. Translated, it is "mushroom".
Not the small button-shaped one of the kitchen, but the larger,
free-growing plant that magnifies and flourishes. That is why we
consider a man from Dimona to be at risk. And why there will be
two of us at your side when you travel.'

After they had gone David Sokarev sat a long time in the room.
    Then he collected together the papers he would require for his
journey, packed them into the old, frayed briefcase, and locked
the door behind him. There were only a few lights on in the office
blocks and laboratories but all around were the brilliantly-lit
wire fences. The watchtowers were manned after darkness, and
as he walked to his car he could see the men high up on the stilted
platforms, and below them the dog-handlers with the proven
attack alsatians. This was the oasis that he knew, safe, rewarding,
isolated.
    When he reached for his keys he found that his hands were
trembling, that he had difficulty in selecting the correct key to
open the door. He got in and sat in the seat for a few moments,
to calm himself and mollify the breathiness that affected him.
Then he drove off for the gates, and the road, and home. At the
three check-points the guards called out a greeting, but this time
won no response.
    He drove home faster than usual, arriving at the flat a full
eight minutes earlier than his established habit would have
permitted. His wife noticed the drawn look in his face and the
tension about his eyes. For the first time in his adult life he was
experiencing fear. It was a fear of the unknown. Of a strange city
of millions of people, but where one man, or two, or three, or
four, had a solitary and inflexible purpose, the destruction of
David Sokarev, of himself. He had seen the photographs of these
men in the Jerusalem Post and the afternoon paper, *Yediot
Aarenot*; they were on their backs, broken and spent, cut down by
gunfire, surrounded by some circle of elated soldiers. They always
died, always seemed to end their missions dragged by the ankles to
an army jeep, flung on to a bloody stretcher with the reverence of a
turnip sack. Garbage. But there was no reason that Sokarev
could see to believe their commitment would be any the less in a
foreign capital.

41

She brought him his meal. Some liver, the money for it dug deep from the housekeeping purse, and watched the way he toyed with the meat, eating to please her. He told her nothing of Mackowicz and Elkin, and what they had said inside his office.

A city is a vulnerable, flaccid target for an act of terrorism. Huge and preoccupied and indifferent – the ideal hunting ground, and never more so than if the stalkers are a small, motivated group of men whose numbers can be counted on the fingers of one hand. In time of war a city can be mobilized, organized and put into uniform with specific tasks to perform. But when peace reigns it absorbs the danger, turns the other cheek, has too much with which to concern itself to be agitated by the tiny cancer flowing at will in its body.

The Provisional IRA proved conclusively how defenceless is a great international capital. One hundred and forty-eight bombs in twenty-two months and the mighty carcase barely knew it was under attack. Cars packed with gelignite disintegrating among shopping crowds, duffle-bags exploding on busy railway platforms, mutilated bodies ferried away in fleets of ambulances. But the next time the sirens went the crowds still gathered to watch, sometimes amused, always interested, never involved.

Where eight million people are gathered together over an area of some four hundred square miles everyone is a stranger. For the terrorist there is anonymity here, the opportunity to blend into whatever background he chooses. If he has funds he can take a smart flat – Mayfair or Belgravia – where a porter will salute as he goes out, but will ask no questions. Otherwise he can turn to the myriad of small hotels behind the big railway termini of North London, pay when he registers, and be left in total privacy. In the big city the man who is careful and patient, and skilled in the art of guerrilla warfare, should survive. He can blame only himself if he fails.

The forces ranged against him are meagre. The principal and

most obvious bastion that he must avoid is the civilian police force, with its headquarters at Scotland Yard, close to Victoria Station. Confronted with the increasing problems of conventional crime, serious and minor, of public apathy and lack of manpower, the metropolitan police have been forced into a crash-course in combating international violence. They started without experience and it was a hard road to make up ground when the luxury of time was not permitted. The whole concept of fighting such an enemy had been far from officials' minds when they moved their offices and files and laboratories into a towering, glass-faced structure so vulnerable to car-bomb attack that policemen had to patrol the pavement outside to prevent any vehicle parking unattended within fifty feet of its walls. But, of the hundreds of detectives who scurry in and out of the main swing doors, flashing their warrant cards at the bemedalled commissionaires, relatively few are engaged in anti-terrorist operations. Those that are belong to Special Branch, the wing formed close on a hundred years ago to counter the Irish Fenian threat.

The Irish problem still dominates their work – tying men down on the long-drawn-out surveillance of buildings, meetings, pubs, airports and homes, along with the constant search for reliable informers.

The Branch men have also to concern themselves with the potential of subversion, and keep their paper work up to date on the fringe anarchist groups, the most militant of the background trade union officials, the activities of the Iron Curtain-bloc diplomats. They are responsible for the protection of principal Britons, from the Prime Minister downward, and also of foreign persons of rank arriving in the country. They are not generously endowed with funds, or with manpower. Less than five hundred men, and the country to cover.

They had been informed of the planned visit of David Sokarev to Britain, but with four days to go to his arrival at Heathrow Airport they were unaware of his crucial importance to Israel, and of the extent of the threat against him. At a later stage there would be a discussion over the telephone between the Middle East desk and the Security Attaché at the Israeli embassy, probably the night before the professor flew in. In the normal way of things the decision on the need for protection would be taken then, with consideration given to the availability of officers, and more pressing priorities.

But for the survival of David Sokarev on his journey through London there was another group of men far more important than the officers of the Special Branch. They worked from little-known premises in one of the most fashionable districts of the capital. Close to the Playboy Club, the London Hilton and the Londonderry Hotel, is a gaunt five-storey building. It is in need of fresh paint, pointing and general repairs. The windows, in the uniform metal-rimmed rows so beloved by architects of the twenties and thirties, are shielded by lace curtains; those on the lower floors are protected by half-inch-thick concertina steel meshes. Side entrances to the block have been bricked up, as have upper windows at the corners of the building that still show the rifle-aiming slits, hurriedly fitted in 1940. There is no plaque on the walls beside the main doorway to give a clue to the occupation of those who work in the building. The parking meters set into the pavements outside the front entrance are masked by red plastic hoods to prevent the casual motorist from leaving his car there. Above the doorway, and needing the attention of the cleaners, are the words 'Leconfield House'. The building carries no other visual identification. It is the nerve-centre of the country's most secret organization, the one responsible for deep undercover counter-espionage and counter-terrorist operations; the British Security Service works from here.

Eleven hours after the tape recording of Ciaran McCoy's conversation with the Arab diplomat had been completed the spools were on the desk of a man who used a small office on the second floor of Leconfield House. A transcript had been taken by the duty clerks, who were the first to listen to the play-back, and that too lay on the high-polished oakwood surface. The room occupied by Philip Whilloughby-Jones was bare to the point of starkness. A regulation square of carpet, determined by his Civil Service grade, covered the centre of the floor and was surrounded by ageing though systematically polished lineoleum. The door to the room was set opposite the only window; on the third wall was a calendar sent out by a firm that specialized in the postal sales of garden bulbs; against the fourth was a steel filing cabinet. Grouped in a semi-circle in front of the desk were four chairs, framed in metal tubing, seats covered with yellow plastic, not designed for comfort but for working men who would leave them when their business was completed. The chair behind the desk offered only a slight concession in two vaguely-cushioned arm-rests.

Jones – he detested the hyphenated name his father had taken to using after his admittance to the masonic order of a small, East Midlands industrial town – was short and sparely built. He had a sharp gull nose that jutted out above his brush moustache, a legacy of his Royal Air Force days. His thin cheeks, merging into the shape of his bone structure, had neither colour nor verve, and were evidence of a man who had spent most of his time indoors. His hair, whispy and greying, was tended hurriedly and carelessly each morning, and remained in shape only for as long as the water used on his comb maintained order. The brightness lay in his eyes; narrow, deep-set, but alert and alive. It was his lower jaw that separated him from other men, the way the skin, lacking in wrinkles and hair, had been transposed from his right buttock to cover the incinerated layers that he had lost so many years before. The replacement had no gloss or animation, and at the point where the new skin had been grafted to the old it irritated and annoyed. Jones was responsible for the general surveillance of the activities of Middle East embassies located in London.

Duggan, of Irish Affairs, would be down in fifteen minutes to talk with him, along with Fairclough, Arab Affairs (Palestinian). Before they came there was time to look again at the file on the embassy in Princes Gate. So much of his work was done from the files; the most thorough and successful course of action followed invariably from the writing down of minutiae – that was the Director General's belief, and the way he expected his subordin-ates to operate. Jones unlocked the second of the three drawers of the cabinet, and rolled it back. Hundreds of typed reports confronted him. Observations, assessments, personal biographies, transcripts of recorded telephone conversations. At the particular embassy several telephone lines were listened to, each extension warranting a separate brown folder. He flicked through them till he came to the one he wanted and lifted it out. Few sheets there. The number was only recently known, and it had been noted that little traffic came through it. Back at his desk he began to read, quickly and expertly, occasionally writing a few words in a neat

45

trained hand on the memory-pad. There was time for a pipe
before the others came, and he lit up, sucking far down into the
charred bowl of the wood.

Wait till there's a big party, then move, they'd told him. Abdel-
El-Famy had delayed going through the French customs and
immigration, waiting till the student group swamped the blue-
uniformed officials. He had merged with them, one moment on
their fringe, the next right among them. But the checks at Boulogne
were casual, guided only by the report from St Omer that they
should watch for someone mud-spattered and probably unshaven.
Famy's delaying tactics were unnecessary. His real protection
came in the orange shirt he now wore, which had been neatly
ironed and that had not suffered from its time in the grip-case;
and in his laundered jeans and hip-length navy corduroy jacket.
He had shaved, too, so that he fitted none of the descriptions
that had been issued to the harbour police. The pistol and the
soiled clothes were buried beneath the previous autumn's windfall
of leaves in a wood to the east of the town. They would be found,
eventually – but long after he had completed the task that had
been set for him.

On the crossing Famy had made a conscious attempt to talk
to a section of the party. His knowledge of French was variable,
but sufficient to allow him to strike up conversation. It was the
start of a holiday and so spirits were high; there was no shortage
of young people to laugh and joke with. The lecturer looking
after the students for their eight days in London was vaguely
aware that a tall, swarthy man, a little older than the others,
and now among them, had not been at the station in Paris. It
puzzled him, but he knew only a few of the group, and had had
little time on the Paris-to-Boulogne leg of the journey to get
close to them. He shrugged it off; perhaps a friend from home, or
from school . . .

Famy saw the white ribbon of cliff as the boat swung to port,
beginning its run to the long jetty. Not the clear white he had
expected, not the formidable barrier he had read of in the University at Beirut, but shallow and with fields coming down toward
the sea. The castle caught his eye, powerful, squat and old-
fashioned. He smiled to himself, savouring it; that was his

enemy, tired now, outdated, unable to compete in the new and modern world that he was seeking, unable to comprehend the hitting power of the Palestinian movement, unable to defend itself against the new philosophy of revolution and attack.

The two girls from Orléans and the boy from St Etienne were a long time getting their baggage together after the complicated process of docking and tying up. Famy was patient, the rest of the group less so. From the lecturer and other students came cries for the three to hurry themselves. It suited Famy well. Out of the delay would come anxiety about the train connections for London, and that would mean a concentrated, excited rush at the customs and immigration barriers.

And that was how it was. As Customs quizzed the first four of the party the lecturer began to shout and wave the folder with the rail tickets. Other students joined in, all hugely enjoying the performance. The officials were good humoured enough, and the party went through. Famy handed over the white immigration card, duly filled in, at the desk, and was talking deeply with the two girls as they swept past the Port Watch Special Branch men. He didn't rate a glance from them. His passport was still in his inner pocket, unrequired, unexamined.

For Famy there was now a moment of indecision. His orders, the orders for the three of them when they left Beirut, had been specific about the next stage of the journey. The instruction was that under no circumstances were they to travel via the direct Dover-to-London rail connection. If for any reason you are suspected, they had said, the authorities have two-and-a-half-hours' grace to make up their minds and intercept at the terminal at Victoria. His people had been adamant about this, and thorough enough to provide the bus time-table that would enable the squad to move down the coast and then link up with a train not connected with the cross-channel services.

Famy reasoned that although he was travelling a full day behind schedule the time-tables would remain constant. He had felt safe with the group and was reluctant to leave them, but his orders made no allowance for personal initiative at this stage. When the girls looked round for him he had disappeared.

There were endless waits at bus stops, interspersing the tedious stages of the journey. Dover to Folkestone, seven miles. Folkestone to Ashford, seventeen miles. Ashford to Maidstone, eighteen miles. And in all that time nobody, with the exception of the ticket men, spoke a word to him – not a greeting, not a smile, not a syllable of conversation.

In Maidstone, a dull, boring little town, it looked to him, as he walked through the streets busy with Friday afternoon shoppers, he reverted to the railway system, and a slow stopping train to London. As he climbed into the carriage he reflected with satisfaction that he was within an hour of his destination, and the streets on which it had been determined that David Sokarev would die.

It was a difficult meeting in Leconfield House – three men round the one desk, close to their copies of the transcript, attempting to read more into the badly typed words than they could find. There were many silences, and an adjournment was forced on them by the necessity for Duggan and Fairclough to return to their offices to search for anything that might throw light on the single brief conversation they had been given. After an hour of sparring round the problem Jones had felt it was time for summary and analysis.

'Let's just stop a minute,' he said, wanting to be back with specifics. 'Let's establish what we have from our own material before we start going elsewhere and picking other people's stuff. First, the number our friend McCoy telephoned is rarely used, but was considered of some importance or that little sod who gave it us wouldn't have looked as though he thought he was doing us the favour. When we spoke to him last he seemed to think we were getting the bargain out of it. So, it's sensitive. That's born out by our second point of reference, the call itself. It's different to other calls on the line, on the number. They've been in some code, but we haven't enough on that yet, and it's not broken.'

He reached among his own papers, taking from one of the files four foolscap sheets, each printed over only three lines.

'Stuff like this. Doesn't make much sense, but this is what we have. "Accommodation one-seven-three, six-five, one-six-two." That was put over three days ago, bit of preamble, not much. English accent, probably disguised. Next night something similar, same sort of style. "Rendezvous as arranged, seven-

seven, one, six." Both times it's the incoming calls that are given the information. On to the message last night. To my mind it represents a failure of rendezvous – clear to the deaf that, nothing remarkable in that piece of deduction. But where the pattern breaks down is that though the voice is the same as the first two calls this time he uses a name. Introduces himself. Doesn't use a code-word, bursts straight in.'

Fairclough spoke. 'Try the simplest way through. McCoy, the name we have and which is perhaps genuine, he's hanging about last night. Cools his heels waiting for someone. Gets fed up. Wants to know what's happening and calls the number, the contact number he's been given. Uses the call box. But he's got to be angry, hopping bloody mad. Too angry to remember the drill he's been given. What's the code-word used in the first two calls?' That he couldn't remember it annoyed Fairclough; a concise, organized man, he liked to have things at his fingers.

'Just one word, it seems,' said Jones. 'Just the word "Mushroom", then straight into the message, and whatever that means. No delay; very professional. No possibility of a trace on a call of the length they've been using.'

'Bloody impossible,' interjected Duggan, who didn't like the way events were shaping – the pattern that was building. Too ominous, too much that smacked of planning, and who was it that plans even on such unimportant details?

'Back to the scene, back to the facts.' Jones knew the way a meeting could disintegrate into side-tracking, into theory, and end up with a morning gone.

'We establish that for last night's call there is no use of the code. We also establish that our little diplomat feels it worth sitting in his miserable hutch half the evening waiting for the incomings, long after the crowd he works for are off swigging sherbert and tomato juice on the merry-go-round. When we look at him, what we have on him, there's damn all. New here, within the last few months. Ostensibly small job – visas and passports. Oil men and few businessmen, not that many, but he has a phone line of his own and an extension not listed in their directory. Takes calls at any time, either arranged or he sleeps in there.'

He paused. He was talking too much, doing his schoolmaster bit again. Shouldn't be like that with his colleagues, but he'd caught the Duggan chill, and didn't want it to spread. Even among friends doubt and apprehension are corrosive. Bloody

49

daft though, wasn't it? Three grown men, playing school-boy riddles, working on a braintease. Fun this one, because they've torn up the answers, won't tell you whether you're right or not. Can change the questions half-way through, can't they, just when you're warming? Their initiative, always the same, always the bastards have the initiative. And the three of them were there, pushing the hot air up, seeking another justification for another lost weekend. Ought to have one's head examined, working oneself into a lather, eighty-hour week, another fraught telephone call home. Bloody stupid. Plough on, Jonesey, they're all waiting.

'So we come finally to the complication. Mysterious Irish voice, the magic accent that gives us all wet dreams at night.' Duggan looked pained; Fairclough smiled.

Jones went on, 'What is McCoy doing – waiting for his mate and, when the blind date doesn't show, phoning a confidential embassy number? Thoughts, gentlemen?'

He'd finished. Let the others pick the bones out of that lot. Nasty smell it left, not too tangible yet, but enough of a stench to alert him.

Duggan's turn. He'd contributed little so far. The area he covered in his work was very different to that of the other two men. They were long-range, working on hypotheses, dealing with the possible, but the unlikely. His concern was the probable, and exact and known threat, that went under the initials of 'PIRA' – Provisional Irish Republican Army. When he had slipped back to his office earlier he had checked against his own list of suspects, and the cross-references, looking for any mentions of Ciaran McCoy. None existed. He had telephoned the head-quarters of Military Intelligence at Lisburn, County Down, in Northern Ireland. They would begin their searches, feed his request into the computer. 'Negative' or 'Positive' would be on the telex by lunch-time at the earliest, mid-afternoon by the latest.

'If the boy's PIRA it's difficult to explain. They've had contacts with this government. Bought arms there. The Claudia and the Klashnikovs that we intercepted, they were from this source. They've had meetings there, discussions, but their politics are the width of the Sahara apart. If there is a liaison then it would be of direct necessity. It's to do one thing, then forget it. They couldn't hold together for anything sustained. But we have to know about this boy, we have to localize him.'

'It's the place we have to start,' Fairclough chipped in. 'Only

50

bloody place we can begin, it's from McCoy we start pulling the pieces together. But if they're talking about a link-up then we're not far off the spectacular. After rendezvous they don't hang about knitting, they move on to target. That's the Arab way — what we have to be thinking about if we believe the liaison exists. They come in late and they hit and they shift. Munich's the best example. The crowd that went into the Olympic village arrived two and three days before the attack. But they'll have done the planning, and with thoroughness. Go back to Munich again: they were setting that up *seven months* earlier.'

'Don't know why we bother,' Duggan, determined to depress.

'Perhaps they're not available to come at all,' Jones murmured, a smile playing round his lips, contorted a little on the graft line, and accentuating the divisions in the age of the skin. 'You saw the morning papers. Shoot-out near Boulogne. Two men believed Arabs cut up at a road block. But nothing from the "Firm" yet.'

'Nice thought,' agreed Fairclough.

There was a gentle knock on the door. The girl who came in was tall, a little plump, fair hair back over her shoulders. Her skirt was an inch too long, her sweater an inch too tight. Too many bulges. She was Helen Anderson, and had been personal secretary to Jones for the last eight years.

'Sorry to interrupt, Sir,' she said quietly.

No, you bloody aren't, thought Duggan. You run this bloody office, come and go when you please. Sorry, my arse.

She repeated, 'Sorry, Sir, I didn't put it through, but there's been a message for Mr Fairclough, from Foreign Office. The Israelis have made a contact with our people in Cyprus. The report will be coming over the wire later on. When they've put it through the mincer, found the right code-book, it'll be sent over. They said it was important, that you should wait on for it.'

She nodded her head, accepted that the message had been understood, and was gone.

'That's the bloody evening gone, for the lot of us,' said Fairclough. 'You'll be waiting all ears and pencils for the phone chat-up, Duggan for trace, me flogging through this lot.'

They all laughed. They bitched and moaned every Friday night when work saturated their desks, and they always stayed.

Only a very few of the businessmen who dropped in for a quick one with their wives or secretaries or mistresses to the White Elephant or the Curzon House Club on the other side of the street would have had any inkling of the work of the men whose lights burned late into the night in the gaunt building opposite.

The Israeli who had flown to the Akrotiri Royal Air Force base in south-west Cyprus was travelling under the direct instructions of the Director of Military Intelligence in Tel Aviv. He came anonymously, the only passenger in an ageing nine-seater Aero Commander. Much of the exchange of information between the various wings of Israel's security services and the British Secret Intelligence Service – SIS or 'the Firm', as the trade called it – was conducted in the immense, sprawling RAF camp. To meet him was one of the resident British team who had driven the seventy-five miles from Nicosia in response to a telephone message from the Israeli embassy there to the British High Commission. The British took note of the warnings that were flashed to London from the island; on at least a half of the occasions that troops had been drafted into Heathrow Airport it followed close on information received via the harsh sun-reflecting tarmac at Akrotiri.

That evening the two men wasted little time, and the Israeli was in the air again less than twenty-five minutes after their conversation had begun. It was sufficient for him to make five points. First, a Palestinian assassination squad had been intercepted on its way through northern France. Second, the Israeli security representative in Paris was both unhappy with the French authorities' follow-up of the incident and uncertain that all the members of the gang had been accounted for. Third, the Israelis had gained the knowledge that the operation was code-named 'Mushroom'. Fourth, his country's premier but largely unknown nuclear scientist would be leaving Tel Aviv for Britain on the following Monday to fulfil a long-standing speaking engagement. And fifth, his government would react extremely unfavourably if any incident should mar the visit. Understatement was the man's style, but he repeated the last three times.

'He is important to us – very important in certain fields that we consider vital to our national defence. You understand what I have said?'

The Englishman looked across at the ground crew standing beside the plane – out of earshot, but curious about the two men.

He asked, 'If he's so important and the threat exists, why not

52

call the visit off, and forget about it?'

'If we did that every time there was a threat we would become immured, sterilized. We don't bend the knee to these bastards, and we expect the support of your agencies in the United Kingdom.'

'Anything else that could help us?' said the Englishman. He thought, the little sod, he's enjoying it. Always do when they can wrap someone else up in their interminable problems.

'Nothing more. Just keep it tight round him, our Professor. As you would say, tight as guinea-pig's arse.'

Always the same, thought the Englishman. They revel in it – the rest of the world jumping to their bloody orders. He too would have a destroyed evening, writing and then encoding his report, but unlike the men in London he would be scratching out of a cocktail party. The big girl from Chancery would have . . . made you bloody sick.

The information Duggan had requested was brought from the basement bank of teletype machines at four o'clock. He read the paper with care, the frown deepening on his forehead as he waded through the lines of blue-punched capitals.

Timing: 15.52 hours. Friday 28/6.
Subject: McCoy, Ciaran Patrick Aloysius.
Address: Ballynafeigh fm, nr Crossmaglen, SArmagh, NI
Age/DOB: 22 years, 14.3.54.
Security File: For last three years McCoy has been member Crossmaglen Bn PIRA . . . After one year was reported I/C Active Service Unit operating Cullyhanna area. Believed expert rifle shot, natural leader. Arrested Sec Forces 8/12/74. ICO and detention order. Held HM Prison Maze where became PIRA cage commandant. Freed on Sec of State's instruction 3/7/75. Since then active in political work and would return again to violence should situation deteriorate. Last is Mil Intelligence and SB assessment. Believed responsible for shootings incidents in SArmagh area, specifically RUC patrol car 17/8/74 and sniping of paratroop killed 10/10/74. Pix and Prints following.
Background: Undermentioned is person-to-person confidential from Mil Intelligence HQ 3BDE Lurgan, NI and not for

release outside your department.

We astonished at release of McCoy and protests were via Commander Land Forces to appropriate political offices. Reply was that as McCoy only detainee from that area and response to local PIRA required in existing cease-fire situation he was being freed. Exclaimer. Regarded as of high calibre and exception to colleagues in that has good educational standards with full secondary education from Armagh City. Deceptive in manner and could pass well in all company.

Re your specific requests:

1. Last seen in area approx 10/12 days ago.
2. No known visits to London, but sister once worked St Mary's Hosp, Paddington London NW.
3. Would have considerable disguise capabilities witness long period before pick-up.
4. Last interrogated by Maj Ian Stewart, Int Corps Rtd, address obtainable Ministry of Defence (Personnel).

Upsummer: Hard boy. Bestest luck.

Duggan photocopied the paper three times. One for Jones, one for Fairclough, one for his departmental head. The original he put into the new folder, marked with McCoy's name on the outside, and which up till then had contained only the transcripts of the phone calls to the embassy.

He read the information again, interpreting the officialese of the message. The implications were fearsome. A top man, in a top-grade Provisional set-up, leader of an active service unit, arrested, served with an Interim Custody Order, then a detention order, and then released by some bloody politician in order to keep a cease-fire going when everyone knew the bastards were on their knees and suing for peace. Responsible for at least two deaths. Poor devils, gunned down, and not even the satisfaction of having their man spend the rest of his natural behind bars. Not even the General able to get the decision reversed. Made you want to pack it in.

So what was little McCoy doing running round London, calling up embassies, missing his links? Duggan hurried to the lift and the floor below where Jones had his office.

5

Sokarev's wife had noted the preoccupation that gripped her husband. There was his listlessness, the unwillingness to contribute anything in conversation, the desire just to slump in his chair, the books at his desk unopened. There were often times when his work had seemed to force him down, literally bowing his shoulders with the pressures of the speed and intricacy and finesse required for the study of nuclear action.

On previous occasions the signs of extreme exhaustion and depression had been well telegraphed, and they had been able to discuss them, thereby lessening the load. But not this time. Her gentle feelers for information were shrugged off, and she was left feeling frustrated and inadequate. She hoped that the arrival later in the day of 'the children', as she still called them, would be enough to rouse him.

Sokarev himself thought continuously of what the security men had told him, wondered why they had found it necessary to take him into their confidence, regretted that they had. He was not used to fear, and could not remember a similar sensation of such intensity. Like an infant afraid to be left alone in an unfamiliar room, he had come in the last twenty-four hours to dread his London visit.

When, just before nightfall succeeded dusk, his wife suggested they should take a walk together he shook his head, heavy with the negative. He heard her sigh her disappointment as she fidgeted with a duster behind his chair.

'We've time,' she said, 'before the children come. We could go down to the new swimming pool, just a few hundred metres, a few minutes. We'll be back well before them.'

He shook his head again, and she left it.

He sat alone for a few more minutes, then got up abruptly.

'I'd like a walk' he said quietly. 'I'd like to go on my own. I won't be long.' Her face clouded, and he watched the pain he had inflicted. Her jaw seemed to tighten, her eyes to close a little. 'There is a problem. I have to think about it. It has no place for

55

you. Not long-term. I'll resolve it very soon. I'm sorry.'

Out on the street there was a warm, dry heat. The children were on the pavement playing football, but they made way for the professor. Hot, spiced smells came to him from the kitchens as he walked mingling with the scents from the flowering trees that had been planted when the flats were built. There was noise: high above him, a couple shouted abuse at each other, fiercely combative.

It was difficult for him to concentrate on the question that dominated his thinking – too many extraneous sights and senses forced their way over him. He walked little more than half a mile, then turned and came slowly back. When he had reached the entrance on the ground floor that led to his apartment he saw the Mini his son drove parked outside, and he went on round to the back of the building where the garages were. He unlocked the door of his own garage, and then the door of the car, on the passenger side, and slid on to the seat.

His hand wavered a moment before he opened the glove compartment. Underneath the duster, where it always was, rested the Mauser pistol. Sokarev took it in his hand, weighing it, feeling the black, hard shape of the butt pressing down on to his palm. The magazine was fastened into position. Live bullets – the power to kill, or to protect. They're dragging you down, old man, he said to himself. Pulling you into their own pit, where crude, insensitive violence settles all. What learning, what thought, what intellectual capacity is demanded to ease the stiff and metallic lever of the safety catch and transform a simple piece of engineering into a killing instrument? So vulgar, so alien. To the men who were to accompany him to London the gun would be as familiar as their shoe-laces, their toothpaste, the belts that held their trousers on their hips.

He would take it with him. Whether they liked it or not, those two young men would have to accept it – a part of his destiny he would keep in his own hands. He put the pistol back in the compartment, and covered it again with the duster.

As he paused at the door of his flat, searching in his pocket for the key, he could hear his wife talking, her voice anxious, excited, and the quieter tones of his son. But he felt calmer now, steadied. When he walked inside there was the smile of greeting on his face.

*

56

At Victoria Station the Arab pushed his way through the crowds of surging, homeward-bound commuters until he reached the telephone kiosks. He waited his turn, and when the box in front of him was vacant nodded his gratitude to the man who held the door open for him, and went inside. It smelled in the dank cubicle. Perhaps a man had vomited there. Looking up at the board above the phone, Famy read the instructions, found a two-pence coin and dialled the number he had memorized. The call was answered, and there was the vibrant noise of the beeps instructing him to feed his money into the appropriate slot. The coin slid through the mechanism, emerging in a small tray below. For a moment he panicked, fumbled for it, and then pushed the coin again into the machine. A pause, then the answering voice. He spoke the number of the extension they had given him, and heard the click that denoted the reconnection. Another voice announced the number he had just asked for, confirming it for him.

Famy said, 'Mushroom, one has arrived.'

From the other end, curt and hurried, 'Same rendezvous, as if you had been here last night. You know it?'

Famy said, 'Yes, I have it memorized, I . . .'

The line was dead, the voice replaced by the purring constancy of the dialling tone. Three hours to kill. Time to be lost, evaporated. Famy walked out into the late evening sunshine and on to the London pavements. In front of him was a tourists' stall. Union Jacks, dolls in guardsmen's uniforms, postcards of Buckingham Palace, cardboard replicas of 'Gentlemen's Lavatory' and 'Piccadilly'.

His voice seemed diffident as he asked the elderly man sitting on a stool beside his counter, 'Excuse me, excuse me. I wonder, do you have the *A-Z Book of London?* A map called the *A-Z?*'

The man looked at him, boring into his face – not for any reason, just a mannerism. He handed the book to Famy.

'A *to* Z,' he said patronizingly, repeating it. There was a look of contempt on his face. 'Thirty pence, it'll cost you.'

Famy moved away with the book. Across the fast-flowing road he could see a sign. 'Sandwiches and Snacks', it proclaimed. He felt hungry and tired. He waited till a group of pedestrians had gathered by the traffic lights, and joined them as they scurried across the wide space. Safety in numbers. He looked at the huge, white-fronted, porticoed houses of Lower Belgrave Street.

It was what he might have imagined of London; grand, majestic, privileged. In the café an Italian waiter brought a coffee to his table, and he also ordered some bread and salad. He flicked at the book, taking in the labyrinthine network of lines and words that made up the Greater London area. When his food came he reached inside his coat for the slim diary he carried, and among a jumble of figures in the section for accounts at the end of it selected the top line. It read '77.1.6'. He shouldn't have written those numbers in his diary. The order had been to memorize them. Dani and Bouchi, they wouldn't have written them on paper. But, Famy had been nervous of forgetting. He was aware that for the first time he had broken an instruction of the mission. The sensation of guilt, though faint, caught him as he started to work the code system that he had been given.

He noted the numbers, printed heavily in black at the top extremes of each page, and went carefully through the book till he came to page 77. There was a '1' printed smaller below it, marking a series of squares. He counted through his alphabet, learned years ago at school, searching for the letter that equalled the number six. On his fingers he came to the letter F. He peered closely at page 77, directing his sight at the square marked laterally by the figure 1 and vertically by the letter F. In the square there was a shaded-in area, a quarter of an inch across, marked 'Waterloo'. They had said the rendezvous would be at a station. If for any reason, his briefing had gone on, it is not suitable for a rendezvous to take place you should go straight to the accommodation. But that was not desirable. He checked with the figures for the accommodation code. '173.65.162'. This time he turned to the back index of the map, sought out page 173 and began to work his way down the extreme left hand column of street names. The sixty-fifth in the descending order read, 'Englefield Road, N.1. 4C 46.' The accommodation address was 162 Englefield Road, on the fringes of Islington and Dalston in north London.

A transcript of Famy's call to the embassy was hurried up to Jones's office.

'There's no chance of a trace,' said the man who brought it. 'Lasted about fourteen seconds, the whole thing, and that includes fumbling with the money, and getting transferred. There's a fair bit of background noise where the call originates, probably a public place, but that's where most of the phone boxes are. It's not inside a building, anyway.'

'Definitely, we can't pick up a call like that?' Jones queried.

'Not a cat in hell. No way at all. Need an awful lot more than that.'

'And the voice?' persisted Jones.

'Need more time with that. Foreign, and we can go a bit further than that. Not USA, not North European, not African, not Asian. I'd put in a bid for Mediterranean, not Latin but East.'

'Thank you,' said Jones, and the man made his way out of the office.

There were those in the department, trained to work at phonetics and speech, who would be able to pin-point the origin of the caller, or at least the region in which he had spent time long enough for it to affect the vowels and consonant construction of the syllables. It would take them no great time, but Jones was certain that whatever they came up with would merely be the professional confirmation of what in his own mind he already knew.

So he had arrived, their little friend. Missed his first appointment, but was now in and ready to make up the lost time for the rendezvous. Right code-word, right part of the world, and ready to meet up with this sodding little Provo.

Jones reached across for his white telephone, the one which carried the department's main number and an extension. The phone beside it was red, and carried a separate number, left clear for incoming calls. He dialled nine for an outside line, and then his home number.

'I'll be late, dear. No, it's just come up. Usual old story, isn't it? I say I'll be late, but it's conceivable I won't be back at all tonight. Boys all right? Good. I'm sorry . . . I always say that. Mean it though. Love you. 'Bye, darling.'

There were two files now. One for the embassy calls, one for McCoy. He took them both with him as he went down to the basement. In cubicles sat the men who listened to the calls that the Director General had authorized as suitable for monitoring. He pulled up a chair beside the man who listened to the number he was concerned with. The man greeted him silently, plugged in a separate pair of earphones, and passed them to him. He offered Jones a cigarette, which was declined. Then they waited, concentration building up, the metal of the earpieces digging into Jones's flesh, as he waited for the next call.

He reflected that there was no complacency among his small team. They were too old for that, too well versed. Each of them appreciated that they were starting late, catching up in a few hours on the homework it had taken the enemy weeks, perhaps months to prepare. There was never enough time in this business for indulgence. Always running from behind, handicapped, catching up against the passing of the calendar.

The major from Intelligence Corps was able to tell Duggan little of McCoy that was not already apparent. He enjoyed his retirement, and the gratuity the army had given him. He devoted his attention, once directed towards interrogation, wholly to his rose garden. He had been there in semi-darkness when Duggan had called the cottage in Wiltshire, and the former officer's mind was more attuned to the problems of green and black aphis-fly and its risk to his blooms than to the young Irishman he had met so many months earlier.

'He was a hard little bugger,' he remembered. 'Very cool, difficult to shake. Cut above the usual cement-between-the-ears boyos. We had more than one session. Didn't budge him at all. Things had got pretty easy for them by then; clamps were well down on what we could do by the stage we got our hands on him. He didn't tell us anything.'

Duggan read him over the first section of the report from Northern Ireland intelligence.

'I didn't see any great political leanings. So few of them have,' said the major. 'He reacts to orders, like most of them. But he's tougher, harder. Has a lot of hate. Patient. One of those that would lie up on the hedgerows for days at a time ready to set off a bomb under an armoured truck. Plans well – we know that from some of his operations. They're a hard breed down there in South Armagh, harder than anywhere else in the bloody place.'

He paused, seeking for anything else that could be of use.

'One thing. If you're looking for him in London. He had a sister, a bit older, perhaps a couple of years. Worked in a hospital, somewhere in London . . .'

Duggan prompted him.

'. . . Well, the girl went a bit haywire. McCoy thought she'd been in the wrong just by coming over. We were told that from other sources. He didn't think she should be working across in the mainland. Seemed quite normal girl, apparently, then got mixed up with a load of hippies. Packed her nursing in and went to live with them. He didn't approve of that. They're a very Puritan crowd, the hard-core Provos. I tried to talk about it to him, tried to shake him up a bit, get him angry. Didn't work. Water off a duck's back.'

'That could be very helpful,' said Duggan.

A courier came by car with the report, decoded, from the meeting at RAF Akrotiri. Fairclough had to come down to the lobby of the building to sign personally for the plain buff envelope that carried only his name on the outside. He waited until he was back in his office before looking at the contents, and then read the typed sheets with attention for detail. It was very thorough, but then SIS in Nicosia were well known for their exactness.

He buzzed through to Jones's extension, received no answer, and tried the outer office. Helen had not gone home.

'He's down below. Eavesdropping. Said he won't be up for some time. He asked me to stay behind. Said there might be some typing to do, some reports to make up.'

Annoyance surged through him. His own girl had disappeared hours ago. Jones's girl was always there, never went home, watching them the whole time when they worked late, amusing herself at their expense.

'Get a message to him,' Fairclough said. 'As soon as he's taken the business down below, we need to see him – Mr Duggan and myself. Say whatever time he's through we'll be waiting.'

When he'd rung off he too phoned his home to warn of a late departure from the office. Duggan had already done the same.

'Here it goes, Sir,' said the man hunched intently in the cubicle, stretching his bulk closer over the machinery. Jones could hear the amplified beeps through his earphones. He winced at the noise.

The man reacted to it, without turning round. 'Have to have 'em up full blast. They can whisper and you've lost the lot while you're fiddling the volume.' He had switched on the tape recorder,

61

the two wheels revolving steadily and without impatience. A third man was behind them, holding to his mouth the receiver of an open telephone to the GPO exchange nearest the embassy.

'It's McCoy,' muttered Jones as the Irish voice came through. The man behind was speaking into the phone, urgently. Jones heard the switch made to the extension inside the embassy, heard the code-word given, and the single sentence in reply before the connection was broken. It had been shorter than the earlier call, by two to three seconds.

'Not a bloody hope,' said the man who was standing at the back. 'It gives them next to nothing to work on.'

'Didn't say much anyway,' Jones spat the words out. 'Two hours waiting for that. Used the code-word, though – that's all.'

His note-pad carried a few hastily scrawled words. 'Mushroom – same as yesterday, but confirmed.'

Helen was standing by the outer door of the basement when he emerged. She said, 'Mr Duggan and Mr Fairclough want to see you. They said they'd wait till you were through with whatever . . .'

'Get them to my office, and quick.' And he was past her, hurrying along the corridor, not waiting for the lift, attacking the broad central staircase, three steps at a time.

From among the crowd by the mobile tea trolley Famy watched McCoy. The Irishman stood in front of the high wooden board that gave out the destinations and the times of the trains from Waterloo Station. He was wearing the right clothes – shirt correct, draped coat correct, sign correct. Nervous, that was as it should be. Not furtive, but anxious. Passengers swayed round the fair head of the Irishman as he swept the concourse, searching for recognition, and his contact. While he waited Famy reflected that this was a completely new departure for him. He had had no contact with foreign groups in the camp: older, more influential men in the movement had, but not Famy. If it had happened as planned, Bouchi would have been the one to go forward. But Bouchi was in a morgue.

Famy drank his tea, his hands scalded through the fragile sides of the plastic cup. His eyes were never far from the Irishman, but intermittently they strayed to take in the rest of the concourse, watching for any other man who might linger overlong. He took many minutes to be satisfied, then began to make his way forward.

He moved deftly, picking his way through the running commuters, avoiding confrontation. McCoy saw him some fifteen feet away, and stiffened. This time it was the Irishman whose breathing came a little faster. His contact was just a few seconds away – a slightly-built figure, with dark chocolate skin, short, well-groomed hair and brightly dressed. A stranger, something separate. McCoy watched him roll his hips and sway past the mass, saw the head turn once for reassurance and look behind, and then he was close, and pausing, and then speaking.

'The mushrooms are – ' Famy broke off. 'I think you are here to meet me?' There was a questioning in his voice. The word they had told him to say, how stupid and idiotic it sounded, spoken by a grown man in the chaos of a railway station.

McCoy just said, 'Come on. No need to hang about. Let's move.' Then, as an afterthought, 'You speak English, understand English?'

Famy nodded. Like all these British, they never believed anyone knew anything but themselves. McCoy was on the move, the Arab half a step behind him. The Irishman pushed a path for himself toward the steps that led down to the bus station in the street below. Almost out into the open again, he shortened his stride and said over his shoulder, 'Where are the others?'

'It is just me,' said Famy.

There was a tint of suspicion in the way McCoy tilted his head towards the other man. 'That's not what they told me,' he rapped out staccato. 'They said there'd be three of you. They told me I'd meet three men.'

'It is just me,' repeated Famy.

'What's happened to change it?' McCoy hissed the question, hurrying again now, confused.

'Read your papers of today. Read of the events in northern France. When you have done that it is simple.' McCoy shook his head, his lack of comprehension overwhelming. They were standing at the bus stop, the street ill-lit from the lights above. Famy went on, 'There was a shooting, at a road block. Yesterday in the early hours. My friends did not survive, only myself.'

McCoy turned round fast, his body close to Famy. Shorter than the Arab, he looked up into his face. 'Dead?' the one word, very quietly.

'They did not survive,' said Famy.

'Is it called off, then, is it over? Finished, the plan?' McCoy

63

was speaking fast, but trying to keep his voice suppressed.

'It is not over. There is no possibility of abandoning the plan. We have been launched. It is not infrequent there should be set-backs. But it is not a thing to talk of here. Later, we can talk.'

McCoy shrugged. He wanted to say more, but it was difficult against the unfamiliar logic spelled out in the curious pitched voice of the other man. McCoy noticed he ran his words together – and very precise, very clear. Like some text book, not natural.

They waited in silence for the approach of the big double-decker bus. What sort of game is this? thought the Irishman. The team shot to pieces, and this little bugger carrying on as if nothing had happened. Daft, bloody mad. He saw the face of the other man – masked, unemotional – staring down the road. Out of their bloody minds, this bugger and the ones who set it all up. What can one man, what can two achieve compared with four? Four was the minimum number, all agreed and locked-up, that had been. Should have been more, but for the problems of shifting a bigger group. And now it's halved, and this idiot says it goes on. God Almighty, put some sense into these thick buggers' heads. He mouthed the oaths, silently rolling his tongue round them, savouring and enjoying the words that somehow diluted the anger he felt. When the bus came he motioned with his head that they should take it, and went up the stairs to the top deck. A couple sat half-way, and the two men took the front seats, Famy pushing his grip underneath his knees.

'We can talk up here,' said McCoy.

'There is no problem, my friend,' said Famy, his voice gentle and lilting as he pronounced the words. There was no rush as he spoke, only a calmness. 'We two are sufficient. There is a plan? I was told there was a plan that could be executed. That is correct?' McCoy nodded, numbness setting in along with the knowledge that he was no longer in control, that the tall stranger had taken command. 'If there is a plan, we can execute it,' said Famy. He broke off as the ticket collector arrived at their seats. McCoy paid, and pocketed the thin white paper strips he received in return. Famy went on. 'He is only one man, the one we seek. He will be guarded, but not thoroughly. If we are determined there is no difficulty that can arise.'

There was no more conversation as the bus jolted its way from stop to stop, leaving the heart of London far behind and climbing the hill beyond King's Cross to Islington's Angel. The upper deck

64

filled, taking on the teenagers disgorged from the cinemas. Occasionally McCoy looked sideways at the Arab, and realized that the man who sat beside him showed no interest in the journey, that his eyes never shifted from their relaxed unseeing gaze straight ahead. The bright fronts of restaurants, advertisement hoardings, pin table arcades, cinema hallways – all passed him by. A group of drunk, noisy West Indians, loud and aggressive, gained no reaction. He's like a train, thought McCoy, on course, all signals green, and couldn't give a damn about anything else. The Irishman tried to put himself into the same situation. New city, contact man he's never met before, close to his target, half the back-up dead behind him, and the bugger doesn't even turn his head. Not a drop of sweat on his head, no perspiration round his balls making his trousers too tight so he has to wriggle for comfort. Just relaxed, as if he's on a coach outing.

The time he had shot the paratrooper was very clear to McCoy. He could recall his nausea as the soldier, in his airborne smock and red beret, had come into sight. He waited so long for him, but when the soldier came he'd hardly been able to focus his eyes down the smooth, crisp barrel of the Armalite. Sweat ran in rivulets under his vest, fashioning freezing paths of movement across his skin. Then the soldier had called to the sergeant patrolling in front of him, a remark that McCoy had tried to overhear, and in the effort recognized his concentration slipping away. He'd fired then, watched the soldier heave and clutch at himself, seen the disbelief that comes before the pain and death. He'd sprinted then, fast with the adrenalin pumping through his veins, and for hours afterward, even in the womb-like safety of the barn where he lay up after missions before returning to the farm, he had panted with the excitement, close to exhilaration, of the moment when he had fired. A near-orgasmic movement of release as the butt of the rifle thudded into his shoulder, his finger coiled on the trigger; he could relive it hour after hour.

But this bugger sitting next to him was something different. It's animal when you don't care, thought McCoy, unnatural when you don't feel the tension. Sub-human. The Irishman had read of these people when they went into Israel. Suicide squads, *kamikaze*, there to kill and be killed. Take the greatest possible number with you. He had seen the pictures on the television of them training with the explosive packs strapped round their waists. Madness, or motivation – McCoy didn't know which.

And the man beside him with the vacant, contented eyes – would he be one of them? Had to be, didn't he? Could be certain of that. One of the hard, mean bastards.

'We get off here. Next stop,' said McCoy. The two men gripped the backs of the seats as they made their way down the centre of the bus to the staircase. They waited by the top step till the bus had come to a halt. On the pavement they began to walk, Famy fractionally behind McCoy. After a hundred yards McCoy turned left, then realized the Arab was not beside him. He turned and saw him pressed against the wall of the pub on the corner. Bloody play acting, said McCoy to himself, and walked on. He'd gone another fifty yards before the running feet caught him up. The explanation was not slow in coming.

'Makes certain we are not being followed. To wait a moment at a corner when one goes on. The tail will hear the feet, and have to keep going. That way you spot him. Nobody is following,' said Famy.

The street was made up of four-storey Victorian terraced houses. Up to fifty years ago these were middle-class homes, complete with maid and cook to work in the basement kitchens and to sleep in the attic bedrooms; expensive and sought-after. But those families had long since abandoned the houses as ghostly, costly white elephants, and fled to the cheaper more territorially secure suburbs. The houses had disintegrated into flatlets owned by landlords who lived far from the premises. McCoy stopped outside a house at the far end of the street.

'Just a word of explanation,' he said. 'We thought about this a fair bit where we were to hole up. We've tried to find quite a new territory this time. None of the haunts our people use, the regular dormitories. It's what we call a "commune" here. Young people, who just couldn't give a fuck for it all and drop out, absolve themselves of the rat race, they say. This place is up for sale, one property owner selling to another, and it's sitting empty. The kids have moved in, taken over, till there's an eviction order, till they get chucked out. But it's safe, safe for us. People come and go at all hours of the day and night. Nobody asks any questions. Just don't get involved with them – don't ask questions, don't give answers. Just keep to yourself, and no one will bother you. I've got them to clear a room for us, when I thought there were four. Just don't let them bother you, and remember, nobody gives a damn who you are here.'

66

They walked up the paving steps to the front door. McCoy pushed the handle and the door swung open. They were met with a flood of hard-rock, shrieking music.

Inside the diplomatic bag sent out of the embassy that night was a cryptic note, in code and in a high-security sealed envelope. It would be flown the next morning to a North African capital. Upon receipt the envelope would be transferred again to Beirut. A telephone call would then be made to the newspaper offices of *Al Nahar*. The call would be person-to-person from the commercial secretary of the embassy in the Lebanese capital to a particular writer. The message that the man code-named 'Saleh Mohammed' was now in London would then be just a drive from the camouflaged tent of the leader of the PFLP-General Command. By Sunday evening he would be aware that his plan was still in motion.

Under the harsh fluorescent light the files in front of the three men who sat round the desk had begun to thicken. Every half hour or so Helen would bring in the mugs of coffee on which the department seemed to exist. The men's jackets were off, their ties were loosened at the collars and their hair dishevelled. Twice the secretary had been called in to type out assessments, handed her without word by Jones. They were all tired now, weary from the strain that had begun more than twelve hours earlier, but aware that no sleep could be taken until the next day's plan was prepared.

Jones knew the danger of exhaustion, had seen it sap men, make them vulnerable. That's how it had been in the war, the last half dozen raids before the end of a tour, but he'd been little more than a boy then. More than thirty years later, and close to the decreed age of retirement, the similar work load was still expected of him. But there was no way around it. No point in mobilizing the forces at their disposal – police, detectives, army – not until there was a plan, something for the masses to do. And that was the problem that he knew confronted him: to find the shape of the threat. Then, and only then, could the big battalions be drawn in. He'd begun to wonder more frequently what retirement would be like, how he'd feel the day after they'd given him the silver pen, or the cut-glass decanter set, or the shining gardening kit: no train to get on in the morning, no conferences to prepare for, no problems . . . he didn't know whether he would welcome it or not. But irrelevant that night.

Past midnight Jones dialled the home number of the Director General. It was rare for him to be called at home, let alone at that hour. To the head of the department, one of the triumvirate who sat on the Joint Intelligence Committee, Jones spoke with deference. He sketched through the outline of the papers that confronted them. The taped conversations, the identification and background of McCoy, the arrival and rendezvous with the unknown man, the Israeli warning. The 'DG' liked his briefs kept short, and listened without interruption as he sat pyjama-clad on the side of his bed, his wife of thirty-one years asleep beside him.

'Suggestions?' the DG asked at the other end of the line.

'Perhaps you could come in tomorrow morning, sir,' Jones replied. 'Have a conference with us. Then I think we should meet Special Branch with a view to hunting the Irishman. The Israeli security attaché will have to be brought in – get the lines buzzing a bit on the newcomer. We'll have to do a card check on airports and ferries, though that will probably narrow down simply to the Channel ports. This Israeli professor comes on Monday, in the afternoon. There's not a lot of time.'

'Right. Thank you, Jones.' The winds on the Sussex Downs wrapped round his house, the central heating was long off, cut on the arrival of spring. The DG shivered. 'I'll be in a bit after eight. Give me a few minutes, then the three of you come in at eight-thirty. Get some sleep in the meantime.' He rang off.

Jones repeated the instructions. Duggan and Fairclough shuffled their papers together.

'Not worth making much of a move at this time of night,' said Duggan. 'I'll doss down in the office.' Fairclough agreed. As they were leaving Helen came in, alerted by the scraping of the chairs on the lino fringe of the carpet.

'What time in the morning?' She said it casually, matter of fact.

'Eight-thirty, my love. We're seeing "DG". You might as well make it then. Far to go tonight? Or Jimmy's, is it? He's the lucky man?'

There was no trace of a blush, just a light laugh. 'Jimmy said he'd sit up, make me some cocoa.'

Lucky bugger, thought Jones. 'Tell lover-boy not to burn the candle too hard. Might be needing him before too long. All fit and fighting fresh. Tell Jimmy that.'

And she was gone, leaving him with the task of setting up the canvas and metal bed – that fitted so snugly when collapsed into the bottom drawer of his filing cabinet, and which took such an age to make sleep-worthy.

6

The music went on throughout the night. It blasted its way through the walls, through the floor boards and under the door, finally merging in the room around the two men. Famy tossed and rolled in his sleeping bag, heaving it about on the narrow canvas sun-bed. They were high in the building, with the walls angled by the roof, but still the noise sought him out, wresting him from sleep. A few feet away McCoy lay still, impervious to the noise, his breathing regular and heavy. For the first hour, after he had undressed down to his underpants and crawled into his envelope-like bag, the Arab had sought refuge, burying his head under the cushion McCoy had given him. But there was a stale smell of perspiration about the faded material. His nostrils had turned and coiled and he had hurled the cushion across the room and then tried to find comfort by drawing himself down into the bag so that his ears were covered. The bag at least was clean. New, with the price tag still on it.

There were no curtains covering the window and the moon threw sufficient light into the room for Famy to make out its bareness. Rough, uncovered boards, indented with nails, peeling floral wallpaper. A length of flex hanging twisted from the low ceiling; a bulb, but no shade. In a corner a bulging plastic bag, and around it a scattering of orange peel, newspapers and cigarette butts. Apart from the sun-beds, and their clothes and their bags, there was nothing else. His shoulders felt the cold of the great unheated house.

When he'd arrived, they'd offered him food, talked of beans and stewed meat and bread. He'd declined, and watched the Irishman help himself from a scarcely washed plate. Later he'd relented sufficiently to take a cup of milk poured from a half-empty bottle. That was all he had allowed himself.

He had waited out in the hall when they had first come to the house while McCoy had entered a downstairs room, and over the music made himself heard. Famy had not been able to distinguish the words. A group, a foraging party, had come to look at him, to survey the visitor. Without meaning to he had smiled at them as they stood by the door. They did not come closer, just watched and evaluated. Long, dank hair, falling straight to their shoulders, boys distinguished from girls by their beards and moustaches, but both in the uniform of tight jeans, sweat-shirts and jerseys. Some had worn sandals, others had been barefoot. There were beads and badges embroidered on the clothes. Famy had been able to look over their shoulders into the rest of the room and in the candlelight had made out others, either sitting on the floor or draped on chairs, all intent on him. McCoy had not led him in, but up the stairs to the room.

There was no life like this in Nablus. Some might live unwashed and in clothes that were little more than rags, but not from choice. No one sought such degradation, or made it a purposeful way of life. In the camp up the hill on the Jerusalem Road, where existence was married to the open drains, where a roof was corrugated iron, where walls were fashioned from wooden or cardboard packing-cases, there was no satisfaction at the awfulness. There was simply no option. Those who lived there had come in 1948, bred their children there, built their shanties, and when the Israeli advance had rushed further forward nineteen years later the movement had been too fast for them to walk on again and seek a new refuge in new filth on the far side of the dividing Jordan river. The tanks had outstripped them.

But the Irishman had said it was safe to stay here. That was sufficient, while the operation went ahead.

There was movement below the floor. Doors opened and closed; he heard shouts on the landings. And then the undulating and controlled heaving of a bed, starting softly, rising minutes later to a frenzy. He had listened, almost ashamed, his mind conjuring the faces and the forms of the olive-skinned girls he had known in Beirut, whose arms he had touched, their gentle skin sensitive to his fingers. He strained to listen, drawn by the steady, driving persistence of the sound. The half-sleep left him. Imagination delving into fantasy; coiled bodies, searching and passion and closeness, enacted in a near room. It was almost nauseating for him to imagine anything so precious, in that stench, in that dirt. In the camp there had been girls – not many, and they had slept in their own tents. They joined in the laughter and the gaiety, shared the training sessions, but at night they left the men to sleep alone on their close-packed trestle beds. In his student days there had been girls too, beautiful, supreme but with mothers awaiting them as the city darkened. He had never slept with a girl, had never known the reality of his imagination, and now close to him two of these creatures, with their smears and the hair, coupled. And then the sound died, and the house was at rest.

It was nearly dawn, when the thin grey light had begun to penetrate the room, that he was alerted by the turning of the door handle. If he had been able to drift back to sleep he would not have noticed the action, as it was done quietly and with care.

He lay very still, tense, eyes like slits, watching the entrance to the room. He saw his coat and trousers, suspended from a metal hanger, move towards him as the door opened. The door was heavy, and the hinges made the sparse, scraping sound. Famy controlled his breathing, reducing it to the same pitch as McCoy's, and watched a darkened shape glide without sound into the room and across the boards. For a moment there was a silhouette against the window and he could make out long hair, and the shape of a coat thrown shawl-like over shoulders, then the figure merged into the blackness of the far side of the room and went beyond his power of vision. A small shaft of light – a hand torch? – edge of his sight field, and he was aware of hands pulling open and probing inside his grip bag. Then the light was doused, and the sound of the feet on the floor boards became muted, as if uncertain where next they should travel. The figure went across the room, back toward the door, hesitating there, at his clothes, those that were not beside him. There was a chink as his belt clasp was shifted, and a smooth rifling of a hand inside his trousers. And then there was the sound of the catch being fastened again, the door closed. Yet there came no movement of footsteps away from the door immediately. He stayed motionless in his sleeping bag. Waiting to see if I am aroused, he told himself. Like a rat that comes for the cheese and lingers by its hole to see if the dogs are out and have the scent. Fifteen seconds passed, perhaps more. Then the noise on the landing, the shuffling of bare feet, finally lost, emptied into the hugeness of the house.

Famy found he was sweating, cold moisture on the folds of his stomach, dampness in the hair at the back of his neck. He would have given anything for the company of Dani and Bouchi, for the presence of his friends from the camp, someone in whom he could confide, someone other than the stranger in the other sleeping bag across the boards.

The fool had said it was a safe place, a place where he could relax, where there would be no requirement to remain vigilant twenty-four hours in the day. Half a night, and both his possessions and clothes had been precisely and systematically searched. Should he have intervened? Thrust himself at the intruder? But how would he have done it? The bag was a strait-jacket, so how to create the element of surprise? It could not have been accomplished, he told himself. He lay on his bag, waiting for McCoy to wake and the morning to come.

It was past seven on his watch when the Irishman began to struggle his way out of the sleep. Famy leaned over to him and shook his shoulder, firmly, communicating his impatience. McCoy awoke, eyes focused instantly.

'What is it? What's the bloody matter?' he said.

'There has been someone in here, someone has been in the room.' Famy said it with urgency, seeking to impress with his information.

'So what? People come and go in these places. Looking for somewhere to doss down, kip for a bit.'

'Not like that. Someone has been to search – the bags and clothes. To examine.'

McCoy stared hard across at him. 'Been in here, giving us a look-over?'

'I was awake,' said Famy. 'I could not sleep, and someone came in, went through the pockets. I didn't move, pretended sleep. Nothing was found. It was about two hours ago, just before the light began to come.'

McCoy forced his lids further open, bruising them with the motion of his arm, and sat up. His white skin seemed curiously weak and without sinew till the body swivelled and Famy saw

72

the reddened, puckered mess of a bullet wound, on McCoy's left side, just below the rib cage.

'Probably just some bugger on the scrounge looking for a few pence . . .'

Famy cut across him, excited, talking fast, 'Nothing was taken. I couldn't see all that was searched, but no sound of money being taken. My trouser pockets, they were looked at, the money remains. It's the wrong place for us here, not the place I was expecting, not *familiar*.'

'Well, it's here you're bloody well staying.' McCoy was close to shouting. 'You'll stay where I bloody well say, and that's here. It's an out-of-the-way, quiet, no-questions place. If some sod comes wandering about in the middle of the night frightening you I can't help it. Shouldn't believe in bloody fairies.'

'And if you're wrong?' Famy asked.

'If I'm wrong? What the hell does that mean? What I say is we're better off here than with the usual crowd, the ones who might want to know about us – our bloody lot.' He quietened suddenly, recognized the anxiety as genuine, and became anxious to allay and calm. 'I'll ask around downstairs, put a bit of heat on, but gently. There's all sorts of buggers just drifting round these places, looking for a bed, or for something to pinch. Nothing extraordinary about the night. Remember it's London you're at now, and it's Saturday, and the man you want is here on Monday, whatever it is you call him . . .'

'Al Kima.'

'Whatever that means.'

'It is the man who grows mushrooms. The mushroom man. My friends would like me to meet him. They would believe that I would avenge them.'

Crisis over, calmed the little bugger down, chance of more sleep. McCoy turned away from Famy to face the wall.

'There's nothing much to do today. Lie up. Tomorrow we start working. For now it's sleep we want, there's nothing today but a walk round the university. Tomorrow it gets interesting.'

The Irishman could not see the gleam in the other's eyes, the brightness that comes from an erotic and compulsive anticipation; the dream of the shudder of gunfire, blood smears on the concrete, the international headlines, and the adulation in the tents far away in Fatahland.

When Famy looked again across the floor of the room he saw

McCoy was asleep, with his left arm high round his head to shut out the light, so that the bullet wound below was exposed. The thought of it bruised the Arab. He who had come so far, and who now assumed leadership, was virgin and unconsummated, had never known the reality of conflict. He could not know how it would affect him, the moment when it came. Famy lay on his back staring at the ceiling, while deep in the sleeping bag his legs trembled.

Jones was padding down a ground-floor corridor at the back of Leconfield House on his way to the canteen kitchens. They'd be empty, but he could heat a kettle there and make himself a cup of tea with the tea bags he kept in his desk drawer. He was without either shoes or socks, having washed his socks last thing before getting into bed. They were still damp, and he would leave putting them on till the last minute, before the walk up the stairs to the early morning meeting. After the tea he would shave, make himself presentable. The way it was supposed to be in the department.

As he stood facing the window, running the water from the taps into the opened top of the kettle, he saw the Director General's Humber turn into the narrow entry to the underground car park, wire portcullis raised as the vehicle was expertly manoeuvred by the young man in the front. In the back there was nothing much to see, an opened newspaper masking the figure, well down in his seat.

The alarm bell, furious, demanding attention, woke Helen.

She reached forward, pressing herself up with one hand, the other straining across Jimmy toward the bedside table and the offending clock, till she found the button and the silence. He hadn't moved all night, the bastard. Sprawled on his back with his eyes tight and hermetically sealed, mouth open, his pyjamas buttoned protectively up to his neck. Bloody good weekend entertainment you make, Jimmy. A great porpoise up a beach, with no prospect of another high tide. She made one more concerted effort to work some life into the marooned carcase next to her, slipping her hands beneath the material and working with her nails at his chest, slowly and with consideration sketching

74

out small patterns of the skin. Jimmy slept on.

'You're bloody hopeless,' she told him, mouth close to his ear. 'Understand, *hopeless*, a great dump of garbage. Come on, wake up! Stir yourself!'

No response. She moved her hands lower, indenting a line where the beginnings of his paunch slunk down to his hips. Then there was movement. Convulsive, total, as his arms came up and around her, gripping the shoulder blades, pulling her down on to him. His eyes opened for a brief flicker, then closed again, and his arms went slack.

'Better Jimmy, fractionally better. One out of ten for trying, zero for everything else.'

He hadn't seen a razor the day before, nor the day before that, and his chin was close-set with a tight brush of hair. It bit into her skin, a myriad of needles.

'Not so fast, lover-boy, or we'll have the bloody department wanting a blow-by-blow account if I turn up with half my face scraped off by your beard.'

He spoke for the first time, but as if the effort were all but beyond him, the ultimate struggle. 'It's Saturday, you're not going in today, and what bloody time did you get here last night? I'm sitting here half the bloody evening waiting for you.'

'I'm going in today, and I'm going in now. Jones's special request. There's a big flap, all hands to action-stations.' She slid out of his grasp and swung her legs over the side of the bed. She wore no clothes. Wishful thinking, you silly bitch, she told herself. Leave him past midnight and you're always the loser.

Jimmy had begun to take an interest. Not in me, she thought, wave him the boobs and the backside, but it'll take second place to the department. He was half up, almost sitting.

'What's going on, what's the flap?'

'Don't worry, lover-boy, you're included in the cast. Some hit-and-runners reached inside base with a nice plum Yiddisher target all to themselves, and second, third and fourth floor are running round like it's Declaration of War day. Big enough for the DG to be arriving before breakfast, then a full scale bit of summitry at zero-eight-thirty hours on the precise stroke.'

He was still trying to focus on her: rounded, pink, but not clear lines yet. Striving for concentration. 'What way is it for me?'

Helen moved off the bed toward the chair draped with her clothes, and began to pull them on. 'Don't know yet. Jones mentioned you just as I was pulling out in the wee small hours. Said he might be needing you. All fit and fighting fresh. Be bloody lucky, won't he? That was all he said, and I was just on my way. Wasn't social chat, I was on my way then.'

'He didn't say anything else?'

'Nothing at all.'

'Bloody fine message for crack-of-dawn Saturday. What am I supposed to do? Sit here all through the weekend hanging on the edge of the phone waiting for him to ring?'

'That's what you do every weekend. God, these tights smell. Not as though anyone will notice. They all slept in. Jones, dreary old Duggan, Fairclough, all doing the boy scouts' bit, kipping on the premises. They'll all be high, smelling to the ceiling. I'll be in good company.' She eased her skirt into position, and grimaced as she looked at herself in the mirror.

'Look like a bloody wreck,' she said.

Jimmy called across from the bed, 'But he said nothing more?'

'Patience, lover-boy, patience. They'll be in touch. It's just that one hell of a panic started up yesterday. Huddles, chats, meetings, files for me to type, despatch riders bombing over from the FO . . . God, I'm late. Never get a taxi at this bloody time, and I said I'd be in. Have to take the car. Now be a good lad, go quietly back to sleep and shed some of that load, so you sound all sweet and sober when the gaffer comes on for you.'

'One more time,' he said. 'Give us a kiss and tell me again what it's all about. Come on.' He said it quietly, the thickness of his voice evaporating.

She leaned over. Let him kiss her on the throat. He was considerate enough not to spoil her make-up. 'I don't know much. Really. But there's an Israeli coming over to stay here, comes some time next weekend, and they've hooked on to a couple of boys. One's IRA, the other they're not sure of, but Phonetics say he's probably Middle East. The codeword they're using is something involving "Mushroom", and the man they're having the flap about is a nuclear scientist. Seems a nice easy equation. Quite a pretty little code-name, better than all those Greek goddesses we're forever calling our fiascos after. But don't tell Jones what I told you. Let it come to virgin, suitably surprised ears. I'll see you tonight – I'll try not to be late again, and we'll cook something.'

Helen stepped up quickly, gave the prone figure a wave and

was on her way out of the flat. Early enough not to meet the neighbours on the stairs, stupid bloody looks they gave her. Two years she'd been coming now. First time after a department party, and Jimmy too drunk to notice she'd driven him home, and waking in the morning and taking his time to remember who she was. And then a habit had set in, and she'd come more often, and taken to cleaning up, and washing his smalls, and cooking him meals. The department directed both their lives, and the few chances of contact with people who did not share an existence governed by the Official Secrets Act ensured a curtailed horizon of friends. They began to accept each other, enough to make love in a perfunctory and clumsy style that satisfied the immediate needs of Jimmy as much as Helen. There was no talk of marriage.

The curtains were still drawn together. Jimmy switched off the bedside light, darkening the room. Be a bugger of a day, he thought, waiting for the telephone to ring the summons. Be by it all day in case Jones called, just as Helen had said he would, just as he always did when there was something rumbling at the department. Wouldn't go out, not even to stock the larder, not even down to the off-licence. Whisky was thin, drained after last night. He could see the bottle over on the table, by the divan in the living part of the room. Barely an inch left, and it had been two-thirds full at the time she should have come back last night.

There was not much else on the table; just the ashtray, a big, cut-glass effort, and piled high with cigarette ends, stubbed and strangled to extinction, and the water jug. He could remember that he'd started by mixing it with water, but the last two inches they'd been neat. Constant refills, the way it generally worked out when he sat up late at night on his own. Need another bottle if any possibility of another late night. But couldn't leave the phone, not if Jones was going to call. There was a nerve-breaking ache in his head now, splitting it from side to side, and a deep throbbing somewhere far inside and behind his temples.

Jimmy lay back, trying to shut out the pain. This was the way it worked out. A big scene down at the department, high level stuff, top men nattering to each other, twisting their knickers, and at the end of the day finding a place for Jimmy somewhere in the set-up. Hadn't been anything for four months, not since the MP, little grovel-merchant. Represented sixty thousand miners and their families and cohorts up in the West Riding. Smug little sod, with too much to say till they worked out the links, the

Hungarians, how he afforded the London flat, the rendezvous points, what he had to offer from the Select Committee on Defence Expenditure. Found it only after Jimmy had slipped the kitchen window at Division Bells' time in the House, picked the lock of the drawer in his working table, and pocketed the over-filled, concisely documented diary. Must have missed it, the little bugger, but he'd never reported it. Just looked crestfallen, as if he might weep when they read the charge out. Asked for his solicitor – lot of good that would do him.

But life had been hard since then. The Department's retainers didn't go that far. For Jimmy existence on the fringe of the department had started a long time ago. Recruitment was haphazard, following few fixed patterns and depending mainly on personal recommendation.

Jimmy owed his connections with the Security Services to his actions on a glorious moonlit night on 24 August 1944. He was aged nineteen, with the exalted wartime rank of Flight Sergeant (Rear Gunner) in a Lancaster bomber squadron. He flew in 'Charley Apple' off one of those eternal concrete runways that littered the flat Lincolnshire countryside. The whole eight-man crew, officer included, had bitched about flying that night.

'Should have their bloody heads examined, those desk bastards,' the pilot had said.

'Sitting bloody duck for whatever they send up,' had been the contribution of the navigator.

Jimmy had been neither old nor experienced enough to add to the condemnation publicly, but he had recognized that the cursing was counterfeit for fear. They were more than a hundred and fifty miles short of the target when the nightfighter was guided on to them. Jimmy had had a fleeting glimpse of it before the firing started, enough time to shout a warning and bring his own machine-guns to bear. Then the cannon began to rake the airframe of the Lancaster. Fire was quick to follow, and then the order to abandon the aircraft. It took Jimmy what seemed endless stretching minutes to realize that the heavy canopy through which he should have made his individual escape would not move. There was one other way out; he crawled more than sixty feet down the length of the belly of the plane to where the roaring wind drove an entry through the forward escape hatch. Six men had already jumped into the night that stretched more than three miles beneath. As Jimmy had been about to lever

78

himself into the hole he saw the movement beyond the flapping door of the cockpit. Then the pilot, edging his way toward him. There was a look of surprise on the officer's face, and he had shouted something like, 'I thought they'd all gone,' and his attention was turned from the effort of movement and the pain from the fire that had caught at the upper fabric of his flying tunic. But Jimmy had not heard him. The words were lost in the noise of the wind and the tearing metal as the superstructure of the aircraft struggled to hold itself together in the face of its unnatural and contorted descent.

They had jumped virtually together. Jimmy first, then the officer. It was the first time for the rear gunner: only the tower and the simulator before. He had felt the moment of stark panic before he had pulled the metal hoop fastened to the harness across his chest, and then had followed the decisive and successive sensation of the jolt of the parachute opening, the surge upward as it billowed out, the silent descent, and then the terror as the earth catapulted up to meet him. The officer had landed less than a hundred yards away, the fire on his body extinguished by the air-rush of his speed of fall.

They had barely disentangled themselves from the cords and webbing of their parachutes when the German soldier reached them, shouting instructions and calling to his colleagues across the fields. Not a front-line man, but middle-aged, a reservist. Jimmy had gestured into the middle distance behind the soldier, and as the man in his inexperience had turned, so Jimmy's heavy flying boot went into his crotch. The German jack-knifed, and simultaneously the hard outside edge of Jimmy's right hand came down on the bare and exposed inch of the man's neck, between the helmet and the thickened collar of the great-coat. The German had died instantly and without a whimper, giving Jimmy and the officer time to fade into the sanctuary and shadow of the trees. When light came the next morning Jimmy had seen the pilot's face, seen the raw, mashed damage, the legacy of the clinging cockpit oil. The sight had not unduly upset him. He had been sympathetic, interested, nothing more.

The pilot's name was Philip Whilloughby-Jones. He was two years older than the rear gunner, and was never to forget the speed and ruthlessness involved in the death of the German. He would never put out of his mind the fresh pleasure that played in Jimmy's eyes, reflected by the moonlight, before they reached the trees, nor the adulation of success that encompassed his young downy mouth. Via the French Resistance they had been smuggled to the Spanish border and after their return home had lost touch – there had been different postings, different stations. Following the war, when Jones became a full-time deskman with the department, he had let it be known there existed a man who could kill without scruple.

His assessment of Jimmy had not been disproved.

The nearest police station to Englefield Road is some six streets away and to the north, beyond Dalston Junction and close to the Balls Pond Road. It is a forbidding, grey-bricked building, dingy and in a general state of disrepair. Inside attempts had been made to brighten the cavernous passages and interview rooms with quantities of paint; they had been largely unsuccessful.

Police Constable Henry Davies, Alsatian dog handler, nine years in the force, was going off duty. That in itself did not entail much work, just signing the time sheet, confirming that his overnight reports were completed and ready for the Day Duty Inspector. It had been a quiet night: no pub fights, no premises broken into. Time for home now – to his ground floor flat to sleep through the daylight hours, with Zero out in the kennel beside the coal box.

As Davies passed the main desk at the end of the front hall the dog on its lead and head pressed close to his left knee, the sergeant, old and cheerful in spite of the surroundings, spoke to him.

'Off home then, Henry? Not been much for you tonight.'

'Not a damn thing, Sarge.'

'Seeing Doris this weekend?' He'd need that for his dossier, knew every damn thing about everyone, the old boy.

Davies paused near the door. 'No way, she's staying in through today and tomorrow. Won't be coming out till Monday.'

'Need a good bath and all, then,' said the sergeant. 'I don't know how she does it. Nice clean girl, living with all that muck.'

The constable smiled. 'She doesn't seem to mind. Gets a bit deep about it all, says it's what police work is all about. Laughs at me for lugging this piece of dog-flesh about.'

'Well, I couldn't do it. Might manage if it was nine to five, Monday to Friday. But not living in among them twenty-four

80

hours, weekends and all.'

The sarcasm was gentle and kindly meant. 'No one's going to ask you to blend into the hippy scene, now are they? Not your style, Sarge. But seriously, she says all the coming and going is at the weekend. When she was at the place behind the Angel they got the pusher at the weekend. You have to be there the whole time – part of the furniture.'

An old lady moved across the hall toward the desk, diverting the sergeant's attention. Lost her bloody cat, most likely, thought Davies. He gave the dog's lead a slight pull, and the Alsatian was up off its haunches. They went together to his van.

He had told Doris, but only half-heartedly, that he wasn't that keen on her living in the commune, and she had dismissed it – told him it was a damned sight more interesting than driving round with a dog for company. But he'd see her on Monday when she came out of the half-world that she'd infiltrated, when she came out to file her twice-weekly report.

7

It was Lord Denning who wrote in his report in the wake of the Profumo scandal: 'The Security Service in this country is not established by Statute, nor is it recognized by Common Law. Even the Official Secrets Acts do not acknowledge its existence.' Since its conception back in the late sixteenth century the department has insisted that its moves and practices are cloaked in total secrecy. For years it was successful, and the Security Service remained shrouded in mystery, with its operators able to congratulate themselves that they had found a near-divine formula for the working of the department. But all good things come to an end, and that very secrecy, once so jealously protected, had now brought the Security Service into hard times. Politicians looking for economic savings in the 1960s and early 1970s found a familiar scapegoat to carry the burden of financial cut-backs; few of them understood what went on in Leconfield House, and those that wanted to discover the strange activities of the personnel there were actively dissuaded from pursuing their inquiries.

The numbers of men employed in the department shrivelled as fewer funds were channelled toward them. Worse followed when their political masters decided that the autonomy of the service should be curtailed, and appointed a career Civil Servant to take charge. Only recently, after a series of publicly castigated mishaps, had the Prime Minister reverted to tradition and put a senior man from the service itself into the Director General's office. His identity was unknown to the mass of the population, and was covered by a 'D' Notice, requesting that the media keep it confidential.

The present DG spent much of his working day wrestling with the budget the Security Service was allowed by Parliament, striving to keep his force efficient, while at the same time remaining solvent. It was a soul-destroying job, and one which he detested. Nor was he paid much for his pains – slightly less than the Fleet Street average for a middle-ranking columnist. But inside the department the new man had revitalized morale simply because his subordinates knew that the man who now controlled them understood their work, was sympathetic to their problems, and was always available. The Irish problem had also played its part in lifting the tempo in Curzon Street. Instead of their dealing almost to the exclusion of everything else with the activities of the Iron Curtain embassies and the huge Soviet trade mission on Highgate Hill, an extra dimension had been brought into the work. On top of that came the more recent wave of Arab terrorism throughout Europe. The DG could note with satisfaction that the building no longer operated on a five-day week, and that many of the heads of key sections were at their desks through the weekend, even in high summer.

The Director General was a short, heavily-built man. Spread across his desk, occasionally breaking off to pencil a few words on a pad, he scanned the files that had been left for him to digest, his eyes only a few inches from the paper. There was monumental concentration, head quite still, seeking for flaws in the arguments, high spots in the information. He believed totally in paperwork, required it to be short and explicit, but demanded all relevant facts to be set out in the files. He had hooked his coat over the end of his chair and undone the top button of his shirt, while his tweed tie hung down loose at the neck. He smoked incessantly, non-tipped and one of the strong brands, drawing deeply till there was hardly enough of the rolled paper left for him to hold without him burning his fingers.

Promptly at eight-thirty came the knock at his door, and Jones, followed by Fairclough and Duggan, came into the bright first-floor office. The DG gestured to them to pull up chairs and continued to read the last pages of the file on Ciaran McCoy. The section heads made a half-moon as they sat down on the far side of the desk, and waited for him to finish. The office was bare, but not to the point of being Spartan: there was a picture of the Queen – the Annigoni print; a water colour of a bowl of fruit; a table littered with yesterday's newspapers; wall-to-wall carpets (as his position decreed); and heavy plain curtains drawn back to let in the sunlight. Not much to gaze at, but they all felt the after-effects from the night just past, and none was in the mood for day-dreaming or staring at irrelevancies.

When he had finished the DG closed the McCoy file, piling it neatly with the others. He threw an eye quickly over the notes he had made, and then looked at the three men facing him. He could see their tiredness. A short meeting was required.

'There's not much time, gentlemen,' he started. Voice calm, easy, fluent from his Welsh background. 'Our guest here on Monday night, his public appearance on Tuesday, and the flight out undecided between Wednesday and Thursday. We can probably ensure that he goes on Wednesday. On what we have at our disposal the threat seems real enough. There is one factor we should consider before recommendations are made to the Home Office. If this were simply an IRA affair saturation protection would probably see us through. They tend to like to make it home all in one piece, so if they see the odds placed heavily against them they like to try again when conditions are more auspicious. But there's the added factor of the Middle East involvement. Different people, different philosophy, more prepared to go with the target. If the other half of the team is Arab – Palestinian – then we must accept he is prepared to die along with our scientist friend. It makes the operation of protection infinitely more complicated. The suicide killer always has things stacked in his favour. It means for us that we have to widen the number of people involved, and mount a much wider screen than I would otherwise advocate. That means police, uniformed and CID.

Thoughts, gentlemen?'

Duggan spoke. 'This McCoy is a hard operator. Given them a long chase across the water, but he's on strange ground here. It's reasonable to suggest he'll need a safe house, somewhere he can hole up with the other man. He has two alternatives. He can go in with the usual crowd, Provo supporters, that lot. On the other hand he can go elsewhere, somewhere right outside the norm. The only line we have on that could be some connection with his sister. She's no longer in London, back in the Republic, but she went through a spell in a commune, one of those in North London, but drifting. McCoy was reported as disapproving, but it could have given him the contact.'

'Half the raids the Special Branch mount are aimed at communes,' said the DG. 'It's a good suggestion, but it'll take time to check out, and that's one for the police.'

'Presuming that the Palestinian has joined up with McCoy – and we have to believe that from the rendezvous call,' said Fairclough, ' – then we can just about guarantee that he's dependent on McCoy for his accommodation, and probably for the guns too. We've had the French report in overnight, and no firearms were found in the car, the one that was shot up and burned out. If the third lad made it away from the car there's little chance he could have carried the necessary firearms, explosives or whatever for three men. And it makes sense that the Arabs would provide the attack team, the Provisionals what local knowledge they needed.'

'It's strange they should have chosen McCoy, then. No history, no past form of operations in London or anywhere else outside his little patch. But with his associations no problem with firearms if he wanted them – plenty of access, could all be fixed. No problem there.' The DG was thinking aloud, picking his words carefully and slowly. 'The firearms would be McCoy's part. But what we have to consider is this. If the original team is decimated, and the one man wants to go on with it, how far does McCoy involve himself?'

'He's a killer,' said Duggan decisively, without hesitation or doubt. 'It's clear from the file. He'll think about it, he'll try and make sure he walks out of it, but he's a killer. He won't step back, not unless the odds are right against him.'

'And our unknown friend will need him?'

'He's essential,' said Duggan. 'The Arab, whoever he is,

84

needs him – and badly. But the two make a formidable threat. Quite a handful.'

'To become more general' – with a slight wave of his hand the DG terminated the conversation – 'to delve into the theory of the attack: what brings these two together? No common ideology . . .'

'Necessity only,' said Duggan. As the protégé of the head of the Security Services, and one whose career was well mapped, and his future charted, he had the confidence to speak his mind. 'The Palestinians must have the accommodation and transport, and if it's provided locally then the trails can be that much better covered. It's infinitely more satisfactory from their point of view, particularly if they can also travel clean of firearms. Same for the Provisionals: they'll have become involved through the advantages that will come to them. They've tried hard enough to get their hands on Iron Curtain weapon systems . . . Europe's difficult as a supply source; nothing coming direct – they don't want to know over there. The American market is inadequate, and difficult on resupply. But the Middle East offers them a major opportunity. If they pull this one in successful harmony then it'll be a guarantee that Klashnikovs, rocket launcher RPG 7s, perhaps even a SAM 7 missile will be turning up on the border for the boys in South Armagh and Tyrone. I'd put it down as a straight swap – immediate help by the Provos, and they get top-grade hardware in the close future. And talk to any army man, not HQ but the guys in the field, and ask them how they'd feel about having that sort of gear on tap for the opposition.'

'And the man Sokarev? . . .'

'Important to the Palestinians, big coup if they drop him. Irrelevant to the Irish. If we lose him – heaven forbid! – the chances are the Provos wouldn't even claim him, nor their part in it.'

'And this bomb that the Israelis keep so much under the table, and that our Mr Sokarev is credited with, what state is that in?'

'The Americans call it the "screwdriver" state. That's a good description. Probably not assembled, but way off the design bench. Just needs putting together.'

There had been enough talking, the DG decided. He straightened in his chair. 'I think we'd better get the following done this morning. Details on McCoy to all police stations in London, particular reference to communes. Run a check on all immigration forms coming in via ferries from Boulogne yesterday, that's for

85

Ports Unit of Special Branch. Liaise with the Israelis, the security attaché – not here, though. Fix a meeting with him at Home Office, and don't let him think that he's running the show. Jones, I'd like you to co-ordinate. Final point. I'd like a man on the ground beside this professor night and day, not just Special Branch – they can look after themselves – but one of our own. So we know what's going on.'

Jones spoke for the first time, mock hesitant, a smile on his face. 'There's Jimmy.'

'Is he on the bottle or off it at the moment?'

'About half-way. He'll fit the job.'

'There are plenty of others,' said the DG.

'He's the best of them.' It was Jones's opinion. None of the other men in the room was prepared to make an issue from it.

For differing reasons both Fairclough and Duggan were disapproving of the choice, but neither spoke. Jones's loyalty to the men who worked for him was familiar to his colleagues. It was recognized there was a personal bond between the section head and Jimmy; the detail of it had never been explained to them. But to criticize the judgement that Jones had made of his man would be futile, and both stayed silent.

The DG nodded. He knew Jimmy, had known him for a long time, liked his results, stayed ignorant of his methods. He said, 'I'm going to see the Minister this morning. I'll be back at lunchtime. If you want me, try about a quarter to one. That's it, gentlemen. Remember, there's very little time.'

From the outer office Helen called the home number of the Commander in charge of Special Branch, and put him through to Jones. Copies of McCoy's file together with the fingerprint and photograph folder that had now arrived from Northern Ireland were sent by motorcycle to Scotland Yard. The conversation also served to activate the search of the immigration forms, thirty-nine thousand of them, representing the number of persons who had crossed to Britain on ferries from Boulogne the previous day.

Helen also called the Israeli Embassy, introduced herself as Home Office, left a number – the direct one to Jones's desk – and asked that the security attaché should call back as soon as he had been located with a view to arranging an urgent meeting in mid-afternoon. Next she traced the Assistant Commissioner (Crime) to a golf club in North Hertfordshire. He arranged to see Jones in his office at Scotland Yard immediately after lunch. That would set in motion the sifting of scores of reports and observations made by undercover drug squad detectives who worked in the communes. The conversation with Jones was impressive enough for him to scratch from the four-ball game he had arranged, make his apologies to his partners, and drive home for a morning's work on the telephone before going into London.

Lastly she raised Jimmy, still waiting beside the receiver, but dressed now. His trousers were creased at the back of his knees, his jacket had great lines carved across the flap at the back, and the shirt was not quite clean. But he was dressed. Would he come in at four-thirty? 'Course he bloody well would. And after that? She didn't know. Going at it like a lot of maniacs, she'd said, and rung off.

The Cabinet Minister who rejoiced in the title of 'Secretary of State for Home Affairs' liked to keep in touch with his constituents. On Saturday mornings he held a 'surgery', where the electors who had returned him to Westminster for the past eighteen years could come to him with their problems. His opponents claimed it was simply window-dressing, and that as he allowed each of his 'patients' a bare four minutes there was little that could effectively be talked about in that time. Clogged-up drains and the lateness of school buses was about all that could be managed. Anything as detailed as council house rents or the redundancies at the local car-body factory could not, to the relief of the Minister, be dealt with in the limited time of his schedule.

He had dealt with fifteen constituents in the straight hour that he set himself, and was preparing for the drive across country to the hall where he would eat a sandwich lunch with the faithful and make a short speech, when the Director General of the Security Services was put through on the telephone in his agent's office on the first floor of the constituency headquarters. On matters of state security the Director General had direct access to the Prime Minister, but there were occasions when that was not suitable. Going too high up the ladder too fast, and then leaving no one senior to fall back if the initial contacts with Government went sour. The DG liked to leave his options a little open, but it was rare for him to seek an interview outside normal working routine with his Minister – rare enough for the Minister to be puzzled, and to be left confused after he had arranged that they should meet at the hall and talk while the tea and food were being consumed.

When the Director General arrived in mid-morning he was shown into a room behind the stage of the hall, and he waited there among the piled chairs and old scenery props for the Minister to come in.

'I'm sorry to trouble you,' he began.

'I'm sure you wouldn't have done so if you hadn't thought it important.' The Minister was wary of the other man. Security was fraught with whirlpools in the political ocean; when everything was going well you never heard from them; they only surfaced when the gales were blowing.

'I think we're running into some bother, something you ought to hear about.'

The Minister acquiesced. The Director General could see he was nervous, uncertain of what was to follow and fearful of its implications, and his voice was subdued as he explained the situation.

The Minister felt trapped. 'What do you want me to do?' he asked.

'It's not so much a case of doing anything, sir. It's a question of your knowing what's going on, what the situation is.'

'How important is this Israeli?' The question was barked, staccato.

'One of their backroom men, not a well-known personality. Named David Sokarev. They regard him as critical to their nuclear programme. He doesn't work on the power station side, not on the civilian programmes. He's with the other crowd, the ones they don't talk about. Sensitive man, sensitive work.'

'Is it an important meeting?'

'Not that we know of. We haven't seen a guest list yet – this has only been developing since yesterday evening. We'll have that sort of thing by tonight. But there's nothing to suggest it's world-shattering . . .'

'Which it would be if the bastards get to him.' He lingered, concentrating his mind on the problem. Always security providing the problems, never any good news, always anguish and heart-searching. And now, with not one of his Civil Servants within

88

fifty miles, with the Prime Minister touring Lanarkshire, a snap decision to be made. I know what this blighter wants, he thought, can read him a mile off. Wants me to tell him he's doing a grand job, let him run off and take charge on his own, and when the fiasco comes, when the scandal breaks, then he can tell the committee sitting under the learned judge 'in camera' that the Minister was aware of the situation right from the start. No way you get me that easily.

'The Prime Minister should be told of this. He takes a great interest in Israeli affairs. He'd want to know. I'll do that. My first reaction is that the Israelis should call off the visit. If it's not an important meeting, not an important personality, then what's the point in risking him?'

'You won't find that so easy, sir,' said the DG. 'Foreign Office have tried that one, down the more tortuous channels rather than the ambassadorial ones. Got a straight shut-out on the suggestion. But I agree it would be the easiest solution to our problem. I'd be grateful if someone could let me know how the suggestion is taken.'

The Minister shook the other man's hand, and walked back into the hall. The plates were empty by this stage, and the tea was getting cold. His words were awaited. He prided himself on talking off the cuff, without a note, but by now his mind was clouded by the conversation that had just terminated. It would be a bad speech.

As the sun rose that Saturday morning so it moved beyond the compass of the attic-floor window to the room that housed Famy and McCoy. While its brightness and warmth streamed through the glass the Arab had dressed, pulling on his clothes secretively and with a shyness that came from never having been separated from his people before. As he dragged his trousers on he had turned his back on the Irishman, who still lay in his sleeping bag picking at the dirt that had accumulated beneath his finger-nails. McCoy called across to him not to worry about shaving. 'Don't want to look too pretty in here. Doesn't fit with the rest of the surroundings.' And then a quiet laugh. After he had dressed Famy paced about the room, taking in its length in a few strides, going continuously to the window to peer down on to the street below, then walking again. He waited for some movement from the other man, and was loath to go beyond the door on his own. The street fascinated him, indistinct voices reaching up the height of the brickwork as he strained to hear what was being said. The dogs that ran free cocking their legs at the lamposts, the black men and women and children, the house along to the right where the old façade had been painted a bright scarlet, the wooden window fittings and the door in vivid yellow – all were strange and beyond his experience.

Beneath him there were more sounds – the music had started up again. It was not so vibrant as when they had arrived, he told himself. That was reserved for the night-time.

Never far from his mind was the image of the darkened, cloaked figure he had seen in the room. He felt a sense of frustration that the Irishman had not taken what he had said more seriously, and felt affronted by the casualness with which his revelation had been greeted. And when the sun was gone, and McCoy still showed no sign of moving, Famy had just squatted down on the sleeping bag and waited for him to get up.

'You can go downstairs if you want to,' McCoy said. Famy shook his head, irritable at his own reluctance.

'They won't eat you, you know. They're just ordinary kids.'

'I'll wait.'

'Please yourself,' McCoy said. He lit a cigarette, smoked it with consideration while Famy silently watched, flicked the ash successively on to the floor, and then when it was spent ground the tip out on the boards. Then he climbed out of the bag.

Standing in his underpants and vest, he stared directly at Famy.

'Have you done this sort of thing before?' he said, not much more than a whisper, but demanding an answer. Famy wavered, avoiding the other man with his eyes, reluctant, hurt.

'No. No, I have not before. It was planned that I should have moved into Israel, that I should fight there, a mission over the fence into the North. Then they had the information on Sokarev, and his visit, and all was changed for me. I was taken from the original plan.'

'Have you been in action before? I mean, have you fired a gun – in anger?'

'Only in training. I have never fought.'

Famy struggled to control what he thought were the inadequacies of his answers.

'It'll be difficult to get near the bastard, you know that?'

'With preparation, there is always a way.'

'You don't mount a thing like this on wishful fucking thinking.' McCoy showed his impatience. 'You have to know what you're about. You can't just breeze in . . .'

'It is unnecessary to talk to me as a child.' Famy cut McCoy in mid-sentence. His speech was clear, soft, almost sing-song. The Irishman retreated.

'Don't get me wrong. I wasn't suggesting . . .'

'Well, don't speak to me as if I were a fool. If you want no part in the rest, say so now. We can separate – your role forgotten.'

'There is no question of that.' McCoy stopped. The voices and music carried up to them. Neither spoke for four, five, six seconds. Then McCoy said, 'I say there's no question of that. I'm under orders. From the Army Council. They've made a decision, and they'll stick to it. They won't go back on it. Our Chief of Staff has given his word.' He smiled, weak at the side of his mouth, feeling the cold on his skin.

The relief flooded through Famy. He reached out and patted McCoy's shoulder, girl-like, but a gesture meant as affection and gratitude.

'What do we do today?' There was excitement in his voice.

'I thought this afternoon we'd take a look at the University. Can't do that on a Sunday, all the students are back in their digs, in their lodging houses. There won't be many of them about, but a few. Would have been better yesterday if you'd showed up on time. Don't worry, I'm not blaming you. You were a bloody genius to make it here at all. I've got a car, and tomorrow we go down into the country. Where the guns are. I've got some grenades. We don't use those much, but I was told to bring them.'

'We know about them,' said Famy.

'We'll try and hit at the meeting. It's a public place. Should offer the best hope.'

'In Lebanon they thought there might be two opportunities. The meeting and at the airport – not as he is coming in, but when he leaves.'

McCoy said, 'The airport will be sealed, it's difficult there. The best chance has to be at the meeting. How close do you need to get to him?'

'As near as is necessary.'

'There has to be a way out.'

'We have not come here to escape. We have come to kill Sokarev.'

McCoy fumbled with his socks, turning them inside out, trying to decide which one belonged to which foot. He felt the chill of the moment. Could see again the pictures. Those arching bodies spilling from the windows of the flats at Beit Shean, crumbling on the paving below and welcomed there with knives and axes and tins of petrol, and then the smoke and the flames; the sack-like shape pulled from the wreckage of Tel Aviv's Savoy Hotel. Palestinians who had gone 'as near as was necessary'.

'There has to be a way that leaves us a chance of escape,' said McCoy.

'Perhaps,' said Famy, and the Irishman left it there. He was a madman, this Arab, a suicide merchant. Well, good bloody luck to him. But what to do about it? Couldn't back out, couldn't fade away from it. Orders too implicit. Just at the time, he'd hold him back. Make his presence felt then, and when the shooting came do it with a bit of skill, with an aimed shot, not close in and blasting over open sights.

But they were not a team, and both men longed for the companionship of their own.

When he had dressed McCoy led the way downstairs. They saw no one till they came to the front hallway, when McCoy opened the door into the main room that faced out on the street. The conversation in the room, carried on in a series of separate huddles, went on uninterrupted, but eyes and heads and bodies turned to look at them. Like the bloody zoo, thought McCoy. He stood in front of the open door, staring back, waiting for someone to speak. They had little resolution against his gaze, and one by one the sitting, standing, crouching youths returned to their own groups. All except one girl. Famy noticed her before McCoy, then the Irishman saw her. Not pretty, rather plain, McCoy thought. A long, loose black dress, and a heavy woollen jersey pulled over her shoulders, shapeless, protection against the cold but nothing else. Ugly, witch clothes, accentuating the dullness of her skin – devoid of make-up, empty of anything feminine.

Doris Lang had noticed that the two new arrivals were out of place from the moment they had come through the door of the

92

house the previous night. She was trained to observe and make deductions from what she saw. These two did not fit the pattern that governed the other young people in the commune. She had seen the Irishman's complexion – too bright, too countrified, too healthy for life amongst the drop-outs – had noticed that his stature and bearing were divorced from those of the hand-to-mouth hippies. There was too much command in his face for him to belong to those who could not cope with the pressures of the life outside. This one, she had decided, was strictly a transit traveller, on his way through, and using the commune for a particular purpose.

She could also sense the nervousness and unease in the movements of the willowy, dark-skinned man who stood a pace behind. He too did not belong there. His hands must have been sweating, because twice he rubbed them against his trouser-legs. He had cold, purposeful eyes, that roamed without settling across the room, always coming back to her. It surprised her that she had found nothing in their possessions last night to give her any indication of their business in the house.

She felt the two men's eyes boring into her, and turned away, unwilling to appear too curious. There was marijuana smoke drifting, cool and gentle, from the far side of the room. Smoking today had started early.

The car of the Israeli Ambassador came to the back door of the Foreign Office.

It was a Mercedes, low on its wheels because of the armour plating that was standard for senior members of that country's diplomatic corps. Unlike the principal transport of other embassies it carried no suggestion in the number plate as to the identity of the passenger. There was a large radio aerial attached to the rear of the bodywork at the side of the boot, and this maintained communications with the embassy building set back from the private Kensington Palace Road. Most ambassadors accredited to the Court of St James travelled with just a chauffeur for company, but in this car there were two other young men, both of whom had been issued with licences from the Home Office to carry Uzi sub-machine-guns. These lay on the floor, one in the front beside the driver, one in the back beside the Ambassador and covered from careless gaze by coats. As it had made its way through the traffic the Mercedes was shadowed by a powerful three-and-a-half-litre Rover, unmarked, and in which sat two men from the Protection Division of Special Branch.

When the car pulled up the bodyguard in the front of the car stayed in his seat, his hand a few inches from the hidden Uzi. The man who had ridden in the back with the Ambassador unlocked the door, climbed out, scanned the pavement where it ran down from Birdcage Walk towards the Horseguards Parade, and nodded. The Ambassador got out quickly, and had been shepherded through the narrow door in a matter of seconds. Both he and his bodyguard ignored the Special Branch man who had also stepped on to the pavement. The London detective assigned to the Israeli embassy was used to that, familiar with being treated as an unnecessary bystander, there to make up the numbers, but not to be consulted.

Through the working part of the week a liveried official would have been there to escort the Ambassador to the second-floor office where the Under Secretary who specialized in Middle East Affairs now waited. But at the weekend there was simply a man in a dark suit. The wide passages were darkened, electricity switched off to save money, leaving the portraits of the great British Foreign Secretaries that lined the walls mysterious and shadowy.

'Thank you for coming, your Excellency,' said the Under Secretary, as the door closed behind the Ambassador. The Israeli said nothing.

'The Minister would like to have been able to see you personally. It is regrettable, but he is out in the country, and cannot return to London in the time we felt was available.' Liar, thought the Ambassador. More likely up to his thighs in a trout stream somewhere in his beloved Yorkshire.

'On the basis of the information with which your own Security Service was able to provide us, and because of additional information that our own departments have obtained, the Minister has asked me to request of your Excellency that further consideration should be given to the visit to Britain of Professor Sokarev.'

The Ambassador said, 'You say "further consideration". To what end?'

Spell it out in words of one syllable, thought the Under Secretary. God protect us, they're a gauche crowd.

'With a view, Excellency, to deciding whether or not the visit should continue as planned, in the face of what your service and ours regard as a serious threat.'

'You are asking me to recommend to Jerusalem that the visit be cancelled?'

'I am asking you nothing. I am merely suggesting, on the direction of my Minister, that you might wish to reconsider the value of the visit.'

'There is only one set of circumstances which would lead me to tell my government that in my personal opinion Professor Sokarev should cancel his lecture on Tuesday night and bypass Britain.'

The Under Secretary inclined his head, and the Ambassador went on.

'If I were to believe that the police forces and other agencies of Britain were incapable of providing the necessary protection for Professor Sokarev, then I would suggest to my Foreign Ministry that the visit should be cancelled.'

Cunning fox, the Under Secretary said to himself.

'There is no question of that. We will provide protection . . .'

'Then there is nothing further to discuss.' The Ambassador's voice was cold. 'When you report back to the Minister about our conversation I would be grateful if you could relay a sentiment of my Government. We are not prepared to be taken simply as a nuisance-child, a bothersome problem that will go away if the door is barred to it. Professor Sokarev has been offered the hospitality of a learned and illustrious body in your capital. We intend to make sure that he honours the engagement. The rest, my dear fellow, is in your hands.'

The Under Secretary bridled. 'You must understand that I was passing on a request from my Minister.'

The Ambassador smiled, without friendship, puckered his eyes fractionally, and said, 'And I will pass on to my Minister that the British Government will be providing – what was the word you used? – yes, "adequate protection". Perhaps you should know, since it seems you have not been informed, that while we have been discussing the suitability of the visit the security attaché

95

at my embassy has been talking with the relevant people on your side on the very question of Professor Sokarev's safety. At times like this, Under Secretary, it is liaison that is needed.'

He turned on his heel and made his own way out of the room.

In the early afternoon McCoy took Famy from the house and to the car parked fifty yards up the road on the far side.

'I didn't bring it down to the station last night,' he said. 'It's nicked – stolen – and that's too public a place to leave it lying around. It's all right in a street like this, half the bloody motors here have separated from their log books.'

It was a two-door Ford Escort, painted green, and unscratched, 'M' registration. 'I got it over in Wembley, that's on the far side of London, out in the suburbs, night before last. Goes okay, though it's a bit small.'

Famy looked at the car, disinterested, and waited for the passenger door to be opened for him. Soon they were heading past the Angel Green and stopping at the lights, indicator clicking, ready to turn right down the Pentonville Road and then into the main university complex. And as they drove McCoy realized the extent to which he was involved. It had begun simply, and without complications; providing back-up, assistance. The shooting in France had changed that, and ensured that if he carried on with the enterprise it would be as an equal partner.

There's no bloody help from this bastard, he thought to himself. Talks in spasms, then goes silent, just gazes into bloody eternity, like no one else exists. Doesn't give a damn whether we come out of it or not. A different war, the hedgerow actions that he had perfected among the fields of South Armagh. Political assassination . . . something that his Active Service Unit had never contemplated. A soldier or a policeman, or a local Proddy councillor, that was different. That was attrition.

This was a totally new concept to him; a killing on such a grand scale that the shock waves would fill the world headlines for a week. It was one thing to drop a Para, to blow a Woolworths, to take out a policeman, but this . . . And he was being drawn into it, he recognized that, and thought even now that the point of retreat was already lost. He was experienced, had known the tension of guerrilla combat in the hills round Crossmaglen, had fired the cumbersome RPG 7 rocket launcher at the tin-fenced,

96

screened and barricaded police station on the edge of his town, had given orders, had had men follow him. And yet this other man who had known none of this was directing him, controlling him – and had outstretched him in commitment.

Perhaps it was the hate. He'd heard of it, read about it, the simple hatred the Palestinian hard men felt for the Israelis, and he knew he couldn't match it. Even in the cage at Long Kesh when he had paced beside the interior perimeter wire and watched the camouflaged uniformed soldiers in their watchtowers, traversing their machine-guns, and jeering down at the men below, even then he could not hate to the exclusion of all else. When these people blasted their hostages, threw their grenades without hesitation, without remorse, into cinemas, they put themselves beyond the reach of McCoy's understanding. His men could never do that. There had to be a purpose to killing. Every victim ought to *know* why he would die at McCoy's hand. But just for the sake of it, just for the gesture . . . that was not enough.

At the bottom of the Euston Road, in the last lap to the university, he asked, 'Why this man? Why Sokarev?'

There was no urgency in the reply. Famy said, 'Three times the Arabs fought the Israelis and were shamed. At their Yom Kippur we fought them again and surprised them with our technique and with our bravery, but we did not win. The next time we fight we will do better, and the time after that we will have greater success. One time in the future we will have them close to defeat. Then they will have no option, then they will threaten their ultimate weapon. They will tell the world of their bomb, how they will use it to survive. Sokarev is an architect of that bomb. To us he represents a symbol of what would be their last throw in desperation. We feel if we kill Sokarev we have demonstrated that we fear nothing from them. If we can eliminate a man so much at the centre of their whole basis of national survival then we have achieved a great victory.'

'There'll be others, others who know as much as this one man,' said McCoy.

'That is unimportant. It is not Sokarev's knowledge that we will deny them. It is the symbol that we attack. It meant nothing in manpower for Israel to lose her athletes at Munich, nothing to lose their attaché in Washington, the man here in London we took with the letter-bomb. It is the symbol that matters. That we can prove to them that we are at war, that we can strike where and when we please.'

McCoy was still silently repeating to himself 'Bloody maniacs' when he drove past the Students' Union building, and pulled up outside the massive mausoleum structure that marked the administrative and academic centre of London University.

'Just relax. Take it easy. If anyone asks, you've left some notes behind, coming back to get them. But don't look furtive, look as though you belong,' McCoy said as they walked up the great cement steps and into the building.

Famy said quietly, 'Do we know which entrance he will use?'

'No, there are a stack of them. This is the main one, the natural one, but there are alternatives.'

There was almost a tranquillity about the Arab's voice, as if it belonged to someone who has had a great rest, and woken refreshed. His breathing was relaxed, unhurried, as he peered round him in the echoing, high-roofed hallway.

'But the room, we know which room he will use?'

'It's marked on the invitation.' McCoy pulled his wallet from an inner pocket. From it he took an embossed square of card, and smiled as he showed it to Famy. 'It's the real thing,' he said. The Arab recognized the name of David Sokarev in ornate, copperplate writing in the centre of the card, followed by a string of initials. He saw also the words 'Lecture Room D, ground floor, Fourth entrance to the Right after entering the Main Hallway.'

'Where did you get it?' Famy asked.

'Acquired it. Long story. I'll tell you some time.'

'What time does he arrive? And when does he speak?'

'He'll come about fifteen minutes before the speech. There's a reception, sherry and sandwiches – he'll probably arrive at the end of that. He's due to talk at eight.'

But Famy was not listening, just scanning the corridor, taking in the pillars, and the various shadowy entrances that led off the hallway to offices and other lecture rooms. He was assessing cover, the room he would need, the speed at which a man could travel across the floor space, the angle required to see him if he were to be surrounded by guards and the welcoming committee. Without seeing the room, he had already decided there would be no

98

possibility of gaining direct admission to the lecture, particularly with the bulky firearms that would be needed for the killing.

'It has to be from outside,' he said, vaguely and to himself.

Famy turned and walked back down the hallway and out into the light. He went left across the car park to the edge of the building, then moved down its side, his attention locked on the windows that were fitted just above the level of his head. Massive, functional and intimidating in its grey strength, the building towered above him in a narrowing column to the topmost point from where half London could be viewed. The fortress to which Sokarev would be brought. But there had been a way, hadn't there, into every citadel? Brick and stone and cement in themselves do not provide protection, Famy thought. There will be a gap, if only one caused by the error of man.

The construction of the lower floors was in the form of a giant and flattened cross, the main doors at the north end, the lecture room off to the west extremity of a protruding arm. Famy hurried across from the front toward the wall where the lecture room would have its windows set, and in his step there was a lightness and excitement. They had taught him the art of what they called 'using dead ground', moving in terrain which was denied to the vision of the enemy. Those who stood at the main door would have no sight of the windows he wanted; the butting corner would deny them. And where would they accumulate the security men that would come with Sokarev? They would be with him inside, and they would be at the doors . . . He came round the corner, McCoy following blindly but uncomprehending, and again there were more windows and beneath them cars, all closely parked and near to the wall. He noted that and was satisfied.

He glanced around him, for the first time a trace of anxiety showing, then scrambled on to the bonnet of a dark saloon. It gave him the elevation to see inside the lecture room, across the rows of pew-like benches, and to the lectern which on Tuesday night would hold the typed notes of David Sokarev. He jumped down from the car.

'Would you go inside,' he said to McCoy, 'and if there are curtains draw them across this window, the middle one of the three?' McCoy stood his ground, confused. 'Just do it,' the Arab said, his voice rising. 'Just this window and draw them tightly. So I can see where they meet.'

He waited a full two minutes after McCoy had gone, then

the curtains swished their way across the broad window. He noted that when they closed they were completely together, letting no light escape from the room. He bent hurriedly down, picked up a small stone from the gravel, scratched the wall at the place where the curtains had met. Almost immediately the drapes opened again. While he waited for McCoy he repeated the scratch in the wall over his original mark. This time he drew a six-pointed star a little more than four inches across from tip to tip. He was still smiling about it when McCoy joined him.

'We must get some gloves,' Famy said. 'Thick ones that will withstand broken glass, cover the hand and the wrist.'

In the mind of Abdel-El-Famy the assassination plan was complete. Beautiful and totally simple.

The drugs scene in London as in any major capital is a brutal and violent one. A below-surface cancer invisible till the skin of society is scraped. Young detectives like Doris Lang, who attempted to infiltrate the market and supply the evidence required by the courts to convict the 'pushers', went through extensive and thorough training before they abandoned their conventional trim clothes for those of the teenagers and drop-outs among whom they would now move.

She had been on a three-week course to learn the medical side of the menace, to be taught the arts of survival in an alien society, and had spent two concentrated days in a gymnasium with an instructor who taught self defence. She was a capable young woman, used to looking after herself, and the Detective Inspector to whom she reported had few fears about her personal safety. What he was looking for from her was first of all, patience, and, when that was rewarded, detail.

She had seen McCoy and Famy leave the house, and then spent another twenty-five minutes reading and gossiping casually and inconsequentially with her new friends before she excused herself and left. On the stair landing on the floor immediately below the room occupied by the two newcomers she had stood stock-still for a full minute, listening to the sounds of the building, convincing herself that in the upper reaches of the house she would be alone.

She had been disappointed with her earlier search in the small hours. She had used the time on the clock that her training suggested, just after 4 a.m., when the psychiatrists say the human physique is at its most vulnerable and yearning for deep sleep. But she had recognized that this search could be only a cursory one, though she had weighed the chances of her discovery as being slight. In daylight she could be slower, more observant.

None of the locks to the rooms was fitted with a key, and she was able to turn the handle and walk in. In her left hand was a small memory-pad and a pencil stub. She worked through the men's possessions for twelve minutes. Much of the time was spent rearranging the clothing in the Arab's grip bag and McCoy's old suitcase so that they would not detect her hand among the socks, and the underclothes and the shirts. She found no papers belonging to either man, no passports, letters, driving licences; no hint of their identity.

There was nothing remarkable in the clothing she looked at that lay in the case. It was the contents of the grip-bag that fascinated her. The clothes in themselves were unexceptional, except that every maker's tag and washing and cleaning instruction had been removed. Not pulled away, but conscientiously unstitched.

She wrote that down on the pad, beneath the times of arrival and departure, and the descriptions she had taken of the two men. She felt the frustration that came from the failure to explain their presence in the commune. Perhaps, she thought, their trip today would provide her with something, perhaps when they returned there would be papers which she could find if she came again in the cold, desolate hours before dawn.

At Scotland Yard Jones saw the Assistant Commissioner (Crime) in his office close to the operations room on the fifth floor of the building. As a result of the meeting two considerable and wide-scale programmes would be put into operation. First, a dragnet to try to locate and then arrest the man McCoy and his unknown partner. Second, the gathering together of the security necessary to protect the Israeli professor when he visited London. It was the first plan that took the majority of their time. Jones sketched through the information the department had collected in the previous twenty-four hours, in some instances withholding sources but allowing the policeman a detailed picture of the circumstances that surrounded the threat to Sokarev. He em-

101

phasized the faint but possible connection between the Irishman and the North London communes.

'You have a difficulty there straight away,' said the Assistant Commissioner. 'We have several under surveillance – from the outside. I can call that sort of information in at any time. If your men are in one of those we can identify them from the logs very quickly. But there are others where we have people living on the inside. I've been on the phone this morning and I'm advised that there are seventeen where that applies. They tend to come out on Monday mornings. There would be a fair deal of opposition if you were to ask me to break all those covers and get the officers out this afternoon or tomorrow. You appreciate a great number of detailed inquiries are going on through these channels. I think to justify such an action I'd need rather more positive information than you've been able to provide me with.'

The Security Service is a force without powers. It can only request. Jones looked pained, acting up a bit. Face set with disappointment.

'I'm sorry, Mr Jones. Tell me it's essential, tell me an address, give me something clear, and we can act. I think that's reasonable.'

'Is there no other way of getting them out other than destroying their position – your people's?'

'What's your suggestion?' The Assistant Commissioner threw it back at him. Like so many others who rarely came into touch with the Security Services, he distrusted them, remaining unconvinced of their effectiveness.

'I don't have one,' said Jones. 'Not ready at hand.' He felt tired, anger growing at the man across the desk, who was so unable to comprehend the scale of the problem – more concerned with marijuana and cocaine than political assassination.

'I'll think about it, ask around,' said the Assistant Commissioner. That was the concession. Trifling, thought Jones. And half another day gone, and nothing new to show for it.

The security attaché of the Israeli embassy was late at the Home Office. Jones's ill humour was not helped by the lack of any apology. But he recognized there were times to bite on it, not to make the scene he would have liked. And the Israeli brought information – time-tables of Sokarev's movements, hotel and room number, invitation list to the speech.

'And he will have two men with him from our own Protection

Division of the Foreign Ministry. I can give you their names. Joseph Mackowicz and Gad Elkin. You know it is our policy, Mr Jones. Since Munich we have become more aware of the dangers. They are expressly charged with the safety of the Professor.'

That was the best news of the day, thought Jones. If the apple-cart goes then those two bastards will be picking up the load along with me. Nice to be in numbers.

He told the attaché what was known of McCoy. The Israeli said, 'With respect, I would suggest from my observations of your own problems and my knowledge of ours that one we have to fear is not the Irishman. If the other man is a Palestinian that is the creature we have to be on guard against.'

Too right, Jones said to himself. And no name, no description, no fingerprints, no file, no bloody history at all.

'We should meet again tomorrow. Same time, and here?'

The Israeli agreed, and Jones hurried to his car, and drove fast back to Curzon Street. It was his complete lack of knowledge on what should be his next move that fanned his impatience. His job only rarely required such a frenzied reaction as was now demanded. It was a sensation he had not experienced before, and he found himself looking at his watch as if the very minutes that slipped away were precious and should not be lost. It was a new form of warfare in which he had become involved, where his enemy was insignificant in stature and strength, had none of the force and intellect that his own side possessed, and yet was an enemy which dominated, and took the initiative. For the first time in close on three decades in the Department he felt a sense of fear and helplessness.

Just before the light faded in the flat the boy suggested it was time for him to be on his way. David Sokarev was not surprised. It was a long, exhausting drive between Beersheba and the IAF fighter-base on the road beyond Afula. He knew his son would be on duty in his flying suit, waiting in the squadron ready-room at five-thirty on the Sunday morning on three minute warning. He would need the sleep, and the drive would take three hours, even in the tuned-up Mini.

As the boy stood up from the chair on the balcony that looked over the town Sokarev said quietly to him, 'There is a matter I want to talk to you about. Can you come to my room? It will not take long.'

And when they were together inside the room Sokarev spoke to his son, shyly, without confidence.

'Don't interrupt me – not till I have finished. And I have not told your mother this. There is a threat against me when I go to London. There were two men from the Foreign Ministry who came to see me two days ago. They are to guard me, and they told me. It is not an important visit. I had been looking forward to it. Just one speech, and the chance to meet old friends and talk. Talk with different people. But it is something that could be cancelled, and the world would not topple. I do not know how to react to the situation. If there was a risk I would have presumed the Ministry, the Government, would have cancelled the visit themselves. But they have not done that. They have just sent men to tell me that I will be guarded. That is all there is. But what should I do?'

He looked at the boy, pleading, seeking for assurance. But his son answered him predictably enough in the language of a serviceman who executed orders, believed in the inviolate authority of his commander.

'If they did not think it was safe they would not allow you to go. You are too precious to us all, father, for them to risk you if there was real danger. If they have not suggested that you cancel, then you should have no fear.'

Sokarev kissed his son on both cheeks, easier in his mind now, dismissing the thought of a telephone call to the Director of Dimona, and together they came out of the office. But the gun, he would take that anyway.

Jimmy had shaved, put on a clean shirt, a suit and the old squadron tie. Finally he cleaned his shoes, and then made his way to Leconfield House. He'd sat in the outer office beyond Jones's door for more than half an hour, exchanging small talk with Helen as she typed, while he waited for his appointment to be kept.

Jimmy was past fifty, and grey-haired. There was not much flesh on his face – the years of living and fending for himself alone had seen to that. There were dark, blotched patches, fierce

104

and red, on his cheeks, not as bad as before he went to the clinic but still evident. A blood vessel had fractured in his left eye, leaving an oasis of crimson in the extreme corner closest to the bridge of his nose. He was tall, and not overweight – partly because he exercised in a private gymnasium, partly because his life style denied him regular food and meals. Helen could see he was ill at ease, almost nervous, as he constantly shifted his position in the chair. Come on, he thought, don't keep me bloody hanging about all day. It was the time he loathed. The time that elapsed before he was briefed, before he was back inside the team again and part of the new operation, when his mind was racing with unsubstantiated ideas. Leaves you like a vegetable, in limbo.

Jones came in, nodded to Jimmy, but spoke first to Helen.

'Any messages, anything new in?'

'Nothing,' she said. 'The DG would like to see you before six. He rang through. Nothing beyond that.'

Jones masked his disappointment. He walked through to his office, opened the door and asked Jimmy to follow. Inside he offered him a chair, and then went to his own behind his desk. Jimmy could see the pile of slim cardboard folders on the desk top.

Jones was expert at setting out the skeleton of a problem. He took Jimmy through the information that was already available. He wasted few words, and there were no interruptions.

'That's the background. Not everything we have – you can pick that out of the paperwork when we've finished. In ideal times we'd concentrate the major effort on lifting the bastards before they hit, but as you'll see from situation reports that we've been doing we're cold on that score.' Just as Jimmy would have wanted it, thought Jones. When the rest of us are getting tired and looking to steer clear of the big ones, Jimmy'll be cheering from the top tower. Proper job for him, one to tax him, one to test him. We're different people. Jones accepted that – the one played-out and trying to avoid the fracas, the other leaping about like a schoolboy. Not quite a smile from Jones. 'We have to be prepared for an actual attack, and I want you, Jimmy, to be right beside our Israeli brother. Adhesive-close, not out of your sight except when he's safely locked in the bloody loo. He'll have his own men with him, a cattle herd from Special Branch, all falling over each other and arguing protocol, but I want you a little bit tighter on him than any of the others. Normally we wouldn't

105

still be in on a thing like this, it would be straight police, but the ramifications are too big if it goes wrong. So you have no doubts about your position, Jimmy, I'll spell it out. If you see anything that bothers you, you act. If you see a gun close to him, you shoot. Don't concern yourself with the bloody paperwork, or the rule book.'

Jones looked thoughtful. Needed to be stronger than that, needed to elaborate, leave him in no doubt, owed it to the man at the sharp end. 'And if you hit some poor devil out for a walk in the park with his dog, we'll cover for you.'

'You always say that,' Jimmy said.

Would he cover? . . . Would he, hell. But it was a form of words. Means not a bloody thing, Jimmy thought – what they feel they have to say. And if the balloon filled up, what price immunity then? In the courts like every other bugger, and double-fast.

'What I need, Jimmy,' Jones went on, ignoring him, best way with Jimmy, 'What I need is the very clear knowledge that I will be informed of every movement Sokarev makes. I don't want it via the Israeli embassy, I don't want it via Scotland Yard, I want it from you.'

'If everyone is twisting their knickers at this rate, why isn't the visit called off?'

'God alone knows. If anybody else does they haven't thought fit to tell me. The Israelis have known for some days of the risk, they haven't opted for cancellation.'

Jimmy left it there. He could see the other man was close to the end of his patience, not ready for a gentle chat on the theoretical.

Jones said: 'I'll circulate your name to the Israelis and to the Special Branch, and have it backed by the Home Office. You'll need some time to work through the papers. Tomorrow I'll want you with me when I see the Israelis. They'll want to run the whole bloody thing. The DG is mildly anxious it doesn't happen that way. You'll need some weapon practice – fix that for the morning. You'd better get back to your place now and pick up some clothes. Fairclough, Duggan and I are sleeping in. You'd better join us. You can have Helen's room.'

As Jimmy walked through the outer office he stopped beside Helen's table.

'Unlucky again tonight, sweetheart. We're all kipping on the job.'

6

After they left the university building McCoy drove across the artery of Tottenham Court Road, and in the maze of side streets behind the Middlesex Hospital found a small Indian restaurant. They spent a long time over the meal. They talked over the abstract background of their lives – the Irishman mostly, with Famy listening, while they picked and pulled at the chappatis, toyed with the rice and the sauces and meats, and fractured the popadums into tiny lasting pieces. And then they took coffee, and after that more beer, as the evening went by.

McCoy talked of Crossmaglen and Cullyhanna. He spoke of the sharply rising hills, with the farms that barely supported life, of the large families, of the economic hardship. He told of the fierce independence of the people who lived there, how they had transferred their old enmity of such everyday figures as the customs men and the tax collector to the soldiers of the British army. He related the story of Mick McVerry, killed in the attack on Keady police station, how they had placed nine gunmen round the building, and a rocket launcher, and how McVerry had been shot down as he planted the bomb against the building that when it went off had left a complete wing demolished. He'd been in the 'Kesh' then himself, he said, otherwise he would have been there. Famy had raised his eyes inquiringly when McCoy mentioned the Kesh, and the Irishman launched into his stories of the prison where he had been held – how they, the prisoners, ran the premises. How they held their courts, and punished those they deemed guilty. How they organized their escape committees, dug their tunnels, worked their switches with visitors. How they held their weapons and explosives classes. How they jeered the Governor as he made his rounds. How they rioted and how they went on hunger strike. How they dominated Catholic opinion in the province outside the wire.

Famy had listened, uncomprehending and disbelieving. He tried to suggest that this was something the Israelis would never have tolerated behind the high yellow walls of the maximum security prison at Ramle, where they held the *fedayeen*. There were so many thing McCoy said that amazed Famy. No penalties against the families and property of those arrested on terrorist charges. Detailed fire control orders for individual soldiers. A piece of paper that gave each soldier the circumstances in which he could shoot. A hundred paratroopers locked up in Crossmaglen police station whose food and ammunition came only by helicopter because it was too dangerous to drive lorries there – too many culvert bombs on the roads, too many control wires in the ditches. But what astonished him most of all was that McCoy was there sitting across the table. 'Why, when they had caught you, when you had done these things, why did they release you?'

And McCoy had just smiled, and laughed, and known it was not possible to explain the gestures of the Secretary of State for Northern Ireland to a man whose knowledge of guerrilla warfare was based on that fought against an enemy as hard and intransigent as the Israelis.

McCoy wanted to talk and Famy was relegated to passive audience. On to the politics of the Irish Republican Army, Provisional wing. Then he spoke of six counties, and twenty-six counties, and thirty-two counties, and of Ulster, which he said was theoretically nine counties. And regionalism and Federalism and Fianna Fail . . . The Arab was lost. As his mind drifted from the slowly slurring speech of McCoy he reflected that about his own cause there was nothing complicated, nothing that could not be taught to a child, nothing that could not be understood by the simplest in the camps.

Because we know what we want, he thought, we are prepared to strive with sacrifice for our victory. Not in a pathetic cowboy world of minimal heroics, shooting down one soldier and claiming that as a victory, killing one middle-aged policeman and believing that changed political strategy; that is no way to fight. Perhaps because they do not know what it is they struggle for, they cannot steel themselves to acts that will shock on the grand scale. But this Irish boy will learn. He will understand what it is to kill when the diplomats of every major capital in the world will react. He will find out what it is to earn the hatred of one half of the world, the gratitude and adulation of the other.

But Famy enjoyed it, felt the security of the restaurant around

108

him, realized that no eyes were transfixed on him, that he belonged
to the scene, and was amused at the conspiratorial whisper with
which McCoy kept up his patter of exploits. It was not till McCoy
was paying the obsequious waiter that Famy thought again of
the darkened figure that had searched his room last night, and
of the girl who had stared at them as they left the large house back
in the mid-afternoon.

When they were in the car, Famy spoke of that.

'We will sleep in different places tonight. You go to the far wall,
and I will be close to the door. If someone comes again they will
have to move deep into the room, and I will be behind them.'

She had seen them come in through the open door of the living
room. They had paused for a few moments as if undecided
whether or not to join the main group, and she had heard their
voices, indistinct against the record-player. Then she had heard
them walk away toward the stairs, and the sound of their feet as
they went up. Through the early part of the night, every half
hour or so, she had turned away from her book to look at her
watch, waiting till the time was right. Gradually the room emptied,
as singly or in pairs people drifted toward their mattresses and
sleeping bags in the rooms above. When nearly everyone had
gone, and there was no longer the music and the conversation to
keep her company, she felt the cold. If she went to bed early the
lack of any heating in the house did not show itself, but by the
small hours the warmth of the day had vanished, dissipated in
the high rooms and the old walls. Few in the building spoke to
her, but that was the life-style they chose. If she had wanted to
talk she would have found people willing to listen. As she did
not she was left to herself.

She wriggled inside the hard wool of her jersey, screwing her
muscles closer to her body, fighting to maintain the personal
warmth that seemed to be steadily eluding her. There was a child
crying on one of the upper floors; it generally did, most of the
night. Its mother had little to give it but a vague animal affection.
In the days she had been in the commune Doris Lang had grown
to hate that woman for her incompetence and her carelessness
in the way she treated a two-year old. She yearned to intervene,
and every time dismissed the possibility as being out of context
with her cover. Probably hungry, poor little bastard, trying to

grow on toast and warmed tins of beans and spaghetti.

At a few minutes before four, the last of those who had sat up in the room with her stretched, and staggered, as if sleep-walking, toward the stairs. She was used to lack of sleep, and was able within moments to drag together the concentration she had allowed to fade and leave her. It was papers she wanted, indications about identity, about purpose – the reason these two unlikely figures, out of shape with the other jigsaw pieces of the commune, had come to spend their time there. Her watch showed just past four o'clock when she slipped out of the room, and went slowly, with great care, testing each footstep, toward the attic.

She wore rubber-soled tennis shoes. They had a dirty exterior, had long been without any whitener, but were totally efficient for moving without noise. With one hand she hitched up her long skirt to prevent it from brushing against the steps. Outside the door of the attic she paused again, listening to the night, to the sounds of traffic, of the heavy breathing of deep sleep, of the distant chorus of an ambulance on emergency call. From behind the door there was silence. Complete quiet. She eased her hand on to the rounded handle of the door, pushed it open an inch, waited and listened again, then went in.

Famy had not heard her on the stairs nor on the landing. But the movement of the door handle mechanism alerted him, the most minute of sounds, as the bar was withdrawn inside the old, unoiled lock. From his half-sleep his eyes focused instantaneously on the white handkerchief he had tied to the handle on the inside of the door. He could see that, however blurred and grey it was in the near-dark. He saw it move, fractionally at first, then swing out, opening into the room. Then his sight of it was obscured as a silhouetted figure came past it. He felt sweat rise high up on his legs, and the sticky cloying moisture search over his skin, finding havens in his armpits, in his groin, behind his knees. He fought to control the regularity of his breathing.

They are in no hurry, thought Famy. Waiting their time, waiting for the light to become natural, easier. Then there was movement again, and with it the soft scuffing of material on the floor. That told Famy that his intruder was a girl, and as he strained into the nothingness of the room he pictured the one he had stared at

110

downstairs with the pale white face, and the hair that had not been brushed, and the cumbersome dress that would reach down to the boards. His own part of the room was the darkest, but the street light made vague shapes at the end where McCoy slept. He could see clearly the girl's outline as she approached his sleeping bag, saw her bend down and open his case, heard her hands among his clothes.

That she had found nothing that she sought he could understand by the way, unhurried, unexcited, she put down the top of the case. Then there was indecision, confusion. She looks for me, the little whore, thought Famy. Remembers where I was last night, is searching with her eyes, but she'll need the torch over here. He closed his eyelids tight, unwilling to risk the involuntary blink if the light should suddenly come on. The footsteps came closer to him, warily, seeking out the ground, testing the pliability of the boards. They were very near when they stopped, and on his face he felt the thin beam of the torch.

He had put the bag close to his head, and he could feel her breath on his face as she bent low over him, painstakingly sliding back the fastener. She shifted a foot, leaving it just three or four inches from the sleeping bag, then her hands were inside the bag, following the line of the torch. It was as she straightened to move away that Famy thrust his hands from under the cover of the bag and grabbed at the leg that was closest to him.

For a moment his fingers were lost in the folds of the skirt, until, just short of panicking, he felt the hardness of her ankle. His whole weight followed, dragging her off balance, pulling her down. The torch fell to the floor boards, clattering and then shining its beam away from them. The surprise was complete. By the time she had realized what had happened she was on the boards, face down, her right arm twisted high behind her back, gripped by Famy, whose knee was indented into the pit of her back. The shock had been too great for her to scream.

'McCoy! McCoy! Come here.' He hissed the command out, and the other man stirred on the far side of the room.

'What is it?' the voice came low across the floor.

'I have the little bitch, I have her here.'

There was a flurry of movement and McCoy crawled through the darkness till he bumped into the mass that was the girl and Famy. His hand reached out for the torch, which he shone into the pale, fear-stricken face. She tried to swing her head away from

111

the light, but he grasped at her hair, and as she cried out he pulled her back into the beam.

'Get your fucking hands off me,' she spat the words at him, and with his free hand he hit her hard across the mouth, and the metal of the battery container caught her lip, bulging and reddening it until the skin broke, and the trickle, highlighted by the softness of her skin, made its way down to the side of her throat. She started to struggle then, without feeling the pain in her head as McCoy clung to her hair, and oblivious of the numbing ache in her arm where Famy had twisted it behind her. With her other hand she reached into the void behind the light, and her fingernails found the flesh of McCoy's face. She heard him cry out in a mixture of pain and astonishment as she raked her nails across his cheeks. The hand let go of the hair, and before she could affect the grip across her back McCoy's foot had lashed into her head. She tried to turn away, but again the foot came, guided now by the light. Accurate and vicious, striking through the long hair that offered no protection to her ear.

Then McCoy was on his knees beside her, hands in her hair again, and this time there was no resistance. She moved her head toward him, following his will, and saw the long weals across his face, saw his eyes, alive with rage.

Famy tightened the grip on her arm, so that she convulsed, then lay inert, the struggle over.

Famy said, 'She searched your things, then mine.'

'Roll the bitch over.' McCoy was panting, and they pushed her so that she lay on her back. The Arab had his weight across her legs, high on her thighs, and he had pinioned her arms to the floor above her head. She closed her eyes and felt McCoy begin to search her. He started at her neck and worked quickly and expertly across her body, running over her breasts, down her waist, rough and uncaring till they fastened on the note-book in the pocket at her hips. Fingers forced their way inside the fold of the material and pulled the pad out. She opened her eyes fractionally and saw him peering at her close, tight handwriting, flicking the pages over, torch close to the paper.

'What does it say?' said Famy, impatience growing as the other man concentrated.

'She's a bloody tout,' said McCoy.

'What's that?' said Famy, his voice rising.

'An informer. A spy. There are names here, people living in the house, times and dates of arrival. We're here too, when we came in, when we went out yesterday. She's a clever little cow. You've no tags, no maker's marks in your clothes, right?'

'We took them out before we came.'

'Well, it's written down here.'

McCoy waited, the big eyes delving into the young face beneath him. She could sense the chill in his voice, horrible and without pity.

He said, 'Who are you? Tell me why you came.' The glazed, fear-filled face peered vacantly back toward him and beyond.

'Who are you, you cow?' He hit her again, this time with the edge of his hand, finding the tip of her chin bone, jerking her head back, banging it on the boards. Still she said nothing, and he struck her with his fist clenched hard into the softness below her rib cage. She gasped for air, fighting to force it down into her lungs, tried to draw up her knees from under the Arab to protect her defenceless body.

'You'll get it again.'

She started to try to speak, but there were no sounds at first, just the effort. Her chest heaved and writhed before the words came. There was a final act of defiance.

'Get off me, you pigs. I'm a police officer. Get your pig-shit hands off me.'

The thought in Famy's mind was immediate. Just two days earlier on the road to Boulogne the police had been waiting for them. Now here, in the supposed 'safe house', the police were again close to him.

'How did they know?' he shouted. 'How did they know we would be here?'

McCoy saw her reaction to what Famy had said, the flick of her head forward to stare at the shadowy face above her. It was that movement that sealed his resolution. His hands came down, settled on her throat, and tightened. She tried to speak of drugs and hippies, but the air was already denied her. Then there was nothing, only the sinking, and pressure of the hands and the blackness when she tried to see.

When McCoy had finished he realized that Famy was no longer beside him. It had been easy. In the world in which he moved and fought the penalty for touts was clear cut. There was coughing in the far corner.

'Pull yourself together, you stupid bugger,' he said. 'Get your

113

things in your bag. We're moving out.'

The house was quiet, at rest, as they went down the stairs, through the door and on to the street.

While McCoy drove, fast and with studied concentration heading south toward the river, Famy sat rock-still beside him. The Arab's mind was moving at pace. It was the first time that he had encountered violent death, and the speed with which life had been crushed from the girl amazed him – its simplicity, its suddenness. And the doubts he had felt about McCoy had vanished in those few seconds. When the time came the Irishman too was prepared to kill. Famy knew, and it was a feeling he had not entertained before, that they were now a team. In the darkness of the attic bedroom the links between the two men had been irreparably joined, and with that his last lingering uncertainties about the success of his mission had gone.

'Where are we going now?' Famy asked.

McCoy did not take his eyes from the road ahead.

'Down into the hills south of London. Into Surrey, where the guns are.'

'And where do we sleep?'

'We sleep rough tonight and tomorrow. We have to ditch this car, get another. Come back to London on Tuesday, probably late. This car will do us for a few hours more, but when the balloon goes up we'll have to have another.'

'How long do you think before they find her?'

'Some time, not immediately. And when they do they'll have the bloody commune on their hands. And they won't make much headway with them.'

'It was necessary to kill her.' Famy said it quietly, but as a statement.

'Course it bloody was.'

'She knew who we were?' The question again.

'Shouldn't think so.' McCoy sensed the other man's surprise at his answer. He went on. 'Probably there on the drugs scene. Could have been bomb squad and out Provo-hunting. You've got two alternatives. Bluff it out, or the other. And when you start knocking shit out of the girl that narrows it down to the other.'

'How far do we have to go?'

'About another hour and a half. Get some sleep.' It was an

instruction. McCoy wanted to drive without chatter in his ear.

Famy closed his eyes. The Irishman, he thought, he would be able to sleep. But with himself there was no possibility of it. As the car jolted its way along the road the image that endlessly repeated itself was of the girl and her eyes that bulged and pleaded, and of the hard calloused fingers on her neck.

But the killing of Doris Lang had not gone entirely unnoticed.

The woman who had nursed her child to sleep a floor below had been unable to sleep herself. She had lain with her eyes wide open, staring at the ceiling. The sounds she had heard baffled her at first. There had been bumps on the boards above, a half-stifled scream, recognizable as such though short and cut off. There had been hurried footsteps across the floor, then the noise of struggle, then shouts, too muffled to understand. There had been scuffling, indeterminate and difficult to follow, and then quietness before the footsteps came hurriedly past her door. The main door had slammed and there had been noise on the pavement, and the sound of a car starting up and driving away.

She had clung to the child that slept, not prepared to go and see for herself whatever had been left in the room. It was light before she summoned up the courage, and by then the men had been gone nearly two hours. When she did go, her child left behind on the mattress still curled foetus-like in sleep, her screams, hysterical and piercing, woke the building.

Henry Davies was drinking tea in the police station canteen. It was thick, strong-brewed, laced with sugar, and hot. He could only sip at it, but always regarded his early morning cup as the essential way to end night duty. He had signed off now, but usually spent fifteen minutes in the canteen, waiting for the day shift handlers to come on, to exchange a few words of gossip and police talk with them.

He had heard on his radio of the flap on the far side of the area covered by the station, but a dog had not been required, and he had methodically continued his patrol, checking factory, shop and warehouse doors.

He was sitting on his own when the sergeant came in.

'Lad, the DI's been on the radio. Wants you down Englefield

Road. Number one-six-two. Wants you down there as fast as you can.' It was the standard joke in the station that he called everyone under the age of forty "lad".'

'What for?' Davies asked.

'I don't know,' the sergeant lied, but did it well, and Davies couldn't read it. 'He asked specifically for you. Slip on down there, lad.'

They'd radioed ahead when he drove out of the station yard, and the Detective Inspector was waiting on the steps of the house for him. There were three police cars parked haphazardly at the side of the street, and a small knot of half-dressed onlookers. Davies got out of the car. A constable who stood on the pavement and who knew him looked away.

Then the inspector walked toward him, unshaven, roused from his Sunday morning bed.

'I've bad news, Henry. I'm very sorry . . . It's Doris. Some bastard's killed her.'

He stopped, letting the words sink in. He saw the mask of overt self-control slide across the police constable's features.

'When did it happen?' Davies said.

'Early this morning. We had a call about forty minutes ago. I've identified her. Do you want to go and see her, Henry?'

'There'll be all the cameras there, prints. All the bloody paraphernalia. I don't want to see her like that. Not with them all working round her.'

'Is there somewhere you can go?'

'I'd like to go to her Mum's. Has she been told?'

'Not yet.'

'I'd like to go there, then. Thank you, sir.'

'I'll get someone to drive you round. Fred can come down and pick up your motor, and take your dog home and give it a meal. You can collect him tomorrow.'

'Do you know who did it?'

'I think so. But they're long gone. Two of them. They're telling us a bit inside. More than they usually do.'

The inhabitants of the commune were herded into the main living room on the ground floor while the coffin with Doris Lang's body in it was carried down the stairs to the unmarked hearse. The Detective Inspector watched it go, then walked back

116

into the room. He had spotted the spokesman for the group, older than most, a fragile and defiant figure. He called him out and went with him to the room behind, used as sleeping quarters. Blankets were strewn on the floor in the position they had been left in when the screaming had started.

'You've been helpful, quite helpful, before I was called out. I want it to go on that way.'

The other man looked up at him, without responding.

'The woman who found the body, she tells me two men left after she heard noises upstairs. Some time after half-past four. Who are those two men?'

The man said nothing, but instead spread out his fingers and pushed them through his hair.

'Now, don't mess me about, sunshine. It's a murder inquiry. We get impatient quickly.'

'We knew one of them.'

'Which one?'

'One was an Irishman.'

'I said, and I said it clearly, don't mess me about. I haven't got all bloody day to be playing games.' Their two faces, the one bearded and with traces of acne, the other stubbled and tired, were less than a foot apart. The man from the commune looked away, then said:

'There was a girl who used to live here. Eilish McCoy. One of the men was her brother. He's called Ciaran. I know because she once showed me a picture of him, in a sort of uniform. Taken back in Ireland. He just turned up here about a week ago, asked for a room, said he had some people coming. Said they needed . . .'

The Inspector said, 'Somewhere quiet, somewhere to lie up?'

'Something like that.'

'And the other one, the second one?'

'We never heard his name.'

'Was he Irish?'

'No.'

'Look, boy, last time, don't screw me about.'

'I'd say he was an Arab.'

'And no name, didn't McCoy call him anything?'

'They didn't mix with us. They were either out or in the room. The second one only came the night before last. There was no name.'

'You say McCoy said he had "some people coming"?'

'He told me there were three others, only the one showed up.'

A detective came into the room. In his hand, held gingerly between thumb and first finger, was a four-by-two-inch note-book.

'It was over in a corner. Left behind. It's Doris Lang's writing, no doubt on that. I've seen it in the station. Her week's log of the comings and goings. Seems she searched these buggers' room on Friday night, again yesterday afternoon. There's a bit about what she found, and a description of the two men. Proper detailed one.'

The inspector went out of earshot into the corridor and said to the detective, 'Get on to Division, tell them to call Special Branch, and shove over all the stuff on McCoy. And tell the people upstairs to get a move on, we'll have half bloody Scotland Yard here by lunch-time.'

When he reached his office back at the police station an hour later the desk sergeant was there to greet him.

'There's been a man called Jones on the phone for you. One of the spoofs from the Security Service. Said something about a note-pad. Wants to come up and see you as soon as you've ten minutes to spare him. Number's on your table.'

'Coming up in the bloody world, aren't we?' said the Detective Inspector as he went into his office.

10

Like an incoming ocean tide that thrusts its way into rock gullies and crevices so the name of Ciaran McCoy swept through the many departments of Scotland Yard. Photographic section, fingerprint section, Special Branch and its Irish section, Murder squad, Criminal Records, Liaison Regional Crime. The name was telephoned to the Commander in charge of Special Branch, and to the Assistant Commissioner (Crime). Meetings were hurriedly convened, and at the centre of them were the suitably doctored files passed on from Leconfield House the previous night. The photograph of McCoy was rapidly reproduced, and despatched to all police stations in the Metropolitan area. The photofit team began work on a compilation of the unknown Arab's features, using principally Doris Lang's written description, written by a trained hand, and also including the sketchier accounts of his appearance as given by the occupants of the commune. Teleprinter messages from the Royal Ulster Constabulary headquarters at Knock Road on the east side of Belfast carried more information on the Irishman. The decision was made to release the picture of McCoy at lunch-time for the Independent Television current affairs programme that would be on air at that time, and for a BBC newsflash.

That was when Norah saw the picture.

Her father always insisted that the television should be on during the formal eating of the Sunday roast, because he liked the farmers' programmes. After the music had faded away and the end-title shot of a threshing machine had disappeared behind a hill the screen went to black before the appearance of the 'Newsflash' symbol. The three people round the table, Norah, her mother and her father, all stopped eating and turned their attention to the set, food still on their forks. The item lasted a minute or so, the first forty seconds taken up by pictures of the comings and goings in Englefield Road. A policewoman had been found in a commune. Dead, strangled.

'Bastards,' Norah's father muttered to himself, 'Bloody bastards.'

Police were anxious to trace a young Irishman. Name – Ciaran McCoy. The picture came up then, and stayed on the screen for twenty seconds. Half this time had elapsed before Norah recognized the boy she had lain beside at the swimming pool, the boy she had kissed, and who had left her so abruptly last Thursday night. She could see it was a police photograph, a man just taken into custody, aggressive and caged. But it was still the same man, the lines of a mouth whether set in anger or friendship change little, only superficially.

'Little swine,' her father said. 'We should string them up. Only thing they understand.'

Norah had said nothing. She put her head down and close to the food lest her parents should see the tears that welled up in her eyes. She had bolted her food, made an excuse and run through the front door. She walked endlessly that afternoon,

119

conscious of an overwhelming feeling of shame, of having been dirtied in some way.

When Jones came back from the police station he brought with him photostats and transcripts of the note-pad. Duggan and Fairclough were waiting in his office.

Duggan said, 'He's blown it, hasn't he, our little boyo? Lost his safe house, lost his base. His picture will be plastered everywhere by tonight, all over the television, and front pages of the papers tomorrow. And now he's running, concerned with his own survival. Not what you'd call an auspicious start for what he's after.'

'Meaning what?' said Jones.

'That it may well be over for him. His concentration now is how to stay free. Does a man in his position go walking through a police cordon, cordon forewarned, cordon with a description? Does he, hell! He stays out. Packs it in.'

'That's one viewpoint.' Jones acknowledged the argument, but looked sceptical.

'The other view takes a different course,' Fairclough joined in. 'If we look at the Palestinian, or Arab, or whatever he is, we can come out with a different answer. He's been through a crisis before, in France on Thursday, and he's still on the move. Look at it from his point of view. If he doesn't go on what does he go back to? They won't welcome him with open arms back in his camp. He'd be a miserable failure. Fiasco. It's when the suicide mentality breaks through. The harder the going gets the more he will be prepared to risk his own life in order to succeed.'

'And the conclusion from that?' asked Jones.

'The conclusion from that is that the Arab is now extremely dangerous. Tiger in the long grass with half his guts shot out. He's a killer still, more so, only thing we can be certain of is that. But he's at a disadvantage, and that's positive, and consolation for us.'

'The picture of one of them, detailed description of the other. Available to every man round Sokarev. That stacks the odds a bit against our two friends.' Jones was able to smile, rare over the last two days. 'But if the Arab wants to go on what about McCoy?'

Again it was Fairclough, hunched forward in his seat, using his hands to emphasize the points he made. 'One of them has killed

120

this morning, but they're both in it together. The critical factor is whether they fall apart, how much of a bond they've made. From what I've read of McCoy I think he'll stay in, right up to the end, providing he thinks there's a chance of living through it.'

Jones wondered how he could be so sure, and envied the younger man the certainty of his opinions. But it was not a time for sarcasm, or for academic discussion. So many of them had breezed through the Department over the years, knowing all the answers, having an explanation for every half-truth situation. The ones that stayed on were the ones who recognized that there were no simple answers in the business. The problem was – and Jones could see that much – that this wasn't the operation the section heads were familiar with, inexperienced at tangling on the short-term affairs. They were pretty good when they had the space to spread themselves, to get through on the inside, to win time to build up the overall picture. But this was a sprint, and didn't really depend on men like himself. Hadn't much to contribute. When there wasn't any time the whole thing came down to Jimmy's level. Who shoots best – us or them? That's why he'd brought Jimmy in on the effort. He liked the man in a distant way, was vaguely fond of him, but to be dependent on him, to recognize he had more to offer now than Jones himself, that left a taste in the mouth.

Jimmy took considerable care over his firearms.

For close protection work he favoured the PPK (Polizei Pistolen Kriminal) Walther. And this was the gun he drew from the armoury, set behind reinforced walls in the basement of Leconfield House just beyond the area used by the monitoring team. The PPK was a small weapon, manufactured with great skill by the workers of the Karl Walther factory at Ulm near Donau in West Germany. Its length was little more than six inches, its weight slightly over a pound. It was not new, manufactured in 1938, and had come into the Department's collection after the war, but the armourer had maintained it with studied attention, knowing that this, among all the others, was the weapon that Jimmy asked for on his occasional visits to the underground room. On most occasions the gun had been returned unused, but a few times the armourer had noticed the magazine no longer contained its seven shells, and that the barrel needed cleaning.

121

The two men had talked about Jimmy's choice at the time that the newspapers were full of how the PPK being used by a Royal detective had jammed during a kidnap attempt, and how it had been withdrawn from use by the bodyguards. Neither the armourer nor the marksmen had been impressed by the reasons made public for the switch-over to the British-made Smith and Wesson, the traditional police weapon. Jimmy's loyalty was unmoved.

With the gun signed for, and two dozen rounds along with it, Jimmy drove north to the police firing range in an old building the far side of Euston Station. There were policemen there, members of a pistol shooting club, complete in denim overalls and earpads, firing at targets twenty-five metres across the floor from the painted white line that ran across one end of the range.

Jimmy showed his identification card to the instructor, and the policemen were called back to the shadows away from the shooting line. They watched as Jimmy loaded the magazine, then stood apparently relaxed facing them and away from the human-shaped target, gun pointing to the floor, loosely held against his trousers. The instructor let fall a box of matches. By the time it had bounced twice and come to rest Jimmy had twisted, body crouched, knees bent, two hands together outstretched and both on the butt of the pistol, and his first shot had hit the target. Three more followed.

'About a six inch group,' the instructor said, and Jimmy acknowledged expressionless. Where else did they expect the bloody things to be? He went to the side wall, by the door, waited a moment for his legs to loosen, then flung himself forward on the floor, rolling all the time before there was an instant of steadiness and he fired twice.

'Eight inches or so apart, both in the chest area,' said the instructor.

Jimmy fired all twenty-four rounds. Some in near darkness, some with a bright light shining at his face, some on the move, some stationary. All hit the target, each puckered hole in the torso area.

'Bit of a bloody show off, isn't he?' said one of the watching policemen, but his whisper was overheard by the instructor, who walked across the room to him.

'Look, boy.' His voice was booming, the result of deafness accrued from eighteen years in the underground range. 'There's a fractional possibility he might miss. And there's a fractional possibility you might hit. That's the difference between you and him.'

Jimmy was well pleased with the morning session, and it was over quickly enough for him to fit in a drink before he was due back at the Department.

The two of them were asleep in the car.

McCoy lay on his side across the front seats, head just beneath the steering wheel. Famy was curled up in the back, his coat off and covering his shoulders. The car was parked deep in a grassy clearing, far from the road and visible through the high summer foliage only to someone who approached to within a few yards of it. There were many such places in the line of Surrey hills between Guildford and Dorking that block the route to London. Later they would become a haven for Sunday walkers and picnickers, but in the early morning the two men had the clearing to themselves.

'We must sleep now, any time we bloody-well can get it,' McCoy had said.

They missed the breaking of the dawn, when the darkness gave way to the half-light, and then the sun began to cast its shortening shadows across the grass. They didn't see the rabbits that came to eat and preen themselves, or the fox that hastened them back to their burrows. It was the noise of children that aroused them. Two boys, little more than ten years old, faces pressed against the steamed-up windows of the car, peering in at them, and running giggling away as McCoy started up from his sleep. He swore inaudibly, and tried to collect his thoughts as he gazed around him. There is always that moment immediately after waking before the bad news of the previous night is remembered. McCoy couldn't immediately place why he was in the car. It came to him soon enough, and with the realization came the memory of the events of five hours earlier.

He shook Famy. 'Come on, lover-boy. Time to be on our way.'

'What's happening? Where are we?' Famy too had woken confused.

'Out in the countryside, taking in the sunshine. Remember?'

Famy inclined his head slowly, deliberately, understanding.

Neither saw the two boys who lay in the thick grass bracken watching the men as they rubbed their eyes and stretched and

123

pawed at the grass, throwing out the stiffness that had accompanied their awkward, limb-twisted sleep. McCoy beckoned with his hand, an abrupt gesture, and the two began to walk the length of the clearing to the path that meandered away among the pine trees and the birches and the undergrowth.

'It's a fair walk, and I don't want to hang about,' said McCoy over his shoulder as he led the way. Neither wore the shoes of the country paths, and both slipped and stumbled where the rain had made the surface muddy.

They walked in silence for more than twenty minutes. Then Famy noticed that McCoy was slowing down his stride, searching for a sign. When he found it he stood still, pleased with himself, beside an old, rusted-up pram chassis.

'That's the first marker,' he said. 'It's easy enough from here to find the place. We go fifty paces now down the path. Measure them out, and we'll be just about there.'

Famy let the distance between them grow as McCoy, his step accentuated by the care he was taking, marked out the distance.

'At home,' said McCoy when he had counted up to fifty out loud, 'we have to hide our guns. We keep them out in the country-side, but somewhere you can get them night or day, so you need markers, so you can find them on a path in the dark. Has to be straightforward and obvious to the man on the pick-up, but giving nothing away to the Brits. Now look, and what's the most prominent tree close to us? Has to be the one with the ivy up it, easy to see, would show up by torch. That's the main marker. Now we have to look for something else that's off the path but equally clear . . . stands out just as much. You walk round the tree, trying to line it up with something that stands out. Right? If you draw a line between this tree, and the big one, over there, the one the lightning hit, you go on and into the bank. There are rabbits' holes all the way down and along the bank. Well, what we're looking for is the hole in the straight line beyond the two trees.'

He walked forward past the ivy-coated branches, past the dead tree. 'The Brits are too bloody impatient to work it out like this. But once there was a chap on the television, and his men called him "Sniffer". He found more of our guns than any other soldier in the province. And what did the buggers do with him? Sent him first to the Tower of London on guard duty, then packed him off to Cyprus for nine months.'

124

McCoy was still laughing as his hands sunk into the rabbit hole. Famy watched fascinated as they emerged again clutching the whitened plastic of a farm bag.

'I had to dig the hole out a bit,' McCoy said. 'But who's going to notice fresh earth at a rabbit burrow?'

He pulled the bag out on to the bank, scanned the path in both directions, listened for a moment and then, satisfied that they were alone, started to unwind the sticking tape that sealed the top. From the bag he took three rifles, small, narrow, seemingly ineffective by their very abbreviation. Each was only marginally more than two feet in length, with the steel skeleton of the shoulder-rest bent back alongside the barrel. He placed them on the plastic, handling them with delicacy and concern, and with them two bulky clothes bags.

'What are they?' asked Famy.

'It's a version of the M1 carbine. World War Two, American. These are the paratroopers' ones, with the folding stock. They wouldn't give me Armalites, the bastards, said three was too many. These are old, but that doesn't mean there's anything wrong with them. They were test-fired ten days ago, across the water, then stripped down and cleaned . . .'

Famy interrupted, anxiety in his voice. 'There were no Klashnikovs?'

'We never get a sight of the bloody things. They've tried to bring them in, but we haven't had any reach us. Our stuff is American. One of the reasons our big men got involved in this was to try and guarantee a supply of Klashnikovs.'

'To you it will sound ridiculous, but I've never trained with any other sort of rifle,' said Famy.

'There's nothing wrong with these. They've packed enough coffins. Three hundred range, more than we need. Fifteen-round magazine – if we need more than three we're screwed anyway. Small, light – just about six pounds. The Yanks ran off more than three and a half million of them in the war. They're untraceable.'

'Why only three? There were going to be three of us, and then you.'

McCoy was taking loaded magazines from one of the cloth bags. He looked up and into Famy's face. 'You were going to do the shooting. The deal was that I looked after the accommodation and the motor. You looked after the rest.'

'And now?'

McCoy laid the magazines out side by side, twelve of them. 'Well, it can't be done by one alone,' he said, still gazing directly at Famy, 'so we'll need two of them, and have one spare.'

There was a huge smile across Famy's face as the strain of the last few hours fled from him. God, the bastard's been suffering, thought McCoy. He's had enough bloody hints and not believed them. McCoy opened the second bag.

'We may not have done you well on the rifles, but on the grenades we've the best. We get a lot of our stuff via the dealers in Holland. These are Dutch, called the "V 40 Mini", less than half the size of a normal grenade. Tiny, but the sales talk is sensational. Four hundred chunks flying out, hundred per cent casualties guaranteed at ten feet. It's what we want, something for close work, not a bloody great bomb that'll demolish half the audience but one that can land nice and near your man, and take him out.'

There were twelve of them. He held one in his hand, nestled in the palm where it fitted snugly, less than an inch and a half in diameter, and deadly. McCoy packed the grenades and the magazines back into their separate bags and dropped them into the bigger plastic one. The rifles followed, and he again taped the top, and then they both walked up the path toward the car. McCoy's mind was now tuned to the next batch of problems. Transport. Where to ditch his present motor, where to get another? And where to sleep, where to lie up for the next two days? Famy could see he was thinking, and did nothing that might break the other's train of thought. He felt complete confidence in the Irishman who carried under his arm the vital weapons that would be used against David Sokarev.

The Prime Minister cut short his Scottish weekend and flew to Northolt, the capital's military airfield. His surprise move aroused little press speculation amongst the journalists covering his foray into the north. It was generally believed, and not denied in official circles, that the country's economic plight had led to the abbreviated schedule. It was less well known outside his immediate entourage that the workings of the Security and Intelligence Services that were ultimately answerable to him fascinated and exhilarated the Head of Government. In his first floor office, overlooking the immaculate flower-decked gardens of his Downing

Street residence, he met the Director General of the Security Service.

The Prime Minister was prepared to listen to the exposition of the problem, and hear the results and actions that would follow from the series of meetings that had gone on through the morning between the police and officials from the Department. He had shown concern that at this stage of the operation no leakage of information to the press should happen, he required maximum detail on the two potential assassins, but already knew of the remarks passed between the Israeli Ambassador and the Foreign Office. When the Director General had finished the Prime Minister turned away to the window, searching for the words he wanted, weighing them before speaking, face serious and intent, pencil twirling in his fingers.

'There is a chance, then, that a massive screen round the man will deter any attack. When I was in Germany for the football some years ago they adopted that policy. Total saturation. Nothing happened, and whether they were successful or not we have no way of knowing. But I think from what you say you don't believe that to be a likely eventuality, the deterrent. We will now move, Director General, into the realm of what is called "Late-at-night thought", not to be attributed to this building. I would like to think that should the Arab, if that is what he is, be taken prisoner, arrested, that he would violently resist such action, and that in his escape attempt he should be shot dead. We've had one package of hostages on a VC10 sitting it out in the Jordan desert, we've had another VC10 wrecked at Schipol, we've had another held at gunpoint in Tunis. I don't want a fourth. I don't want to have to hand this man over at the point of a rifle with a plane-load of lives at stake, and that is what will happen if this man is taken and put through the courts. The Irishman in that context is unimportant.'

The Prime Minister wished the Director General luck, smiled bleakly at him as they shook hands, and showed him to the door.

In their small bedroom the Sokarevs were both involved in the packing of his suitcase for the visit to Europe and the United States. While his wife took the clothes, folded them and laid them on the bed, Sokarev placed them with care into his old suitcase. He chided her against giving him too many shirts, and

127

spoke of the services of hotel laundries, but she said she was not concerned with that, and had her way. The shoes, the shirts, the underclothes and the socks, pyjamas and dressing gown, a thick jersey, all went into the case before his two suits. The suits were the only two he possessed, one for best, for making his speech, one for wearing during the day. And for travelling she selected his jacket and a pair of slacks and hung them out on the edge of the wardrobe. When they had finished the case was bulging and both of them had to press hard down on it for the locks to fasten. The case meant something special to him, and he had cared well for it since it had brought his many fewer belongings to Israel on the long journey from Frankfurt thirty-nine years ago. It was rarely used and treated with consideration, and had taken on special importance for David Sokarev, because his father had brought it for him, and carried it to the station, and handed it up into the train before waving goodbye. His father had disappeared from view as the train had pulled out from the platform, lost in the pall of engine smoke, and had then returned home to wind up the family affairs. He had been full of promises and assurances that he would follow his wife and son to Israel when that was completed. David Sokarev never saw him again.

The key that locked the case had long since been lost, and Sokarev used a wide leather belt to hold down the top in case the clasps should fail during the journey.

She fussed around him that evening in the bedroom. It was a rare event for him to be away from home for anything more than a single night, but she could see that the anxieties and worries that had oppressed him two and three nights before were now something of the past. They laughed with each other, and smiled a lot and sometimes he put his arm round her shoulders, and he talked of the friends that he would be going to see in London, men that he had met on previous visits or who had come to Israel, and with whom he corresponded. When the packing was finished he went to his study to work on the draft of his speech while his wife moved to the kitchen to cook his dinner; it would be something light with cheese, as he liked it.

He wrote the speech in spidery long-hand, frequently crossing out what he had already set down and placing the corrections in smaller writing over the top. He would talk on the need of his country for atomic power to ensure self sufficiency in the fields of agriculture and industry and reduce the necessity of oil. It

128

would not be a fine speech, he knew that. He shared the problem of many brilliant men that he found it arduous and awkward to cannibalize his detailed laboratory work into the language of a lecture theatre. He had sketched what he would say – unsatisfactory, but the best he could manage. There would be no mention of the energy of the atom when directed for military purposes, and in the well-mannered and professional group to which he would be speaking there would be no questions on that count. It was understood. Accepted.

He had worked for more than an hour, and was still regretting that Anna would not be accompanying him and that he would be dependent on a typist from the embassy in London, when the telephone rang.

'Mackowicz here,' said the distant voice, after Sokarev had given the number. Thoughts of neutrons and atomic piles and reactors fled from him, as his mind cleared. In their place was nothing. Clouded, vacant and hesitant.

'What do you want?' his voice showing the resentment he felt at the other man's intrusion into the private oasis of his study.

'I was just ringing to make sure that all would be well for you tomorrow.'

'There are no problems,' said Sokarev.

'You need have no fears of the visit to London. The British authorities are taking many steps to ensure that no incident will take place.'

'I have no fears.' Sokarev spoke sharply.

There was a pause at the other end of the line. What more do you want to say? thought Sokarev. Why burden me at my home? For the next ten days you will be there to hold my hand, dictate my movements, govern my actions.

'I will be picking you up myself tomorrow . . .'

'But I have a taxi ordered. It is all arranged. There is no need.' He was close to anger.

'It has been decided that I shall take you to Ben Gurion. Elkin will be with me. You can cancel the taxi.'

'Who has decided it?'

'It has been decided in the Ministry, by the superiors in our Department.'

Sokarev sank back in his chair, the telephone still to his ear. There was no fighting them; they had taken charge. The depression surged again through him. He was weak, pliable again in the hands of the young men who would accompany him, a toy passed from hand to hand.

The younger of the two boys that had played in the clearing in the early morning saw and recognized the picture of McCoy when it was shown again at tea-time on television. His father telephoned the village policeman. There were a series of calls that followed the sighting, and from County headquarters at Guildford some twelve miles away a tracker dog was sent. Special Branch officers drove down from London, and in the fading light the dog found the rabbit hole where McCoy had secreted the rifles and grenades. It had taken the Labrador a long time to discover the hiding place, but eventually he stood by the entrance whining and impatient. The policemen had moved with caution lest they should disturb the footprints in the fresh soil. They would return again on Monday morning for a more detailed examination, but in the meantime the ten yards square in front of the hole was covered with plastic sheeting, and a constable was left to spend a lonely night to prevent interference with the evidence.

From Scotland Yard the report of the identification and subsequent discovery were passed on to Jones, along with the conclusions that had been drawn from the find in the woods. So Fairclough had been right, and Duggan wrong in his assessment. The bastards weren't running, they were on course still, and visiting a cache. Collecting something. And only one thing they'd need such a hiding place for. They'd have their guns now, thought Jones. He looked at the picture of McCoy on his desk, face puffed out where he'd tried to distort his face as the shutter had gone on the army camera – old trick, to try to make the official record useless. Hard, mean face, thought Jones. The photokit picture of the Arab was with him now, fresh from the printing press, and alongside it an artist's impression in semi-profile.

Jimmy came into the office, following his knock by a couple of seconds. Jones could see the well-scrubbed chin and cheeks, bright and shining, knew it was the sign of too many at lunch-time and a head under the tap. Cold water, to regain control. Jones pushed the pictures across his desk towards Jimmy and said, 'Those are our little boys. Get those bloody faces stuck in your mind.'

130

11

From behind the driving wheel Elkin watched Mackowicz emerge from the doorway of the flats carrying the professor's case, and a few steps behind him came Sokarev and his wife. He saw the scientist kiss his wife hard on both cheeks and cling to her for several seconds before breaking away and almost run to the car door Mackowicz had opened for him. She stood and waved long after the car had gone away up the road, but through his mirror Elkin could see that the passenger in the back never turned his head. The face behind was taut, stretched with emotion, that much Elkin could see before he settled into the long, winding road to Ben Gurion Airport.

There was little talk during the journey; Mackowicz tried several times to get conversation going, but was rebuffed by Sokarev. By the time they were through Kryat Gat, nearly half-way there, he had given up and sat quietly beside Elkin, leaving the passenger to whatever thoughts with which he cared to occupy himself.

The two security men were not unused to this. It was frequent that men who required bodyguard protection should resent the presence of those sent to ensure their safety. If the man didn't want to talk then that was his concern, thought Mackowicz; he and Elkin had enough to concern themselves with.

They had been out of Israel on this duty before, but always in a bigger team, once with the then Prime Minister Golda Meir, when the detail had been nine men, once with Abba Eban in his days as Foreign Minister, when there had been four others. This was a different situation – just the two of them, which made their success or failure more dependent on the effectiveness of forces completely outside their control. In particular, when they had travelled with the Prime Minister they had been in sufficient numbers to organize a complete security screen around their charge. They had not been obliged to rely on the departments of the countries they visited. But when they were simply a pair

131

they would be forced to accept the guidance and knowledge of the British police. It was not the way they liked to operate.

Their selection for the task of watching over the small, stout man who slumped across the back seat of the car was no accident. Both were expert shots with hand guns, and both were thorough and painstaking. When the threat had become known they had been the two obvious choices. The Head of the Protection Division of the Foreign Ministry had had no doubts that among the men under his control Mackowicz and Elkin were the most efficient and professional. They travelled light, just two canvas bags in the boot alongside the professor's larger bag. They contained a few changes of clothes, while the suits they wore in the car would see them through the public functions. In one bag were the files, marked 'secret', that contained all the available Israeli intelligence information on the threat, and a complete dossier on Sokarev from his blood group to details of his family and his financial arrangements. In the other bag, wrapped in shirts, were the personal two-way radios that would be modified to the wavelengths of the Israeli Embassy by the resident communications and wireless expert, and the issued firearms.

They had left at seven and turned into the driveway of the airport seventy-five minutes later, which left them a little over an hour before take-off. Sokarev could sense that the two men in the front of the car understood his hostility to them. He was dominated by feelings of isolation and loneliness, and an inability to communicate with the two men with him. They were so much younger, so assured. There was nothing to talk to them about, no mutual point of sympathy. Killers, he decided: so how different were they to the men who awaited him – if the fears were true? Cloaked in legality, given the seal of approval, how much were they separated from the terrorists? Both groups killed from a sense of duty, both acted without hesitation, ferret-fast. He recognized that he was afraid of the men he had been given as travel companions. Only the gun could give him confidence, his own gun, the unused Mauser, and that was a step into their world, one with which he could never sympathize, barely understand. It rested in his coat pocket, beside his spectacle case, awkward, forcing out the material of the jacket, the single magazine in his inside breast pocket placed within the fold of his wallet.

The baggage check took half an hour. Thirty minutes of

shuffling the cases forward inch by inch as he stood behind a crocodile of blue-rinsed lady tourists who even at that early stage of the morning were strident in their retelling of alimony suits, lost husbands and necessary hysterectomies. He was surprised he was not taken through a side door and spared the routine, but neither Mackowicz nor Elkin made any move to suggest that that were possible. When they came to the young man in the orange jerkin who was searching the cases it was only Sokarev's that was opened. When it had been checked, closed again, and scribbled on with chalk his bodyguards produced their identity cards, exchanged a quiet word with the airport security man, and were allowed on their way to the ticket desk. Sokarev felt the indignity, near-humiliation of it. Elkin saw the chin jutting out and the thin-lipped anger of his mouth, and said – not with pomposity but a degree of kindness – 'It's routine, Professor Sokarev. It's nothing personal about you. All passengers are searched. All, that is, except us. We carry papers and equipment. Perhaps it would not be suitable for those to be seen by others standing in a line. So we go through. If it is of comfort to you we are all searched when we leave Heathrow.'

Sokarev fumbled for a reply, unnerved by the accuracy with which the other had interpreted his thoughts.

From the ticket desk the three of them walked toward the staircase that led to the departure lounge. Sokarev noticed now that Mackowicz was to his right, Elkin to the left. Not out of my own country, and already they have taken up their positions, he thought, leaving me like a prisoner under escort. They dwarfed him, eyes already watchful and rotating through an arc. Elkin's jacket was buttoned, and Sokarev could see the bulging shape of a strap-fastened holster. They went through passport control, the official barely looking up as he flicked through the passports, stamped them and handed them back.

Elkin said, 'You have to go through the body search now, Professor. We again are excused that. We will collect you on the far side.'

In front was a long row of curtain-fronted cubicles where from time to time a young man or woman, also in an orange jerkin, would appear. Like a whore waiting for trade, thought Sokarev. And the next customer would step inside and the curtain would be drawn back. Once a man, swarthy in complexion, was led back out of the cubicle, his face betraying self-consciousness as he

133

walked in his stockinged feet, the security man behind him holding his shoes outstretched, as they went to the counter that contained the X-ray equipment.

It was the embarrassment on the face of the victim that jolted Sokarev's mind to the weight in his pocket. It was a situation he had not considered. He had not thought out how he would carry the Mauser on board the aircraft; he had vaguely presumed that his escorts would be with him, and would see it as a *fait accompli*, looked pained for a moment, perhaps have shrugged, and allowed him to carry on. The curtain was opened again, the man gestured him to come forward.

He stood with his legs apart and arms outstretched shoulder high. There was fear now. Fear of discovery. The fear that comes to a small boy caught stealing, found playing truant away from school. The hands started at his collars, feeling under the material, tested the area under his armpits, loitered for a moment on the shape of his wallet in the breast pocket. Sokarev thought he was going to be sick. He watched as the wallet was taken out and opened. The magazine lay there, pristine, unbelonging among his papers. The security man stiffened, set his face, muscles tensed on the top of his wrists.

'Do you have a pistol to go with this ammunition?' said the security man evenly.

Sokarev nodded. 'In the pocket,' he said, still keeping his hands out. The hands found the Mauser there, withdrew it sharply. There was a moment when the security man's eyes were off him as he checked the breech of the pistol, assuring himself it was not loaded.

'I am Professor David Sokarev. I am a nuclear scientist. My work is at Dimona. My flight is to Europe . . .' Waves of wretchedness overcame him, and his voice tailed away. His eyes were now fixed on the floor, not caring to see the keen gaze of the man who stood close to him in the cubicle. When he had collected himself sufficiently he went on, his speech barely audible. 'There are two men from the Foreign Ministry travelling with me. They are to guard me. They are waiting on the far side. I had not told them that I was taking the weapon.'

Ten minutes after they had taken Sokarev to the offices of the security department of the airport Mackowicz was shown in. His face was controlled, betraying no emotion, and he spoke in a huddle with the senior officer there. He never looked once at the

Mauser that lay on the desk, the single rectangular magazine beside it. Whatever business was conducted Sokarev took no part in it. Then Mackowicz walked to the door, opened it and waited for the scientist to go through. When they were alone in the concourse Mackowicz said, 'It was unwise of you to try to take the gun through. There is an important thing that we must now establish. Neither my colleague or myself would consider ourselves fit to make judgements on your work, at which you are an expert. We expect that you would treat us with similar generosity. We do not expect you to make judgements on security matters. If you have no confidence in Elkin and myself you are at liberty, as you have been since we got to Dimona, to telephone to Jerusalem and explain your objections to our superiors.'

The voice scythed through Sokarev's defences. He shook his head, staggered now by his own stupidity.

'I am sorry,' he said. 'It has been a great strain, since you came to see me.'

'We are responsible for your security. We have the right to demand your full co-operation. There will be no repetitions of this situation. Not when you are in our care.'

Sokarev's head was down on his chest as he shambled after his captor toward the lounge seat where Elkin sat. The three men sat in total silence till the flight was called, the guards reading newspapers, the professor staring emptily through the windows and out on to the tarmac. He felt he wanted to discard the whole journey, go home to his wife and to his laboratory and shut out for ever the nightmare world of guns, searches and terrorists. When the flight was called Mackowicz was up first, athletically rising on to the balls of his feet, then he bent down and took the professor's arm and helped him out of the low leather seat.

Elkin said, 'I think we should remember, Professor, that we are going to be together for some time now. Whatever has happened is in the past. It should not linger on.' And he smiled. Sokarev attempted again an apology, but Elkin shook his head.

'It is in the past. Forgotten.'

They walked together down the steps, and past the young soldier who wore an automatic rifle slung across his shoulders, and out into the blazing heat of an August morning in Israel. The sun beat into Sokarev's eyes, causing him to pull the lids together to keep out the very brightness that sprang up at him from the tarmac. Away to the front, acting as a giant reflector,

135

was the 747 Boeing jet, its white underbelly and roof gleaming in the harsh light. There is no going back now, thought the scientist. There is no escape. Whatever happens now it is out of my control.

Sokarev mounted the steps to the plane. Mackowicz and Elkin were a pace behind him.

Along the corridor from the control room, and high in the Scotland Yard tower block, they had taken over the main lecture theatre for the Monday briefing of all those detectives and senior uniformed officers involved in the hunt for McCoy and his colleague and in the protection of David Sokarev.

Jimmy sat at the back, far behind the rows of neatly-clipped necks, looking down on the proceedings. If anyone had turned to watch him they would have detected a faintly bored, disinterested face – that of a man who has been through it all before. Not that Jimmy ever felt totally at ease in the company of policemen. And they didn't react well to the presence alongside them of what was virtually a freelance operator, unconditioned to their code of discipline and their rule books.

The details read out concerning the timings and locations of the visit failed to hold his attention. A big man in uniform did the talking. Like evidence in a dangerous driving case, thought Jimmy. Solid, monotonous, dull. Never make it on the stage, you won't, brother. Drawing on the blackboard isn't much better. All those lovely coloured chalks. How they adore it, like dressing up for the pantomime. Green lines and red circles and blue crosses.

What a way to go to war. Has McCoy got a big map, does he stick his finger in it like bloody Rommel? Can't fight these bastards with maps and diagrams, old soldier. Looks good, sounds good, doesn't work that way. There's only one place you'll get Master McCoy and his little friend, and that's beside Sokarev. That's the only place those bastards will show. Wasting your time with all the motorcades and all the escort riders. Doesn't happen there. Happens when he's on the pavement or at the speech. Stands to reason, if you're planning a show like this for a dozen weeks, you're not going to risk everything on the off chance you might manage a pot shot during a cavalcade. And when the old drone had finished, time then to get up to the university, and have a look, and come back via the hotel, and still have some minutes to spare before the plane arrived. Should have done the reconnaissance yesterday Jimmy-lad, not been in that boozer half the afternoon. Should have given the place the look-over, not a thing that ought to be done in a hurry. Should have been thought out, Jimmy.

He knew it, didn't have to argue the toss about it, and comforted himself only with the thought that he would be close to Sokarev. Human wall, and no pension rights. But perhaps it was a safe old number, for all that. Whoever heard of the bodyguard catching it? JFK, RFK, right down to Faisal; all had the detail round them, who lived to file the reports on what went wrong, and still had time to go to the funeral.

Forty men in the room, all of them brass, and how many taking orders . . . another three hundred, four hundred? And they're just two. What real chance have they got?

That was where Jimmy's thoughts came to a stop. Below him, pinned to the side of the blackboard, were the pictures, McCoy's and the man whose name they still searched for. Nasty, rough bastards, Jimmy said to himself, very hard, very serious people. And what do we have against them? This crowd, dragged in from murder inquiries, bank robberies and demonstrations on Sunday afternoons in Trafalgar Square. His eye rolled around the room. Many of the officers were taking notes, all listened intently, following the speaker as he took them slowly through the maps and diagrams. If these two bastards decide to come in close, thought Jimmy, then this lot'll find themselves in a different league. They'll wish they'd never got out of bed.

The big jet had swung out over the sea, deep and distant beneath them. Sokarev saw the beach at Herzliya, could make out the people on the sand who looked up at the wallowing giant as it surged toward its cruising altitude. Four and a half hours would take them to London, thirty-one-thousand feet and a cruising speed of six hundred miles an hour, hurtling across the Mediterranean, then the Italian coast and the huge expanse of France before the descent and the shore-line of Britain.

Elkin sat beside the window, his charge beside him, and then Mackowicz in the aisle seat. Sokarev dozed till Mackowicz's voice overrode the hazy thoughts he was entertaining, and he opened his eyes. The man talking to his guard was like a replica, thought the scientist. Same assurance, strength, poise and ease of movement. And wearing the same heavy jacket, even in the sweat-making atmosphere of the cabin, to hide his gun from the sensibilities of the passengers.

Mackowicz turned to Sokarev. 'We used to work together, this layabout, Elkin and I. Then he took the easy life. He just flies with the airline. Logs more hours than the pilots.'

Sokarev said, 'I did not know that you people were on board . . .'

'Two, sometimes four. Always two. We have no option. The orders are very clear. Our planes are not to fly to Arab countries. If there is a hi-jack attempt all you can do is shoot, and hope.'

'And the pressurization, what if that is broken?'

'The pilot will dive. He will try and throw the terrorist off balance. He will also attempt to get below ten thousand feet. If he is unsuccessful and there is a fracture then there is a disaster – nothing he can do. So he falls for two reasons: to get below the pressurization problem but also to confuse the man or woman, give us time to act. It has all been practised.'

'And the passengers, what of them?' asked Sokarev, impatience in his voice.

'If they are Israelis they will understand. If they are not . . . then they use another airline.'

'But the guns you have. The moment you fire you will puncture the fuselage.'

'The bullets are restricted velocity. You need have no fears, Professor, it has all been worked out.'

So they were at war. Even in the womb-like casing of the airliner they were in a state of conflict. Not great armies, just tiny fragments of platoons. But just as lethal, just as capable of inflicting misery as the big battalions. Sokarev reflected that the front line was now under two hours away. It might be in a car on a three-lane motorway into the capital, it might be the pavement outside a hotel, it might be a lecture hall packed with distinguished academics. It was a new war as unfamiliar to him as it was commonplace to the men who now rested, their eyes closed, mouths sagging in relaxation, on either side of his seat.

Jones was a long time staring down at the twin pictures that lay on his cluttered desk. They'd found their way to the top of the pile of files and maps of central London, and the plan of the university complex and the surrounding streets. He supposed he was expected to loathe the pair, have a great and consuming hatred of them, but it never worked that way. Before they'd pushed him into 'Middle East' he'd laboured for a dozen years on the Soviet bloc (Czechoslovakia) desk – where the then DG said the real work was done. Not hard to remember the attaché, trade of some description, that they'd picked up after months of trailing and surveillance. Was reckoned to have been a big man – 'incalculable damage to the national interest' was what the judge had said – but he hadn't seemed that formidable in the interview room of the police station they'd taken him to after the lift. Rather ordinary, more anxious that someone should give him a cigarette than anything else. Hadn't said anything, of course, just smiled at their questions in an apologetic way, embarrassed that they had to play such games. The Section had used a major manpower quota to track him, classified it as a 'priority' operation, and Jones was one of those closely involved. Afterwards it was just anti-climax, unimportant, devoid of stimulus.

He wondered how much different he'd find McCoy and his friend, whether they'd be any more fearsome face to face than the quiet little man from Prague. McCoy was easier to evaluate; his photograph had been taken in custody and his eyes and mouth showed all the aggressiveness of a trapped man. But the other picture, that was the one that held Jones's interest. Quite a pleasant mouth the photokit and the artist had given him, and eyes that were large and not set with fear. Hard to see him as something special, something to be exterminated, because the threat he carried was so contagious. Didn't look like the rabid fox he was categorized as. Just a boy, really, and nothing in his features to betray his potential.

Helen came in, no knock, walked across the room and peered past his shoulder at the pictures.

'Those the clever pair, causing all the fuss?'

'Those are the ones.'

'And you've set the big, bad Jimmy loose after them?'

'Slipped his collar, right.'

'And how good are they, compared with our Jimmy boy?'

'They'll do all right. They'll give him a good run, he won't have to worry about that. He'll get his full out of them.'

'And then they'll send him home in one piece?'

'Probably,' Jones said. Before she went back to the outer

office he saw the whiteness of her cheeks. Should have taken it more gently. But it was the one point that nagged at him, worrying at his composure as to whether Jimmy would beat these two at the close quarters where he was certain they would meet. It was difficult to believe in the danger if he stared at the face with the close mesh of curled hair that the police artist and the eye-witnesses had given to it. To find the real man he had to go to the file, and that was still sparse and without flesh to hang on the skeleton information they had so far accumulated.

He took a drawing pin from his desk drawer and used it to hang the Arab's picture on the wall beside his filing cabinet. Where he could see it at any time he wanted, where he could study it, learn from it, understand it.

The effect on McCoy was less violent than on Famy. The Arab looked with ill-concealed horror at the pictures blazoned across the front pages of the papers. They were standing outside a small newsagent's shop in South West London beside a bus stop where they hoped to board the transport they needed to return to the inner suburbs. The pictures had been blown-up hugely, and in the squat popular papers covered half the front page. There were banner headlines, screaming at them across the pavement: 'The Killers', 'The Most Wanted Men in Britain', 'Have You Seen These Men?'

'Don't bloody gawp at them,' McCoy hissed in Famy's ear.

'It was that-note-book. The one that we left behind, that is where they have taken it from,' said Famy.

'Bullshit. They'll have talked in the commune. Got my name there. That's a Northern Ireland picture of me, taken when I was nicked. They've got an artist to do yours from all the descriptions. It's not particularly good, yours.'

'It is sufficient for them to discard many men. They have given a height, and a weight, the general detail. Not adequate for positive identification, but enough to come close. And they have the clothes, the trousers and shirt that we still wear . . .'

'Get back, can't you? There's no place better for anyone to spot you than if you're pressed tight up against the damn thing.'

'They have no name on me,' Famy said, as he moved away from the shop front and the two men resumed their position at the back of the queue.

Famy felt the uncertainty again that had dogged him throughout his first hours in London. It should not have been happening in this way. They should have been safe and secure in the house, not needing to venture out, dependent on the Irishman for their supplies. There was to have been no question of them hanging about in crowded streets; orders had been specific on that point. Every time a man or woman or child turned to him he imagined the dawning of recognition, and he shuffled his feet, attempting, badly, to maintain a casual, relaxed front. How do people make the recognition? he wondered. How can they translate something so distant from their lives as a wanted picture in a newspaper into the flesh and-blood beside them on the street? It's a difficult and long step to take, Famy told himself. It would take great certainty, requiring a person to peer again and again to convince himself he were right, and that there was more than similarity with a picture he had merely glanced at.

To McCoy it was a less awesome experience. He was accustomed to having his picture in the front pocket of the bottle-green RUC uniforms and the camouflage tunics of British soldiers. He was familiar with life on the run, avoiding capture under the very eyes of men who had studied his features. But he realized a fundamental danger in their present position. The newspapers put two men together, identified them as a partnership, and that was how they were travelling, in tandem, linked to each other. But isolated, moving as loners, how much safer they would be. It was turning over in his mind when the single-decker green bus pulled in at the shop, and the queue moved forward. They must separate, but where to? It was easy enough for him, but what to do with the Arab? Couldn't have him wandering the streets solo, insecure and liable to panic. So what to do with him? There was no immediate answer, only a vague plan, slowly taking shape.

McCoy bought the tickets from the bus driver, and they made their way to the back seats where they would be behind the other passengers, where their faces would suffer least exposure. Famy had the grip-bag, containing a selection of both their clothes, and the rifles, magazines and grenades. It was heavy, and the handle straps strained against the metal hoops that held them to the framework of the bag. His own case had been left in the boot of the Escort, packed with some of his own clothes, some of Famy's. The car itself was off the road in the woods that surrounded the Surrey town of Esher. It would be difficult to find, and he had prised off the number plates, throwing them far into the undergrowth. The ground had been hard, the tyre marks slight, and anyway they had brushed the ground with hazel saplings, leaving a light scuff covering the trail of the wheels.

As the bus made its way toward Hampton Court the two men sat in silence, McCoy working on his next move, Famy suffering from the tension of having seen the photograph and the drawings. By the time they had become locked in the traffic flow McCoy spoke, low and direct, talking from the side of his mouth and close to Famy's ear.

'We have to separate today. The danger lies in us being together.'

There was startled surprise on the other's face, the flash in the eyes that suggests the feeling of being betrayed. McCoy saw it.

'There's nothing for you to worry about. But we have to be apart for today at least. There are eight more hours till darkness, when we should meet again.'

Famy turned his head, the tightly clamped lips giving warning of his suspicion. 'Where would I go? What do I do?' he said.

'I don't know yet. We can talk about it. But we have to get apart. The two of us together is too much of a risk.'

'We could have stayed with the car in the woods . . .'

McCoy cut into him, anxious lest he should lose control and sacrifice the initiative to the Arab.

'It would have been possible. But we could not take another car there, and we have to change motors. We have to get a car in the town. In the country they can block you too easily; it would be reported faster.'

Famy did not reply.

'Look, you silly bugger,' McCoy was talking quickly, urgently – 'I've told you I'm in this with you. You don't have to worry. I'm not bolting on you. It's a judgement I've made, and a necessary one. Am I going to ditch on you now? Think about it. After the girl, after taking you to the guns, am I going to bunk out?'

Famy nodded. He was exhausted from four nights without adequate sleep; there was no spirit in him for argument.

'Where do we get off?' the Arab asked.

'Further on there's a town – about another fifteen minutes. There's tubes and trains there, cinemas. Whatever you want.'

'And you, where will you go?'

Famy saw the hesitation, and had the ability to sense a lie.

142

'I'll just lose myself for a few hours,' McCoy said, 'till the night has gone. Till we can meet up and get a car.'

Again the Arab had no reply. A sense of loneliness and isolation welled up inside him. How far could he trust the Irishman? He was unsure now, certain there was a further reason for the split, certain that he was not being confided in. What could he do? On a bus, where ears would flap and quicken if he raised his voice? He was powerless.

Five stops later McCoy rose out of his seat and went down the length of the aisle. Famy took his cue and followed. Then they were out on the pavement, amid people who hurried past them, intent on their own business. The two men stood for a moment before McCoy saw a tea bar down the road and across the street, and began to walk toward it.

'Just round the corner and up the main street, that's where the cinemas are. There's one there that shows three films, separate theatres, all divided up. That'll lose you for some time, and it's dark in there, you'll be okay. We'll meet back in the tea bar. Eight o'clock. Now don't just walk around, get somewhere like the cinema and bloody-well stay there.'

Famy looked at him as they went in through the door of the café, quizzing McCoy with his eyes, searching for the truth of the other man's decision. He found no answer.

When McCoy left the grip-bag and its contents stayed with Famy. 'Safer with you,' he'd said, 'tucked under your legs in the cinema. Out of harm's way, better than me lugging them round.'

He ducked out into the sunlight, and vanished beyond the doorway, hurrying along the pavements, side-stepping to avoid the crowds of lunch-time shoppers. Free of the bugger, he thought to himself. Free at last without the nursemaid millstone round my neck and pulling down. The relief at being on his own again flowed through him, a river that has broken a dam and finds again the dry stone bed, its expression rampant and without check. He was half-running when he reached the supermarket.

McCoy went inside, through the electrically controlled glass sliding doors. The cash registers, a bank of them where the girls punched the keys and took the money, were at the far end. He took a basket, put a single bar of chocolate in it, something that would stave off the hurting pain of hunger, and walked down past the stacked counters and shelves to the queue that had formed for the privilege of paying. He watched the girl as she deftly handled

143

the bags and packages and tins, eyes never on the customer she served, always on what she took from the wire baskets and put down on the flat surface beside her, while her hands played the numbers on the machine. Her face was set, expressionless, dedicated to the task of extracting the right money, giving the right change.

When he put the basket down the slim hand was there in an instant, pulling clear the chocolate, while the girl mouthed the amount that showed on her machine, as a tiny row of trading stamps reached out from the mechanism.

'Hello, Norah,' he said, very quietly, conscious of the people behind him bustling and impatient at being delayed. She looked up at him. There was startled recognition, then fear, like a rabbit's because she was sitting down and he loomed above her. Taut, strained, wide eyes pierced into him. The will to say something but no voice.

'I have to see you.' He angled the words to give the stress of dependence, and waited for her to react.

'What are you doing here?' Bewilderment, but conspiracy also, hushed so that the words would carry no further than the two of them.

'I have to see you,' he repeated the words, only with greater insistence. 'Outside, make an excuse. I have to be with you this afternoon. I'll be outside and waiting.' He put down two ten-pence coins, the amount shown on the cash machine, took the chocolate and walked back out on to the street.

On the far side of the street he waited. Twenty minutes, perhaps, then she was there looking for a gap in the traffic. Blouse and jeans instead of the overalls she wore for her work. Just before she saw the opportunity to cross she looked across to where he stood. His smile was not returned, and then she was concentrating on the cars and the lorries.

He took her hand. Soft, small, fitting inside his fist. He kissed her without pressure on the side of the cheek, and felt her drag herself back from him.

'You didn't tell me inside there. What are you doing here?'

'I've come to see you.' Inadequate, need more than that.

'You've seen the pictures. You're in the papers, on the telly.'

'I know.'

'Well, what have you come here for?'

'I wanted to see you, girl. I wanted to be with you. I wanted ...'

144

He did not finish. What could he tell her? He clenched her hand tight in his. How could he tell her, that he had to get away from it? That he wasn't just a machine, a killing apparatus. That there was a need for a break, to get away from the awfulness of the running, from the concealment and the chase and the ultimate confrontation. There was a girl on the farm near Cullyhanna, and a place in the gorse and bracken on Mullyash Mountain where she would go with him and let him talk to her and love her and relax with her, till the sleep came and the understanding. Then he could go back to his war. But how to tell the little shop girl from South West London that a man who fights must one time fall asleep in arms that hold no danger? That the time comes when the company of men is repulsive and rejected? Another day beside that bloody man and he'd come to loathe him, not through any fault of the Arab's. McCoy knew there was no fault in him. But it did not lessen the need to escape, and to exist again in the world which he had denied himself.

'I needed to talk to you, somewhere where we could be alone,' he said.

They walked together through the town and into the vast open expanse of the Royal Park. There were roads that cut across the landscape, leaving great segments of virgin ground covered by sprouting grass, and the delicate shaped fronds of the bracken, where the sun shone down. And there were woods where the birches and oaks filtered the light and cast a haze of shadow. It was as he had wanted. He had found what he sought.

They went deep into the bracken, along a path used only by the big red deer that scampered and leapt as they approached, making good their escape. He put his coat down on the broken stems and they sat together. There was no horizon beyond the immediate wall of green that surrounded them, hiding them from all eyes. McCoy sank on to his back, reaching up with his arms and pulling the girl down on to his chest. Her head rested underneath his chin, and against his mouth he could feel the strands of her hair, and there was a scent to them, freshly washed and clean. They lay there a long time, and his thoughts were of the hill farms, and the other girl who was dark and more heavily built and who comprehended the need for release that overwhelmed him, and of the buzzards that would circle and swoop above them across the hills of Armagh County.

It was Norah who broke the spell.

'It is you they are hunting? It was your picture on the TV that we saw?' Frightened, small voice, and his dreaming reply failed to take her fear away.

'It was me. I'm the one they're looking for. They're a long way behind me, and they won't find me.'

'But you killed a girl, strangled her, that's what it said.'

'What do you want me to say? What do you want me to pretend?' He rolled over on to his stomach, and leant on one bent elbow above her, his free hand in her hair, stroking, caressing it into shapes. 'It has nothing to do with your life. It is something separate. I won't tell you I didn't, and you wouldn't believe me if I did. There's nothing I can say, nothing you should know.'

His hand came down from her hair, and a finger nail flicked carelessly at the plastic buttons of her blouse, held by frail cotton to the material. He saw the tears coming, the tightening of the muscles close to her eyes and the reflection from the moisture that ran beside her nose, and found a track that skirted the fullness of her cheek and then was lost on the grass. He came down to her mouth and kissed her, and there was no room for her to back away. She felt her body pressed hard against the unevenness of the ground. And his hands began to go free, and search out the places they quested for. When they had unfastened the clasp behind her back and removed the soft protective covering on her breasts, she put her arms round his neck, and, sobbing, dragged his head close down beside her. She could not account for her actions, could not justify the tenderness with which she ran her hands over the harsh bristles below the hair at the back of his neck, could not reason why she flexed her legs slowly apart in the hope that his hand would find its way. When she opened her eyes his face was very close, and he kissed the lids, closing them, and there was just the darkness and the sensation and the knowledge that the hands were moving again, demanding ownership, seeking new territory. The button slipped loose at the waist of her jeans and she wriggled as his hands eased them below her knees, and still there was the darkness and the desperate requirement for him to move on. He lingered at the scarce-formed line that led down to the gentleness of the soft hair, and she moaned his name without sound into the roughened cheek joined to her own. When he came into her there was pain, and a power she had not known before, and she writhed and tried to escape. But there was only the thrashing, pinioning weight that held her, till at last he

146

sagged, spent and exhausted.

Norah lay on the ground unmoving, the sun playing on her skin, the wind blowing its patterns, while the man beside her slept, his face with the quietness of a child's, the smoothness of his skin broken only by the tramlines worked by the nails of Doris Lang.

From the bank where he had cha ged a ten-pound travellers' cheque, Famy looked for the red cubicle he now identified as a telephone box. It took him fifteen minutes and brought him back to the railway station he had walked past when seeking the bank. The bag was heavy, and it was with relief that he dropped it down on to the floor of the box. He closed the door behind him, and felt in his pockets for a two-pence piece. He had no difficulty remembering the number, nor the extension to ask for when the switchboard operator answered. As he had expected, the figures of the extension were given remotely and above the crackle of the connection.

'It's "Mushroom" here,' Famy said.

There was a scuffling on the line, the sound he recognized as a receiver being placed against the material of a shirt or jacket, and indistinct words spoken into a void. Clearing the room, thought Famy.

'What is it you wish to say?' the telephone was active again.

'I wanted to know whether there were further orders, whether there were new instructions.' Was that all he had telephoned to discover, when there was no chance of further orders? His tone echoed the hollowness of his request.

'Nothing has come through.'

Famy paused, waiting, wondering what to say. He could not speak of his desolation, his fears, of the horror of seeing his picture in the newspapers.

'Nothing at all? There is no word from home?' Perhaps the man at the embassy sensed something of his feelings, recognized the helplessness of the other.

'There is nothing, but that was not to be expected. It is the style of the leadership to allow a free hand in such matters. Your arrival has been communicated.' There was a sharp click on the line, and the sound for a moment was blanked out. In less than a second it returned, and Famy was able to hear the breathing,

147

regular and unemotional, of the man he spoke to.

'There are difficulties?'

'It is so confused now. We have lost our place, because of the girl . . .'

The voice cut in, interrupting. 'There was a clicking noise on the line. We must not speak any more. Ring off, and move away. Do not stay near the telephone. Very briefly, is there anything else?'

Famy was confused. He had heard the noise, but had not interpreted it.

'The Irishman. I do not know at what stage I can trust him, whether I am better on my own. We have the guns now, but . . .'

'Is there nothing of importance that you have to say? If not, ring off.'

'. . . it is the Irishman. He said we must separate for today . . .'

'Ring off. And get away from the telephone box. Right away from it.'

The voice was at shouting pitch, and the line went dead, returning to its continual, miasmic purr. The urgency had at last communicated.

Famy picked up the bag and ran from the station hallway.

12

With the talkative, restless Jimmy out of the office and on his way to the airport for the reception committee, Jones's room had reverted to its normal hushed calm. He was poring over the files, alternately concentrating on the growing information on McCoy and the maps and plans that covered the Professor Sokarev visit when his internal phone rang.

'Monitoring section here, Mr Jones. Your embassy number is on. Chatting away. We've routed through to intercept . . .'

He did not wait to hear any more. He ran through the open connecting door, past the desk where Helen was typing, and out into the corridor. Fifteen paces to the staircase, not bothering to wait for the lift, and down the six flights in a headlong race to get to the basement before the call terminated. He was panting when he arrived. Inside the cubicle the big man was hunched, checking the dials for sound level as the tapes beside him spun slowly round. The spare earphones were already plugged in, and Jones jammed them lopsidedly over his head.

'They've just heard the intercept switch go. The Embassy's trying to wind it up,' he was told.

He was in time to hear the reference to 'guns', then the shouts of the other voice. One more half-hearted sentence and the line was cut.

A white telephone on the table inside the cubicle rang and Jones instinctively reached and picked it up.

'Intercept here. The call was made from Richmond, a public telephone. Checking the location now.'

Jones dialled the special number that had been assigned to the Scotland Yard operations room that was concerned exclusively with the hunt for McCoy and the unknown Arab. He spoke briefly, passing on the relevant material. No more, and rang off. Time to get out of their hair, leave them a chance to get moving. Best break we've had, thought Jones. Something real to bite on for a change. They played him back the tape, which he heard through four more times.

When he walked into Fairclough's office Jones said. 'The nerves are fraying a bit in the team. The Arab on to the Embassy, doubting McCoy. Says he's been left on his ownsome, and doesn't like it. Sounded depressed, miserable, not having a happy time, wanting instructions from home. But he says they've retrieved the guns, which confirms that stuff from the hills we had in last night. But he sounded unhappy, really miserable.'

'Did he say whether or not they were still going to have a go at it?'

'Nothing about that. Said McCoy had told him they must separate for today.'

'Well, that's clear enough then. And not bad thinking. They're more vulnerable like that, together. They'll resume harness tonight. I suggest they're still operational.'

Jones made a slow way back to his own office. He knew what he had to do when he reached its quietness and sanctuary – had to understand them, had to find a way into their thought processes, had to make the men who were just pictures and closely-typed words into human beings. That was the way, the only way, you could anticipate their next decision and action. But they were so remote, and he so out of touch with their world, that he evaluated his chances as minimal. That was why he was not hurrying.

In the town on the outskirts of London police radios had begun to chatter instructions, locations, descriptions, facial features, clothes. Men were hauled from traffic duties, serving summonses, investigating larceny and vandalism.

The Chief Superintendent who controlled the local police station concentrated deploying his men in three directions. First, he blocked all major roads leading out of the area; that was his major and initial priority. Second, a van-load of police took over the hallway of the station that served British Rail Southern Region and London Transport District Line Underground. Third, he concentrated cars not involved in the road blocks in the centre of the town, cruising and observing the hundreds who swarmed on the pavements and around the shops. Revolvers were issued to car crews leaving the station, the required and formal paperwork left till the end of the day. When he was satisfied that the town was sealed as well as possible in the time, he came on the radio net himself to issue a clear and uncompromising instruction.

'The man we are searching for is dangerous, is probably armed, and should not be approached by any police officer who is unarmed. If you see him call in; we'll have the reinforcements you need.'

That was the message that first excited the radio ham who sat in his terraced house whiling away the time till his night shift began at the Hawker Siddeley factory down the road in Kingston. He ignored the stringent code set down by the Wireless Telegraphy Act that forbade any member of the public to listen to police messages and make use of them, and left his set tuned in to the area police frequency. He had turned the set up when he had noticed the rapid upsurge in traffic, and was in time to hear in full the words of the Chief Superintendent. He had a list of the numbers of the news desks of the Fleet Street papers, and being a conscientious man, had taken a note of their edition times. The *Daily Express* were traditionally the best payers for news tips,

150

and there was no need to explain from where the information originated.

As the net was closing around the town, Famy was paying his money underneath the glass grill at the cash desk of the cinema. James Bond was in town – double feature.

'You've nothing to fear. Just do as we say, don't hesitate, whatever it is, and everything will be fine. The British have a big force out. Our own people from the embassy will be close by. But do as Elkin and I say with no questions.'

Those were the last words Mackowicz said to Sokarev on the flight itself. Then the plane finished its long taxi, and the doors to the stiflingly hot cabin were at last opened. Other passengers were already in the aisle waiting to leave when the chief steward and the man that Sokarev knew as El Al security transposed themselves across the corridor, leaving the route to the steps clear for Mackowicz to lead, followed by Sokarev and Elkin. The scientist saw the resentment etched in the faces of those delayed, and wondered why people always looked so hurt and embittered when they have just successfully negotiated an air flight. What have they to face, he thought, that justifies their puckered and peevish stares, and all because they must wait another seventy-five seconds before following down the steps?

It was a comfortable, gentle heat, not aggressive like that in Israel, that greeted them on the tarmac. And there were the Special Branch men. Six of them forming up, three on each side of Sokarev and walking with him, faces turned outward, toward the black Mercedes of the embassy that waited close to the steps. The security attaché spoke briefly to Mackowicz, shook his hand and then came alongside the professor.

'There are people to welcome you, Sir. They are in the lounge at the Terminal building.'

Sokarev started to speak of his baggage.

'Just give me the tag, Sir. On your ticket. It will all be taken care of while you are in the terminal.'

As the car started up Sokarev could see two heavily-laden unmarked vehicles take up position in convoy behind. He sat in the back seat squashed between the attaché and Mackowicz. Elkin was in the front with the driver, and between them another man who was middle-aged and had a faded, autumn look in his features, a man to whom nothing had the freshness of surprise. From the window Sokarev looked into the expressionless faces of uniformed policemen who waved and gestured the car across the traffic lanes. There were dog handlers in the background, and men who stood in civilian clothes but with their right hands resting on the top buttons of their coats. More policemen were at the entrance to the VIP suite, tall men in their serge-blue uniforms, who discussed his progress from the car to the doorway via handheld radios, and who failed to meet the almost apologetic smile that he gave as he walked by them.

They sat him down in an easy, low-slung settee in the suite, choosing one far from the door, and a lady in black with a white apron brought him tea with a china cup and saucer and offered him with her other hand a plate of biscuits. She at least returned his smile, muttered the word 'love' to him and was gone through a doorway, not to be seen again. The man who sat in the front of the Mercedes was moving across the room toward him. Sokarev could see that his suit was old and uncared for, there was a nick of blood of his collar, his tie was sufficiently loosened to reveal the top button of his shirt, and his shoes had been cleaned but in haste and without thoroughness.

'The name's "Jimmy", Sir. Security. I'm to be with you right through your stay here. I hope we'll get along. Which are your men?'

Sokarev gestured first towards Mackowicz who hovered close to his shoulder then pointed to Elkin who stood across the room by the door.

'There is Mr Mackowicz and Mr Elkin. I am glad to meet you . . . Jimmy,' he laughed quietly waiting for the other to offer a surname. None was forthcoming. 'I had been told that I would be offered help on the visit. I am grateful to you.'

'There's more than just me, Sir. About another two hundred. The ones you'll see, at any rate. But I'm the one you'll be aware of. I'll be beside you the whole way.'

'You'll have competition, then,' Sokarev quipped, warming at his first impression of the man. 'Mr Mackowicz and Mr Elkin have told me they booked those places for themselves.'

'Well, it should be crowded then. Which is about right.'

Thank God, thought Sokarev, they are not all like those men that have come with me. This one at least I can talk to. He has a

152

sense of humour, not like those who pad round in my wake, with their orders and ultimatums and their soured faces. He could see the man who called himself Jimmy talking out of earshot with Mackowicz, folders passing between them. All the men in the room were in huddles, talking, chattering like sparrows, exchanging sheets of white paper, drawing them from folders of green and blue and red and brown. And I am the supernumerary, thought Sokarev. Nobody talks to me, nobody has even the time to say a 'hello', or a 'welcome'. Everybody talks about me, about my movements, my sleep, my meals, but I am not consulted. Even the one that joked with me has nothing substantial to say. All that is kept for Mackowicz. If I wanted to attract attention I would have to shout, throw an epileptic fit, take my trousers off. Otherwise they would all go on as if I did not exist. Perhaps for some I am an exercise in strategy, a game to be played with, and when the time has come for me to leave I must be packaged up, shipped home, and then forgotten. For others I am a source of anxiety. Not that they would mourn David Sokarev if his body lay in the gutter; what they would mourn would be their careers, their futures, and above all their reputations.

He was far away and enjoying the self-pity when the security attaché spoke to him.

'We have your bag now, Professor. We are ready to leave.' His tea was half-finished in the cup. It mattered to no one. The circus was ready to entrain. It was not intended David Sokarev should delay it.

A reporter with the airport news agency, Brenards, with a clearance pass that gave her access to the area of the VIP lounge, saw the convoy leave. She was there to interview a prominent industrialist returning with major export orders from the United States. Courteously but firmly a uniformed policeman told her she was not permitted to go within twenty-five yards of the lounge doorway. She had already watched the cordon stiffen up, seen the drivers start their motors, taken in the scale of the police operation when the little man was brought out of the VIP suite. He was barely visible between the larger bodies of the Special Branch men who hemmed him in. As soon as the last of the guards had clambered aboard the cars were on the move. She would not have known by what airline the passenger who warranted so much attention had flown with if she had not recognized the features of the El Al station manager. When the cars had gone she had moved up beside him and asked him the identity of his passenger. He had shaken his head, given no explanation, and turned on his heel to walk back to his own transport. There are few things that irritate reporters, even trainees, as much as the studied brush-off.

Her telephoned call to her news editor reported 'massive security, an unknown and anonymous Israeli VIP, police tracker dogs on the tarmac, an escort of armed Special Branch men, the waiving of customs formalities, and a high speed convoy into London'. The news editor liked it too, gave it a further gloss of his own, and put it on the wires, along which it would be carried to the newsrooms of all Fleet Street papers.

Immured between the shoulders of the security attaché and Mackowicz, Professor Sokarev saw little of the countryside bordering the M4 motorway between the airport and central London. If he strained his head there were occasional glimpses of fields and football pitches before the cars sped on to a stilted flyover, and only the roofs and upper office windows of the taller buildings were visible. He could sense the tension that now gripped Mackowicz, the way he peered into the cars that they passed, or, when they slowed, clogged in traffic as the motorway narrowed from three lanes of traffic to two, the way he heaved himself across the window pressing his whole upper torso against the glass. Sokarev had stared in the other direction for the moment or so before the convoy had started off, while the bodyguard had loaded the heavy black-painted pistol before returning it to his shoulder holster. It was an unpleasant, angular weapon, outside the scientist's experience, and he was unable to give it a name.

In thirty-five minutes they were at the door of the hotel that had been chosen for him. More detectives were waiting here, easily recognizable. His own car had jerked to a halt, and Mackowicz had said in his ear, 'Don't stop, don't hesitate, straight inside.' Then an arm had taken his and half-bundled him through the moving swing doors.

Across the hall a man stood with one foot in the lift, holding the button to keep the door open. Sokarev was kept moving,

154

across the lavish carpet, then bustled into the lift. As the doors closed he found himself pressured by the shapes of his own men, the attaché, the one who called himself Jimmy, and the elegant, dark-suited fellow he presumed to be from the hotel. They went to the fourth and top floor. At the extreme right-hand end he saw two men rise from their chairs, one of them turning to unlock and open the door of a corner room. The pace was maintained till the door slammed shut behind him.

'Welcome to our hotel, Professor Sokarev,' intoned the man in the dark suit. He spoke with the necessary formality that concealed the management's displeasure at playing host and having responsibility for such a guest. There had been no breath of this when the reservation had been made, no mention of policemen, or of detectives who wanted to sleep in corridors, watch the front desk, and slump in lounge chairs. That had all started early in the morning, too late to insist on a cancellation.

'There is a connecting door to the other room and your two colleagues.'

One room only for the two of them, thought Sokarev. The attaché read his thoughts.

'At night one will be sleeping, the other awake. They will take it in shifts. In addition there are the men outside.'

Soon the group dispersed, the manager through the main door, Mackowicz, Elkin, Jimmy and the attaché into the adjoining room. Sokarev was alone, able to unstrap his case, and begin to put in the drawers the clothes that his wife had folded with such care. He could reflect that whatever fears he himself entertained for his own safety they were matched by the anxiety of the Security Services of Israel and of Britain. The realization chilled him.

Next door Jimmy was on the telephone, through to Jones, and the other men waited in silence for him to finish speaking and then relay to them the latest information. Jimmy gave nothing away to those who looked for a sign. He listened poker-faced, said he'd be in later that evening, and rang off.

'There's been a flap since Friday morning, but it's really buzzing now. Bit over an hour ago one of them called the contact man. We've traced the call to the south-west. They're saturating a town called Richmond. Nice, comfortable, posh place. And it's crawling with coppers now. They think there's a good chance they have the bastards bottled up. But then they always say that.

And then make the excuses twenty-four hours later.'

'How many of them are there?' Elkin asked.

'Just two,' said Jimmy. 'One from Northern Ireland. Cut above the usual grade. Good record, good operator. The other we think is from your part of the world. No name, but we've a face, not a bad one we think, to fit to him. He's a bit homesick, made a phone call he shouldn't have. That's how we're pressuring them right now. Special Branch will be round in about twenty minutes, an inspector; he'll have the files and the pictures for you.'

Jimmy sensed he was the odd man out in the room, that they wanted to talk in their own tongue, discuss their problems among themselves. It was the time for him to assert himself, make the position clear. There must be no doubts, no misunderstandings.

'My orders, gentlemen,' he said, 'are very clear. I have to be beside your man every moment he's out of that room. Not five yards, or four yards, or three yards away from him. Right beside him. My orders are very explicit on that. He's not to leave this building without me knowing it. This isn't a scene you'll run yourselves. We are in charge, and you will listen to us. And a final point. If I see something out on the street and open fire and hit the wrong bloody target there'll be a hell of a row, but it'll blow over. If one of you does it, you'll be in court before you know what's hit you; it'll stink for months. So go a bit careful.'

Jimmy went out into the corridor – to have a smoke, chat up the Branch men, and to allow the men he'd left behind in the room to vent their feelings. With amusement he heard the raised voice that he recognized as Mackowicz's, rich in aggrieved anger, and Elkin's quieter but in a harmony of protest, and then the calmer tones of the attaché soothing the hurt pride, salving the wounds.

That poor little sod in the other room, Jimmy thought. Lonely, frightened and going through this hoop just to make one bloody speech. He could just as well have put it in the post, all neatly typed out, and everyone would be just as wise. But that's not the way it works. He's going to stand out there like a tethered goat, put out as bait, with us up in the trees and him praying we get the bastards before they get him.

Jimmy went back into the room. Mackowicz was still hard-eyed, uptight; Elkin was a bit better, not much, but they both knew where they stood. The attaché had done a good job. Their clothes were already scattered around the room. The radios and the Uzis were on one of the bedspreads. They were settling in.

'No appointments tonight, right?' Jimmy said to the attaché.

'Correct. He was to have dined at the university. We've put that off, said he had a heavy cold. He'll eat in the room tonight. He'll be tired from the journey. Tomorrow he can stay in till we go out in the evening.'

'And Wednesday to the States?'

'He goes to New York on Thursday. His arrangements there are from that day. We saw no reason to change them.'

'I hope he likes his room then,' snapped Jimmy. 'Because if he's going to be here for an extra day that's where he's going to have to stay.'

The wind had raised its pitch, gathering power and determination as it swept across the great open spaces of the park. It sought out the body of McCoy where he lay, shirt unbuttoned to the waist, forced its currents across his chest so that in his sleep he shivered, and wriggled to hunch his frame and protect himself. And then he woke. He saw the girl beside him with her clothes still in the casual disarray that he had left them, legs outflung, arms behind her head, staring vacant and uncaring into the deep distances of the sky.

He looked at his watch. Past seven. Less than an hour to the rendezvous, and the light beginning to drift away. The afternoon had been lost, and soon would come the cover of darkness that he needed for movement.

'Come on, girl. Time to be on our way.' He said it without noise, but there was none of the tenderness in his voice that she sought and expected. She lay motionless, unwilling to look at him.

'Come on, girl. I said it was time to move.' There was a cutting edge in his voice, sharp and unfamiliar. She reacted, fumbling with her jeans, pulling them over the slight hips. She turned away from him to contort her arms round her back to refasten the clasp he had unhooked. He brushed the grass and dried earth from their clothes and together they started to walk toward the heavy wrought-iron gates, through which the cars flowed in and out of the park. They walked in silence, Norah with her head down, avoiding him.

157

They were still a hundred yards from the gates when McCoy saw the policemen operating the road block. He counted six of them. One was far in the distance on the road toward the town waving his arm languidly in the air, slowing and warning the oncoming traffic. Another had a clip-board and was taking down registration numbers. Another talked to the drivers, peering inside to scrutinize the passengers. A fourth and fifth searched under bonnets and in the boots of the cars, and a sixth sat in a police car facing away from the block, his engine ticking over. McCoy understood the scene. Last man there for a break out, revved and ready to give chase. It was professional, he accepted that.

Too many for anything routine. Too heavy a force for local crime. Then he thought of Famy. Unwilling to be left on his own, nervous of what might happen to him if he were abandoned to his own devices for just a few hours, suspicious of where McCoy had gone. And now the road block; not a casual one, but thorough and painstaking. He had to be sure where the bloody Arab was, had to know what had happened.

Stretching on either side of the gates were the eight-foot-high walls of matured brick that ringed the park.

'I can't go through the check,' he said. 'I have to get across the wall, somewhere away from the main roads, but near to the town.' The girl hesitated, uncertain. The policemen would hear her if she shouted. One scream and they would be running, sprinting towards her. And what then? That was where the equation defeated her. What would she say? Tell them the man they sought had lain with her, that she had opened her legs to him, pulled him down on to her?

She was not long in deciding. She took McCoy's hand and led him across the grass, cut short by the sheep, past the great oak trees, and then where the wall dipped down following the contours of a gully she stopped.

She had chosen well, he could see that.

McCoy reached up to the top of the wall and levered himself a foot or so off the ground. It was perfect. The wrong end of a cemetery where the trees grew close together, where the leaf-mould and grass-cuttings had been piled against the bricks. He slipped over, landing easily on the piled vegetation. He put his right arm back over the wall, grabbed Norah's wrist and heaved her over the barrier. They crouched behind one of the big yews, the necessary precaution till he was certain they had not been observed.

'I want somewhere that I can lie up, somewhere safe,' he whispered to her.

'Just out of the cemetery there's a building site they've cleared. There's nothing there now. Just scrub and that. What are you going to do then?'

'Get me there, I'll tell you then.'

They walked along the narrow tarmac path between the disordered rows of stones, past the jam jars that held single wilting tulip-stems, skirted the fresh rectangular shapes of earth, and came to the gate.

'Where to from here?' McCoy said.

'Across the road, and about a hundred yards down, that's where the site is.'

'But there's a bloody great fence round it. I can't climb that on the main road.'

'Down at the side, the second turning, no one'll see you there.'

She was involved now, part of his team. The moment of crisis had gone. She would do as he told her, he had no doubt of that. Usually did, the little bitches. He sensed he now had in his possession something quite priceless. He had a courier. Someone who could run for him, who could be his eyes and ears. God knows why they want to dip their fingers in, he thought, but they do. Don't think it out, too stupid to do the addition and multiplication.

There was traffic on the road, but no policemen. He had his arm round her shoulder as they waited for an opening and then crossed. They fitted a conventional image, boy and girl, out for a walk, fond of each other, and very distant from the picture any motorist who saw them might have had of a hunted killer of the Provisional IRA. They walked down the side road, not fast, taking their time. McCoy spoke to her closely, and anyone who saw them would have imagined it was endearments he was whispering against her hair.

'Listen carefully,' he said. 'Do exactly as I say. Near the station there's a tea bar, on the far side of the road, toward the river. You'll find a man in there, a darkie. Taller than me, no moustache or anything, short hair. He'll have a grip-bag with him. Just say the word "Mushroom" to him, and tell him to follow you. Take him through to here, not on the big roads, down the side streets and get him here. And tell him to go carefully.'

'Is he the other one they're looking for?' Norah said it with excitement pitched in her voice.

'I've told you. You don't need to know. Just go and do it, girl. The way I've told you. If he's not there, wait for him. At least an hour. But get him here.'

He scanned each end of the road. Empty, deserted. Then he was on the buckling, bending wire, monkey-like, before he tumbled down on the far side and was gone. She heard his running feet crashing in the undergrowth, and after that nothing.

From his seat in the cinema Famy heard the sirens in the street outside. He remembered the urgency of the instructions over the telephone to set distance between himself and the station, and he huddled in the darkened seat as the raucous noise blotted out the sound track of the film whenever the police cars passed outside the cinema. He bit at his fingernails as he watched the technicolour heroics that filled the screen. The images meant nothing, failed even to divert his attention from the problem that now preyed upon him. It was the immediate problem of survival. The bag was there against his legs, reassuring in its bulk, and he quietly slid open the zip and felt with his hand for the cotton surface under which were the awkward, angled shapes of the grenades. He lifted one out, small, the size of a shrunken apple, and put it in the pocket of his coat. The rifles were too large, too cumbersome, but one grenade would be sufficient to stave off immediate pursuit. It could be concealed, not like the guns, and it gave him the confidence that he would need to walk out into the unknown of the middle-light of the evening.

Sometimes his thoughts wandered back to his friends, the men he had hardly known, but whose companionship in the short term he had valued, to Dani and Bouchi. Their laughter on the plane out of Beirut, the banter about Nablus and the olive groves as they had driven across France, and the fear that had bound them on the route to Boulogne. He recaptured again, so that it overwhelmed him and blotted out the meaningless antics of the celluloid pictures, the blood of his friends that had spattered and soaked the seats of the car. He could still hear Dani's words. Their exhortation before the colour in his soft brown cheeks had faded to the greyness that preceded death. The words knifed through his subconscious, controlling him, providing the momen-

160

tum he needed to go on.

He left the cinema before the completion of the second film. He'd already seen well into the second reel, and the story had still not attracted him. But his motives were clear. He wanted to be away before the big rush to the doors, and the exit he chose was at the side. It was simple reasoning that if a hunt for him were in progress that the entrance hall of a cinema would be an obvious place for them to look. With the bag in his hand and the grenade in his pocket, he slid back the iron bar that kept the fire door shut. He went unnoticed and without impediment.

It took him many minutes to make his way to the rendezvous. He walked with a shuffling, almost sideways gait along the front of the shop windows, ready to spin his head toward the loaded shelves of merchandise on the occasions that the squad cars cruised past. There were men on foot too, and to avoid them he twice entered shops, mingling in front of the counters till he had seen through the plate-glass windows that the danger had passed. With each step he took there was greater confidence. They're stumbling about, he told himself, uncertain what and whom they seek, thrashing in the dark.

In the café he took a seat at the back, again sideways on to the door, so he could observe the comings and goings and at the same time swing his head away should he wish to obscure his face.

He saw the girl come in, noticed the nervous, switching eyes that took in the customers sitting at the tables and on the stools at the counter. The look of grateful recognition she gave him stiffened Famy and his hand moved instinctively to the pocket that held the grenade, his fingers seeking out the circular pin that was the safety device of the V40. He stared at her, hand clasped round the metalwork as she came closer, eyes riveted to her pale, pretty face.

She bent down toward him as she reached the table. She was trembling, and when her lips moved, at first there was no sound.

'Mushroom.' She blurted it. 'He said you were to follow me. I'll take you to him.'

And Famy understood. Why had he been so anxious to split up that afternoon? Needed a girl. Not a woman who would reason things out, but a girl who would follow blindly where he led. Dangerous, he thought, but probably better than someone older. As she turned back toward the door he saw the hard-etched creases in her blouse. Not bad, McCoy, he thought. A roll in the grass and you have the loyalty of the whore.

She took him through the back streets of the old town, climbing the hill over which sprawled the fashionable residential homes of the previous century. Past alms houses and churches, past homes that had been neatly outlined in white gloss, past blocks of flats where those for sale were advertised as 'luxury' on the estate agents' boards. Sometimes the streets were narrow, in other places they widened out, but none of them was busy with cars. There were children playing their games with balls, men walking in company to the pubs, women hurrying home with their baskets of late shopping, and no policemen. Famy held the girl's hand, and she let it rest there, inanimate and without feeling. But it was better that way, more secure. They went mostly in silence, Famy occasionally speaking, but meeting only non-committal response.

In front of them was a wall and daubed on it the words 'Park Hill was Home to Me' – a relic of the time there had been a great house set in its own grounds on the site, and when there had been protests before the demolition men came. Now there was only a tangle of bushes, cut-down trees and neglected shrubs.

'That's where he is,' she said. Her voice was detached – as if she realized thought Famy, that her usefulness was expended, and was resigned to it.

'It's time I was getting home, my Mam'll be spare. Going out of her mind.'

'Where do you live?' asked Famy.

'Chisholm Road. Just round the corner. At twenty-five.'

'I hope we see you again. You have been very kind to me . . .'

She was away running into the night. He was different to the other one. More gentle, wouldn't have hurt her like that Irishman. But probably wouldn't have done anything, sat there all afternoon pulling grass up. It still ached where McCoy had been, and there was a bruised, raw feeling at the top of her thighs. And he hadn't used anything, the bastard.

13

Even as security-conscious a building as Scotland Yard is susceptible to leakage of classified information. In the drably-painted ground floor press room the crime correspondent of the *Express* heard the first whispers of the mounting of a major security operation to protect an unnamed Israeli VIP.

The anonymity of the man being guarded was broken by the paper's science correspondent, who had received an invitation seventeen days earlier to attend a lecture by Professor David Sokarev of the Dimona Nuclear Research Establishment. His casual call to the Israeli Embassy's press spokesman, and the flat refusal to his request for information on the professor's itinerary, served to confirm that Sokarev was the man being subjected to intensive security. The Brenards' report of armed Special Branch men at the airport to guard an El Al passenger added further colour to the story. But it was the chief sub-editor's intuition that turned the story into the front-page splash. At his desk where he collected the various type-written sheets and the agency copy, he began to shuffle together what had up to then figured as quite separate material. He had in his hand the stories now catchlined 'Sokarev' along with those on which he had scrawled 'Manhunt'. And it made good sense. Heavy protection of an Israeli nuclear scientist married with a vast police dragnet for a known Provisional IRA killer, travelling in the company of an unidentified Arab.

By the time the third edition was on its way by van to various rail terminals the headline 'Arab Death Threat to Israeli H-Bomb Scientist' blasted its way across the top of the front page.

The Prime Minister's anger when he read the story before retiring to his Downing Street flat for the night was stonily rejected by the Director General.

'No leaks from this department,' was his riposte. It was his policy to strike an independent posture for the Security Services, and one thing with which he was traditionally quick to show intolerance was ill-informed criticism of its work.

'From what you've told me, sir' – the deference was purely formal – 'I think you'll find it's straightforward reporting of a series of facts visible to any trained eye.'

That went some way to calming the Head of Government. 'But it doesn't help the position,' the Prime Minister said.

'There's not very much that does help the situation in times like this.'

'What I mean,' said the Prime Minister, 'is that if anything happens to this man Sokarev after this, we are all going to look almighty stupid.'

'That's a fair point, sir,' the Director General replied.

Not a great deal to say after that. Only the obvious, that they had problems, that they were coming from behind, that there was huge ground to be made up. The silences grew longer, till the conversation reached its natural end. He wished the Prime Minister a good night's sleep.

So they'd the wind-up in Whitehall. It always amused him. Meant the telephone would be going every five minutes in the morning. Politicians crawling in on the act, and nothing they could do about it. For that matter, he thought, not much any of us can do. He checked with Jones, still in his office too, but with no new developments to report from Richmond. It would be a long day tomorrow, long and trying.

Before they had set out into the darkened park there had been fierce words between Famy and McCoy. Ostensibly it was over the question of whether or not they should leave the seeming security of the undergrowth at Park Hill, but in effect it concerned the leadership of the two-man team. Famy had wanted to stay put, and was impressed by the semi-concealed basement of an old, long-gone building that McCoy had been hiding in while waiting for the Arab's arrival. The Irishman was for getting on the move immediately.

'We have to sleep somewhere tonight. We have to have some rest, and this is as good a place as any,' Famy had said.

'With the police about we have to quit, get out and fast,' had come the answer from McCoy, who was accustomed to command, was used to men reacting to his orders without hesitation and arguments. He had assessed his colleague sufficiently, felt the time of deference had died its death.

164

'We are completely hidden here. We would not be found.'

'All we are doing is staying inside whatever cordon they've round us. Giving them time to get organized, bring in reinforcements. It helps them, louses us. And in the morning, at first light, there'll be dogs, helicopters, the whole bloody works. They know we're here. Christ knows how, but they know it, and we have to shift our arses, and on foot, and in the dark.' McCoy was suppressing his wish to shout, turning his voice to a subdued snarl.

'But they will concentrate their efforts while they believe in their information. When they have been unsuccessful they will relax. Tomorrow it will be easier to move; we should stay till tomorrow.' The top of his cheeks were flushed red. Famy stabbed with his finger at McCoy's chest to reinforce his point.

'They don't work that way, little boy. They're bloody policemen, not soldiers. They do it by the book, solid and thorough, they don't get bored and go home to put their feet up . . .'

'You have endangered us,' Famy interrupted, unwilling to let McCoy dominate. He threw his ace card, unsure where it would take him, what dividend it would bring. 'You have risked us. And what for? So you could lie with that girl for the afternoon . . .'

'Shut your fucking mouth,' McCoy spat the words at him. Famy could not see him, just hear his breathing, feel the closeness of his body. 'Shut your face and don't open it again. And just think back a bit, over what you've done today, try and remember where they picked you up.'

The memory of the agitated diplomat on the far end of the telephone seared through Famy's mind. The sense of shame was too great for him to tell the Irishman what had happened. He was defeated.

'Where do we go?' he said. McCoy made no capital from the submission, applied no salt, and spoke with the heat gone from his voice. Silently Famy thanked him for the concession. The pivot that controlled who dominated the team had shifted – it was inevitable given the circumstances, and irreversible.

'We're going on foot into the park. There's a place near here where we can get over the wall. It's a couple of miles across. If we keep off the roads we'll be all right, and out the other side. Another couple of miles, and if we're lucky we'll get ourselves a motor.'

Famy followed as McCoy led, blindly. The truth of his situation was clear to him; without the Irishman he was doomed. He could yearn till it bled for the companionship of Dani and Bouchi, for the warmth of comradeship at the camp in Fatahland, but on his own in another continent, in a strange country, he needed the Irishman.

They blundered across the rough ground, tripping on fallen branches, stumbling in water ditches, always seeking the total black void away from the lights of cars. Once they saw the revolving blue light on the roof of a police car and flung themselves flat on the ground, and waited long after it had gone before resuming their progress. They climbed the chain-link fence that demarcated the boundary between the park and a golf club, handing over the weighted bag, one to the other, made their way across the greens and fairways till they came to another fence which shielded a neat, tended row of back gardens. They went with care over that fence, having sought out a garden into which no lights shone, and then were out in a short and rounded cul-de-sac, well illuminated by the tall sodium lights.

McCoy said, 'I'll go ahead. Twenty yards or so, and on the other side. You take the bag. That way we're not so bloody easy to notice. And go slow. Look as though you belong.'

They walked another hour and a half till they were in the wide and deserted Wandsworth High Street.

'Somewhere off here,' said McCoy. 'Out of the main stream we'll collect a motor. The new ones'll have locking devices on the wheels. We want an old one, something with a "D" or "E" or "F" after the numbers.' They were together now, the immediate threat of the police cordon far behind them.

'It was easy, as it turned out,' Famy smiled, shy, wanting to end what tension still existed between them.

'There's no way they can stand shoulder to shoulder round a town that size. All they can do is block the main routes and hope to luck. If you keep your cool you'll win.'

McCoy didn't regret the hard words of their clash. Be something wrong if we weren't at each other's throats on a caper like this. Not enough sleep, not enough food, eyes running the pavements over your bloody shoulder half the day. Less than a full day to go, and then, Holy Mother . . . the mad scramble to get clear of the sodding place. No clear escape route, not like it had been planned. Should have been sitting quietly in that attic hearing the fuzz and the politicoes spouting on the radio, spieling their inanities to the goddam reporters. Should have been all ready and

166

waiting, safe in the nest at the top of the house, stacked up there while the temperature stayed cool. And now . . . Where to go now? Where to shift to, where to lie up? . . .

One at a time, my Provie boy. Let it work itself when you get there. Get the priorities sealed up first. But this bloody carry-on is not the way you do it. You don't stand up in Crossmaglen market square and blast a para and then wonder where you'll scarper. Doesn't work that way. You plan it all out, think about it, have your watchers and your spotters and the woman who'll take the gun in her pram and the man who'll leave his back door open and the car that'll be waiting. You don't leave it to chance. Donal hadn't a route planned when he fired – seventeen and couldn't read. He'd died in the alleyway behind his house, and everyone in the section shot him, big, bloody guardsmen, and they'd laughed. Sean hadn't thought it out when he drove the bomb to Newtown Hamilton and they stopped him at the checkpoint. Wasn't usually one there, not on that cross-roads, and he's fifteen years in the Crumlin Gaol to think on it. The bloody eejit way of getting stuffed, he'd told his men, to be out on the business without the preparation. You don't survive if you're in a hurry.

They'd expect something better of you, Ciaran McCoy, he thought. Piss themselves laughing in the boozer. Off on the big one, off on the spectacular, and no plan out. The beer would swill round their guts but there'd be no tears if the bastards shoot you, no protests if they nick you alive and lock you up the rest of your natural. Drink themselves stupid and talk and talk, and all to say that Ciaran McCoy had done a job across the water, and hadn't thought the way out. They'd hiccup and belch their way home, down the streets off the square and think: 'Stupid little bugger, and him the one that was always telling the rest.'

But there'd be no more trouble from the Arab. He saw that, the way Famy followed him, like a dog, half a step behind, frightened of disapproval. There'll be no more shouting. He'll do as he's bloody told.

Off the main roads the streets were deserted. Television had played the national anthem and was now quietened, the bed-time cocoa had been taken upstairs, the doors locked and bolted, cats shoved into the night. No one curious of the sounds came to an upstair window as McCoy prised open the bonnet of an ageing Ford Cortina. From his pocket he drew a packet of cigarettes

167

and took one out. He slid his thumbnail down the join where the
two ends of paper met and brushed out the shredded tobacco,
then squeezed off the filter, letting it fall into the gutter. With
one hand he felt across the iron frame on the top of the engine
till his fingers, guided by knowledge and experience, rested on the
vital terminals. Into the gap between them he inserted the sliver
of paper. Without asking he moved to Famy, took the grip from
him, unzipped it and pulled out a shirt. He placed it against the
triangular glass partition at the front of the driver's window,
paused and then smashed his hand against the cotton. The blow
was sufficiently muffled. There was no alert from those who slept
in the houses around. The glass tilted on its axis. There was room
for him to insert his hand down alongside the interior handle and
carefully release it. When he had opened the driver's door he
leaned across and freed the lock on the passenger side, then
motioned for Famy to take his seat. When the Arab was there,
door closed and the bag on his knees, McCoy returned his
attention to the engine. Again his hands moved across the greased
bulk searching for the rubber, nipple-like button that he needed.
When he found it he glanced again toward Famy, gave him the
half-smile that meant success, and pressed. As the mechanism
shook into life he eased the bonnet down and slipped into the
driving seat. There was a last look up at the undisturbed drapes
across the windows and he had edged the car out into the road
and driven off.

He headed east, away from the policemen who shivered, bored
and listless, at their road blocks.

'Piece of bloody cake,' he muttered to himself.

'What now?' Famy asked, cautious and uncertain of the
Irishman's mood.

'Get some distance behind us. About half an hour's worth, and
across the river. Find somewhere off the tracks, and get some
sleep. We'll need a garage when it's light where we'll get some
keys to this bloody heap. Out on the other side of town where
there are woods and we'll lose ourselves there for the day. We
don't come back into town till the evening.'

Famy nodded. He was conscious he was being told what he
needed to know, nothing more. No frills on it, no embroidery,
and above all no discussion.

McCoy sensed the mood.

'Don't fret yourself, lover-boy. This is your day, not mine.

168

I'll get you there. I'll prop you up just when the curtain rises. You think about that and leave the transportation to McCoy. Don't concern yourself with how we get there. You'll be on hand, just when you need to be, to see your man. There's a lot to get through before that, but it'll come soon enough. The time won't stand back for you, it goes on its way, till it's you and your man. And don't go ballsing it on me.'

McCoy laughed, selfish and introverted. Private thoughts, not to be shared, and as they drifted along the broad empty vistas of a deserted night-laden city he sang, quietly ignoring his audience. They were the songs of his movement that passed over his lips, soft, delicate, finely woven words of death, martyrdom, adulation for the fallen hero. They're all like that, he thought bitterly. Need to be stiff, cold, and shrouded before the music-men get round to you. Get their fiddles and accordions out then, when the grass is sitting on you. Not before. Don't find you the price of a pair of shoes till then. But let some bastard soldier gouge your guts out, and they'll be round the clubs, strumming and crooning your name. That's the way of the music-men. Never a song about the living, only the dead. Only the little bastard stupid enough to get in the way.

He'd walked at Donal's funeral, tramped his way far behind the family, deep in a mass of bodies and far from the army cameras and snatch squads, hidden and anonymous, and made a lone exit from the graveside while orations and epitaphs were in full flow. But they had an effect on him, those great and endless trails of silent men and women who formed the processions behind the cheap box, draped with the flag and mounted by the black beret. He could recognize the emotional dragnet that caught him up and welded him further into the cause. When they buried one of his men there was immediate retaliation – a soldier died. It followed as inevitably as night after day. Clear, easy to understand. But the death of the Israeli – was that worth getting blasted for, put in the box, was it worth the journey, bumping on the shoulders across the long, ill-cut grass of the churchyard? Never heard of the sod, hardly knew what he looked like, one piss-poor photograph. Fat, insignificant little bugger, living on the other side of the world. Just an order, McCoy. Leave it at that, and leave the thinking to your superiors. Do as you're told, obey your orders. Somebody else's war, this one, but can't be fought unless McCoy stands in the line. Famy would die, no

169

hesitation, but Ciaran McCoy, what would he do? How hard would he press home his attack? His mind was too tired to react to the intricacies of the problem. Shelve it. Pray Jesus that it doesn't come to that. And if it does . . .? Think about it then.

Famy was asleep when McCoy brought the car to a halt. They were back north of the river, and the rough ground behind the flats would suit him for the two to three hours before the growing dawn and the light of the day would drive him once again to seek obscurity and a more settled hiding place to while away the hours before David Sokarev was to make his speech.

It was hours now since the planes had come. Without warning, the sound of their vast thrusting engines left far behind as they swooped over the hills, flying the contours of the ground, hurtling towards the plotted co-ordinates of a map reference. Young men, expert and trained in the sunshine of far-away Arizona till they could handle the multi-million dollar complexities of the Phantom cockpit, straining with their eyes for the criss-cross of wheel tracks on the sand five hundred feet beneath them, then searching for discreet, camouflaged outlines of the tents before they let loose the awkward torpedo-shaped cannisters containing the petroleum jelly that had been given by a nameless scientist the title of 'napalm'. The pilots carried their planes away toward the next target that had been designated, and so did not see where the cannisters landed. The navigator would twist his body – difficult in the all-encompassing, padded-out 'G' suit – but he too would recognize only the column of thick black smoke and have no knowledge whether the mission had been successful or not.

The leader of the General Command was in his tent. The stubbled, worn face resting on his clenched hands. There was a candle held upright in a Pepsi Cola bottle, on the same table where he leaned his elbows. The light faded and rose, at the whim of the cool night that eddied through the flap on the tent, finding the flame and bending and brushing it. It was a time that he loathed and detested, a time when he was helpless and unable to hit back. Four men dead, burned beyond recognition, life cut short as they had screamed. And the technology of his enemy, his speed and his knowledge, took him far away from the puny retaliation possible to the men on the ground. Nothing, only the oaths and obscenities shouted into the dirt as they had lain in the fragile cover between the rocks and waited for the echoing noise to pass. And the men who had died, buried already, not deep down – the parched ground prevented that – but hurried into shallow pits at dusk.

His subordinates, recognizing the signs that he wished to be alone had left him when he had retired to the tent. Others would care for the morale of the young men who had filed past the bodies, would take care that the sight fanned their hatred of the enemy across the border. There was a solitary piece of paper on his table brought by the journalist from Beirut, who had visited and left before the arrival of the jets. He had read it over and over again, keeping the information even from his closest colleagues, savouring among the disaster and horror of the day the news that it carried. The one they called Saleh Mohammed was there, on target and meeting his rendezvous contact. The best boy that he had, the one he had willed to survive.

It would devastate them, he knew that. A plan of such detail and skill that he had hugged and kissed the shy bespectacled recruit who had worked on its conception, not a youth who could go himself across the border, the right claw foot controlled that, but one with brains and with foresight and who had talked not just of the operation but of its consequences, its wounding potential to the state of Israel. It would hurt them, twist behind the nation's rib-cage . . .

The old man who acted as his bodyguard came noiselessly into the tent.

'Some food for you, Ahmed. It is time to eat. One cannot sit and starve and grieve.' He was the only one in the camp who would call the leader by his given name. It went back a long time, eight years. They had held the house together at Karameh when the Israelis had swarmed in brigade strength into the refugee village beside the river Jordan ten months after the Six Day War. It should have been so easy for them, but for the first time the Palestinians had stood and fought. The cynics said it was because they had been left no escape route. There was truth in that, but for once the *fedayeen* had not thrown down their guns and surrendered. There had been mourning in Israel when the casualty figures were announced, more than twenty dead, more than seventy wounded. There had been dancing in Amman as the captured Centurion armour was driven in triumph through the ancient, winding hill-streets, and among the Palestinians there

171

had been much to remember and heady praise and the start of resistance. The hours in the wrecked building, hammered by the tanks and hitting back with the rocket launchers and the Klashnikovs, had forged the bond between the two men, one a leader and the other a follower. The relationship had not changed. It was acceptable, and the old man knew when he was required.

He put the plate in front of the leader. A mess of beans and rice and sauce with lamb's meat cut in small squares.

'They have had their day, the Israelis. We will have ours. There is no sudden way to victory,' said the old man.

'What they have accomplished against us is a mere nothing to the blow that awaits them.' The old man was rarely taken into the leader's inner confidence. He said nothing and arranged a spoon and fork alongside the plate in front of the sitting man. 'Within the next hours, perhaps as long as two days,' the leader went on, 'we shall hit them so that they yelp like dogs.'

'Across the border?' With a burden of sadness. He knew the risks, had cleared too many bundles of the possessions left behind by the suicide squads.

'Across many borders. Far from here. Bouchi, Dani and the third one, you remember? They went to Europe. Bouchi and Dani are dead, the other alone has gone through. He is on course, on target. Today or tomorrow he will move, and then the world will know of him.' He spoke the words hurriedly, interspersing them with pauses as he scooped up the food from the plate, cramming it without finesse into his mouth. He did not look at the man that stood behind him. When the plate was cleared he sat back in his chair and addressed himself to the empty screen of canvas to his front.

'His target is David Sokarev. Of the utmost importance to them, but a man of whom you will never have heard. He is from the world of science, of the very fundamentals of science. He concerns himself with the structure of the atom, and with the breaking of the atom, and with the release of its energies. They are jealous of their anonymity, these men, they do not seek to be answerable to their fellow species. They hide themselves away like slugs underneath wet rocks. It is rare for them to emerge into the open light, but Sokarev has come out. To London. That is where we will meet him, and will kill him.'

The old man watched as the leader turned toward him. He saw the excitement in the eyes, deep and brown and shadowed in

172

their sockets. Not since they had waited for news of the raid into Kiryat Shmona when the orders had been to eliminate as many of the enemy as were within range of the guns, men or women or children, had the old man seen a similar look – the fanatic awaiting his fulfilment.

'Eight bombs they have, perhaps nine by now,' the leader went on staring into the other's face, the voice quavering on the verge of self control. 'Not big – the size of Hiroshima and Nagasaki. In a city they would kill ninety thousand, up to one hundred thousand. Suck the air from their lungs, burn the bodies of our people, blind them, maim them, infect them so that those that live from their breeding would produce grotesque mutations. They would not make what their American allies call the "clean bomb". They will not waste effort and expense on such refinements. It will be a weapon of filth and of poison, and it is their ultimate defence. They hide behind it in the knowledge that the very mystery of its existence gives them strength. The man that we will shoot is the man who has created this bomb, loved it, succoured it, spent his working life refining the effectiveness of its yield.'

'And when he is dead, what will have changed?' said the old man.

'It will take the elimination of Sokarev to awake the world to the Israeli power. When he is dead and the news has been carried from continent to continent the world will wonder why the Palestinian people have chosen to exact retribution on one who seemed so mild, so harmless. And we will tell them why he was chosen, we will tell them of Dimona, of the plutonium schemes, of the reactors there. And with their knowledge so too will come their fears. Fears of a mushroom cloud settling the "Middle East problem", as they call it, fears of an annihilation more ghastly than the world has experienced since its cleverer men developed this horror. All the world will be talking about the bomb of the Israelis, not just the peasant peoples but in the embassies and the chancellories and the senates and the palaces. There will be demands for inspections and controls – the Americans will want that if only to silence their critics. If their bomb is muzzled their ultimate defence is taken from them, and then they are weak, then they can be beaten. All their men are replaceable. Dayan was replaceable, and Sharon of the Canal, and Rabin, and Eban, and Peres, all have others who wait to take their places. Sokarev, too. Other scientists can move behind his desk, but nothing can replace the bomb. It is final, the complete answer to their defensive strategy when future war goes against them. If it happens as we believe it will, if the governments of the world demand to know of this weapon, exercise control over it, then ultimately Israel will lose and go down stripped of her last and most powerful weapon of defence. That is why we will kill Sokarev.'

The old man ran his fingernails across the bristle of his chin, pondered, his brows lined with deep confusion.

The leader smiled like a man who has outlined to his friends his plans for the conquest of a woman they all consider beyond reach. The older man had not heard him talk in that way before.

'It is strange,' he said quietly, 'how the death of a man can move the world more than the life he has so long striven to perfect.'

He let himself out of the tent, taking the plate with him, and was gone, moving his way with familiarity across the sand, bypassing the ropes that held the tents. The night was very clear, a slight moon and the endless abyss of stars.

The leader snuffed out the candle with his thumb and forefinger, and stripped off his denim coat and trousers. He felt his way across to the narrow canvas bed and edged his body under the single blanket that he allowed himself. He had no difficulty in finding sleep. The images of the four burned carcases had long since passed, and he dreamed of the small, sad-faced man whose picture he had seen. And the face dissolved into terror, and there was a gun blotting out the picture, and he could hear the man's scream and then the staccato roar of the automatic rifle.

Beyond his canvas walls the camp was quiet. Only the shuffling movement of the sentries and, at the village a mile away, a dog calling for its bitch.

It was past three on the Tuesday morning when Jimmy returned to his flat. He had been conscientious enough, nothing to drink, and he had made his calls. He had been to Leconfield House and reported back to Jones, he'd returned to the hotel and seen that Sokarev was in his bed. For half an hour he had padded round the hotel checking the fire doors to convince himself they were closed to outside entry, satisfying himself that the Branch men were in position. He had spoken briefly to the Israeli who was sitting up; the one called Elkin. The other slept noisily in the bed close to where they had talked in whispers. The connecting door to the

174

scientist's room was open, and the Uzi lay on the bed beside them. They talked inanities, Jimmy cheerfully, and Elkin with caution, as if unsure of himself with the strange man. Jimmy had said he'd be back by early morning and repeated that under no circumstances were there to be visitors allowed to see Sokarev or that the man under threat should be permitted to leave his room.

There was a Branch man in the corridor outside the room, another beside the lift-shaft, two more in the ground floor lobby of the hotel. Too many for them, thought Jimmy, hopeless for the opposition. It relaxed him enough for him to wander out of the front door easy in his mind that no harm could come to his charge during the night.

From the hotel he drove south and west for twenty minutes till he reached Richmond. The road blocks were in position still, searching the cars travelling in the other direction. He found the police station easily enough, in a side street close to the bridge where the scent of the low water river drifted up to him. It was a chill, damp night, and he hurried from the car across the parking area at the back of the station to the rear door. There was a bustle of activity there, an ants' nest into which a spade had pitched.

In more normal times there would have been three, perhaps four officers on duty, whiling away the darkness and waiting for their reliefs to come in. Instead the lights were on, blazing throughout the building; corridors were noisy with hurrying men – some in uniform and some in plain clothes; teleprinters chattered messages to and from Scotland Yard; telephones rang. At the front-hall desk Jimmy showed his identification card, and watched as the bored features of the sergeant who looked at it awoke with interest. He was ushered up two flights of stairs and shown the open door of an office where a group of men sat round a table. The air was heavy with tobacco, the flat surfaces littered with maps and plastic coffee beakers.

The senior officers didn't waste Jimmy's time. He was grateful for that. They explained what they had done, in what they were currently involved, what they planned for the morning. It was thorough and painstaking, and left nothing out. They showed him where they had already searched, where their road blocks were in force, where their patrols, foot and mobile, were operating, the locations of the houses they planned to raid at first light. But

175

he could read the answer he was looking for in their drawn, humourless faces. There was none of the anticipation that catches hold of a huntsman's eyes when he thinks he is closing on his goal. It was routine, good routine, and that he conceded, but there was insufficient material for them to go on, and they knew it, and understood that for them to catch the men whose descriptions were plastered across the district they would need extraordinary luck. Policemen don't expect luck, don't count on it, Jimmy knew that. He sensed that for all the effort being put into the search there were few in the room in which he sat who expected that the night would be crowned by success.

As he drove back to the flat he could reflect that it had not been a totally wasted journey. Jimmy liked to know where he stood and the monotone description of the police action in the town had provided him with the information he sought. They were loose again, the two little bastards. Free and with their guns and with a plan and inching their way closer to the target. They had two full days in which to launch their attack. When they're that close, Jimmy boy, then they have to be in with a chance. No doubt about that. You're enjoying it, you little bugger, he said to himself, it's the way you would have wanted it. You'd have crapped yourself if they'd been picked up, and you'd had to hand the PPK in, unsoiled and unused. Nobody likes a fox that won't run, that goes to earth too fast, and you, you're looking for a good long ride and a good kill at the end.

He let himself into the flat, took off his shoes by the door and tip-toed into the bedroom. Helen was there, scarcely covered by the sheets, arms and legs heaved apart in the abandon of sleep. Not a stitch on her, poor girl. Destined for disappointment again. He undressed, letting his clothes mingle on the carpet with hers, and eased his way on to the bed, careful not to wake her. Something in his presence must have aroused the girl. She hooked an arm across his waist, feeling out the crevice underneath his armpit, but she did not waken, and Jimmy lay still till sleep came to him too.

He never found it difficult, not even on the nights before he might shoot or be shot at, or when another man's life might rest on his wits and alertness. There was no tension. Killing was not important to Jimmy, which was why the sleep came to him fast, which was why Jones championed him, and why the Director General tolerated his presence on the payroll.

14

It was the cold that woke Famy. He had been in a half-sleep, tossing under his coat in the back seat of the car searching for warmth, wriggling to escape the chill that had settled on his body and gnawed its way beneath the light cotton of his clothes. For a few moments he could not place where he was as he stared up at the roof of the car, then swung his head up to peer through the window. There was a noise, but far away, the sound of children shrieking to each other, the revving of starting cars. Beyond the glass he saw the tired, untidy shapes of the tower flats, grey and streaked from years of exposure to the weather, soaring up in composite and identical rows to high beyond his view. There was a woman there shouting into the void instructions to a man going to his work. Between the flats and his own position were the lines of prefabricated garages, and then nearer still seven feet of chain-wire fence, buckled and bent where children had scaled it. To the far side of the rough, broken ground where the car was parked was another fence and beyond that a railway line. There were other cars alongside, but different from the Cortina, without bonnets, without tyres, wheels even, doors gaping open, deserted as useless and too complicated to dispose of.

Famy stretched to see over the back of the seat, anticipating the huddled shape of McCoy prone across the width of the car. It hit him a cruel, winding, sledge-hammer blow. The emptiness that he saw. He rose on the back seat, jerking his sleep-stiff limbs forward searching for confirmation as the messages raced through his brain. Two seats, gear handle, steering wheel, dashboard, nothing else. The sweat started to run. He peered again through the windows, turned round in all directions, before sagging down upright on the seat. With a quick movement he felt for the grip-bag and ran his fingers over the outside till they rested on the hard shape of the rifles. The guns were there, but where was the bastard Irishman?

The argument and the hard words of the previous evening came back to him, and the long silences as they had walked and then driven through London. You cannot trust any but your own, he should have known that. Putting trust in a stranger, one whose involvement was no more than partial, it had been madness. Famy felt a great exhaustion sweeping across him. On his own how could he go forward? Was it possible to continue by himself? He started to cry. He had no strength to fight the tears, interrupt their path to the stiffness of his collar. He had not wept for many years, not since his youngest sister had died at the age of a few days in the front room of the bungalow in Nablus. But he had been only a boy then, and since adulthood he'd prided himself on his ability to keep his emotions tight and controlled. But that the Irishman had left him asleep and defenceless, betrayed him, made an escape without having the courage to face him directly . . . that was a total wound, painful and throbbing.

He opened the door of the car and eased himself out. His watch showed past eight and the sun was coming high from behind the flats, casting great shadows and playing patterns on the weeds that grew unchecked on the open ground. He walked warily away from the vehicle taking in his surroundings till he came to the opened gateway which led to the made-up road and further away to the lines of sand-brick, terraced houses that lay behind the long tin fence. There were more people there, none concerning themselves with the tall young figure who watched them. As his eyes played on the short horizon of chimney tops and television aerials it took him little effort to realize that he had no knowledge of his whereabouts. They had driven a long way since crossing the bridge, he had known that as he jolted in the seat with the motion of the car. Then he remembered the *A to Z* street guide he had bought, that had stayed in the grip, and he looked for a street name that would help him to identify his location. It would be at the far end of the line of houses, where the junction was. But there were too many people out on the pavements readying themselves for work and school and shopping. Later they would be gone, and that would be the time to walk the whole length of the street to find its name.

By the time he turned on his heel and drifted slowly back toward the car his mind was made up. There was no possibility that he could follow the path of abject defeat taken by the Irishman. When the men of the General Command went across the enemy's border there was no retreat if they were cut off and

178

surrounded short of their target. They stood and fought and died where they were trapped. Few returned to receive the adulation of their comrades after a successful mission, none returned to admit failure. Failure and surrender were the cancer growths in a movement such as his; despair would be close behind, and hopelessness, and then the victory for the enemy. If we lose our courage, he thought, we can lay down our rifles, fold away the denim fatigues and go back to ploughing the fields of Lebanon and Jordan; we will never see the hills of Nablus and the groves of Haifa.

There was a poem he had read in Beirut, written after the degradation of the Six Days' War. One verse alone remained in his mind, clear and without complication.

People may be divided into two classes, those who grin
Vacant and lopsidedly,
Who've given in,
And the rest of us who grin
To prove he isn't there,
The worm within.

It would be a sentence of death to go on. A conscious and measured decision. But it had been so for his brothers at Beit She'an, or on the sea front of Tel Aviv, or at Nahariya. They had stayed to die, had accepted its inevitability. He felt a great calmness after his mind was concentrated. The tears ceased to roll on his face, and deep in his belly the tightness had gone. There would be no insinuating, creeping rottenness, no worm.

Mackowicz did not inform David Sokarev that a visitor had arrived at the hotel expecting to take breakfast with the scientist. He was left in his room playing with the toast and the little packets of butter and the plastic marmalade jars, unaware of the heated dispute being fought out in the lobby. When the tall, white-haired, upright figure of Sir Humphrey Talbot, Fellow of the Royal Society, glasses half-moon and far down the bridge of his nose, had come to the reception desk and asked for the Israeli's room number a Special Branch man had folded the newspaper he had been reading and walked to Sir Humphrey's shoulder, indicating to the girl behind the desk the information should not be given.

'Can I help you, sir?' His voice was pitched low, inaudible to the other guests who milled about the counter handing in keys, seeking directions, writing travellers' cheques.

'I don't think so.' He turned back toward the girl. 'Young lady, I was asking you the room number where Professor Sokarev is staying.'

'He's not taking visitors, sir,' said the detective.

'And who might you be?' snapped the other man, already in poor humour at the frustration of the delay, coupled with the early hour he had risen in order to travel from his home in Cambridge to keep the appointment.

'Detective Sergeant Harvey, Special Branch, Scotland Yard. I'm afraid the Professor is not able to see anyone this morning. It's a very clear instruction we've had, sir. I hope you haven't been inconvenienced.'

'Of course I've been inconvenienced. I've come up from the country to see the man. I have a letter from him inviting me.' Sir Humphrey reached into his faded leather briefcase, rifled through the papers, and with a look of triumph on his face produced a single page letter. 'There, read that. Very simple, I would have thought. Clearly typed and with his signature at the bottom, on headed paper from Dimona.'

The detective read it through, motioned for the visitor to wait, and picked up a house phone. He spoke quickly and out of Sir Humphrey's earshot, put the receiver down and came back to Sir Humphrey's side.

'One of the Professor's colleagues will be down to see you directly, sir. To explain the position.'

'But he's travelling on his own. It says so in the letter . . .'

'I think you will find that things have changed somewhat, sir, in the last few hours. Have you seen a newspaper this morning?'

'Of course I haven't. Not read one anyway – just glanced. Been travelling, haven't I?'

'If you had, perhaps it would be clearer to you, sir.'

The lift door opened and Mackowicz emerged. His coat had been hurriedly put on, tangling with his shirt collar. At least he's hiding his shoulder holster, bloody cowboy, thought the detective. Might have shaved by this time in the morning. Mackowicz read the letter, and handed it back.

'I regret that your journey had been unnecessary. Professor Sokarev is receiving no visitors before his speech this evening. I am sorry.'

Sir Humphrey's voice rose in anger. 'But this is absolutely ridiculous, damned ridiculous. I've travelled half-way across southern England to get here at the Professor's invitation, and you, without even the courtesy of introducing yourself, tell me I shouldn't have come. What sort of nonsense is this?'

'My name is Mackowicz, I am with the Professor's party. I can only repeat my apologies that you were not forewarned by our embassy that it would be impossible for Professor Sokarev to keep his appointment with you.'

'I demand to speak to him on the telephone. He's an old friend.'

'That, too, I am afraid, will not be possible. He is taking no calls. I am sorry, sir.'

Sir Humphrey was not used to being spoken to in such a way. He was accustomed to deference, a smoothing of his way. He was uncertain how to react toward the young man with his open shirt, casual leather jacket and a day's growth on his chin, who met his gaze so unswervingly.

'Well, when in heaven's name will I be able to see him?'

'Are you going to the Professor's speech this evening?'

'Of course I'm going. I'm chairing the damned thing.'

'There will be an opportunity then,' said Mackowicz. 'I see from the Professor's letter that he was expecting you to drive him to his speech this evening. That, too, I am afraid, has been changed. But at the university you will have an opportunity to meet with him and talk.'

'And perhaps you would be so kind as to inform me the reason for this lunatic carry on?'

The detective sergeant handed him a morning paper. 'You seem not to have taken in the news, sir. Perhaps that will help you to understand our problems . . .'

'Of course I've seen the headlines, but you're not for a moment considering that I pose a threat to . . .?'

Mackowicz cut him off. 'Because of the situation it has been decided that the Professor will receive no visitors. There are no exceptions.' He went back to the lift and disappeared. Flushed with embarrassment, Sir Humphrey walked to the door and the Special Branch officer settled again in his chair, moulding into the background, inconspicuous and unnoticed.

Four floors above, Sokarev had finished with his breakfast, and paced dejectedly about the room. Elkin was now asleep and Mackowicz made poor company. More than an hour to go before

181

the typist came from the embassy to take the dictation of his speech, but that at least would distract him from the company of the young men and their sub-machine-guns and radios and who shuffled about with their fixed, humourless stares. The speech would take the morning to prepare, and after that perhaps he could sleep. There would be many distinguished men of learning to hear him in the evening, and he wished to be at his best and most incisive. An afternoon rest would help.

Jimmy slept late, deep in a meaningless dream that involved images of the countryside, hedgerows, overgrown fields and the animals who made their homes there. He fought to retain it against the increasing competition of the daylight that surged through the window, curtains not drawn. Silly bitch, he thought, when he woke up, always leaves them open, probably undresses there as well, right in front of the glass, handing out orgasms to half Holborn.

He hadn't noticed it when he'd come back to the flat. Stayed up too long. Too much talking with Jones before going to the hotel and to Richmond. Bloody man didn't seem to want him to go. Wants to be loved, Jimmy could see that, lonely boss-man with all the chaos piling up on his desk and having to rely on someone else to steer him through it. Jones under strain, talking more than he usually did, fidgeting with his pipe and pulling at the skin at the graft points below his mouth, reddening and irritating the lines. And he'd wished him luck when Jimmy went on his way. Never done that before. It had been a bit ridiculous, a sort of paternal send-off, and Jimmy not three years younger and as much in his twilight as the other man.

The girl was still sleeping. One of them always was – it seemed the most consistent fact about their life together. They laughed about it to each other, and cursed privately. She looked good, always did when she was asleep, and too vulnerable to be woken. She'd be late already for the dingy room where she spent her days sandwiched between Jones's office and the corridor. He wouldn't wake her yet – Jones could wait. It wouldn't do any harm, slave labour he had from the girl. Jimmy told her that often enough, and she ignored him. Jones could get impatient for one morning, wouldn't take her so much for granted.

He reached across her prone form, careful not to disturb her

182

and deny to the girl the deep relaxation of sleep that showed in the way her mouth had drifted open, awkward but at peace, too many teeth showing. Not at your best, sweetheart. There were lines beside her lips, alongside her eyes, under her chin, that in a few hours would be camouflaged by the cosmetics. Jimmy wasn't concerned with that; the rivulets of age that were forming on her features caused him no dismay.

From the bedside table he lifted the telephone receiver and dialled the number of the hotel where Sokarev was staying. When it was connected to the top-floor rooms where the Israelis were encamped Jimmy recognized Elkin's voice, softer and more conciliatory than the other bastard's. He sounded cheerful, said they'd had an uneventful night, that their charge had woken, taken his breakfast and was now working on his speech for the evening.

'And no visitors, under any circumstances, right?' Jimmy said.

'That is the instruction. A guy came and wanted to see him, a scientist. Mack dealt with it. He was a bit bothered, but left.'

Jimmy shuddered at the prospect. He could imagine the tact that Mackowicz would have employed to make his point.

He said, 'I'll be down quite soon. A few things to sort out, but it'll be before lunch, and for God's sake no room service or anything sent up from the kitchens direct to the room. If he wants something he'll either have to do without or you get it yourselves.'

'There's enough of your police outside the door to serve a banquet, cook it, and wash the dishes afterwards.'

'Don't worry about them. They're there to make up the numbers, make the circus look good. Do it yourself. I'll be there round about twelve.'

Jimmy crawled out of his bed and made for the bathroom out through the door and across the corridor. There wasn't much else of the flat, just a kitchen. Bachelor Towers, and he wanted it that way. He needed someone like Helen to visit, once or twice a week, and clean the place up while she was waiting for him. But not to live there, they'd be on top of each other, arguing, pulling hair out, claustrophobic. It was not a bad arrangement. Gave each sufficient companionship, and the minimum of commitment. Those in the Department who knew them both and who knew of the limitations of the arrangement put the bond down to a mutual passed-over loneliness. Jimmy would have denied that, perhaps violently. Helen would have smiled and changed the conversation. It was generally agreed among their friends that neither allowed the relationship to impair their individual effectiveness at the Department.

After he'd shaved and scrubbed with his toothbrush to eradicate the taste of last night's cigarettes, he dressed. He did it slowly and with thought, as if getting himself prepared for an important engagement, an interview for a new job, an evening out with a girl-friend. But it was the clothes themselves that let him down. His trousers were heavily creased, not just at the seams down his legs but all over, a legacy of the night-time hours that they had lain crumpled on the carpet after he had kicked them off. The shirt that he chose was clean, not worn yesterday, but it had been on his back for many other days before that and the collar showed the frayed outline where the cotton had rubbed worn against the unshaven bristles on his neck. A button was missing, but would be hidden by his tie. The socks too were clean, unholed, perfect, and he could smile quietly and secretly to himself as he pulled them on. Three pairs he'd bought, one of his few concessions to the semi-domestication Helen had tried to enforce on him. Beside the bed were his shoes, brown and lace-ups. The toes were scuffed and needed the attention of polish and a duster. He pulled the handkerchief from his trouser pocket, checked to see that Helen was still asleep, and then rubbed the white cloth square hard across the leather work. She'd seen him do that once and screamed a protest. His habits hadn't changed; only now he employed discretion.

From the drawer of the table on which the telephone stood he took the pistol he had drawn from Leconfield House, and the shoulder holster apparatus that was his own. The holster, of strengthened black plastic, fitted across his upper back and chest like a carthorse harness. It had been made to fit, and until he placed the gun itself in the pouch provided he was hardly aware of the straps that looped round his arms and across his back. But the gun gave the holster a weight and presence. His jacket hung across the chair he had draped it over, and when that was worn the PPK and its props were decisively hidden. Same tie as yesterday – RAF Escapers Club. Nothing dramatic for the motif, just a pelican bird, and not many who would pass Jimmy on the street would know its meaning.

He shook her shoulder, gently and with a kindness that few who knew him casually would have guessed he possessed.

184

'Wake up girl, time to be on our way.'

'What time is it?' She said it sleepily, resisting the intrusion, eyes squinting into the sudden light.

'Bit after nine.'

'You pig!' she shouted, scrambling from the warm security of the bed clothes.

'It's a beautiful sight to start the day with.' Jimmy was laughing as she struggled to cover her thighs and breasts with the scraps of lace and nylon that she scooped from the chair near her side of the bed.

'You're a pig, Jimmy. A mean, miserable pig. All bloody dressed yourself, and not calling me. Jones'll be off his rocker when I drift in at this time.' She wriggled her long legs into the trousers she had used the day before. Jimmy didn't like her keeping spare clothes at the flat, so what she arrived in the previous night she went out with the next morning.

'Won't do him any harm. Let him sweat a bit,' Jimmy said.

She said nothing else, fiercely concentrating on her dressing and then the attack on her face in front of the mirror. Hunched over it, eyes intent on the reflection as she worked the pencils and brushes around her eyes. The lipstick she put on with a bravado that ensured disaster. There was a low oath, in a pitch she seldom used, as she tidied the indulgence with a flick of the *Kleenex* tissue that had remained overnight on the dressing table.

'Are you coming down to the speech tonight?' Jimmy asked as they stood on the pavement beside her Maxi car.

'Only if I'm needed. I don't want to be there just to rubber-neck. I don't know whether Jones is going.'

'I'd like you to come, might want the car there. If I've one from the Department I'm saddled with the damned thing. If you come, slot in behind the convoy and when we've dumped the little bugger back in his bed we can shove off somewhere. I can call you later on.'

'There can't be much chance of Jones going. He may want to be at the Yard, or by his phone, but it's not like him just to be there if there's no purpose to it. There's enough of the thickies, you included, lined up for the evening without him shoving in and getting in the way.'

'Whether he comes or not I'd like you to be there with the car.'

She unlocked the driving door and sat far back into the seat. As she fastened the safety belt across her chest she said quietly and with a suspicion of mockery, 'Want me to see the hero boy in action? Roy of the Rovers defies Amazing Odds. Triumph of Virtue. Good wins Through. That it?'

When it came to needling Jimmy she was the great expert.

'Bugger off to your boring office,' he shouted. 'I'll call you, and I want you there. If you want a bloody meal on the house, that is.'

The car was away and lost in the traffic, leaving Jimmy searching the street for a black cab. They were not easy to find in the final throes of the capital's rush-hour, and he paced impatiently for a full fifteen minutes before he could hail one and then sprint a weaving path between the oncoming cars to the other side of the road where the driver waited for him.

When they were on the move Jimmy sagged deep into the seat, half-aware of the scurrying masses going about their business beyond the perspex. This was the ideal guerrilla country, the perfect territory on which to wage the sharp and cruel form of warfare that the enemy had perfected. Thousands of faces were swept past his vision from the window, their preoccupation with their own affairs total, their knowledge of the threat miniscule. The perfect, unnoticing hiding-ground, where anonymity remains a virtue. In this huge, ant-like society what hope could there ever be of selecting out just two who were different from the rest by the virtue of the fact that they had declared hostilities? Where to find them – where to start to look?

There can be only one killing ground. The one right beside David Sokarev. Not ten yards from him, or even five, but right up against his shoulder. Jimmy felt no sense of fear at the prospect of physical injury. What screwed up his guts was the possibility of failure. It always dogged him, that horror. That he would end up the ultimate loser. He could picture the little man with the blood and the surprise in his face, and the look of betrayal that would dominate his eyes. That would be the awfulness for Jimmy. The unmentionable and unspeakable disaster, if he lost Sokarev.

By the time he reached the hotel where he would spend the rest of the day before leaving for the Senate House, the very image of failure and the chance of it that had crossed his mind had rendered him irritable and tensed.

From where he crouched inside the small car Famy saw McCoy

appear round the corner from the street and walk warily towards their hiding place. Twice he looked behind, to satisfy himself he was not under surveillance. He jogged the last ten yards to the car.

Under his arm was a brown paper bag, and he reached inside his pocket on the left of his trousers when he reached the window through which Famy stared at him. McCoy took in the numbed astonishment in the other's face, and the sad, emotion-drained look in his mouth.

'I've got the keys. No problem, an old fool in a garage up the road, spilled him a yarn and had them straight away. Got the whole bunch and said I'd return them later. Piece of cake. I've got the gloves we need for the window, too, motor-cycle sort with protection half-way up the arm. Made of leather and bloody expensive. Hope your mob are good on expenses.'

He laughed, then let the humour dissolve as Famy's face failed to react.

'What's the matter?' McCoy said. 'You look like someone's just parachuted you into bloody Jerusalem.'

'I thought you'd gone,' Famy whispered, frightened of the words, but with no option but to speak them.

' 'Course I'd bloody gone,' said McCoy. 'I told you last night we'd need the keys. You said we'd need gloves. What's special about that?'

'I thought you'd gone for all time. That you were not coming back.'

McCoy spat back at him, 'How many times do I have to fucking-well tell you? We're in this together. I've told you that. For once in your suspicious miserable life try believing what you're told.'

He stomped round the car, angry, kicking at a tin and clattering it away across the stones and debris of the site. Famy climbed out of the car.

'I'm sorry,' he said. 'It was shameful to doubt you. I am abject to you.' He paused, letting the seconds of confrontation flitter away. 'How do we spend the rest of the day?'

McCoy nodded. He had the imagination to feel the Arab's sentiments on waking in the empty car.

'I should have woken you. Forget it now. We stay for the rest of the day. It's as good as anywhere. We'll go direct from here to the Senate. No sense in just moving about unnecessarily. What we

187

need now is some sleep. I don't want to be yawning and looking for my bed tonight.'

The few tourists who had gathered on the pavement across the road were unaware of the identity of the man who stepped from the black Humber car and hurried into the extended and tranquil-lit hallway of Ten Downing Street. No better informed was the police constable on the door, nor the morning-suited usher who glanced from the proferred card to the book listing the day's appointments to the Prime Minister, and matched the printed name on the card he had been given with the typed list that rested on the lobby table.

The Director General was taken by lift to the flat on the top floor that the country's senior politician had turned into a miniature home when pressure of work prevented him from using his more substantial town house. It was well known that the Prime Minister's wife disliked having her living rooms trampled on by Civil Servants and Members of Parliament and visiting delegations, and so when her husband had early business to conduct he 'slept over the shop' as he delighted to tell those who called on him at the start of his day.

He was at breakfast, but immaculate and ready to present a public face, the absence of a jacket to cover his waistcoat his only concession to informality. As he pushed the marmalade on to his squares of toast he motioned to the head of the Security Services to take a chair opposite and pushed in his direction the china coffee jug.

'I've seen the Home Secretary this morning,' the Prime Minister said. 'He's told me what the police are doing concerning the Professor and his problems. I wanted to know your feelings about the affair as we go into these crucial hours. No minutes to be kept or anything like that, just your opinions, and what your own department's state of readiness is. That sort of thing.'

The memoir business into which retiring political leaders entered with such enthusiasm on retirement was sufficient to keep the Director General on his guard. He regarded the Prime Minister's request for information as legitimate, but saw no need to expand at too great length.

He chose a cautious path, describing what the other man would already know. He started with the police operation at the hotel,

188

listed the precautions that would be taken to transport Sokarev across the city. Official-style decoy car driving from the hotel at high speed, while the target left via the kitchens in a closed police van, switching to a more formal type of transport in the concealed yard of Tottenham Court Road Police Station before arriving at a normally locked side-entrance at the university main building. He spoke of the scale of the escort that would be used during the transit period, and also of the numbers of men on guard at the building and of the search procedures that had been adopted inside and outside the hall where Sokarev was to speak. He mentioned the gelignite-sniffer Labradors, and the metal detectors that plain-clothes troops had employed before the room was sealed the previous night. He talked of the police liaison with his own department that had been set up. He went into the degree to which invitation holders to the lecture had been vetted, and lingered for a moment on the problems of body searches without giving offence to the members of some of the most learned institutions of the country. He touched on the convoy and the protection screen that would be used to return the professor to his hotel. And then he stopped and waited for the Prime Minister's questions. They were not slow in following.

'Well, that covers the police side of things. Everything in fact that the Secretary of State told me. What are you doing?'

The Director General was in no hurry. His long pauses could be infuriating and he knew it, but did nothing to alter the pace at which he delivered his answers.

'I have the men who head the various departments involved in constant meeting, and they have a liaison line to Scotland Yard. We have endeavoured to provide the Metropolitan force with all information, relevant information, that is at our disposal.'

'Do you have a man on the ground with Sokarev?'

'I have a man right beside him. He is my direct liaison with the police protection force and with the Israeli Foreign Ministry protection team that is accompanying Sokarev.'

'What sort of man?'

'Experienced,' said the Director General.

'Experienced in what? Running an office, liaison, Arab affairs?'

'He's a marksman.' The Prime Minister stopped, swinging his head from the window to stare directly at the DG. A piece of toast remained uneaten, half an inch from his mouth.

'There are enough police there for that, surely? I would have

189

thought that you would have put a senior man with liaison capabilities rather than a gunman.'

The Director General was patient, leading a small boy through an algebraic problem that he might one day answer, but not in this school year.

'I have placed a "gunman", as you describe him, alongside Sokarev because the greatest risk to the life of our guest is close-range shooting. The man I have there is far in advance of anything the Metropolitan Police can provide. He will not be taking a subordinate role in this day's movements . . .'

'It would seem,' said the Prime Minister, 'from the way you have dispensed your priorities that you regard an act of violence as a major possibility.'

For the first time since he had sat down the DG poured himself a cup of now lukewarm coffee. Before he began to drink it he said, 'Considering the known opposition I regard it as inevitable.'

15

As David Sokarev walked through the door of the lecture room in the Senate Building of London University he came unnoticed. He was late, and the attention of the three hundred men who made their living from the study of nuclear physics had long since been diverted from the huddle of plain-clothes policemen with their bulging suits who blocked the only entrance.

He was close to half-way down the side of the room and heading toward the table adorned only with a stand microphone and a glass water jug sitting on a tray between four glasses when those he had passed reacted to the short figure in the grey suit who shuffled past them, hemmed in like a convict by the taller and more heavily-set bodyguards who jockeyed for space at his side. There were few who had come to listen who had not read their morning papers, listened to radio news broadcasts or watched a television news bulletin. All day the headlines had blared the information that a major terrorist plot existed with the sole purpose of assassinating the scientist now making his way the

190

length of the room. Those who first recognized him, from the pictures they had seen in the last few hours, or who had met him in the past, rose from their seats and began to clap. Within seconds the entire room had taken their cue from those who had initiated the applause. The noise spilled into a cheer, self-conscious at first, the men used to working in silence and unaccustomed to venting their thoughts in such public manner. Those that were close enough saw the sad eyes of Sokarev, saw his tongue run with anxiety over his lips seeking to moisten their desert dryness. Perhaps the acclamation confused him, but as he turned to look behind to gauge the size of the room his feet became entangled and he pitched forward a few inches before one of the many hands of the men who surrounded him arrested his stumble.

By the time he reached the top table everyone in the room, excepting the security men, was standing pulping their palms together in a concerted gesture of solidarity. The smile that dawned on his face was one of helpless gratitude. He tried not to look as they beamed and shouted their support for him, instead contenting himself with cleaning his spectacles, and when that was exhausted sorting his notes for the address.

It all meant little to Jimmy. He had permitted Mackowicz and Elkin to flank the scientist and had positioned himself a pace or so behind. That had been the inner yoke of the shell around the Israeli. Beyond had been the Special Branch men, six of them, two car loads who could get no closer than five to six feet from the man they had been ordered to protect. Now the shell fragmented as the guards moved to their appointed places. The only door had been locked behind him, a plain-clothes and unmistakable police guard on either side and equipped with walkie-talkie personal sets to co-ordinate any turning of the key. There could be no sudden surprise entry from that quarter.

The two Israelis were at the raised table, Elkin standing to the side the door was found, Mackowicz opposite and close to the windows now draped in brown velveteen curtains. Jimmy saw that Mackowicz had brought his macintosh; warm summer evening, clear sky, indisputable weather forecast of sunshine for at least the next three days. The coat, held across his thighs, meant the Uzi was concealed there. Wonder if he's put the catch off, thought Jimmy, put one up the spout. Down the long walls that stretched the length of the room were four of the Branch men, two on each side. The remaining two were at the far end, facing Sokarev and the committee that had assembled to host the meeting. Nine armed and trained men in the room. Has to be enough, Jimmy said to himself, has to guarantee it. But the knowledge that Mackowicz had the sub-machine-gun grasped in his right hand aggravated him. Without permitting anyone in the packed ranks of seats to observe his action he drew the PPK from his holster and held it low behind him against the wall, and positioned himself so that he faced the windows, and could see Sokarev to his left and the men by the door to his right.

When silence at last settled on the hall the chairman rose to speak. He had already glanced with as great a force of anger and contempt as he could command at Mackowicz. He found no reaction, but his experience of the morning in the hotel lobby still stung.

'Ladies and Gentlemen,' he threw his voice to the back of the hall, correctly gauging that some of the elderly might have difficulty in hearing in spite of the amplification system. 'It gives me the very greatest of pleasure to welcome to our gathering this evening that most distinguished of colleagues from the State of Israel, Professor David Sokarev.' He paused, and the clapping began immediately and with great fervour, till Christ-like he raised his hands to quell it. 'I think we are all aware that the Professor has done us a great honour in coming to visit us. If we believe only a half of what we read in our daily journals then there is no doubt in my mind that Professor Sokarev has displayed great courage in coming to our shores to honour this engagement. I think we can accept that in the highest offices of our land the dangers that Professor Sokarev is running are believed to be genuine – witness the number of gentlemen with us this evening who I regret wholeheartedly are going to find this evening's lecture extremely tedious.' There was a ripple of laughter as the greyed and balding heads of the audience strayed around the walls searching out the men with their close-cuts, two-button suits and suede shoes. But the laughter did not last, and it was at best brittle and nervous. The presence of the interlopers was a factor beyond the experience of the men who had come to listen to the professor.

'Because of the difficulties that have surrounded Professor Sokarev since his arrival here I myself have not yet had the opportunity of speaking to him, but when I extended the invitation that he should come and talk to us I suggested he might care to

192

discuss in our company the distinguished work connected with lasers that has been associated with his name. Now whether that is what he has eventually decided on, I do not know . . .' It was clear the chairman had more to say, and Jimmy was prepared to shut out the rest.

The gun, he had now decided, was unnecessary. It could rest as easily in the holster, enough of the melodrama. He turned to the wall, as a child does when it wishes to urinate out of sight of adults. With the PPK again weighted against his chest he faced back into the room, wondering how many had seen his movement. The speech of introduction droned on. Jimmy felt himself beginning to relax. Two moments of priority danger, he told himself, and one already successfully negotiated. Arrival and Departure – those were the hitting times for the opposition. Not in here, not with the screened and searched and checked out audience. The departure would be the time for maximum vigilance, not Jimmy's phrase but Jones's. And Helen was out there waiting. Soft and comfortable. She'd follow them back to the hotel, and when they'd dropped Sokarev off, all tucked up in his pit, they'd go back to the flat together, and stay awake together.

The policemen who were beyond the locked door, outside in the corridor, shared Jimmy's feelings. They had formed a close knot together, sufficiently at ease to light up their cigarettes and talk about the ordinariness that dominated their lives. Mortgage rates were swapped, the cost of holidays, gossip about superiors and desk men. And in the creeping darkness beside the towering shape of Britain's largest university complex the officers posted there also felt an easing of the tension that had gripped and alerted them at the time the professor had driven to the building. There would be ample warning of his exit. Then the pocket radios would chatter and there would be the noise of the car engines revving. Time enough to supervise their closely chosen watching points. One group had gathered at the main entrance, dwarfing and formidable. Another had drawn together by the side door through which Sokarev had entered the building. From neither position was it possible to view the windows of the lecture hall; that part of the building butted out too far for them to see beyond its corners.

The constable who had been assigned the duty of watching the windows of the lecture hall now lay at McCoy's feet. He had not been armed, and even if he had carried a gun he would not have had the opportunity to use it. Nor had he spoken into his radio, attached to his tunic lapel, before the crashing blow came down on the soft rear area of his head, below the line of his reinforced helmet and where skull base and vertebrae come together. It had been mercilessly simple, Famy advancing with his tourist map, stuttering in ineffective English, distracting the constable's attention as they peered together at the street divisions while McCoy moved cougar-quick with the metal tube of plumber's piping. The thieves' charter of keys McCoy had gained at the garage in the morning was next employed. A parked car opened, hand-brake suppressed, and the vehicle pushed in silence to the place of the scratched star underneath the window.

Famy saw that the Irishman never looked at the sprawled figure beneath him. Again the glossy coldness that meant there would be no hesitation at the moment of contact, and all who trespassed in their way obliterated without concern. It was as he would be when the time of firing came. Famy was aware of the flooding excitement bursting through him. Now at last they would savour victory, triumph over endless obstacles. It was the ultimate moment of his mission.

McCoy said, quietly and slowly, so that he did not have to repeat it, 'There's been one round of clapping. That's the entry. The next one means he's on his feet. We go, straight then.'

Famy extended the shoulder rest of the M1, locked it in its extended position, checked the magazine was in place, cocked the gun – quickly and fearfully lest the noise of the mechanism would arouse curiosity – and eased off the safety catch.

Beside him McCoy had pulled the heavy black glove on to his right hand, the metal tube grasped in the grotesque finger-shapes. But no gun, Famy saw he had picked up no weapon.

'You should have the other M1 with you,' he hissed, amplifying his worry.

'No need. Your pigeon now, remember? I'm going to give you the clear shot, then it's all yours.'

'It will be a famous success for our people . . .'

'Keep that fucking nonsense till you've hit the bastard.'

They heard the swell of applause build behind the blackness of the curtain, prolonged fierce clapping and shouts. Famy went up the back of the car and on to the roof that buckled and heaved

194

under his weight. He needed to steady himself with his free hand, nerves gripping at his legs. McCoy came the other way, climbing over the bonnet and stretching up past the windscreen till both stood together, uncertain of balance on the shifting platform. They were exactly above the mark Famy had drawn against the wall, and level with the join of the curtains. The Irishman pushed his face close to Famy's.

'Remember it then. When I've done the window and got the curtain back he'll be forty-five degrees to you. And don't bugger about. If they all start blasting chuck the grenades. Right?'

He waited for Famy to bring the rifle up to his shoulder in the aim position, waited till it was snug against the shoulder and the right cheek, and then smashed the tubing into the expanse of glass. Famy winced away from the noise as McCoy's fist, protected by the glove, beat at the obstinate and remaining slivers still fastened in the mortarwork of the frame. The hand grabbed for the curtain and pulled it back; instinctively Famy lunged forward, still in the fire posture, raking the brightness of the room for his target.

Where was he? Where was the whore? Which was the one he sought? Which of the uncomprehending, blank faces that had turned and now stayed motionless and transfixed peering at the source of the commotion? The answer was not long coming. The man who stood at the table while all around him sat, the man who had begun to cower, who knew the blow was near and sought to avoid it, who could not urge his muscles to follow the racing orders of his brain. That one, that one was Sokarev.

Famy steadied to fire, aiming for the chest where the white shirt and the dark tie disappeared into the greyness of his suit. So big, so easy, through the shape of the gunsight.

'Speed it up, for Christ's sake,' screamed McCoy, and as the finger closed round the trigger, squeezing as he'd been told, Famy twisted his gaze to the agony of impatience on the Irishman's face.

When he looked back he saw the man at the far end of the table thrusting a way toward Sokarev, and the man closer to him was wrestling with a coat swinging the billowed shape of it up toward his shoulder.

Famy fired.

As the curtain exploded with the noise of the breaking glass,

195

Jimmy's hand moved to the holster under the breast pocket of his jacket. His fingers found the harshness of the handle, fastening on the ridging there to aid his grip. Then there was the protruding gun barrel, barely thirty feet from him. The pistol was coming fast, out in front, arm extended, level with the eyes as he heard the shout from far in the night, and then the first shot. Fractionally later Jimmy pulled the hair trigger, without finesse and conscious of the need not for accuracy but for a volume of shots. Some were to hit the curtain, some to disappear he knew not where.

Jimmy fired six times, shouting all the time in the direction of Sokarev.

'Get him down. Get the bloody man on the floor. Get him under the table.'

Elkin reached the scientist first, taking off in a leap when still five feet from him to pinion Sokarev to the floor among the tangle of chair and table supports and feet. Jimmy saw the chairman sag in his chair and then fall forward, casually and without effort on to the open surface of the table.

Again and again the rifle at the window fired and with each succeeding shot Jimmy was surer in his knowledge.

'He's missed the little mother fucker, and he knows it!' It was almost a shout, exhilaration at the contact, half-smile playing on his mouth. But the eyes were cold – focused, taking in the scene around him.

The two Branch men along the same wall as Jimmy had begun to fire, not standing but crouched, in the taught posture, classic but slower. He's not going to take it, too much for him, it'll finish him, the little rat, thought Jimmy. He saw Sokarev far under the table, Elkin covering him, saw Mackowicz bring the Uzi to his shoulder, rid himself of that useless coat, and he began to make for the door. He had reached it, elbowing aside the policemen, shouting for the door to be opened above the nerve-shattering noise of the long burst fired by Mackowicz, when from the corner of his eye he saw the puny, dark grey and rounded shape loop its way from the window toward the top table.

Mackowicz far back in the room shouted the one terrifying choked word, 'Grenade!'

It bounced, seemingly consumed with inertia, on to the floor between the table and the front row of the audience's seats, made a gentle parabola before bouncing again and then rolling

196

unevenly, toward the shelter of the table where Elkin protected Sokarev. Mackowicz jumped for it. There was a moment when he was airborne and Jimmy could see the grenade wobbling, nearly stationary, then it disappeared beneath the big body. Stillness, fractional but complete. Then Mackowicz was lifted high toward the ceiling. Jimmy did not see him fall – he was through the door, now unlocked and running toward the main entrance.

The detonation of the grenade was still battering in Jimmy's ears as he went down the corridor through the confusion of the milling policemen. Because the shots and explosion had come from inside the lecture room every man, in or out of uniform, saw it as his duty to crowd as close as physically possible to the source of the gunfire. Behind Jimmy as he shouldered his way through the advancing charge came a cry for 'Stretchers'. He knew where to go. He dug his heels into the soft gravel immediately outside the doorway, ran out into the night and to his left and then swerved again to get himself along the side of the building and to the marksman's position. In the shadows far in front he saw two men jump from the roof of a parked car and start to run for the low boundary wall that separated the university precincts from Malet Street and the free-flowing traffic. Still sprinting, Jimmy fired – stupid really – carried away with the cowboy game, only one shot, and the magazine was expended. There was a shot in return, wide and high and to the right, barely close enough for him to distinguish the 'crack' that signalled its incoming. As his finger moved uselessly on the trigger, bringing home the message of his wastefulness, he slowed, couldn't get close now, not with an empty bloody shooter. Across the road he heard the frantic, piercing sound of dispute, and the noise, belatedly, of a car revving. Jimmy was panting now, out of condition, not enough time in the gym, striving to fill his lungs with air.

'Helen. Helen. Where in God's name are you?'

It seemed deep eternity before the car pulled up sharp alongside him.

'Get out. Get out of the bloody thing.' His voice came in short staccato bursts. She hesitated, disorientated by the distant noise of gunfire and now the heaving wild-eyed form of Jimmy.

'Get out, you stupid bitch. Get out of the bloody car.'

She began to unfasten the clasp of her safety belt worn across her body. Always in position, however far she went, reflex.

197

Jimmy wrenched open the door, took hold of the collar of her coat and pulled her from the wheel. One action, out of the seat and clear of the door. The background cacophony; of police whistles blowing, of a radio screeching with static, of orders bellowed. Jimmy had taken her place and the car was already spinning in a one-hundred-and-eighty-degree half-circle as he headed for the one gap in the wall and toward where he had seen the running men and heard the starting car.

Seventy yards in front the Cortina struck out into the mainstream. It was a laboured movement, that of a winged animal, one certain in the knowledge that it must escape but with its limbs damaged and impaired. Jimmy heaved with relief. He was in contact, the vacuum space between the cars would lessen. He cut right from the centre of the road to avoid a racing police car, light revolving, siren at volume, travelling in the other direction. Flashed his headlights, but it was past him, his gesture unseen by driver or navigator. No system of communication from Helen's car, no radio telephone. He pulled out again, avoided the bus that lumbered in front and cursed that the girl had purchased a slow-acceleration family car. But the gap would close.

The Cortina went through the traffic lights on red and was in Goodge Street, long, Georgian and geometric, heading south. Jimmy followed, was faintly aware of a car skidding to an emergency stop to avoid collision, and settled himself easily into the seat. Not good yet, Jimmy, had you with your Y-fronts on your knees, not often it goes that way, but it'll get better, and the little bastards up front'll wonder what hit them. The PPK rested on his lap. Another magazine was in his jacket, right pocket. He would wait for an opportunity to reload.

They had run from the window close together, Famy with his head bent round, covering the area behind them, the small rifle ready to fire, ready to head off pursuit, McCoy leading with his right arm pressed hard against the upper shoulder. When Famy had turned once to fire away into the distance McCoy had savagely pulled him forward, destroying his aim.

'It's distance we have to have. Hang on here and we're screwed.' The words sobbed out, but with little tone as they emerged from the clamped and pain-creased mouth.

When they reached the Cortina McCoy had thrust his left hand

198

across his body into the opposite trouser pocket and pulled clear the laden key ring. It took him several seconds to select the one he wanted, small and bright and fresh-cut. He tossed it to Famy.

'You drive,' he said, and flung open the passenger door, left unlocked when they had parked the bare forty minutes earlier. Should have left the keys in the ignition.

Famy had the rifle to his shoulder. It was small, a child's toy, too insignificant to be a killing weapon. The people who had paused on the far pavement did not believe in it and now stood and watched – not with great fear, not petrified beyond movement, but curious. Famy was jolted from the image by McCoy's words.

'Come on, you stupid bloody eejit. You'll have to drive.'

Still Famy held the rifle up, peering over its sights, watchful of pursuit.

'Shift yourself, you bastard.'

Famy lowered the rifle, and held it at his side, as a man who walks with a stick, and is resting. 'I cannot,' he said.

McCoy seemed not to have heard him. 'Don't piss about. Get behind the bloody wheel.'

'I cannot drive.' Famy said it slowly. Humiliation, abject and total.

'Course you can bloody drive,' McCoy's voice rose in exasperation and temper.

'I don't know how. I have never driven.'

McCoy waved his right arm in Famy's face. 'Can't you see, there's a bloody great bullet in there? Stop farting about and move the car off.'

'It is impossible. I have never driven. I cannot.'

The monotonous recitation slid home to McCoy. The obscenity he yelled at the Arab was vicious and wounding. McCoy ran round the car and draped himself into the driving seat. He laid his right arm along the wheel for support and from the street light Famy could see his face whitened. With his left hand McCoy inserted the key into the ignition, and then put the car into gear. By pushing his whole body forward he was able to turn the wheel toward the direction of the road before he could bring his left hand into play again with the gear stick.

Famy wondered whether the Irishman would faint. He wound down the passenger window and looked back across the road, rifle aimed again. In his jacket pocket were three grenades – he could run his fingers over them. Grip-bag in the rear, where it

199

had been left, more ammunition, more grenades, needed the reassurance, and then the car was moving. He cringed as they went through the lights, bracing himself for an impact that did not happen. And another car came through the lights, clearly visible to him, unmistakable.

'Another car followed us,' near-panic, near-hysteria.

'What am I supposed to do about it?'

'I cannot see it now, not as an individual car, there are just lights.'

'Forget it,' said McCoy. 'If it gets close blast it. If not forget it.'

McCoy could tell that his concentration was sapping, felt the weakness drifting uncontrollably over him. The wound itself fascinated him. Little to see, but he glanced obsessively at it. Just the neatly driven hole that lay in the centre of the blood patch where the cloth had darkened and stained on the upper forearm. The pain ebbed, rising only when he tried to use the hand, and then sliding into numbness when he rested his fingers on the wheel.

'Did you get the bastard?' McCoy said.

They were on the move now. If he did not have to go fast, and drive under pressure, then he could manage. If there was pursuit ... There was a vagueness, an absence of care, caused by the loss of blood, but that was the option that he did not care to consider.

'I don't know.' Famy's reply was little more than a whisper.

'Course you bloody know. Either saw him go down or you didn't. You know when you've hit a man, the way he goes.' McCoy said it with patronizing knowledge. Seen it at first hand – the way a man was raised in the air, thrown up rag-doll, and the way he then slumped out of control, unable to protect his head. There was a lapse of the co-ordination that maintained the living.

'It was difficult to know.' Famy paused. He studied the road in front, the thinning traffic of late evening in central London, then glanced behind. Only a myriad of jumbled lights, some stationary, some on the move, none so close as to threaten danger. Famy wanted to explain, wanted the other man to understand. 'I was about to fire at Sokarev when you shouted. There was distraction. As I fired there was a man across the room who began to shoot. One of the men pulled Sokarev under the table, I was firing all the time he did that, but he was on the ground and then was gone from my sight. The man who sat beside Sokarev, he was hit ...'

200

'Big deal, they'll be singing and dancing in Beirut if you've drilled a Brit geriatric.'

McCoy was almost amused at the other man's discomfiture. And it was a failure, that much had penetrated to him, through the cloud and the haze. Without his wound he would have felt savage hatred at being associated with the fiasco, but the injury dissipated his anger, rendered it obsolete.

'. . . There was shooting from the wall facing us. Three or four men. And the bodyguard near the table, another one, not the one that went to Sokarev, he had the small machine-gun. He had started to fire when I threw the grenade. The grenade would have taken Sokarev, but the man fell on it. Then I could see nothing. He just exploded, and then there was smoke. The men who were shooting had an aim by then, one could not stay at the window.'

'One of those bastards took me.' There was finality in McCoy's words. To Famy it seemed the pain of the inquest was over, and the car was still moving, McCoy could cope with the disability. Famy watched the cars behind and those alongside but could find nothing to sustain his earlier anxiety. He put the M1 on the floor, under his legs, easy to reach but invisible to any driver who might glance at them casually from an adjacent car.

McCoy said, the trace of a smile playing at the side of his mouth, 'I thought this was the one where you stood up and had yourself counted, where you took Sokarev, or they took you. Bugged out early, didn't we?'

'It was impossible to continue shooting with all the firing from the wall.'

'Hand gun stuff, not accurate at that range. Lucky shot that hit me.'

'You started to run, and you were pulling at me.'

'But it's not my war, remember? You could have stayed. You were the bloody marksman. I'm just the chauffeur. So, why did you do the scamper?'

'I couldn't see any more . . . only the smoke . . . I couldn't aim.' But Famy knew they were just words. There was no recollection of making a decision to run. He was already moving long before the awareness of it. There had never been a moment when he had the choice, choice of life and death.

They had swung to the west now, and the traffic was lighter as they navigated a by-pass route which avoided the heart of the city. McCoy was able to keep the speedometer flickering a path between twenty and thirty miles an hour.

'They won't react well, your masters. Won't have wanted you hanging about able to fight another day and Mr bloody Sokarev coming out clean.' McCoy was turning the screw. Knew it, and enjoyed the process. Retribution for his pain.

Famy stayed silent.

'My crowd wouldn't take kindly to it – not with all the investment. If it's cocked then it would have been better it had never started. Victory for them, bad news in your parish.'

McCoy was talking as if to himself, softly and winning no response.

'The Provies have their own way if it doesn't work out. If it's yellow, if the bugger sprinted to save his neck, then it's court martial. Not as formal as all that, nothing pompous. Half a dozen guys, in a barn in a garage. Sentence comes a bit formal, though. Hood and a pistol shot behind the ear. Leave a note on them too, so the next lot know why.'

Famy had his eyes closed, lids tightly drawn together, but was unable to shut out the message as McCoy expanded.

'If it's just because they didn't think, mucked the scene, then it's easier. Call it knee-capping. Bullet through each, from the back. They walk again, but they never run, and they stand out from the crowd because they're on sticks for weeks. The Proddies, the other mob, they're worse . . . use a Black and Decker. It's a drill, used for putting holes in the wall. Takes longer than a bullet – obvious, isn't it? But they're real bastards, those Proddies.'

Famy said, 'There was one who went into Israel, and came back alone. All the rest were taken or killed, only this one survived and they found his Klashnikov had not been fired. And they took him with ten of his friends to the open ground. He had a start of fifty metres, and then his friends began to fire. They all had to shoot, and the guns were checked afterwards, and they were watched to see they did not shoot wide. He did not go many metres, and it only happened once. There was no need for a repetition.'

'You'd better think of something good to say,' said McCoy. The game had gone far enough. There were other preoccupations for McCoy. Where to go, what to do about the wound? All men who go to the lonely war, the guerrilla's war, have a common fear, multiplied in their fantasies till it controls and dominates them. It is the horror of sepsis, of gangrene, of the putrefaction of their

202

flesh. McCoy needed a den, where he could go and curl his legs and watch the entrance, and be safe, and needed it for many days, with hot water and clean towels . . . What to do with the bloody Arab? No place for him in the den, the lair for one only. Perhaps kill him – easiest solution, attractive. Something to think on, half an hour more for the driving, and a decision by then.

The problem engrossed him as he drove, and Famy too was quiet, but with what thoughts McCoy neither knew nor cared.

For a full three minutes after the firing of the last shot Elkin covered Sokarev's body. When the scientist tried to move and shift his suppressed left arm from under his body the security man firmly pressed him down again flat on to the polished boards of the floor. There was a great calmness about Elkin's face, and the eyes were very clear, traversing the room for any further threat, and outstretched in front of him as an antenna his arm and the service revolver he preferred to the Uzi.

The Branch man who had taken a position nearest the table had bent down and asked the one inevitable question. Was Sokarev hurt? Elkin had shaken his head.

'Keep him there, then,' the detective said. 'First we'll clear the casualties, then empty the room. After that we'll work out how to shift him.'

Sokarev was aware that his legs were trembling, uncontrollably, the flesh of his upper thighs lapping together, and he was power-less to stop it. He could remember little of what had happened, just the noise of the window, and then the sight of the shortened barrel of the rifle poking and weaving in the curtain gap, locking on to him. He could recall the moment that Elkin had hit his legs and pulled him down, and then the horrific, unending exchange of gunfire. He had seen Mackowicz dive and lie still and then lift off into the air, and his ears felt pierced by the sound of the grenade.

The stretchers came fast. That on which the chairman lay was covered, end to end, by a grey hospital blanket and left at the far end of the room. What remained of Mackowicz was beside. The policeman who had helped the ambulance team to lift the Israeli's disembowelled corpse on to the stretcher had vomited as soon as the pink and softened organs were covered over. The ambulances had come from University College Hospital less than half a mile away. It was to there that seven casualties were hurried; four suffering from gunshot wounds, one from grenade shrapnel injuries and two from coronary heart attacks.

The detectives had already started to examine the fire position outside the window when one of their number, walking beside the car used as the platform, stumbled on the body of the constable. When they lifted the young man on to the stretcher it was with care, a degree of gentleness, conscious they were handling their own.

In strange, shuffling silence the guests were ushered from the room and across the wide corridor to a similar lecture hall. Their patience was requested and it was explained to them that though they would not be detained for long it was impossible that they could be allowed to wander from the building while the large-scale search of the immediate area of the university was still under way. After the door had been closed on them few had anything to say. The conflict between Israel and her neighbours was not a thing that many understood. For a few moments they had been exposed to the unfamiliar; but the experience would do little to aid their comprehension.

When everyone had gone Sokarev was helped to his feet. They stood him back to the wall and hemmed in by policemen, Elkin right beside him, the gun still in his hand but resting against his trouser pocket. Later they brought him a glass of water. He found he could scarcely hold it, and Elkin took the glass and put it against the professor's lips and tilted it to such an angle that some spilled from his mouth and dribbled on to the front of his suit.

Jones had stayed in his office alone that night. Helen, vague about her movements, had been gone three hours. From a long way down the empty corridors he heard the laboured footsteps of the messenger from communications. Too old to hurry, and why should he in his ignorance of the message he carried to Room 3/146? He was a little out of breath when he knocked on the outer door, and surprised that the Section head had bounced across two offices to be there to snatch the paper from his hand. There were no thanks from Jones who now concentrated on what the other man could see were three bare lines of type.

They didn't explain much. An attack on Sokarev – unsuccessful, rifle fire and an explosion – casualties, large local-scale hunt

204

started for two men – no immediate result. In his office again Jones sagged back into his chair, read the message three, four times, looking unsuccessfully for any word or interpretation that he might earlier have missed. And nothing from Jimmy. Where was he when all this was going on? Why hadn't he intervened? Why hadn't he called? Half the reason for the man being there was that he'd be on the phone, so the Department wasn't relying on the police for information. Should have called in by now. He swivelled half round in his chair and looked at the picture, in deep shadow now because of the angle at which the lights were hung. Pretty little boy, nice smile, big eyes, neat head, looked as harmless as a butterfly, but he'd concealed the wasp sting. Bloody-near pulled it off, him and that Irishman. Jones felt a great sadness that pulled him down, his head deep in his arms on the table. What was the point of it all, when all the king's horses and all the king's men could be pushed off centre-stage by that little rat? Shouldn't have been an equal contest, shouldn't have been allowed to throw the sucker punch, and he had, and nearly won.

The Soviets sniffing round the Defence establishments, or the Czechs, or East Germans . . . they were so straightforward. Bit of a game when you became involved with them. Reckoned on the odds, didn't they? And if they didn't think they could win they didn't come in. But this little sod, he hadn't worked out his chances of survival – couldn't have done, or he'd have stayed at home – and yet he was, in there kicking. Jones didn't know what his feelings were toward the young Arab. Probably there was a tinge of admiration, that of the older man for youth which does something no longer possible for the other through age. But it was balanced quickly by the anger and frustration that the Arab had put them through the hoops, and laughed at them and lived.

Had to be brave, too, Jones acknowledged that. The old labels weren't any good. Courage if he was from your lot, fanatacism if he was on the other side. He'd learned the futility of the tags when he was still young, when he saw an ME 110 night fighter with its two-man crew peel away in its tail of flame, known they wouldn't survive, and known too that they'd pressed their attack long after the chance of success had vanished. They were brave men, and they were the enemy, and they'd earned respect, and been prepared to die. The Arab had been prepared to die too, as a

205

sacrifice for his army, whatever bunch of twisted idiots they turned out to be. And all such a waste, and everyone scared out of their wits by the implications of it all – everyone except his Jimmy.

The telephone broke in, shrill and insistent, bursting over the quietened room. Helen on the line, chill and matter of fact. Jimmy in her car . . . hot pursuit . . . a get-away vehicle disappearing from the scene . . . God only knows where he's gone . . . shots in the street . . . she was coming back to the office. Just the staccato statements, without emotion or involvement, and then she'd rung off. Jones put the receiver down. Funny the way she'd used Jimmy's name, usually a laugh when she mentioned him, but not this time. Jones, long sensitive to intonation and emphasis, noted it, and wondered what the hell she was doing there anyway. Then he put it from his mind. Unimportant, silly girl – should have stayed at home. His thoughts were surging with Jimmy. Just what he would have wanted, he thought, the big challenge and the chance to prove himself where all else had failed. And he'd have to kill them, wouldn't he? Have to kill the Arab. Only way now.

Under pressure Jones would normally have resorted to the palliative of work, buried himself in the paperwork of the operation, twisted his mind away from the generalities with the specifics of detail. But he had no function now; it was all out of his hands. There was nothing he could usefully do. That's how far down those bastards have brought us, he thought, right down to the base area, where the Jimmys are waiting.

He screwed up the teletype message, crumpled the paper in his fist and tossed it unsuccessfully in the direction of his waste-bin.

None of the photographers and television crews who had been covering the arrivals and who were scheduled to film the departures had any worth-while pictures of the event. Now they crowded against the side door from which they believed the Israeli scientist would emerge. A fierce argument broke out when a police inspector called them to silence and informed the gathering that under no circumstances would flash bulbs or arc lights be permitted. Thirty voices were raised in protest, but when they died the inspector's message was even more explicit.

'Gentlemen,' he said. 'I am not prepared to have the person of

206

Mr Sokarev either impeded or in any way illuminated on this step. If you think about it there's no way I can say anything else. If you don't play ball you're down the station, charged and in court tomorrow, and I wouldn't vouch your cameras will survive.'

The Prime Minister, called from the dinner table, suffered three agonizing minutes of uncertainty. The first message relayed to him by the Commissioner, telephoning from Scotland Yard, merely stated that there was heavy shooting and an explosion inside the room where Professor Sokarev was speaking. More details would follow.

He had waited for them alone in his personal office, unwilling to face his guests again before he knew the worst. When the telephone rang again he expected catastrophe, but was told that whereas there were casualties the professor was not among them. There was no more reliable and confirmed information.

He had barely resumed his meal when his Parliamentary Private Secretary brought in a folded slip of paper. The Israeli Ambassador was demanding a meeting, and that night.

'Put the bloody man off till the morning,' he said, and motioned for the butler to replenish his glass. 'Right to the top,' he urged.

16

It satisfied Jimmy that the car he tailed should be unaware of his presence. Like a marriage, tied together, but neither showing any indication of the bond that linked them. It was as it should be, professional but not easy, not one for the kids in the department – they'd have been up close, blowing the contact, but Jimmy kept back from the other car, leaving it room to manœuvre, far from the bumper and the rear red lights that shone at him, that gripped his attention. No question of an attempt to ram or force it off the road. Idiocy if he tried it. Would leave him with two men to handle, both armed and with all the dangers of losing them both

207

in a foot chase. It was better this way. Eventually the bastards would stop and that would be time enough for him to make his presence known. They went slowly, and so were not hard to follow, yet he was surprised that there was not more speed and more effort to put greater distance between themselves and the university. Jimmy sought to interpret his opponents, fancied he could understand them, all part of his training, but this lack of urgency confused him.

There was a road block outside Richmond. Uniformed police, torches, arms waving, but all in the lane that ran toward the city and with no interest shown in the cars that travelled the other way, from the direction of London. Typical, thought Jimmy, no bloody liaison. The wireless nets must be jammed with traffic on what's been happening, and nobody's told these poor sods that the birds have upped and flown, and that the only purpose of the law being there is because they might come back to the nest to roost. It was a wide and open road, well laid down by a fully endowed local authority with a grass space with bushes and small trees separating the two routes. Slow as it was the car he followed went through, carried by the flow, too fast for him to shout and attract the attention of the policemen on the other carriageway. No chance of stopping, couldn't risk severing the thread that bound him to the Cortina.

The PPK was loaded now, empty magazine discarded on the floor by the foot-brake. It had not been difficult to rearm the pistol, and he now weighed in his mind when would be the moment to open fire. Perhaps when they stopped the car, when they were out on the pavement and unaware, when he was in the darkness of the saloon and they were in the open, free for him and naked, illuminated by the streetlights. A possibility, a good one. Attractive because then there was the chance that they would be close together, and the burst of shots might cover the two of them. When the traffic closed and he was but two or three car-lengths away from the Cortina he could see the two heads. That of the driver bent low, in supplication over the wheel, the other more upright and turning every two minutes or so to look behind him. How did they rate themselves? Jimmy wondered. He knew where he'd have put it. Fifty-fifty, at best. Escaped but hadn't taken the professor. Perhaps not as good as fifty-fifty. Chap needed a score to measure his performance against, important that, competitive world. Not as good as evens, Jimmy reckoned.

Perhaps only the professor counted. Buggered it up, hadn't they? And for all the security they'd won their surprise – must have wanted the surprise factor above all else, and they'd achieved that. Good ground work, but the rest screwed. Not like McCoy, that, Jimmy thought, not if you read his file. Couldn't have been him on the gun, must have been the other bastard. Taken too long, hadn't he, not the way you'd have done it Jimmy, you wouldn't have left the rifle hanging through the window half the night. Silly bastards. Should have been on champagne now, and instead they're running, and don't even know what's right up their backsides and waiting to belt them.

Jimmy could see they had slowed in front of him. Nearly there, he told himself, but they must be unsure of the right turning. Lost their way, but they wouldn't be in the side streets unless that's where they're heading for.

The pistol was in his right hand, flat against the wheel. His window was down. Not long now, my little darling. He muttered casually and without emotion, but would not have denied the excitement.

To kill the Arab or not. It had bounced round McCoy those last miles into the town. Famy was expendable, and from the way he turned and fidgeted in his seat was aware of it. Knew what his own people would do to him if he crawled home, the surviving straggler, in the first true flush of failure. Better off face down on the refuge of the building site, with the weeds and undergrowth and rats for company. Had had his chance of immortality, if that mattered to him, and had messed it. The alternative, to rot in a cell as a lifer in the Scrubs, and no one coming in a hi-jack jet, the freedom bird, to lift him out and take him home. Good-for-nothing, wasted material. A bloody great beacon of a fiasco to his colleagues and commander – McCoy liked that, rolled off his tongue well. He'd be paraded, sunken and sheepish, through the British courts, after the spooks had finished with him, after the chatter, after the 'debrief'. Be a killing for the Ministry of Information back in Jerusalem, worth a public holiday to them – 'Day of Arab Balls up'. And the bugger knew it all, could see that from the way he sat, misery from ear to ear, the little chokes, the set firmness of the mouth. And his chances of making out on his own, getting clear, McCoy assessed them as minimal to nil.

209

If he needed his hand held for the attack, how much more would he depend on the nanny protection for escape.

McCoy was close to resolve when Famy broke the long silence that had permitted the flow and insinuation of the Irishman's thoughts.

'You are going to the girl's home, right? To the place where you hid when she came for me? That is the place that I will leave you.' Perhaps he looked for reaction, expected surprise, but there was none from McCoy, just eyes on the road, hands on the wheel, and the bead of lit sweat high on the forehead. 'There was an idea when we were planning the mission at home, that the attack should be mounted at Heathrow, at the airport as he flew to the United States. It will be harder without my friends, but it is the only possibility. I will go on foot, across country, to the airport. They told us that it was not difficult to gain entry to the perimeter, and I will see the El Al land. He will not board till the end, and I will have time, with the rifle, to get as close as I need.'

'Impossible.' McCoy never moved his head, just the word of dismissal.

'It is not impossible, only difficult. I have the resolution now, not earlier but it has come to me. It was different earlier. I have now the will that I should have possessed when Sokarev was on the gun. But it was the first time that I had ever fired on a man. It is not easy, not the first time. It is not simple to stand and expose oneself to gunfire. I have learned much in the last hour, more than they taught me in the camp. More in the hour than in three months.'

'They'll gun you down before you set foot within two hundred yards of the plane, and you don't even know which one it will be.' Perhaps McCoy was less certain of himself, the quietness of the Arab disconcerting him. There was a strange confidence he hadn't witnessed before, something novel, delicate, and which he did not wish to fracture.

'The plane will be the one that is most heavily guarded. I have ideas, and there are many grenades. The Israelis say, and they are right, that if one intends to kill there is no favour to be found in starting far back, relying on aim and the steadiness of the hand. The Israelis say you have to be close, body to body, that you have to be prepared to die yourself. They are correct. They are experts in the art of killing, and we are not. We can only learn from them.'

'We part company then. It's not part of my game.'

210

'Your side is more than complete. You carried me to the target, you placed the rifle in my hand. You have fulfilled your order. As long as I live I shall remember you with friendship.'

No risk of that being long, thought McCoy. Right hornet's bed we've put our stick into. But if the boy wants to go gloriously that is his concern. Not the style of Crossmaglen. Happened once in Ballymurphy, up in Belfast, when they were all twisted after Internment, and half a dozen guys went for a trot down the road and firing Thompsons from the hip at the biggest pile of sandbags and bunkers you ever saw. Had their bloody heads blown off, one after the other. Did anyone thank them for it the next week, or the next month, or the next anniversary? Did they, shit. Just called them 'eejit bastards'.

'I'm going to the house,' McCoy said. 'She'll put me up somewhere. I have to wash the arm. Doesn't hurt so much now, but it needs cleaning. Last time they had me over the border, into Dundalk General and on the table with the knife in less than half an hour. You can't bugger with gunshot, have to clean it.'

'Where will you put the car?' asked Famy.

'At the end of the street by the house. It's a dead-end, no one'll see it there, come looking for us. We'll do the goodbye bit then.'

He'd hesitated at several of the road junctions in the last half-mile, searching for the landmarks of the streets known from the single occasion that he had walked the girl to her front door. And then there was the spread of ivy on the end brick wall, and the tree with the white-washed number on it, that was cancered by disease and that would have to be cut. She had said it was a shame, for the tree. He turned into the girl's road.

After McCoy had stopped the car he reached awkwardly toward the back floor space of the car, feeling for one of the M1s in the grip bag and for another magazine. From the cloth sack he took two of the grenades, slipping them into his pocket where they banged together, making a dull, hidden noise, without the ring of softer, less lethal metal. The gun he crooked under his shoulder. Then with his left hand he opened the door of the car. Famy waited for him, then pulled the bag over his seat. His rifle was loose, trailing one-handed as he walked round the front of the car. Simultaneous with McCoy he was aware of the lights of another vehicle that turned into the street, and reacted as fast as the Irishman in shielding his firearm alongside the silhouette of the leg.

211

'Stay still till he's parked and switched off,' McCoy snapped at Famy, concerned at the intrusion, wanting to be on his way, unwilling to face interruption. They were both illuminated by the powerful undipped beams that blazed at them from twenty yards down the road. There was a sense of foolishness, of conspiracy, that was unnerving.

'As soon as he's gone disappear.' McCoy tried to take control, knew it was for the last time, but a pride dictated that at this moment, even as he relieved himself of his commitments and responsibilities, he should still lead. 'It's been strange. Not much to say now . . . but I'm sorry, for your sake . . . and I mean it . . . I'm sorry it loused up . . . What's the matter with the bastard, why doesn't he kill those bloody lights . . . ?'

McCoy felt the searing surprise of pain as the first bullet struck his shoulder. It spun him half-round in the fraction of time that it tore a path deep into the softness of the flesh, smashing into the boned strips of his upper ribs, before disintegrating, the aerosol of smoothed and roughened particles. Famy reacted well. Crouched beside the car door he fired six aimed shots at the car, hunting for the lights, seeking to destroy them, and when that was complete blasting into the darkness above his memory of the bulbs. He paused, studied the silence that had spread at desolate speed across the street, and grasped for a grenade. Pin out, lever free, left arm extended, and then he hurled it, as the instructor had taught them, overarm and toward the car. The moment before the blast he saw a shadow, down low near the pavement, scurrying for the protection of the nearest front garden.

Drunkenly McCoy regained his feet and lurched through the wicket gate to the front door of the girl's home. With his rifle held one-handed and high he hammered at the wooded panelling. There was one more shot, but wide and far into the night, insufficient to deter him.

'It's a pistol. Out of range, give him a few more. Have the bastard keep his head down. And listen: when we get inside just do as I say, don't bloody argue.' Famy saw he was ashen, his face screwed tight around the mouth and chin, the reaction sharper and more acute than the previous bullet had achieved.

The door opened. Silhouetted by a light from the back of the hallway was the girl. There was an older woman behind her. Further back a man, top collar button undone, staring without understanding.

McCoy pushed the girl savagely to one side, sending her spinning on to the carpet. Satisfied that Famy had followed him in he kicked back with his heel and heard the door slam behind him, the Yale lock engage, the portcullis down on the outside world of the street.

'Whoever the bugger is that's out there' – McCoy was speaking only to the Arab, ignoring the others as if they did not exist, had not yet been reached in his agenda of priorities – 'he's seen us both go in. Double yourself out the back, through the kitchen door, over whatever fence there is, and run, run till your legs won't carry you. I'll hold here with this crowd. It'll take the fuzz light years to work out what to do, and all the time they'll be thinking it's the two of us that are sitting inside. It'll give you hours of start on the bastards. But don't hang about now. Move yourself . . .' The pain came in a great spasm, seeming to catch hold of the wound and pluck ruthlessly at it before letting the sinews fall back into their torn but ordered place. 'For Christ's sake don't mess me, be on your bloody way.'

Famy said nothing, just ran on past them. Past McCoy and the girl, past her parents. The light from the kitchen ceiling threw the small garden into shape and he saw the fence, five feet high and sixty feet away. He trampled through some plants that clung to his ankles then swung himself on to the wattle embroidered barrier and was over. There was a path, and beyond his eyes nothing but darkness.

When McCoy spoke again it was with great deliberation, his defence bunker against the flowing agony.

'I have a rifle, fully loaded, twenty-six rounds in the magazine. I have hand grenades. There will be no hesitation in killing you if you do not do exactly as I say. And any bloody heroics and the women get it first. The old one right at the start. If the police come God help you.' The girl, upright now, and joined in fear to her mother, began to weep – quick, sudden, little choking sounds, delicate convulsions at her throat, head hanging. 'You, father.' – McCoy gestured with the rifle barrel to the man – 'You're to go round the house. I want all the outside doors and windows locked, and I want every curtain in the house drawn, and I want the keys brought to me.'

He looked at them for the first time, turning his head from face to face lingering on each till they averted their heads, unable and unwilling to meet and sustain the gaze of the deep, hate-

213

consumed eyes. 'I've explained it then? And it's understood? Don't mess me about. Don't play games with me. I've said what it means if you fool with me.'

As he took the mother and daughter upstairs he could hear the noise of the locks being turned, the bolts driven home, and the curtains sliding on their plastic runners. He was so very tired, so near to sleep. He yearned for it, for an escape from the pain, and the awful hallucination of fighting in another man's army, another man's war.

On all fours Jimmy edged his way along the pavement toward the end house of the terrace. Helen's car was alight, flames careering through the interior. In a few moments it would explode, when the heat reached the petrol tank. Shouldn't have happened to her, not her pride and joy, only bloody girl he knew who washed her motor, poor cow. He went without haste, feeling the growing heat playing at a distance on the seat of his trousers, watching all the time at the house, expecting the gun, the black barrel. Next round due, bell should be clanging, and he was short of seconds, no one to hold the stool – but no one that he would have wanted there. What you joined for, Jimmy-boy, the licence to play the grown-up games. He saw the curtains in an upstairs room abruptly jolt across the window frame, noted it as an essential step in the protection and precaution process against siege and eventual attack. Nothing else he could register on, and then he smiled to himself, nothing but the tacky and small pool of blood, reflecting, by the front gate. One of the bastards with problems. The Irishman, it would be his cupful. That was the one he'd aimed for and who had spun against the bodywork of the old Cortina too fast for him to be on the evading kick. The move of a man who's been hit, and the blood, the amount of it, that meant an effective and hurting wound. 'Incapacitating' was what old Jonesey would have called it. Cuts the odds, getting on to an even chance now, Jimmy. One by one the lights were doused in the house. Good thinking again – obvious, really – but meant the homework had been done, necessary if they want to see out. Only have to move the curtains a fraction of an inch and they can see the whole street, while they stay hidden, invisible. Four houses down and on the same side of the street a front door opened and Jimmy could see a man peering at the burning car. Others would follow when curiosity overwhelmed the baser instincts of self-preservation and the barricading of doors in response to the gunfire.

The man backed away when he saw Jimmy's gun, seemed to see it before he fastened on to the crouched figure beside his hedge-enclosed front garden, and hurried toward his door, seeking to shut out the threat. But Jimmy was faster, had his foot there, his worn leather taking the force of the swinging woodwork.

'I want the telephone,' Jimmy said. 'And while I'm talking write me the names of the people in the end house, this side, everyone who might be in the house at the moment. And don't go back on the street, not unless you want to make the front page of the papers, picture and all.'

For the man it was instant nightmare, too consuming for him to question Jimmy's identity, and there was the gun. Meekly he led the stranger to the back room and pointed to the telephone. It was an automatic response that led him to subdue the volume of the television programme he had been watching. Fingers spun the dial. Jones's direct outside line number.

'Jimmy here, Mr Jones. They're holed up in Richmond. Chisholm Road, just by the park. One's in difficulty, not fatal, but he'll have a hard time. They've rifles and grenades, same stuff as earlier. Police aren't here yet, but they'll be coming when the local worthies report gunfire up and down their discreet little track. First impression is that they know what they're at, taking all the basic precautions . . .'

Through the house Jimmy heard the penetrating wail of a police siren. He put the telephone down without explanation and ran back through the house and front door, careering into the centre of the road to wave down the patrol car. He saw the officers inside flinch away, then remembered he still held the PPK. He showed them his plastic coated identity card – the answer to all problems – with the black and white mug shot from the days before his face filled out with age.

'Don't go any further,' he snapped. 'First thing, one of you get round the back, the other clear the street. Boyos from the London effort tonight are in the end house, one on the right side. They're littered with hardware, so go careful.' As an afterthought he asked the obvious. 'Have they issued you with firearms?'

215

The policemen were both young, not out of their twenties. They shook their heads, apprehension running deep.

'Well, don't just sit there. If you haven't got them it's tough. Showbiz. One of you'll still have to shift round the back, the other call up the bloody cavalcade.'

Within a quarter of an hour the house was sealed to the outside world. Police marksmen with FN rifles had taken up positions across the street facing the house. Others lay in the garden at right-angles to its front door. Four were against the back fence and with them were the local force's two attack-trained Alsatian dogs. A portable searchlight, short and tubular, erected on a tripod and powered by a noisy insistent generator, projected its high intensity beam against the face of the house. The building itself was eerily still, as if contaminated by plague, quarantined, no movement and no noise around it, great shadows thrown on the brickwork by the roses that the family had so carefully nurtured. At the bottom of the street were the fire engines, motors ticking over, blue hazard lights circling perpetually, and further back the ambulances with their rear doors opened and the red-blanketed stretchers laid ready at the road side. This was where the other residents of the street had gathered. Adults still dressed, children in their night clothes and wrapped in anoraks and overcoats against the chill of the evening. There was little talk among them, just the overwhelming sensation of shock that such a thing should happen in their street, in their private preserve.

The order had already been issued that no instruction concerning reaction operations should be broadcast over police short-wave radio, and no information issued to the press unless from authorized police public relations at Scotland Yard.

'We have to cocoon them,' the station superintendent said. 'Cut them right off till the VIPs arrive and announce the Great Plan. In the meantime no sense letting them just twiddle a few knobs on a radio set and have an earful of what we're up to.'

'Who's coming down?' asked Jimmy.

'Half bloody London. They're leaving the PM and the Queen in charge, far as I can make out. The rest are hot-footing it over here. Assistant Commissioner, Home Secretary, Defence people, a man called Jones from your crowd, scores of them.'

'Let's hope they bring some changes of socks,' said Jimmy. 'They can take a long time, these things.'

216

'It can take a long time or it can take five minutes. That's a political decision.' The superintendent walked away.

In the back of the official car that sped south-west out of London toward Richmond Jones felt an overwhelming sense of relief. Had the pair of them boxed up: that had been the gist of the message from the Scotland Yard Operations Room. Would just be a matter of sitting it out, waiting for them to get tired of their predicament once they'd been convinced of the hopelessness of their situation. Might lose a hostage or two – unlikely, though, and anyway they were expendable, weren't they? Probably get everyone out alive; it was reasonable to assume so on past performance. That would tie it up neatly, avoid the martyrdom that Jimmy would want to award the Arab. No more killing, no more slaughter, and a finish to this lunatic hysteria that had been gripping everyone in the Department the last five days. And the Department had done well; that would have been noticed.

The Prime Minister sat at the end of the table, the cigar nestling in the fingers of his right hand. It was unlit and little more than a theatrical prop, but he liked to have it there, particularly when decisions had to be made. There were four other men at the table. On the Prime Minister's right the Commissioner of Police for the capital and the Permanent Under Secretary for the Ministry of Defence. On his left the Director General of the Security Services, and further away a middle-ranking Civil Servant from the Home Office.

The Prime Minister had opened the meeting – begun as his dinner guests were still finding their way on to the pavement outside Number Ten – by asking the Commissioner to report on the latest situation at the house.

A detailed, clipped account. Without waste, no adjectives for effect, rhetoric removed. The policeman concluded, 'It's basically a classic siege situation, of which we have some experience of our own but on which there is much international information to fall back on. They have three hostages, they are proven killers, one of them is confirmed injured. As yet we have no demands, but it's early for that. They'll follow, and when they do they'll be wanting a plane out. These men are liable to be in a highly un-

217

stable condition after their failure earlier in the evening. In my submission, time as much as anything else will calm them down. Otherwise you have a potential bloodbath.'

The Prime Minister shifted his weight, faced the Director General.

'I've not much to add to that. Except that we believe that our man has wounded . . .'

'Your marksman,' the Prime Minister interrupted, 'the one that you put such faith in.'

'. . . our man has wounded the Irishman, McCoy. Our assessment is that McCoy would probably be the more skilful of the pair, in the tactical sense, that is, but that his resolve may not equal the Arab's. We would believe that if it came to a shoot-out in the house then the greater threat to the lives of the hostages and of the storm party would come from the Arab.'

So ridiculous, thought the Prime Minister. Intelligent men, all of us, people to see, work to be done, beds and families to be getting to, and all sitting round a table in the seat of Government discussing the form, the betting card on who kills best – the Celt or the Oriental. Nonsensical.

'Mr Dawson, we move into your realm. What are the considerations we have to weigh in contemplating the storming of the house?' The Prime Minister was looking past the Director General to the young, lean and shadow-pallored man who had to that moment taken no part in the discussion only scribbled comprehensive short-hand notes on a small lined pad.

'With respect, sir,' – Dawson spoke at a speed that matched his writing, not looking up from his papers, but in a low voice so that the others had to strain forward to hear him – 'the business we face is not that different to the proceedings of the Lord Chief Justice's Court. We can only deal with previous case histories, with other judgements. It is unlikely that there will be special circumstances that will give us an option that has not faced other authorities here or on the Continent or in the United States when challenged with the same problem. I submit that we have to look at the solutions that have been attempted or discarded in the past. First, the best documented: the Olympics attack. In Munich the Germans were confronted with an end of terrace building, but they were dealing with a larger group of hostages, and many more men in the attack squad. The Police President of the City considered the use of incapacitating gases and eliminated them

218

as too slow. They also considered gaining access to the house next door and placing explosive charges against the common wall and blasting an entry that way. This was rejected, too: potentially dangerous to the hostages and also unsatisfactory if their exact location in the building could not be pin-pointed. So they relied in the end on luring the Black September team into the open and assaulting them with selected marksmen. Result: a fiasco. In the United States, in the Washington Court House siege, the authorities took their time, stalled. After many hours they managed to provide a key to the hostages, secreted in the supplies they were permitted to send in, but they had some high-quality people imprisoned who were able to make decisive use of the help given to them. I think that is unlikely to apply in this case. The Israelis themselves – and they believe they have a certain unmatched expertise in these matters – stake all on heavy frontal assault backed by diversionary fire, heavy fire. They risk everything on speed and finely worked-out timing. You will be aware, sir, that the terrorists die, but they take a high proportion of the hostages with them. Probably unacceptable in our circumstances.'

There was no shuffling of papers, scraping of feet, stifled coughs. Dawson was the expert, with a mastery of a vague and untested subject. It was easy to see that on his ability and conclusions rested the lives of many.

'The Dutch faced a different type of situation in the prison siege at Scheveningen in the autumn of 1974. They determined to enter one heavily locked door, the only point of access to the prison chapel. But they had certain knowledge through eye-witnesses and electronic aids of the precise positions of hostages and captors. They waited till they were satisfied the terrorist faction had been lulled into false confidence, then used a laser beam to burn out the lock, accompanied by massive diversionary noise. That operation was completely successful. I should stress that British experience is in the field of the waiting game. It is the tactic most generally advocated. As a strategy it is probably applicable more to the domestic problem of criminals or IRA-type terrorists, less useful in dealing with international groups – Palestinians or Red Army of Japan. If you freeze the latter type out you are then faced with the legal processes and the probability of reprisals with the aim of freeing your prisoners.'

'How soon could we mount an effective attack on the house?' The Prime Minister wanted it over, completed. The other men

219

could see that. Easy to recognize, the fear of a drawn-out bartering for life. Endless negotiations as they had witnessed in Germany and France and Greece and Italy, and then government capitulation to the power of the automatic rifle, the primed explosives.

Dawson said, 'It's well documented that the most favoured time for assault is just before dawn. Give or take a few minutes, but it's round four o'clock. Doctors will tell you that medically this is the time of least resistance – it's when the elderly die, the blood gets colder then. And we start with the advantage that these men will be tired. They have been under pressure for many hours now, since the weekend. They need to rest. If one is hurt then that puts greater stress on the other, but he too must relax at some stage. So tomorrow morning – it could be done then, as soon as that. But the earlier you attack the greater the risk. Whatever their capabilities these two men will still be attempting maximum performance. You would be leaving no time to wear them down, blind-alley them.'

The idea of the laser appealed to the Prime Minister. He talked frequently in his public speeches of the need for technological advance in the country; his opponents said he was obsessed with gadgetry, more interested in the machines of industry than the men and women who manipulated them. He was close now to the decision for which the four men waited.

'Two questions, Mr Dawson. Could we produce the laser by the time tomorrow morning that you have specified? And what sort of diversions would you think necessary?'

It was William Dawson's value to those that he advised that he seldom answered unless certain of his information. The availability of the cutting beam caused him to hesitate before committing himself.

'Probably we could get a laser from industry, certainly from Imperial College. It does not have to be a particularly refined or sophisticated model. Whether the necessary authorization and personnel could be obtained in the next five hours . . .? As for the diversions, I would suggest considerable noise for five minute periods, every twenty minutes or so. Engines revving, fire brigade sirens, shouting radio chatter. Build it up, then let it fade, but keep it up in the pattern through the night till the small hours. They'll be accustomed to it, familiar, by the time we want to use the laser, its noise covered, it would take about fifteen seconds to open the front door, not more.'

220

'You have the authorization, Mr Dawson. Get the damned thing.' The Prime Minister was bubbling now, effervescent, decision-taking, the broth of politics. Facing the Civil Servant who sat beyond the police commissioner, he said, 'Mr Harrison, I want the Special Air Service to assault the house in the small hours of tomorrow morning. I would be unconcerned if the Arab should not survive the entry.'

The commissioner reacted quickly. 'With respect, this is a Metropolitan Police district. Several serious crimes have been committed in that overall responsibility area, and we are quite capable through our Special Patrol Group of mounting the necessary assault. It's a slur . . .'

'Commissioner,' said the Prime Minister coldly, folding his spectacles, the discussion completed. 'I am interested in results, not sensibilities. If you ask Mr Dawson I am sure that he will explain in great detail that one of the few successful legacies handed down by the Munich police after Furstenfeldbruck was the certain knowledge that in future all similar operations should be placed squarely in the hands of the military.'

The messages went out, coded and fast. Thirty-five minutes after the Prime Minister's advisers had taken their leave, and still short of midnight, the SAS anti-hi-jack force had been lifted by Wessex helicopter from their base camp in Herefordshire. They represented some of the most highly trained and resourceful troops in the British armed forces. There was little equipment stowed on the floor of the helicopter, just an awesome variety of firearms.

The spasms in his shoulder came and went with increasing frequency as McCoy moved about the house, so that he needed to steel himself for the onset of pain that caused him to stop and lean against the nearest wall. There was much movement, much that he had to do, aggravating the wound, but his persistence was uppermost. Structure had to be built, the rest would come after that. He took the parents upstairs, one at a time, and laid them face down on the beds, one in the main sleeping room and the other in the spare bedroom. It required great effort for him to rip up the top sheet of the front room double bed into the narrow

221

strips that he sought. Using his undamaged hand and his teeth he tore at the lengths that he needed to tie them. Neither of the elderly people were in a state of mind to resist him, too horrified by the suddenness of the incursion. But if they had then one well-placed blow would have won them their freedom. As it was they obeyed meekly and followed exactly the orders that he gave. When they were prone on the beds he bound their hands behind their backs, threatening to each that he would be watching the lifetime partner, and that if he heard the sound of attempted escape then he would kill.

When he had finished he felt his strength drain until he was totally weak. Mingling now with the pain was a rising nausea. He flopped back against the wall behind the headboard, on the sparse single bed in the girl's room, his feet on the yellow coverlet, smearing it with street dirt. He angled his body so that his weight was borne on the left side, and in that hand he held the rifle, pistol-like, the shoulder support still folded. Like a grotesque interloper he dominated the tiny room, blond hair dishevelled and lost in a myriad of Medusa patterns, his face, with its colour from the fields of South Armagh now vanished, showing only the anger of the eyes and the ferrule lines of exertion. The stains on his jacket were not rich and red but stark, damp and soiled. He laid the rifle across his lap and pulled from his pocket the grenades, which he placed beside his hip. The good hand, the one he now relied on, resumed hold on the trigger guard of the M1.

Till she followed him into the room the girl had not seen the wounds, but when he shifted on the bed, awkwardly and seeking the comfort that the pain denied him, the blood run was visible, and she saw too the twin holes in the cloth. She sat on the end of the bed.

'Why have you come back here? What do you want of us?'

'Time, my little girl. Time for a friend.'

'For the Arab?'

'Time for the Arab. Time for him to stretch his legs, get on his wings.'

'He has gone?'

'You saw him, he's moved on. Further to go than I have. This is where I finish; his post is a long way yet. It's as if he hadn't left the starting line. He's the whole course to run. I'm his handicapper. Big Ciaran ensures he starts in front, out ahead of the bastards. That's the way it is, my little cash-machine girl.'

222

No need to talk to her, nothing could be said that mattered, just an empty face and fingers that punched a till. Meaningless. Time to think of yourself, Ciaran-boy. Famy off on course, but the fences are higher and the ditches are deeper and they've extended the track, the bastards. We held all the cards, he thought. Now we've none of them, and the silly bugger's gone on, and to his death, and he's taking you with him. His eyes were open, but he did not see the girl, just stared to the darkness of the ceiling. He wondered how he'd go, how death would close in on him. Had thought it might be in a ditch, or in the mess of a farm yard as the cordon tightened, or on the high wire of the Kesh, or being pulled by the legs from a sniper pit by a para. But never thought of it like this, not in a room eight by ten with rabbits and daffodils on the wall, and the smell of scent and a folded nightdress under his arse.

But even as the barometer of pain circled to hideous levels, so the preciousness of life remained hard to pass up. His eyes closed, clamped shut, his upper teeth hard down on the bottom lip, and he waved with the rifle barrel for her to come closer. He put the gun down beside the grenades and began to drag with his left hand at the jacket. She slid along the bed to him, and as he levered himself away from the wall she looped the jacket over his shoulders and down his arms. Once he cried out. When the jacket was off and he was free of it she dropped the garment on the fluffed, sky-blue rug. He rolled on his side, doubled up and panting for relief.

'Get some water, and something to clean it.' She barely heard the words. She was gone briefly, and came back into the room with a saucepan, the steam rising from it, and a wad of bright cotton wool. When she switched on the light he opened his eyes again, and then, with his help, she took off his shirt. With care she lifted his vest over his head. The blood had caked far down his chest – dark, dried rivulets leading to his navel. With the swabs she worked her path closer to the neat, circular wounds in the flesh. Not much time on the arm, priority to the shoulder. She felt the skin tighten, striving for escape as she neared the place of the second bullet's entry. Instinctively she pulled him forward so she could clean the expected exit wound in his back, and saw only the skin, unbroken and stretched across the tightened back muscles.

'It's still in there,' half a statement, half a question.

He nodded, and for the first time she saw him smile.

'It has to come out. It'll kill you.'

'All in good time,' said McCoy. 'The lad has a long way to travel. I want him far on his journey before the heavies find it's just wee Ciaran McCoy that's holding the baby.'

'What will they do, the police?'

'They'll huff and puff a few more hours, then they'll call for surrender, and we'll do nothing, then they'll have a bash at us . . . Switch the light off!' His voice was suddenly urgent, incisive. When the room was in darkness again she could listen. Close by, down the road, there was the roar of a heavy engine as if the driver was pumping his foot up and down on the accelerator. Across from the window muffled shouts. She eased the curtain back, giving herself visibility of the road immediately in front of the house.

'There's nothing moving there,' she said.

There was some brightness from a street light, augmented by the searchlight beam, and though his face was half in shadow she could make out the line of his features. 'Why is it necessary to do what you have done to my parents?'

He anticipated her. 'They stay tied, and they stay separate.'

'They couldn't do anything, they couldn't hurt you.'

'I said they stay like that . . .'

'You said the police would break in. How soon?'

'Not for a day or so. They'll want time to work out a plan. Take them half a week.' He reached forward with his left hand and took hold of her arm, then pulled her so that she stretched across the width of the bed, and his head sank into her lap where her thighs came together. He remembered the afternoon in the park. Not thirty hours before, yet half a lifetime. In the darkness his breathing slowed and he lay still. Had to rest, had to go back to Cullyhanna, had to climb the hills again.

'Why didn't you use anything yesterday?' she said.

'I don't know,' said McCoy. 'I don't know.'

17

Once the doctor had gone they left David Sokarev alone in his room.

The tablet he had taken, washed down with tap water from the tooth mug, had taken effect quickly, bringing on the drowsiness that conquered the terror of the earlier part of the evening. After the noise-filled, siren-blasting convoy had carried him to the hotel they had hurried him to his room, aided his undressing and readied him in his bed for the arrival of the Jewish doctor. Elkin had hovered close and maternal as the doctor bent over his patient, but Sokarev could see that his bodyguard's calm acceptance of the situation was waning, to be replaced by a morose silence. The lion had lost its mate. The two men had hunted together, worked, planned, eaten and rested together, bound in their opposites by comradeship. That was all destroyed now, by a pathetic and harmless-seeming grenade.

The assurance and confidence around the scientist when they had left for the university was another casualty of the attack, replaced with a diffidence that alternated with the fraying tempers. The Englishman should have been there, the one Sokarev remembered above all others, the one with only a given name and with the old suit. He was the one who had promised he would be beside Sokarev, who had made a joke of it all, who had laid his professionalism out for all to see in the very relaxation he had demonstrated since they had met. But he was absent, the one who was needed now. The man among all others in whom Sokarev had believed, in whom he had placed his trust. There had been a promise.

Sokarev felt a great helplessness, isolated and remote when he spoke from his bed, the neatly folded hotel blankets high up against his striped pyjamas and across his chest.

'Where is the Englishman, the one who called himself Jimmy?' It was an interruption and cut across the low-pitched conversations that were being pursued out of his earshot across the width of the room.

'He left in chase,' said Elkin. 'After Mackowicz was killed he ran for the door. He had been shooting, there is no word of him since then.'

'He said he would be with us. Continuously.'

'Well, he's not here. No sign of him. Running the streets, no doubt, trying to pull back something from the chaos. But something dramatic it has to be, after what has happened. The security was like a sieve. Disorganized, unprepared. A shambles they made for us.'

He came close to the bed, words barely under control, spitting his anger. 'You can understand, Professor, that from now it will be we who supervise all movements. There will be no more outsiders making decisions, no more delegation. The Englishman that you want beside you made a grand speech about "responsibility" to Mackowicz. Where is Mackowicz now? Where is the man who gave those orders?'

The Special Branch Inspector, already feeling the ice wall that divided him from the Israelis, made no comment. Irretrievable situation. No verbal points worth scoring, and short of currency anyway.

With the arrival of the Ambassador the men had withdrawn through the communicating door. The Ambassador, not attempting to disguise his fury, the security attaché, Elkin, two more men from the embassy that Sokarev had not seen before but who carried hand radio sets. They closed the door after them, and the English policeman, unwanted and ignored, made his way into the corridor outside. Last to go had been the doctor. Just a specimen to them, thought Sokarev. Like a box of bullion, to be displayed when necessary, shifted when convenient. Not to be consulted, not to be taken into confidence. In the last minutes before the pill took its action he heard the raised voices seeping through from the next room. Shouting, and Elkin's voice loud and demanding to be listened to, the security attaché attempting to act as intermediary and being driven into irrelevance by the deep, clear-cut words of the Ambassador.

The point at issue was simple enough: the movements of Sokarev. Elkin insisted on an immediate return to Tel Aviv. The Ambassador with his superior diplomatic rank but without the specific responsibility for Sokarev's safety, required clearance from Jerusalem before the visit to New York could be cancelled.

'It is impossible to justify the continuance of his journey,' shouted Elkin.

It is a way of life in the Israeli community that title and position count for little when the question of security is at stake. He could browbeat a senior diplomat in a way unthought of throughout Europe.

'If they can attack here they can attack in the United States. One of our men has died already that this one speech could be made. How many more do we lose protecting him if we go to America? And for what . . . ?'

'He goes for precisely the reason that he came here in the first instance. The threat was known, but we do not bow to threats . . .'

'He was a scientist, not a target dummy.'

'. . . The decision was made at cabinet level that he should come. We will not be cowed by these people.'

'Before that was a reasonable risk. Not now. They did well tonight, those bastards. That they missed was our luck. Not credit to us. Luck, and Mackowicz.'

'The decision must come from Jerusalem'. The Ambassador spoke with finality.

'The decision is easy, Excellency. Very simple, no doubt you can answer it for me. Which way is the Professor more important? A household name, famous, and dead; a martyr to the cause of the survival of our country. That is one option. Or more important in his office, in his anonymity, with his papers and his tables and his work. It is sad you cannot consult with Mackowicz, he would pick between the options.'

There was a purple, veined flush high on the Ambassador's cheeks. He turned to the door. 'As I have said, the decision must come from the Foreign Ministry. I will relay your comments, and they will have consideration.'

'And what of Sokarev? What of his ability to go on? Will that have consideration?'

But the Ambassador and the security attaché were gone. Elkin looked at the two new men who were to share the room with him, then twisted away lest they should see the tears that now lapped at his eyelids. Like a brother to him, Mackowicz. An elder brother, protective, dominating. And now without his stomach, intestines splayed to the winds. He crumpled himself full length on his bed.

227

That Sokarev was alive and breathing heavily a few feet away was an inadequate consolation.

The Ambassador, an experienced diplomat, was well versed in the art of self-preservation. His request to Jerusalem for guidance contained no suggestions of his own, and added with prominence the concern of Sokarev's remaining bodyguard. The coded reply he awaited, a jumble of numbers, arrived in the embassy communications room within two hours. After it had been deciphered it was brought to him.

XXCLL478219
FOREIGNMINISTRY JERUSALEM
0018208 PERSONAL FOREIGN MINISTER TO AMBASSADORUK ITEM HIS EYES ONLY ITEM AFTER URGENT CONSIDERATIONS SOKAREV'S MOVEMENTS EYE INFORMING SIMULTANEOUSLY AMBASSADORUSA TO ANNOUNCE CANCELLATION OF ABOVE'S TRAVEL AND SPEAKING ARRANGEMENTS IN NY AND OTHERS ITEM SOKAREV SHOULD RETURN ISRAEL FIRST AVAILABLE NONSTOP ELAL FLIGHT ITEM WE DEMAND FULLEST SECURITY DURING REMAINING HOURS SOKAREV'S PRESENCE UK PARTICULAR LONDON HEATHROW DEPARTURE ITEM YOU WILL ISSUE STRONGEST PROTEST TO UK GOVERNMENT AT LEVEL NOT BELOW FOREIGN MINISTER PREFERABLY PRIME MINISTER AT LAX UK SECURITY STRESSING FULL INFORMATION AND WARNING PROVIDED BY OUR SECURITY SERVICE PRIOR SOKAREV ARRIVAL ITEM WE REQUIRE PUBLIC EXPRESSION REGRET ITEM COMMUNICATION COMPLETE
XXDYY478219

Alone in the flat in Beersheba the scientist's wife heard over the Israeli Broadcasting Corporation's final radio news bulletin of the attack on her husband. The information came without warning, as the news media transmitted the story faster than those Government authorities responsible for her husband's welfare could react.

In desperation she tried to telephone first her son; on operational stand-by and not available to take messages. Next her daughters; both out of their student hostels and not expected back till later. The Director at Dimona, an old friend; away at a conference in Tiberias. The seemingly endless lingering of the disappointments as she waited four times for a familiar voice to come on the line, and on each occasion had her hopes dashed, took a heavy toll. She sat in David Sokarev's chair, beside the fire that would not be lit till the winter came and the cold over the desert and waited for the early morning light still five hours away. That she knew her man was safe was of some small help. What caused her to sob soundlessly into the half-darkness of the centre of the room was the knowledge of the deep fear and terror he would have suffered. So inoffensive, so mild, without enemies, without a voice that was ever raised in anger. Buried away in a cramped office, insulated against the hatred and hostility that lay rampant beyond the wire fences of Dimona. But would his work, and the implications of his study, provide him with an insight into this obscenity? She wondered. The preparation of the bomb itself, awful, grotesque, multi-destructive, would that have prepared him to confront the viciousness of the last hours? It was not his way to see the bomb as a finished and completed article of war. Just figures and notes on paper. Drawings that were meaningless to others. Long hours and days and months of work. Calculations and equations.

He would not have understood. He had been too long absent from the world of men who now fought round him to take and protect his life. He would be alone, defenceless. That was why she wept for him.

The Special Air Service squad were brought to Chisholm Road in two Black Maria police vans from an improvised helicopter landing pad on the football pitches beside the main road that ran out of Richmond to the south. They wore full-length black dungarees, were not encumbered with webbing and equipment and none boasted badges of rank on their upper arms or shoulders. They jumped casually and with ease from the open doors at the back of the vans, and then the heavy canvas bags were handed down.

Jimmy stood in the shadows and watched them. Not youngsters, but most of them still half his age, hair cut close, clean shaven, disinterested faces visible only when the lights rotating on the roofs of the fire engines illuminated the path across which they walked. The killing squad. Different to Jimmy, not self-taught as he had been. Trained and practised, funded by Government that their expertise should be developed. Selected with care and

229

toughened and primed. Taught not to act independently, but in the pack, deadly and irreversible when the leash was slipped. If they felt excitement they did not show it, just trooped after the one who was their leader across the road to where the Home Office man waited. Some squatted low over sheets of paper held flat on the pavement, others stood in a circle peering into the area lit by torches.

William Dawson was a thorough man. He took them through the diagram of the outside of the house, all windows and doors marked in red, first the ground floor, then the upper storey. The squad said nothing, two taking notes, the others watching and silent. Then came the plans of the interior of the end of terrace home. Drawn to scale. Red marking the doorways again, and blue crosses on those that the neighbours had reported to be fitted with locks and bolts. Fingers ran along the routes of the hallway, the stairs and the landing. Occasionally those at the back would crane their necks up the street to relate the floodlit frontage with the paperwork. Jimmy stood half a dozen paces back from the huddle; Jones was far behind him at the steps of the police control vehicle.

Dawson was talking, fast and coherent, sketching the plan he had described to the Prime Minister. Diversions, and time factors, and entry points, and opposition capability, and of the laser. There were precedents, and case histories and suggestions. The attention that the squad gave the Civil Servant was the accolade that he had done his work, was as expert in the planning as they would be in the execution.

When the group broke up it was to appointed tasks. Four to unload the firepower they had brought with them, to lay the weapons out and to load them. Four more to begin a scrounging expedition among the fire brigades, for ropes and axes and the fifteen-foot ladders that would carry them to the first-floor windows. The officer and his sergeant detached themselves, and in the company of a ranking police officer made their way past the front doors of the houses, traversing the front gardens, working closer to the house that they would storm. When they had seen the front they moved, silent and catlike, through another house and across its back garden till they came without warning on the police who watched the rear of Number 25. From the outside there was little to tell them of the situation beyond the brick walls. All curtains drawn, windows darkened.

'They had the light on a bit ago. In the front, upstairs, the small room where the girl sleeps. It was off within a minute. The men across the road from the front think the curtain there moved once, but it's bloody difficult to be sure. It was when we first started the noise business that the Home Office chap wanted. The second time we did it nothing happened, not that we saw. There's been three more times we've used the noise since then, and nothing. No movement that we've seen.'

The Chief Inspector was depressed. That this was not police work he acknowledged, was grateful he was not asking among his men for volunteers for an attack party, but the very competence and hardness of the new arrivals had shaken and concerned him.

'What chance have you got of getting those people out alive?' That was the nub of the problem as he saw it, and he raised the question as they slipped back toward the concentration of vehicles and men.

'Can't say,' replied the officer quietly, as if their voices would carry. 'Depends where the family are, whether they're together. What state the wounded fellow is in. How much speed we can muster. If we're fast enough there's a good chance. The theory is that it's difficult for a man to turn his gun on his hostages as we're coming through the door. He has no protection. He goes with them. There's not many relish that – that's what the handbook says, at any rate. But it's all theory. There's nothing cut and dried.'

Before they reached the fire engine closest to the house, and where men in uniform had gathered, and where there would be ears to listen to their conversation, the officer said, 'Don't misunderstand me, but isn't there some question about priorities? The hostages aren't at the top of the list as I see it. If they were we'd be talking, negotiating. Spinning it out. I have the priority as the two blokes. If we get the family out that's a bonus. Hitting those two buggers in there is what we're here for.'

Jimmy's eyes had seldom left the house. Its very ordinariness fascinated him. Uninteresting, unremarkable, undistinguished. Forty-nine others like it in the road. An inhabited box. Lived in by people who were as stereotype produced as the bricks and mortar they surrounded themselves with. And their visitors, they also were from the depths of mediocrity, without identity – totally irrelevant without the guns and the grenades. The only thing of significance about them were their rifles and the explosives. But that to Jimmy was muscle, that was the core of terrorism. It was this power that lifted the nonentity on to the pedestal he sought. Jimmy had heard that in a lecture in the Department, had listened – which was rare – and agreed. Behind him was the Home Secretary, arms either akimbo or flattened against his backside as he looked solemnly at the tarmac and heard out the Assistant Commissioner. Only one reason he's here, thought Jimmy, the hardware. Doesn't matter how screwed up are the little bastards with their hands on it, the hardware brings the big men out. To all of them standing round the house with their guns and their dogs and their truncheons McCoy and the Arab were just pictures, two-dimensional, black and white. Not to Jimmy. Jimmy had seen them, seen the character of their faces, the shape of their mouths, the slouch of their movements. And Jimmy had tried to kill them that evening, counted himself unlucky that he hadn't. It tied them together, Jimmy and McCoy and the Arab, in a perverse but brutal liaison. And they had seen him, twenty yards away, and there had been the rifle fire and the thrown grenade. So they knew each other, understood the stake money. When he looked away from the house Jimmy could see the SAS men making their preparations. But these were outsiders, not a part of it till little more than an hour earlier when their helicopter had lifted off from the far west.

Jimmy walked across the road to where the army officer stood, concentrating on his note-book. He tapped the other man's shoulder and pushed forward his identity card. The officer glanced at it, and acknowledged him by diverting his gaze to Jimmy's eyes. He's impatient, the bastard.

'Jimmy's the name. From the Security Services.'

'George Martin, Captain.'

'I've been on this one. Full time. Since the flap started. I'd like to go along with you.'

There was a faint smile at the extremes of Martin's mouth. Not quite as tall as Jimmy, looking up at him. Unsettling, unhelpful, difficult to communicate. Jimmy went on, 'I'd like to go into the house with you. I know what they both look like, could be of use to you.'

The smile broadened. 'Sorry, father, no passengers this time round. If you want to come and identify them after there'll be no problem.'

232

'Don't give me the father crap . . .'

'And don't get in my way. We've work, and no time . . .'

'Listen,' said Jimmy, face close to the soldier's. 'I'm in the protection team. Right beside Sokarev, the Israeli, this evening, appointed to guard him.'

'You're a touch off course then. Nobody told us he'd joined the party in there. I'd have thought your best place was at the hotel holding your baby's hand. Must be looking for a bit of a lullaby after the hoop you put him through tonight.'

Your cool's going Jimmy. Double fast, like it always does with these uptight swine. 'If it hadn't been for me he'd be in the morgue now. And when you get in there you'll find one of the bastards half-dead with my bullet in him . . .'

'Come to the wrong chap then. It's the Birthday Honours you're looking for. I don't hand medals out. Right now I'm busy, got my hands full, and no one goes in alongside my team. Understood?'

'You stupid bastard,' said Jimmy.

The captain smiled again, almost a laugh, and walked away.

It took Jimmy some minutes to find Jones. He was in a group among men of equal status, discussing the problems that confronted them. How to introduce before the scheduled dawn attack the fish-eye visual surveillance lens that would arrive in a few hours from London, the merits of the various audio-electronic devices that were available, the question of news releases. Jones was rarely in such company, unfamiliar with the bright excitement his companions felt at whiling their evening away waiting for whatever disaster or success the morning might bring. He felt his years shackled to the desk had cheated him of something he vaguely saw as precious. Too much time on paperwork, while the knowledge of the techniques that dominated the world of his new companions was denied him. That he was accepted among them pleased him, but he recognized it was not because of his contribution but through his rank and title. And then Jimmy was at his side, pulling at his coat, just as he was in mid-sentence, and drawing him away. Jones saw the warning signs, noticed the blink in Jimmy's left upper eyelid, knew it from years back. And Jimmy launched off: 'Bloody army, bloody pigs. I've been

233

with this one right the way through, did you well tonight, bloody well, and now I want to go in there and finish the bloody thing, and that little prig, the bloody army man, treats me like I'm out for some bloody Cook's Tour. All patronizing and "Come in when we've finished" and that crap.'

'What do you want to go in for, Jimmy?' said Jones.

'To finish the bloody thing, finish what started this evening.'

'Be in at the killing, right? That's what you want?'

'Right first time. I bloody started and . . .'

'It's not a quota job, Jimmy-boy. You don't need notches on your pension book. What's the matter, short this year on your numbers? You're not a policeman. You haven't got to get twenty traffic bookings a month to hold down a reputation.'

'You mean you're not going to tell them to count me in?' There was doubt in his voice. Jones had always backed him in the past. Why different now?

'Of course I'm not. What do you expect me to say? I've got a man on my books who's a bit short of stiffs this month. Comes out in a rash if he doesn't nab a couple each thirty days. Snap out of it, Jimmy. You've had your scene tonight, done well. You should be off home, and in your pit by now and sleeping so you're not a zombie tomorrow when God knows what happens.'

'Straight bloody heave, then?'

'If you see it that way, Jimmy, that's your problem. But do us all a favour and shove off back to town so you're not knackered in the morning.'

'I thought there'd be some bloody clout from you,' Jimmy was shouting, his words carrying across the still of the night, loud enough for those who could not avoid hearing to shuffle their feet and cough.

Jimmy swung on his heel and walked through the rope cordon, side-stepped the newspaper and television photographers, past the sightseers who would wait till there was any action of any sort at whatever advanced hour. He walked down the hill toward the town. There would be a taxi rank there and then there would be the hotel close to the flat where the night porter would fix him up with a half bottle. As he went he wondered about the life and times inside Number 25. He thought of McCoy with the hole in him, and of the Arab. Pictured the faces as he'd seen them in the glare of his headlights the moment before he'd fired. Wondered

234

how they'd cope when the military came in. Wanted to be there, missing his bloody treat, and God he'd deserved the party. The tin that he kicked in his frustration careered clumsily and raucously down the road in front of him.

She knew that if she moved McCoy would wake. It was awkward, half-propped on one arm, and lying across the narrow width of the bed, with the weight of his shoulders and his head flattened against her stomach. His sleep was light, punctuated by convulsions when he twisted his body over from right to left, felt the pain, and swung back on to the undamaged arm. The wound through the upper chest was near to her head and it oozed strange and unknown fluids that showed in the half-light as opaque dribblings. Sometimes she turned her eyes away from the hole and its debris, but then her imagination took over and besieged her more fearfully than the reality. Nightmarishly she could see the stunted column of lead striking the softness of the skin, could feel the splitting and carving of the tissues and wonder at the sensation of the fragments making their uninterrupted passage in the void beneath the flesh. And he had said it would all happen again. Had told her that they would come. Policemen with rifles, more bullets, bursting through the door, kicking their way across the tiny floor-space, brushing aside the whitewood and wicker chair on which she had laid his stained jacket and shirt and undervest. And what would he do when they came? His rifle was half under his legs, still held close to the trigger guard by the left hand. So small, and beside its shallow length the grenades, miniaturized. They didn't have the scale and size for her to believe in them as killing weapons. Too sparse, too insignificant. But when they came, when the police came, he would try to fire, try to pull the absurd circular pin on the grenade. And they would shoot. They would be quicker, organized, without pity. Then there would be the profusion of holes, beating formations in his chest, slicing through the rib cage that showed clear as he lay in his sleep. When they came it would be to kill, not to capture. Norah knew that.

Even had she not been so tired she could not have analysed her feelings for Ciaran McCoy. 'Love' was the magazine word, written in stories with windswept hills and boys who were dark

235

and tidy, and girls with wasp waists and unbuttoned blouses and long hair. Infatuation she understood, read of it in the agony columns, real enough, able to match it with her own emotions; the boy last year who worked under Father at the factory. Temporary and heartrending, nice to cry over. But McCoy, this was something unique for her and surpassing her understanding. She could not envisage herself in love with a man capable of such horror as the strangulation of the policewoman whose picture the television had shown, not in love with the man of the hateful, animal-wild eyes imprinted in her mind from the newspaper picture. Yet she had lain with him in the grass of the park, and taken him in her arms, and pressed his head against her breasts, and said his name, and felt the warmth and the pain of him deep between her legs. And he was to die. Snuffed out. Shot dead by the guns of men in uniform.

Norah reached down to the floor, to the square of carpet that covered the centre of the room inside the vinyl surround, and felt under her bed for her shoes, careful not to disturb his sleep. All her shoes were under the bed; the room was too small to provide the adequate cupboard space she required. Two pairs were there, her evening going-out ones, and the flats for work in the supermarket. Further under were the back numbers of the magazines that came on Thursday mornings and that caused her to linger in bed and be late for breakfast and run for the bus. She straightened, gently and slowly, taking time till she could ease out the pillow that had nestled in the small of her back. Together they were sufficient. First the magazines, then the shoes, then the pillow. With one hand she steadied his sleeping head while she wormed as far back toward the wall as her body had room to move, and then there was the space for her to build the counterfeit lap. The height was the same, and when she eased his head on to the softness of the pillow his eyes stayed tight shut, and there was only the forced and erratic breathing.

She was not betraying him, she told herself, only offering him salvation. This way he would survive. Go out of her life, that was inevitable, but survive. On her window-sill were the keys to the outside doors he had brought upstairs with him. It was easy for her to select the one that opened the front door.

Past three she saw on her watch when she stepped out on to the landing of the house and went barefoot, and on her toes, without

236

sound toward the staircase. At the head of the stairs she stopped to listen to the night noises of the house. McCoy's breathing, audible, painful. Fainter movements from the rooms where her parents lay.

Pray God he doesn't wake, she said to herself, and eased on to the first step.

Famy had gone over the wall and into the park. Once inside he ran till his legs would carry him no further. Fast, hard and direct toward the south-west, sprinting so that many times he had plunged without warning into bushes, stumbled in the grassed-over drains. His hands were cut, and there were tears round the knees of his trousers. The rifle made it difficult, clutched as a talisman, with only one hand free to protect him when he pitched forward. But McCoy had made the sacrifice. McCoy had stayed behind to win him the distance he now sought to put between himself and the pursuit. No idea how many hours start he would have, whether the hunt had in fact already begun, whether it would come at dawn or not for a full day. But the Irishman had sacrificed himself, probably given his life to gain him the ground he now swept over. It clinched his motivation, and when his legs sagged under him he rested only for the muscles to tighten, the control to be regained, before starting once more.

When the brickwork of the park wall swung away from the direction he sought, exhausting its usefulness, he looked for escape in the streets and roads outside. It took great effort for him to force his way up on to the summit of its height, and he toppled rather than jumped on to the ground on the far side. Soon he was out of the cover of the trees and under street lights, passed by late traffic, and running by houses where lights still shone and from which came the flicker, blue-grey on the wall-papers, of television sets. When he came to the river he walked along the bank, anxious lest he should miss the bridge marked on his pocket-book map. But when he had found it he quickened his step. There would be no more such barriers for him now, the map showed that, just a network of streets and roads and gardens stretching across his path, separating him from the great open space of flattened concrete that was the airport and from which David Sokarev would fly.

237

He knew his way, was unerring in tracking his route. Every ninety-five seconds a jet-powered passenger air liner roared above him on its descent to the tarmac, red and green belly lights flashing the message to the Arab far beneath that he was on his course.

18

It was the policeman crouched in the shadows of the doorway directly opposite Number 25 who first heard the faint sound of the bolt being withdrawn behind the door across the road. He stiffened into an aim position, his FN rifle at his shoulder, barrel pointed across at the floodlit porch, and talking all the time into the radio clipped to his tunic. Within seconds of his first message he could hear the scraping of activity around him, others alerted, more marksmen preparing themselves. The superintendent's voice was relayed to him over the miniature loudspeaker set into the same instrument. Disembodied and unreal came the instruction, 'If the men come out, shoot. Only if their hands are up and they are obviously not armed do you hold your fire. If they have hostages with them, shoot. Under no circumstances are they to reach the darkness, either of them.'

All right for him to say that, the policeman thought, all right if you're down in the control vehicle. The door edged open, two inches at first, time for the constable to ease off the safety clip on the right side of the rifle, an inch or so above the magazine. He was sweating, could feel the moisture on his hands. He'd only ever fired in practice, and the last time eight months before. Then the door swung fully back on its hinges, but the light from the beam down the road came at such an acute angle that the hallway was only a black rectangle of darkness. He strained without success to see into it. They'll come in a rush, he told himself, all together, the parents and the girl in front, the men behind. And his orders were to shoot. God help us all, he thought, lips bitten tightly, hands shaking, causing the sight on the end of the barrel to waver in gentle helpless meanders. In normal times he drove a squad car; a marksman's role was something he had never taken on before. Only his eyesight, that was superb, qualified him for the shooting position he occupied twenty short paces from the doorway.

His finger tightened round the trigger, and then he saw the girl come from the shadow and hesitate on the step. There was a surge of relief through him. At least the bastards were not right behind her. It would give him a chance to miss her, perhaps hit them. Very quietly, little more than an aside, he broadcast her progress along the four yards of paved path to the front wicket gate. Here again she stopped, and the fifteen rifles that had covered her as she walked forward traversed their aim back to the dark recess of the doorway.

A hundred yards away and watching now through binoculars the superintendent called into his microphone, 'Tell her to get into the middle of the road, and keep the bloody door covered.'

The constable stretched up, straightening his legs against the stiffness that had long crippled his knee joints. The girl wouldn't have seen him yet, wouldn't have seen any of them, would be bewildered by the silence and the emptiness of the street.

'Keep walking,' he said, more staccato than he would have wanted. Nerves, he put it down to. 'Come out into the street, hands high. Out in the middle.'

Still the girl seemed unaware of his presence, simply obeyed the commands. She came to the centre of the road, and the constable could see the glazed eyes, could see the bloodstains, too, on the white of her blouse, the scattered hair strands, and the uncertain steps. Like a sleepwalker, he thought, like someone learning to walk again in a hospital. 'Walk down the road, and slowly. There's a rope across it about a hundred yards down. They'll meet you there. And don't run.' The girl veered to her right, and began to walk, and the policeman's concentration returned to the open doorway, rifle grip marginally relaxed, waiting.

When she reached the rope a host of hands greeted her. Under her shoulders lest she should faint, hands of comfort around her back. She felt weakness till two detectives frisked her, and she was alive again, backing away from the fingers that ran down her body, circling her waist, on the inside and outside of her legs. 'Just formality,' said the voice behind her, but close and reassuring, and then there was one arm around her, strong, protective. She made no effort to stem the flow of tears that wracked

239

her as they led her to the control van. They helped her up the steps, and the superintendent muttered to his men, 'Keep it very gentle. When she starts to talk I want it coming easily. Rush it now and we'll screw it for all time.' He was old enough in the business of interrogation to know that hasty, capsulated and impatient questioning could cause the girl to freeze, make the progress endlessly slow and confusing.

They gave her a chair, and the superintendent said, 'It's Norah, isn't it?'

She nodded, blank agreement.

'Tell us what's happening, Norah, in your own words.'

She smeared her arm across the upper face, diverting the tears, snuffled, and started to talk. Her voice was very low and the policemen and the SAS captain who had crowded into the van had to stretch forward to hear.

'He said you'd attack, and when you came in you'd be shooting. You'll kill, I know you'll kill him. You'll murder him in there.' The faces of her listeners were impassive, showing no reaction. 'I couldn't see him die, not like that. He's hurt, there's a terrible wound, blood . . . and he got me to clean it. He's sleeping now, he was when I left him . . . I made a pile for his head so that he wouldn't know I'd gone. He needs help, needs a hospital. I thought if I let you in you'd take him alive, you wouldn't shoot him.'

Behind her a detective whispered, half to himself but not subdued, 'Little cow. Little bitch.' She seemed not to hear.

'The door's open. He's up the stairs, in the small room at the front. It's my room. He's on the bed there. Asleep. He doesn't know I've come. He'd kill me . . .' The tears came again and her head sank forward on the smallness of her chest.

The army captain leaned close, one question to ask, 'What sort of guns does he have? Where are they?'

'There's a rifle, a little one. It's in his hand, and there are some grenade things. They're beside the rifle, that's all he has.'

'Norah, listen, because this is very important if we are to help this man' – the superintendent spoke softly, paternal, a voice to be trusted – 'you have to tell us where in the house is the other man. The one on your bed is the Irishman, where is the other one, the Arab?'

She looked into the face that was very near to her tired and haggard eyes, stubble beginning to show, white collar fringed with

240

grime. So he knew what he was up to, the man McCoy. She wanted to scream with laughter. It was as he'd said it would be. Buying time for his friend, and how much purchased? How many hours? Four, five perhaps? And they didn't know. Tricked by a man with one good arm and half his chest shot out. All these coppers, and McCoy had done them. But there was no hysteria, too exhausted for that. Only a slow smile that rimmed the bottom of the young fresh cheeks, almost of sympathy.

'He's been gone a long time,' she said. 'He went right at the start. Just ran through the house. There's only Ciaran . . .'

'Bloody hell,' said the superintendent, kindness evaporating from his mouth.

'We'll go and get the bastard.' The captain said it over his shoulder, already half out of the van.

The superintendent sat back in his chair. 'And you haven't come to tell us this to save your father and mother, haven't mentioned them. Nor to help the troops who were going to break in, less than an hour from now, and risk their bloody lives. Not on your list, right? Only thing that matters is that Ciaran gets his bloody treatment. Straight in on the National Health. Makes you want to puke.'

She was satisfied with herself now. They saw the defiance come to her, chin jutting out.

'So where's the Arab?' Different tone, harsher, games completed.

'He didn't say. Just ran through the house. Went through the back. Hours ago.' The last spat out with relish.

'Where to, for Christ's sake?'

'I said, he didn't say. Ciaran said the whole thing was to win him time.'

'And how long have you known him, this McCoy?'

'Two weeks.'

'And you knew what he'd done?'

'I knew.' And she smiled again. Pretty smile, the superintendent thought, pretty face. Just as stupid as they all are when they meet their McCoys. Screwed her, and screwed her life. Par for the course. He climbed out of the van to begin formulating his plans for the manhunt that would not get operational till first light, still more than ninety minutes away.

*

The split board that Norah's father had so long meant to repair betrayed to Ciaran McCoy the approach up the stairs of the SAS sergeant. The creaking whine when the soldier eased his weight on to the divided wood broke through the thin sleep, causing him to sit up sharply, a reflex before the agony jolted him down. He was aware of the rifle immediately, nestling in his hand and pressed to his thigh, but when he motioned his shoulders seeking the shape and familiarity of the girl he realized she had gone. He took his hand from the butt of the rifle and felt the pillow and the shoes and the magazines. Confirmation if he had needed it. There was a whisper from the stairs, a hiss for quiet, then the drumming of feet, the moment of assault. For a fraction of time he had the capability to make the decision that would determine whether he raised his gun and armed the grenades, or whether he submitted . . . but his mind was incapable of clear thought, and his instinctive reactions too dulled. When the sergeant came through the door, finger poised on the trigger of the Stirling sub-machine-gun, McCoy lay where he had slept, gun barrel prone on the bedspread and offering no threat. That he lived through those three seconds as the SAS man acclimatized himself to the light of the room was dependent on the soldier's training and expertise, and his knowledge of when it was necessary to shoot, when not. He assimilated the atmosphere of the room, saw the crumpled figure, the barrel that pointed nowhere, the hand removed from the immediate proximity of the grenades. And then there were others crowding into the bedroom, three, four and five more, standing high over McCoy. The light was switched on. One pulled the gun from his hand, removed the bullet from the breach, scooped up the grenades. They ran their hands over McCoy's trousers, checking him for more weapons and lifted him without violence from the bed-clothes before ripping back the pale blue sheets. When they laid him down again it was on the hard coiled springs of the bed.

Ciaran watched them as they worked quickly and with thoroughness round the room, no words spoken, acknowledgement that each knew what was expected of him. End of the road, Ciaran boy, but not the end his imagination had ever entertained when he played his war games. He'd thought they'd shoot. Flattering himself. Couldn't take the great Ciaran alive, without a whimper, without the mighty bang out. Too big just to finish up this way. Deceived himself. Unimportant, though, and he didn't care. Get

242

so tired, such exhaustion, that you don't give a damn what happens. Glad in a way that it's over. Which ever way, with the living or the dead, unimportant, just the relief that it's completed. And the Arab had had his start, had his opportunity. And he must go through it all again, the poor bastard. And on his own. And you're out of it, Ciaran boy, clear and finished and safe.

The captain bent over him.

'Get the doctor up here.' He said it without emotion, matter of fact. 'Pity the bloody thing wasn't six inches across. Would have saved us all a load of trouble.'

Through the door McCoy could hear the voices of Norah's parents, frightened, gabbled and seeking the reassurance of the soldiers. There were feet on the staircase, a diffusion of voices, orders being given, and then the arrival of the doctor.

'Make a habit of this caper?' The doctor had his hand on McCoy's pulse, but his eyes, puckered with the distress of an old man, wandered from the wounds to the already healed scar in McCoy's side.

'I don't mind shifting him,' said the superintendent. 'But I don't want him under anaesthetic yet. He's some talking to do before we get that far. We'll chat him in the ambulance and when they're cleaning him up.'

The father and mother were still on the landing when they carried McCoy, bound to the stretcher, past them. They looked at him as if staring at a rodent, vermin. Hate-consumed, but schooled by fear. The progress down the narrow stairs was difficult and slow, and before they were half-way, and manoeuvring on the bend McCoy heard Norah's mother, plaintive and appealing.

'Where's our girl? What's happened to our Norah? What did he do to her?'

You'll find out soon enough, thought the Irishman. It amused him, and without the pain he would have laughed. You'll find out and wish you'd never asked, and if they tell you you'll wish they hadn't. Always the same. Always the girls in tow, attracted like dogs to a bitch's fanny, flies in a jam pot. And always they cock it up. You're not the first, Ciaran. Just like the big boyo in Belfast. Took his bird along when they holed up in the big posh house, in the posh road and she still went in her slippers and curlers to fetch the morning milk from the corner shop. Rest of

243

the road had it delivered. Gave it away a mile off, once the copper on car patrol spotted her. Got him nicked.

He was still wondering why the girl had betrayed him when the stretcher party carried him out on to the street.

There were television arc lights there. They'd allowed the cameramen up from the corral at the bottom of the hill. Give 'em a show, McCoy. Give 'em a picture. Don't let the bastards see you down. The spot lights were aimed at his face and blanched the skin on his bared chest, accentuating the whiteness that surrounded the bullet hole with its sparse patch of covering lint.

He shouted, 'Up the Provos,' and the policeman holding the stretcher handles behind his head jolted them hard, sending the rivers of pain flowing fast and deep. Bastards. And all up to the bloody Arab to wipe the victory smile off their faces. The bloody Arab and his Mushroom Man.

Before they lifted him into the ambulance McCoy had lost consciousness.

The cures he'd been on, the expensive, the unpleasant and the not-so-cosseted varieties, had never lasted for Jimmy. The craving and desire for excess of alcohol, a dose sufficient to immunize him against pressure and anxiety, remained, lingering and nagging in his life. They'd tried most of the accepted methods to wean him away. The health farm in Hampshire had cost the most, and lasted the least time when he was back in the outside world. The withdrawal programme practised at the clinic behind Brixton Station had been the most ferocious, the most scarring and the longest running. But each broke down at the stage when Jimmy went back to his breadwinning and the sepia world of his activities demanded some softening. He was now a low-capability drinker, a short-capacity man. When rational he could recognize the problem, when angry and disappointed he turned away from the consequences.

The flat had been empty when he returned. Helen was not there, gone to her own place. Could hardly blame her, didn't know what time he might have shown up, or in what state of tiredness. Bed hadn't been made from the previous sleeping. Washing up not done, never was, tea leaves settled in an eddy round the plug hole of the sink. Clothes not picked up. If she'd come back she would have done the tidying ritual. But at least he wouldn't have to tell her about the car. Insurance?... Didn't know, be some difficult talking. She'd hate him for it. Couldn't blame her. Pride and joy ... and up in smoke.

He unscrewed the top of the bottle, cheap brand. Filthy expensive by the time he'd paid the porter his chip, lose it all on expenses. They looked at them hard in the Department, but he could lose that, hadn't eaten all day, funnel it through there. Straight, no water. Tap water would be warm, and he hadn't filled the ice cube box in the fridge. About an inch to start with, four gulps, needed forcing down, coiled up his guts, blazed a trail through them. Sagged in the chair, the easy one, springs still kept in check by the upholstery, feet just reaching the table, laces at eye-level, loosened his collar. Coughed a couple of times then corkscrewed his body forward to reach the bottle and the first refill. So tired, seemed to have been moving for ever. No thoughts, just wanting to shut it all out. Jones pulling his bloody rank, the SAS captain, and those bastards in the house. Should have been your day, Jimmy, and yet you're sent home early, and told to work a bloody shift pattern.

At first the telephone was an accompaniment to his thoughts. It took time for it to communicate urgency, and even more for it to instil the submission required for him to give up the comfort he had established for himself and hobble across the room to the table beside his bed. He deliberated whether to answer, but discipline won through. He picked up the receiver and gave out the number, had it right, too, which surprised him.

'It's Jones here, Jimmy. It's all over down at this end.'

'Congratulations.' Jimmy had difficulties, the word was slow coming.

'It's not like that, Jimmy. We have McCoy, but the Arab's gone. He's loose.'

'Not so bright then. Which clever bastard let him slip?'

'He went when you were there, Jimmy, so cut the quips, before the cordon ...'

'I was on my bloody own, wasn't I? Can't be round the whole house. He didn't come through the front.' All the same, bloody buckpassers brigade.

'Don't come the maudlin, Jimmy. No one's criticizing you. It's a statement of fact. He's loose with a minimum of five hours' start. I want you at the West Middlesex, and now. Not hanging about, but down there now. They're patching McCoy up, and

245

we're keeping the surgeons off him till we've had a preliminary. After that he goes under, has his surgery, and they dig your bullet out of him.'

'Leave the bloody thing there.'

'Don't screw me about, Jimmy. We have to know what the Arab is at. McCoy has to tell us.'

'You've got others who can go and do it.' Why wouldn't the bloody man get off the line and leave him to the bottle and the chair? Why Jimmy, why not one of the young ones who fancied their hand at interrogation? Budding Skardons all of them, looking for another Klaus Fuchs to break, looking for a reputation.

'Jimmy, stop waffling, stop boozing, and get off your arse. The Yard's down there. I'm on my way. I've sent a car for you, be at your door in about ten minutes. Put your head under the tap and be there. I want you to talk to McCoy, that's all.'

Even with the drink Jimmy knew why he had been called. Just like Jones, the way his mind worked. Who'd be on the same wavelength as this Irish bastard, who'd be able to frighten him, or win him, or batter it out of him? Not a copper, not one of the bright lads transferred from Intelligence Corps, not old Jonesey himself. Another thug, that's what he wanted, and put them together. Two rats, both hungry, in the same hole. Two cockroaches disputing the one patch.

Jimmy sat up, breaking his cat-nap as the car drove through the wide gateway and into the hospital forecourt. Sleep when you can, basic rule, fit it in with the opportunity, always the same when the other lot dictate the time-table, hold the initiative. Time now to regret the whisky, hadn't been much left in the bottle, motion of the car didn't help. Head spinning, uncontrollable circles. The half-light was beginning to simper through and the nineteenth-century blocks were heavily outlined against the coming dawn. Blue and white signs pointed in every direction. CASUALTY. MATERNITY. X-RAY, OUTPATIENTS. Ward names, recalling local dignataries and benefactors. He saw the police van and the group of uniformed men outside casualty, and the car pulled up there. Jones was waiting for him. He saw Jimmy's appearance and winced, distaste on his face.

'We don't have long. The surgeons are impatient. Want to get

246

their hands on him. Police haven't had anything out of him. Laughs at them. He's weak, but should survive. Reckons he's the cat's whiskers – probably the morphine.' Jones led the way through the corridors beyond 'Casualty', past the red-eyed junior doctors and nurses who whiled the night away waiting for the road accidents and the self-damaged drunks. By the staircase there were plain-clothes men, cigarettes cupped in their hands, the whole place deathly quiet and accentuating their echoing steps. They went up the stairs on to the first floor and toward the ward entrance to their right.

Jones said, 'Fifteen minutes maximum. You and me, I'll take the notes. Just get the bastard talking.' He showed his I/D card to the two policemen outside the door short of the main communal ward area, and went into the private room. It was barely big enough for a bed, a table and an upright chair. They'd worked a small chest in there as well, and the two men had to ease their way round the obstacles to get to the bedside. There was a nurse sitting at McCoy's feet, short and West Indian, her feet dangling above the floor, waiting the requisite time before removing the thermometer that stuck out like a battleship's gun from the Irishman's mouth. The two men said nothing, allowed her to examine the thin glass tube, write down the results of her study on her clip board, and go when she was ready. She moved past them, avoiding their eyes, and went out into the corridor. The detective who had been sitting in the room followed her. Jimmy took the nurse's place on the bed, Jones the vacated chair.

Picking at his nose, Jimmy said, 'My name's Jimmy. I'm here till we've finished with you. After that you'll get the surgeon. But not until we've chatted. Doesn't matter to us whether it's ten minutes, ten hours, ten days . . .'

'That's not what the doctor . . .' McCoy spoke with a faintness, whispering.

'Fuck the doctor, McCoy. The medics come back through that door when we say so.'

'They said – '

'Well, they got it wrong. Don't you follow in their tracks. We've all the time in the world. You haven't. You're short of an exit wound, right?'

McCoy turned his head toward Jimmy, managed to lift himself fractionally so that he could see into the eyes, grey-blue and pitiless, rimmed with red. There was a man like that in Armagh

247

City, came to do the executions, seemed to matter less to him than culling a pig on market Thursdays.

'I know about that bullet. I fired it. Not a good shot, should have killed you. Was ahead of you all yesterday. Fired first at the meeting when your gun was still waving about, followed you out, trailed you all the way. Then you gave me a good clear shot while you stood on the pavement, couple of bloody gooks. Pathetic stuff, McCoy, and you supposed to be an expert. Short of men on your side of the water, are they?'

Good stuff, Jimmy-boy, thought Jones. Nothing to write down yet on the pad, but setting him up well. Kicking the boy's vanity, needling him and hard.

McCoy could remember, though his concentration surged and ebbed, the time the army had lifted him years before. There had been a roughness, but a certain set of rules about it all. Pinioned him not gently, but they'd never given him the fear that they'd kill him. This man was different. Not a soldier, not a policeman ... different. An enemy.

'Wasn't me on the gun.'

' 'Course it wasn't you on the gun. That was the sharp end, wasn't it? Didn't expect you'd be there, didn't expect you'd be standing by the window when we all started blasting. Left the man's bit to the kiddie, did you?'

'Famy wanted to shoot, that's what he came for.'

Jones's pencil started to move, first words on the virgin paper. A name at last to put to the face. Not really important, but tidier. Made it all neater when you had a caption for the picture. And all those hours they'd put in just to get the name, and now they had it it was irrelevant – not worth a damn alongside the usefulness of having the face. Jimmy would have registered it, too: it would have given him the kick he needed to get on top. Be no stopping him now.

'He's worse than you, and that's fucking useless.' Jimmy's voice was quiet, casual. As if the conversation were about the visiting centre-forward between strangers on the terraces. McCoy could follow the technique, was aware of it, but too tired, too hurt, too drugged to combat his adversary.

'He's not finished, the boy.'

'Only because he's running. Running with the mess in his pants, and the bog paper in his hand.'

'He'll bloody show you, you Britisher pig.' Out in the corridor where nurses and doctors waited, gathered beside the police guard, they heard the Irishman struggling to shout. They looked at their watches, noting how much longer the questioning could continue.

'He'll show us how fast he can run.'

'He's not finished. What do you think I stayed behind for? Why hole up, if not to give him time? I wasn't there just so he could scarper. He's set to blast you, you and the Yiddisher.'

Jimmy laughed, exaggerated, loud, ridicule. 'He'll never see him.'

'He'll see him and he'll get him.'

'What do you think we're going to do, you pig-thick ape? Parade him up Whitehall? Stick him in a coconut shy? You had your chance, and you buggered it.'

'You can't keep him close all the time. He'll have to put his feet on the ground . . .'

'There's only one place.'

'Right,' hissed McCoy. Jimmy could see him quivering, chest shaking, breath panted in the emotion of the dispute.

'The airport. Up the steps the little man goes and your hero makes his last stand,' Jimmy gabbled the words out, maintaining the momentum. McCoy was with him.

'Right, right first bloody time.'

Jimmy said nothing. Sudden, total silence. The noise still-born, the voices aborted. McCoy's eyes closed tight shut. The enormity of what he'd said, slow in dawning then overwhelming. Betrayed him. Ciaran McCoy, volunteer and officer of the Irish Republican Army, had betrayed him.

'Holy Mother of Jesus, forgive me.' His lips barely moved with the formation of the words that Jimmy did not hear.

Jimmy stretched off the bed and walked towards the door, Jones a pace behind. He said, distant, matter of fact, 'The surgeon only gave us fifteen minutes. We reckoned that would be enough. And we were right, Ciaran, we've four and a half to spare. So it's over to his tender hands now. Hope the bloody knife's blunt.'

McCoy did not see him go. In his life he had never known such abject misery.

The diversion along the park wall and then the search for the bridge crossing of the Thames had cost Famy a considerable detour, switching his journey from six miles to nearly nine. The pale shiver of light was spreading as he came to the cohorts of warehouses and offices that marked the outer perimeter of Heathrow. He felt new confidence now that he was alone and on his back the new clothes, blue jeans and a pale-green shirt. It had been a clear night and the housewife who worked a long day's shift had seen the opportunity to leave her husband's washing out on the garden line. A bonus for Famy as he had gone on his way. New clothes that would render obsolete the description given to the police in Richmond.

Famy recognized the danger of moving too far a distance inside the airport before he had solidified the cover that he regarded as essential to protect himself later in the day. The detail he had studied and accepted as he had run. Now all he needed, he told himself, was time. Time to move to the position that he must have. Time to be ready for when the El Al landed. Must be there for the first one. They'd take him out, send him home, rid themselves of Sokarev. And so easy to know, once he was there. Can always tell when a big man is flying, or one they think highly of. The security, that's what gives it away, what makes it so obvious. But had to get there, and then stay and wait and watch, watch for the signs that meant Sokarev was coming. Had to get there, to where the first El Al flight would take on its passengers, and then be patient and observe, and look for the security men; the hard-faced men who would tell him the quarry was close.

In Fatahland they would be waking now. In the tents set among the scrub and the rocks his colleagues in arms had passed a night spent dreaming of an opportunity such as he had been given, awaiting it as their own one-time destiny. The new day would be coming over the camp. The same sun rising across the mountain to the east of Nablus where the road ran on down to the Jordan valley, where his father would be out of his bed, and his mother already in the kitchen outhouse behind the bungalow, and his brothers dressing for school. And in Haifa and Netanya and Ashkelon and Beersheba the Jews would be waking too. All would say his name when the next evening came. Some with adulation, some with resignation, some with detestation. The blow he prepared to strike would be mighty, to many millions it would shatter the foetid complacency, and to those who lived on the far side of the wire and the minefields and who longed to cross over he would bring hope and aspiration. There was a

250

pounding of excitement, close to purest happiness.

Inside the perimeter he skirted the road that ran adjacent to the runways and across the acres of dividing clipped grass, keeping back from the vague traffic flow, seeking the shadows. He appeared to any who might notice him as one more from the ranks of the thousands of immigrant workers, the life-blood of the airport, on his way to another day at work, washing dishes, sweeping concourses, cleaning lavatories. His bag seemed not to weigh so heavily, the roar of the big engines lightening the load. He was very near to the estuary of his mission.

Back in Lebanon they had told him about the tunnel that was the sole route from the outside conurbation to the heart of the airport complex. They had showed him a photograph of its entry, pointing out the footpath that ran separate to the vehicle road. If there was security that path could be guarded – too simple, too easy, and risks should not be taken, not when the scent was so strong. He saw the bus queue, a short hundred yards up the hill from the entry tunnel, a straggled line of brown faces, of turbans and saris, many carrying the bags that contained their working overalls, bags that were so similar to the one that rested by his feet when he joined them. Infiltrate where you will not be noticed, that is what they had told him; there is a time for combat uniform and a time for camouflage. And the bus when it came would take him to the central terminals. He must look there for the canteens and rest rooms where the workers gathered for their breaks. He must look for a man whose job, whose appearance, and whose identity papers would give Famy the passport to the tarmac where the Jumbo would refuel, reload its seats.

One man, one man from so many who would be there, one man alone would be necessary.

19

The bus was hideously slow through the tunnel. Worrying its way down the underground passage, sandwiched between the cars and lorries and coaches, it had no speed, no hurry, no urgency. Flashes of illumination thrown into the interior from the big yellow lights fastened to the angle where the sides met the roof, causing Famy to turn outward toward the windows, obscuring his features from his fellow passengers. There was little talk on the bus. The eyes of the inmates were remote and insular, men and women compartmentalizing themselves from their seated neighbours, minds dulled by the time of day and the anticipation of the boredom and frustration of their service tasks through the next nine hours. They were soft, thought Famy, unthinking fodder, with neither the power nor desire to question the humiliation of the role that had been awarded to them. Poverty of initiative, absence of hope. Facing another day of averted eyes, stumbling submission, far from their own country. Plucked from a great distance and brought here to serve. Pathetic people, without the arm of Famy and his strength, incapable of insurrection, shackled. And they would have little comprehension of the Arab, fail to understand his mission and what he tried to achieve for them. They would be unable to accept that the M1 and its hitting capability represented a blow for them as much for them as the men and women and children in the Chatila and Sabra camps. Did not all colonialists support the Israeli State? They paid lip service to the enemies of Israel, but only superficially, only for their gasoline. There was no sincerity. The white man identified with the Jew. When the day was over and they sat again on the bus that would reverse its route and they went back to their homes, how would these people have reacted to the operation that Abdel-El-Famy planned for the last hours of their work shift? Too stupid, most of them. Few would acknowledge that his act was for them, for all the majorities that lacked wealth and opportunity. They were trapped, these people, as trapped and imprisoned as the Palestinians. Without homelands, without fields, without flocks, without expression. It is a daydream, Famy; tomorrow will be the time of dreams, tomorrow . . . but today there is not time. The bus increased its speed, surged into the brightness at the end of the encasing tunnel, and pulled up the hill in the selected lane that would direct it to the central airport buildings.

They swung across the traffic lanes, paused at the traffic lights, and then turned right toward the bus shelter where the night shift workers waited. Inside the bus many were already standing up, lifting their bags with them, and the sudden jolt of the brakes as the bus finally came to a standstill made several lose their balance. Then they were hurrying down the aisle, afraid of being late, and in their rush they swept Famy forward with them.

He watched the way the men went as they left the bus halt. The procession had divided, men taking one course, women another, a splitting of the human confluence. There were other buses behind him, more in front that had already disgorged and were pulling away, and the stream took him toward the opened double doors of the red brick building surmounted by the blue-tinged windows of the octagonal control tower. There were signs beside the entrance. 'Canteen' and 'Admittance to Staff Only'. No security checks, none that was visible anyway, but it was early for that. Nothing sensitive here, no threat presented. But it suited him well to be out of the rising sunlight, anonymous among the mass of people who belonged to the System. They would not be looking for him here. It was a place where he could rest, where his legs that ached and protested could relax, where he could doze and regain the sharpness of thought he must have by mid-afternoon.

The woman who served him at the long counter was surprised at the way his cup and saucer rattled as he carried them away from the cash machine. She put it down to nerves. Like half these Asians, she thought, scared out of their wits, and what do they have to do? Only clean out the loos and push a broom round. It amused her, gave a cherished feeling of superiority. But she was wrong. There was no fear in Famy now. That his hand shook was from the strain of carrying the bag for so many hours, fingers entwined around the plastic strap. But no fear, not now he was without the Irishman. And confidence is of critical value to the assassin. The killer has to believe in his prowess as much as his cause, must believe in his ability as much as the God-given right to exact retribution. Those who saw the unfamiliar face sitting at the clothless table by the window would have latched on to the great contentment on his features, the gentleness that comes from peace of mind and the patience to consume time. He was now a more dangerous and potentially lethal figure than at any time since he had landed in England. He had come to terms with his mission, and with its implications. He was ready to kill.

253

He put three spoonfuls of sugar into the coffee, stirred it slowly and looked about him.

Along the Great West Road leading toward London from Windsor huge queues of traffic formed up behind the military convoy.

Land-Rovers front and rear, fifteen three-ton trucks, each carrying twenty soldiers. Alpha, Bravo and Headquarters Company. Grenadier Guards, long lines of battle honours stretching back into three hundred years of history. Thin red-line tunics of the ceremonial discarded for mottled camouflage denims, the uniform of urban guerrilla warfare of the streets of Northern Ireland. Four hundred men in all. FN rifles. General purpose machine-guns. Hand-held Carl Gustav rocket launchers. All there to protect one man from the hands of an equally solitary threat. Many times the resident Battalion at Windsor Barracks had practised on exercise their recent responsibilities of Heathrow security, but there was a tightness and silence about the men who sat on the slatted seats in the backs of the lorries. Never before had they been told the risk was real, confirmed.

Interspersed among the trucks were the armoured cars of two Hussar squadrons, Saladins with khaki cloth tied across the muzzle of the big gun, and the Saracen personnel carriers.

Police reinforcements were being mobilized from Divisional forces in the Metropolitan area. More would come from the rural Thames Valley strength. By nine in the morning the perimeter of the airport would be sealed, the concourses would be under guard, the tarmac patrolled. Later the plans for the security of the El Al flight to Tel Aviv would be thrashed out in the squat police station on the far side of the tunnel where the various security forces would set up their control and communication posts.

The Prime Minister had rubber-stamped the guidance from Home Office and Defence. Saturation. Forces of such strength that the Arab would turn his back on his target, dismayed. Box the bastard out, deny him any chink of light, any opportunity to attack.

*

254

Through the window Famy saw the deployment. Little strung-out columns of troops. Rifles carried warily and diagonally across their bodies, letting the bustling civilians fan out and find a path to the side. Some were draped in the belts of machine-gun ammunition, worn in cross-over sashes. One man in each patrol hunched forward to compensate for the weight of the radio set perched high on his back. Among the conventional throb of the traffic he heard the piercing and complaining squeal of the big Rolls-Royce engines of the armoured cars, and saw the pedestrians out on the pavement pause and turn and stare at them. All had read their morning papers, heard the radio news bulletins. They would wait for the five-minute call, for the show to begin. And all would stay for the curtain call. It amused Famy. One against so many. No one to share the footlights with him. After a while he became tired of watching the criss-cross motions of his enemy, and finished his coffee. He walked back to the counter, ordered a fresh cup, and with it a sandwich filled with dried and crumbling cheese and slices of over-ripe tomato.

There were many hours to be consumed before it would be time for him to move, but the sights beyond the window fanned his confidence, spread it as a brushfire. His best hopes were confirmed. The troops and the guns had not come just to hunt down Abdel-El-Famy. There was another more cogent and potent reason. The Mushroom Man would be travelling, on course for their rendezvous. The fly into the web, the lion toward the pit. And all the soldiers and police would be as extras, as onlookers.

From the next table he took a discarded newspaper and read a version of the previous night's events. His English was adequate, sufficient for him to understand what had been written. He was 'fleeing', he was 'probably on drugs', he was a 'fanatic'. The public were warned to keep away from him, not to 'have a go', told to phone the police if he were sighted. Guns had been widely distributed to the police. He would be shot on sight, the journalist had written. On the front page there was a smudged and meaningless picture of the house where he had left McCoy, a policeman there and a rifle in his hand, and the story was topped with the news of the capture of his friend. Described as 'late news'. He read that McCoy, though injured, would live, and he was thankful. But they do not understand, he thought. There is no word of Palestine, no word of the bomb, no word of the camps and the suffering. It raged through him so that he wanted to scream at those who shared the canteen with him. Do they care so little for Palestine that they take no trouble to understand why? Why do they think we are prepared to die? Stupid, goat-shit bastards, do we enjoy death? Can there be no sanity in what we do? Can we never be right, justified, driven beyond the boundaries? And then his temper calmed. On the centre pages of the tabloid was a photograph, blown large, of David Sokarev. It was more recent than the old snap shot they had shown him in Lebanon. He could dwell on the face in a way that had not been possible in the split seconds that he had peered into the artificial light of the hall. Remember it closely, study its detail. There will be little time when he is between the car and the steps, and he will be hurrying, and there will be men round him. Recognition must be instinctive, not as it was in the hall, when his eyes had to search. Faster this time.

He would know him. Whether he was crouched low, whether he wore a hat, whether he had his coat collar turned up, however fast he went, he would know him.

The alcohol Jimmy had drunk in the small hours needed greater time to disperse through the bloodstream than Jimmy had permitted. Short of sleep and still wound at wire tension he came to the hotel. The adrenalin that for a short period had fought and overcome the whisky for control of his veins as he confronted McCoy was now bested. Johnny Walker supreme. His head ached with the pressure, trying to break out and expand from the confines of his skull. Splitting pain, and self-administered. Wanted to rest, wanted just to fold up and sleep it off. But no rest was permitted. Told where he had to be, and that was with Sokarev. Back on course again, Jimmy, taking orders, doing as the gaffer said.

The Branch man in the foyer recognized him from the previous days, nodded a greeting and described his passage into the lift over a small radio transmitter. New, that, souping things up a bit, and so they should. On the fourth floor he was met again, quizzically and with suspicion, by a man he had not seen before and who blocked his way down the corridor to the Israelis' rooms. Jimmy fumbled for his wallet and searched among the folds for his card. Should have been able to spot it straight away.

256

Knew where he put the bloody thing, but couldn't find it. Always put it in the same place, but where? And then it was there, clearly to be seen where he should have looked in the first place. Jimmy mouthed an apology, embarrassed. The detective was clean-shirted, shaved, dressed for work. And you, you look a bloody wreck, Jimmy. A shambles. The policeman examined the card, searched back again into Jimmy's face, handed the card back and stepped sideways to allow him through. There were more men outside the doors of the two rooms. They would have seen the initial checking, but went through the routine again. Bloody coppers. Jimmy knocked on the first door, opened in response by Elkin.

The greeting was mutually cool. Had to be after last night. No source of congratulations. Jimmy noted that the curtains of the room were drawn, bed-side light on, no possibility of anyone outside the building being able to see inside the room – basic precaution, as it should be. Everyone learning what it's all about. There was a new man slouched on the far bed, the Uzi not more than six inches from his right hand. Elkin went straight into the attack, had been accumulating it.

'It will be different from yesterday. We have taken charge of the arrangements. Any plan will go through us, be approved by us.'

'You'll do as you're bloody well told.' Hadn't expected the assault that fast.

'After last night we make the decisions.'

'You'll make the decisions when you're on that fucking aircraft . . .'

'We left it to you, and it was a fiasco.'

'You'll be told what's going to happen, and if you don't like it you can get out on the pavement and walk to the airport.' When Jimmy shouted the sledgehammer reverberated behind his eyes. He closed them. All so bloody daft, childish. When he forced the lids hard together he could squeeze out the pain. 'Calm yourself down for God's sake.' He spoke like a man who wants to end the full drama of a domestic row, wants to pack it in and forget it by the morning. 'Did you sleep last night?'

Elkin shook his head. Bags big and bulged, sack full, spreading to his cheeks, high red flush beneath them, eyes above soft and watery. Been crying, Jimmy saw.

'We have the Irishman. Only leaves the one other. Fancies

himself at the airport when your man goes out this afternoon. Be out of his depth. Less chance than a chicken in Biafra. He's no hope. They'll be working out a route later in the morning, nothing for you till that gets in the pipeline. You should put your head down till then.'

Elkin walked back to his bed, sat on it heavily. Jimmy recognized he would struggle to stay awake and lose. Poor sod, doesn't rate us – and why should he? Fearful what we'll cock-up while he's kipping. And everyone so bloody tired, never known an operation when they weren't all walking round like zombies . . . what Jones had said, wasn't it? Stupid old bugger. Jimmy took off his coat and slung it on the floor, lifted the pistol from the shoulder-holster and pressed it into the waist of his trousers before dumping himself into a brocaded arm-chair. He had thought that sleep would come easily to him, pleaded for it, aware of how much faster the incapacity of exhaustion came to him as he veered between middle and old age. But the liberation was not at hand, and was made harder by the still figure of Elkin on his bed. Jimmy willed himself to follow, but without success. And his head throbbed, with the blood scarlet flashes across his vision.

Beyond the partition door David Sokarev too was asleep. Jimmy had heard no movement, no creaking of restless bed springs, and turned the door handle giving himself a few inches of vision. Like a little angel. No nightmares, the pills had seen to that. Dead to the world, blanked out, insensitive to it all. Pray the drug keeps him there. Met a man once in a pub – where you meet them all, Jimmy – in his cups, deep. Said he'd been a prison screw. Once done the death cell stint. Hadn't volunteered, the sick list had seen him on the rota, usual guys not available. Not the actual night, but the one before. And the man had slept, and they'd all marvelled, and known the news the governor had brought the previous evening. Even slept through the shift change, and the new screws had tip-toed in. They'd let his breakfast get cold, fearful for him when the protection of sleep was gone. He'd been a crude bugger, the one who'd told him the story, but different when he spoke of this. And the more that Sokarev slept the better. Cushion him from the carry-on. Only bloody defence he had. A weak face he had, unprotected, with its old man's stubble.

And by the late afternoon Sokarev would be gone, and his

hands would be washed and he'd be back with his girl, and no phone calls, and he'd retrieve the bottle. God, he wished his head would call a cease-fire. He'd be in lousy shape in the afternoon. Lousy.

Famy had studied many of the men who came into the canteen through the early and middle morning. Some he dismissed immediately as being of no use to him, others he toyed with for longer, examining their features and their build, before rejecting them too as unsuitable for his purpose.

It was gone eleven when he saw the man he wanted. Indian, correct height, at a little below six feet. Youngish, early twenties, and not yet filled out with the obesity of his race. A turban, good because it distracted from the facial images, white and cleanly furled. A faint moustache, hardly visible, but there was time for Famy to use his battery razor and match that. White overalls, emblazoned across the left chest with the British Airways sign and, more important, specked with oil spots and smeared with grease. Maintenance. A man who worked on the engines, tended the beasts when they were tethered, had access to them when they lay crippled. And where did the work go on? At the piers, on the tarmac, on the big concreted open spaces where the aircraft sojourned. Access dominated his thinking. The need to find an identity that ensured access. A job that provided access to the hidden and secret areas denied to ordinary civilians, the ticket behind the wire fences and the control points.

Famy left his table, and holding his bag moved across the floor of the canteen toward the table where the Sikh sat, solitary, unaware of the man who approached him.

As his car drove away from the cul-de-sac of Downing Street the Israeli Ambassador's concern was defused. He had taken his security attaché with him to the meeting with the British Prime Minister, but in the event had left him outside the heavy oakwood doors to the personal office. Alone for an hour with the British Head of Government, he had discussed the previous night's attack. They had moved on from the past to the plans that had been drawn up for the departure of David Sokarev in the late afternoon.

'The Prime Minister put it to me,' said the Ambassador to his companion, 'that his Government could in no way be accused of dragging their heels on this matter. He said it was his personal order that preparations were made for an assault on the house where it was thought the terrorists had taken refuge. He said that the safety of the hostages was put at secondary priority compared with the need to avoid negotiating with these people. I cannot counter that. It was to be done as we would have hoped. And they have been fast with the interrogation of the one man they hold. They tell me that the Arab will attempt a final attack at the airport. It is admitted that there was laxity at the university, but I have assurances that it will not be repeated. It would have been difficult for me to relay the instructions of the Foreign Ministry.'

The security attaché was unconcerned with the private diplomatic innuendo that had passed between the two men out of his hearing.

'What are their plans for the airport?' More important, to what had his civilian master, short of a military background, agreed?

'They have moved troops to Heathrow. Guardsmen and light cavalry. They are bringing in more police. There will be around a thousand men from their security forces, many armed, they tell me. The Prime Minister informs me that the Arab is in possession of an M1 carbine with a maximum effective range of three hundred metres. Therefore they will put an army and police cordon in position of a circle with a radius of four hundred metres around the jet-liner. There will be no admittance inside that area other than to vetted personnel, our own people, and the security men. The plane will already be loaded when Sokarev boards . . .'

'How is he transferred to the airport?'

'It is the assessment of the British that a motor convoy is the best method. There are many points of entry into Heathrow, and they maintain that it would be impossible for the Arab to be correctly positioned, and knowing which one they will use. I see no reason for disputing that. It is their hope that the demonstration of force will be so great as to deter the man until Professor Sokarev is safely in the air. After that they will concentrate on his capture.'

'So again they have not consulted us.' The attaché spoke evenly, not looking at the Ambassador, watching the oncoming traffic.

260

'They have consulted me.'

'You are not an expert in these matters.'

'That is offensive.'

'You would not know whether there were flaws in the plan or not.'

'Where are the flaws that your experience warns you of?'

'How can I tell? How can I estimate? I had hoped to see the plans. Discuss them. Negotiate them. Be given alternatives, told of the contingency fall-backs. There is no chance of that now.'

The Ambassador was silent, thoughtful of the way he had committed himself so few minutes earlier. Career, future, promotion to permanent position in the Ministry in Jerusalem, all might rest on the agreement he had made with the Prime Minister. The attaché said nothing else. The point had been made, there was no value in returning to it. They would do their best, the British. Probably haphazard, but their best. Only they were not experts. Europeans did not understand the Palestinian fighters, were naïve in the new science of counter-terrorism. But so proud of their integrity, so determined to make their own decisions. And their own mistakes. So there had been no talk of decoys, or of helicopters, or of military aircraft. Do they comprehend the resourcefulness of the assassin who is prepared to die that he should reach his target? He doubted it.

Mohan Singh was happy at the other man's company. It was rare for him to have conversation during the early lunch break when his shift pattern decreed he went off sooner for his food than many of his work colleagues. The stranger listened to his problems, to the description of his life and his education, the circumstances that had brought him to England, and his difficulties in finding a job as rewarding financially as the one he now held. He spoke of his family – his wife and the three small children – how they lived in two rooms at the back of an uncle's house in Hounslow, how he was obliged to send money back to Amritsar to maintain his elderly parents. He was not aware as he chattered on that the man with him spoke little, just nodded and smiled and encouraged.

There was not long, Famy knew that. Sitting at the table already for fifteen minutes, there for another fifteen before the approach. How many more before he returned to his work?

High wall clock turning, not much time. And all the while the plans racing, wasp-fast, through his mind. They had more coffee, Famy going up to the counter and collecting the two cups. His hands no longer shook, relaxed and supple now, fingers eased, pliant . . . He set the coffee cups down and inclined his head to hear again what the Indian wanted to pour out to him. He had no feeling about the clear knowledge that he would kill this man. He was as nothing. An arcade machine, activated by a coin. Not an enemy, not a friend, just a carriage to take him to his destination, to his destiny. McCoy would have done it better, but McCoy had made the sacrifice for him, and he must fulfil his trust.

The man was tedious to Famy. Grumbling but frightened to be considered in that light, without the courage to fight for what he wanted. As a carpet that complains but cannot shift itself from the trampling boots. He would die quickly, compliant with his fate. The Indian had finished his coffee, coughed and cleared the sinuses of his nose, loud and guttural.

'I must return, or I will be late for the afternoon's work. It has been nice . . .'

Famy interrupted. 'I have to wash my hands. You will show me the lavatory?' A stranger, helpless, needing a friend.

The Indian responded. 'I will show you. It is difficult to find if one is new here.'

They walked together down the corridor further into the building and away from the canteen. Twenty yards, perhaps thirty, and round two corners till they came to the door with the male, trousered symbol set high on it.

The Indian smiled, 'It is here. Not easy to find.'

His inclination then would have been to leave and walk away, but Famy spoke quickly and at the same time pushed open the door, moving inside.

'I would like to see you again. Where could we meet?' Mohan Singh followed him. Famy was no longer listening, was taking in the lay-out, the cubicles at the far end of the long side walls past the stand-up urinals. There was a man there, nearly completed, heaving his hips to shake off the last drops. He would be gone in a moment. It was not a place that men delayed beyond their business.

At the washbasin, the water running, loud, interfering, he pretended not to hear.

'Wait a minute. Till I have finished,' he said over his shoulder.

262

In the mirror he saw the man move toward the door, heard it slam in his wake.

Famy swept the water from his hands on to the front of his jeans and spun to face the Indian. No words now, and how many seconds before another man came in? The Indian had started to talk again when Famy's forearm, swung from far back, hit him on the protuberance of his throat, at the Adam's apple. A gurgling, choking moment of protest. Surprise in the eyes before the misting of insensibility. Famy caught him as he collapsed and pulled him, limp now and unprotesting, to the furthest of the lavatory cubicles. Then through the door into the constricted space in front of the pan. Not dead yet, not a body. But had to be killed, had to be silenced. He worked the shape in front of him so that the head faced inward and he had room to close the door behind him and fasten the catch. 'Engaged' it would say to any who came. And he would hear the door into the main corridor if it were opened and an intruder entered. That would hold him up. He had waited all morning for his man, and now was impatient.

He closed his eyes, settled himself as if in a moment of prayer, seeking the strength that now was essential, knuckles whitened, nails in his palms. He raised up the Indian's head, took the turban from it, placed it carefully on the door hook, particular not to dissarange it, aware that he would not know how to rebind it. Then he pulled the zip fastener of the overalls down to the level of the upper waist and clawed the arms of the garment from round the shoulders till it rested in a concertinaed mess on the Indian's hips. The overalls as much as the turban were too vital to be defiled if they were to serve his purpose. And now he was ready. A fearful clarity, in slow, stopped motion. He lifted the head again and with all the force in his shoulders slammed it down on the hard polished white china of the rim of the bowl. Once, twice, three times till the bone of the skull no longer resisted the impact. Crude, irreversible damage was what he sought. He could not hold the man in the upright position any more. It slumped on to its knees, blood finding independent paths into the water held at the bottom of the pan, suffusing pinks and reds together.

There was no movement. The man had become matter. Insignificant, finished. Famy heaved him once again upward so that he could observe the hurt he had inflicted, and more practically to see that the ribbons of blood had not passed on to the overalls. These he stripped off, twisting the body, lifting it, pushing it so that he could slip the garment down its length and over the shoes. It had been a hot day, and the Indian wore only a singlet – deep-stained now – and pants underneath, not clean and with their own faint smell that competed with the urine stains on the floor.

He left the body still kneeling but with the head deep in the pan. An obscenity, but necessary to remove totally the horror of the face and the damage that he had brought to it. In the breast pocket of Mohan Singh's overalls he found the small, plastic-coated polaroid card, read the name of the man he had executed in the cause of Palestine, and looked at the photograph, un-recognizable from the smashed features of the man he had killed. Three minutes later, now wearing the overalls, he climbed up over the dividing wooden wall and into the next cubicle. He hurried across to the washbasins, scrubbed his hands in liquid soap to rid himself of the few blood-spots that rested there, then checked in the mirror that the turban was straight and still fastened. His bag was where he had left it, under the basins.

Out in the corridor Famy glanced at his watch. If the Jumbo were on time it would be landing in three hours and forty minutes. There would be another sixty minutes of refuelling. He had far to go, each step more hazardous than the last. And he had killed for the first time, the first time in his short life. There had been men who had slumped in his gunsight in the lecture hall, but they were different – abstract, unconnected. This was with his own hands, using his own strength, his own will. It had been the irreversible step, and he had taken it.

20

It had been four years since the British had first awoken, and then tardily, to the threat confronting their premier airport. The familiar continental backdrop of patrolling troops and armed para-military police on the runways and in the terminals had been thought just another European eccentricity, until the Guards

264

and their armour had deserted Windsor and rolled into Heathrow for the first time. Many had seen that as an erosion of something peculiarly British, a departure from a way of life long established, a further weakening of the nation's aloofness from the violent habits of the neighbours. But times changed, and the troops came more often, the frequency of their alerts reducing the bizarre appearance of their initial arrival. And the British Airports Authority, the managing body for the 2700 acres of billiard-flat grass and concrete that played host on a summer's day to close on a thousand aircraft, had called its charge a 'national defence priority', and written in an annual review of the 'formidable tasks posed by the new warfare' of terrorist attack. Familiarity, though, dulled the fascination of the armed men, the excitement died its death. Twenty million passengers came and went each year, and few could boast to their friends of having seen a rifle, a semi-hidden pistol handle at the hip of a policeman, let alone a light tank.

So on this Wednesday there was again a refreshing novelty about it all, and enough sunshine to bring out the crowds. Those who were flying arrived earlier than they otherwise would have done. Those landing lingered in the anticipation of an event. Around the army, the work of the airport continued uninterrupted; but ears were cocked listening for sirens and gunfire, and above all the ceaseless drone of uninformed and ceaseless rumour.

The turban felt strange and unfamiliar on Famy's head. Not that it was heavy or ill-fitting, but as a constriction, the mark and uniqueness of an identity that he had not fully taken over. The overalls were right, loose and baggy, presenting no pressures on the shape of his body, and masking the rifle now pinioned, barrel down, in the belt at the front of his trousers. It was one of the small pieces of advice that they had given to him: secrete a barrelled weapon in the very front of your body. The hands always search at the sides, examine the flanks. The grenades would have been harder to dispose of on his person had the Indian not carried the small, yellow lunch box in the pocket of his trousers. The V40s wrapped well in the greaseproof paper that the nameless and faceless wife packaged round her man's food.

Famy walked toward the security check-point between the two giant structures that formed Terminal Three. 'Departures to Right', 'Arrivals to Left', and straight ahead the pendulum bar, unmistakeable in its red and white message, with the notice slung beneath, large and decisive, 'Stop.' Beyond was the inner world that he had to join, the realm of the loaders and mechanics and airline personnel, passengers excluded unless they moved in their corralled herds on specific walkways. The BAA security man, blue uniform, white-rimmed cap, operated the movement of the bar from a glass-cased booth at the side. A soldier had crammed in beside him, and there was a Land-Rover behind daubed with the standard NATO camouflage parabolas. More soldiers beside the barrier itself. They were relaxed, confident, safe in the knowledge of their numbers and their firepower. Briefings had passed that down to them. Battalion commander to company commander, company commander to platoon commander, platoon commander to section leader. The word had been spread, circulated. One man was the risk. They had his picture in their minds, the description of his clothes.

An Indian in British Airways livery went no way toward fitting the requirement for vigilance and care that had been stressed on the Guardsmen. They looked in the bag, but cursorily and laughed when he asked in a voice, high-pitched by nerves, but which they took to be the flavour of his homeland, whether he should remove his turban. As they waved him through he shouted to the men in the booth.

'Good luck.'

And their smiles turned to the sneers of the young. A thousand against one. So who needed luck? With those odds half a day more and the rifles would be back in the armoury and they'd be in the pub under the castle wall. They watched him go, and their attention was taken up by the next vehicle. An airport catering van, and there was the need for the tedium of climbing inside and searching.

Pier 7, they had said back at the camp, was the one where the El Al would come to rest. Right at the extremity of the glass and prefabricated buttress down which the passengers would walk to the aircraft. Some days they would board through the tunnel that billowed out from the main construction, sometimes they would walk a few yards across the tarmac. One thing was constant, they had said, always the El Al was removed and remote

266

from the other aircraft. Nearer to him was Pier 6, clogged with its quota of Jumbo 747s . . . British Airways, Pan American, Trans World Airlines, Japan Airlines, Middle East Airlines. He skirted them, measuring a distance that would cause no offence, draw no attention to him. Neither too close to the machinery nor so far out on the tarmac that his basic unfamiliarity with the surroundings would be exposed.

There were more soldiers to his front, and an armoured car dwarfing them. Awaiting an arrival. Sitting and crouched among their packs, close to the one who had unslung the burden of the radio. Watchful, but not yet on alert. They had been right at the camp, and he praised their thoroughness, wondered where they accrued such information. This was where Sokarev would come. There were police standing in separate groups, distant and unwanted by the soldiers, a lesser force, while dogs sat with patience beside their handlers. As he crossed beyond Pier 6 more of the reception group came into his view. Two more armoured cars sheltered under the raised flooring of the further and final pier. Big, ugly, powerful. Huge engines. Mounted machine-guns silhouetted against the sky. Firing power, hitting power, killing power. All there for Abdel-El-Famy. Twice he had seen the wounds on McCoy, seen his man's blood flowing from his body, seen the pain take his face. But they were pistol shots, not fatal, not lethal. Different to the force and velocity of the weapons that were now arrayed in front of him. These were stopping guns. Men did not climb up again, did not drive cars, did not see another day-break, not when they were struck by this power. The M1, difficult to forget, pressed against his groin, was unequalled. Only the Klashnikov could compete – superior perhaps. The rifle he had been trained on, a soldier's rifle, a rifle of war. Trained? Trained for what? So easy in the dry heat of the camp to talk of war, and to wave the farewells to the men who went without hope of return and whose places at the trestle tables would be filled by others with the bright eyes and the solutions and the unquestioning confidence. But what war was this? In an alien, hateful world. Reviled. Hunted. A war with only one victory, consummated only with the death of Sokarev. And if toward that victory Famy died it was of no consequence. Erased without trace if the big rifles took him. That Famy was prepared to die for Palestine was not important. An aggregate of irrelevance. Forgotten with the last tremors of his heart-beat, as if he had never been. But in the camp would they not care there? Only from success can the martyrdom come. Success and only success, no other criteria. As in a dream he walked, argument and counter-argument, punching and confusing him, seeking answers his intellect could not provide. Why knowing the forfeit did he strive so willingly to be remembered? Why, when we know we will be dust, worm fodder, do we seek so hard to be recalled in friends' minds and in their voices? Famy did not know, did not have the comprehension. He yearned only to be mourned. But understood the currency. To be remembered with tears, then Sokarev must die. Only then would they weep for him, the boys with the abyss-brown eyes who shared his tent in the camp.

'Where the bloody hell do you think you're going?' – strident, beating in through his fantasies. The voice was rough, aged and foreign to him. 'Get out the bloody way.'

Famy was rigid. Horror at discovery, disaster. His eyes flickered, body still. The fork-lift cargo transport was five feet away from him, directly in his path, painted strident yellow and blue. El Al colours.

'You want to look where you're bloody going, mate.'

'I'm sorry,' Famy stuttered the words.

'Not half you won't be sorry, not if this lot runs over you. What do you think those bloody lines are for, the white ones? 'Cos it's for trucks, right? Trucks corridor.'

'I was watching the soldiers.'

'Stupid buggers, goofing about because of this Arab and the Yiddisher. If you worked for El Al you'd see enough of them. Troops, police and their own crowd and they're right bastards . . .'

Famy had recovered, was steadier. He was not one of them, this man. An employee, but not of their blood.

'It will be a big show this afternoon, all the troops and things, when the Israeli comes.'

'Not here it won't.'

'But when he boards there will be great security, surely?'

'Not putting him on here. Stands to reason. They're not bloody fools, these people. Load up here, taxi on to 28L, across to the VIP suite, lift him on, and up, up and away, and the squaddies and coppers can go home.'

'I didn't know there was a VIP area there.' Fishing, Famy. Deep, black water, unable to detect what is nibbling at the bait, uncertain of the reward.

'The new one. The one the old girl uses when she's off to Balmoral, where they put Kissinger down, right beside Cargo.'

'I'm sorry that I was in your way.' Famy smiled, and turned and began to walk toward the nearest British Airways plane.

A fleet of company trucks hovered underneath the fuselage belly. There would be a lift there. He would say he was urgently required at Cargo. It would only take a man a few minutes to drive him, and he would be close then. As close as he needed. Within range, within the range even of his M1.

The fleeting relief to which Jimmy had succumbed was broken by the arrival of Jones in the hotel room. He was aware of the voices, dim and thudding through his consciousness before his eyes reluctantly took in the scene, lids prised apart in protest to the sounds. Elkin looked to have benefited from the rest. He stood now on the far side of the room and close to Jones. They were examining a sheaf of type-written sheets. The security attaché was with them, and before he let his presence back with the living be known Jimmy accepted that the conversation was between Elkin and Jones, attaché on the outside, present but not partaking of the feast. No sign of Sokarev. Poor bugger, thought Jimmy, still holed up in his patch and waiting to be consigned. Wonder they don't give him a waybill, stick a number on his arse and freight him home. His head still hurt, not as acutely as before, but intermittently. Take the bloody pledge, man. Your age, and still don't know better.

Jones acknowledged him. Not with friendship, not with warmth, just recognition. Doesn't really like me, after all these years, tolerates me around. Accepts he needs me today, knows he won't have to go through the charade tomorrow. That'll be the ditching time, usefulness used up. Quick handshake it'll be, then piss off and don't show your face till it's been under the long-term tap and washed the bloody booze out. No obligation, not till the next time, till there's a bit of filth that needs scooping off the carpet, a drain that needs cleaning that stinks too much for him to put his pure white hands down.

'Glad to have you back with us, Jimmy,' Jones said. 'I was summoning the courage to kick you, you've been snoring like a sow in labour.'

'Why didn't you wake me when the confab started?'

'Nothing too complicated there, and you were much too pretty to disturb. Mr Elkin and I have gone over it.'

Pompous bugger. Wasn't like that when he wanted McCoy talked to. Means he thinks it's a piece of cake from now, all sewn up and can't go wrong. And it had to be. He'd be a gutsy bastard, the Arab, if they saw him again. If he puts his nose into this crab hole, then you'd have to hand it to him.

'What's my part in this show from now?' Jimmy asked, still slumped in the chair.

'You travel with him to the airport. Hold his hand all the way. Take him carefully up the steps, fasten his seat belt, and last thing before they shut up shop you vamoose down the ramp again. Very simple, very straightforward.'

'Where's he going from?'

'South side, the VIP area. The plane will taxi across from Terminal Three and lift him up right under our supervision. For once it's all planned, nothing for your right index to get twitchy about.'

'What news of Famy . . .?'

Jones was growing irritable. Not pleased at being spoken to with such lack of deference in public, in front of foreigners, strangers.

'No word of him. But the airport's sealed. Troops, police, armour, no need for you to be worried.'

'It's not me that's worried. It's not my job that hangs on knowing where the little runt is.'

Six thousand men work at the Heathrow Cargo terminal, there to despatch and unload more than a thousand tons of freight a day. That an outsider, an alien, should be in their midst would not be noticed.

Famy squatted low on his bag in the sunshine in the front of the big British Airways transit shed. There were others around him, watching the soldiers in the distance, statuesque and guarding a circle of empty tarmac. He spoke to no one, nor received any words of greeting or enquiry. It was of no concern to him, he did not seek communication and conversation. More troops on the corner of the building before the open ground that stretched to the white wooden fence that shielded the bungalow VIP lounge

270

from his sight. The presence of the turbaned stranger would not arouse comment; freighters were traditionally the veterans of the fleet, converted as their passenger days were exhausted, and it was accepted that maintenance was in frequent demand.

There was a warmth in the air, and in the distance the shapes jumped and bounced and faded, made hazy by the heat. He had to blink to hold his concentration on the big plane in full view across the tarmac. The sheen played and gleamed on the outline of the El Al jet less than six hundred yards from him. He could make out the armoured cars, black in shadow against the light, and occasionally the figures of the soldiers around them would press into focus. Beneath the upright zip of his overalls the rifle worried against his body. It hurt, and would continue to hurt. There were many minutes before the plane would be ready to take Sokarev on board. He felt a curious calm now. No anguish and no stress. The desire to dream and fantasize was conquered. All so very clear. In limbo, sucked into a void, and awaiting the inevitability of the rendezvous. It was beyond interference.

Sokarev was past complaining or feeling any degree of independence as they led him through the kitchens of the hotel and then into the delivery area where food and provisions were unloaded in built-up bays. The escort seemed to the scientist to be too preoccupied with their problems and anxieties to explain or justify the departure plan that had been decided on. The van that waited was painted blue, unmarked and with the windows smoked to prevent those on the outside looking in. There were five men with him to share the two rows of seating behind the driver. The security attaché, still defensive and introverted. Jones, who ignored all around him. Elkin, fidgeting, willing the journey over, the Uzi across his knees and constantly referring to his wrist watch. Special Branch convoy co-ordinator, talking all the while into his handset, and then fiddling with the dials as his answers came back in differing volume. And there was Jimmy, picking with a matchstick at the dirt under his nails, with his coat open, and his gun exposed, and his head down thoughtful and concerned, and not sharing his mind. Behind was a car, more Branch men, and with them the replacement for Mackowicz, unhappy and pained at being separated from his man.

271

It is as if they are punishing me, thought Sokarev. As if I am in some way culpable for what has happened. He was still tired, not rested by the capsule that the doctor had given him. They put me out of their way while they worked out their plans, needed me absent, and the easiest way was with the pill, he told himself. But it does not bring real sleep. And he recognized that the men with him were tired, had seen it in their faces, and in their clothes, the way they snapped at each other, their impatience. The equation for him had often been proved in the work at Dimona; tired men operate at reduced efficiency, and that frightened him. He felt a shortness of breath and searched for air, loosening his collar and slipping off the suit jacket he had put on for the journey. All the ventilation slats in the van were closed. He would have liked one open, to release the engine fumes and the body smells, but did not feel he had the authority to ask for it. Incapable of soaking up more humiliations he sat in his seat and suffered till he felt a shiver in his limbs and deep under his clothes, and a feeling of cold and sickness. There was nobody to tell.

In the yard of Hammersmith police station, a third of the way to Heathrow and behind closed doors, he was transferred to a car. There were escorts front and back, but nothing for the casual observer of the convoy to recognize.

The security attaché now drove, Jones and Special Branch crowded into the front beside him. Sokarev was sandwiched between Elkin and Jimmy.

As they climbed on to the pillared flyover that they had crossed two days ago Sokarev felt a tug at his sleeve and looked at Jimmy.

'Don't take too much notice of these buggers,' Jimmy said, for all the car to hear, 'they're all as shit-scared as you are. And will be till we've waved you on your way.'

Famy's whole being was riveted to the movement of the big jet. Three hundred and fifty tons of it, making the solemn progress from the end of Pier 7 toward the axis of the runways. Two Saracens came in front, where he could see them, dwarfed by the huge concentric lines of the nose. Small cockpit windows, high above the ground, where the pilot and his crew were sitting. All of them able to see him, but not capable of recognizing the face of their enemy. Remember Dani, remember Bouchi, remember

272

McCoy. Endless, indistinct faces played through his vision, sometimes blotting out and obscuring the reality of the plane. The faces of his friends, of those who had believed in him.

The plane was waved inside the cordon of soldiers. More armoured cars were awaiting it, policemen beginning to scurry, and the wind brought the talk of their radios, faint but recognizable. The soldiers faced out of their arc, stern-eyed now, keyed up, expectant. The nearest was barely twenty feet from Famy. A corporal, two blackened V-stripes on his tunic arm, self-loading rifle, water bottle, emergency field dressing strapped to his webbing belt. Famy saw his hands as they cradled the rifle. Finger on the lip of the trigger guard, thumb for the safety catch, a movement of a second and the gun was armed, deadly. The soldier did not return his stare, gazed through him, used to being looked at. The Guards always were. And his position, the square of concrete on which he stood, had chosen to stand, made him Famy's opponent. As inconsequential as that, where a man placed his feet. That decided whether he would kill or be killed.

'Juno turning into Hatton perimeter entrance, sir.'

Corporal on the Land-Rover radio set to his company commander. The major raised his hand in acknowledgement. Bloody stupid names they always gave these affairs.

'Sunray getting it on the net?' the major asked.

'All getting it, sir, not just the CO, the convoy's hooked into all stations.'

'Put out the Instant Readiness.'

'Roger, sir.'

The major saw beyond his cordon a line of civilian trucks and cars and lorries held back a quarter of a mile from the plane. Have to wait till the show was over. No non-involved persons inside his line, perfect field of fire around three-sixty degrees. Just about perfect, anyway. Only the corner hangar of the British Airways cargo complex jutting in and breaking the geometry of his protective circle. Saw the loaders there, standing and sitting and watching, anything for a chance not to work. Shouldn't have been there, but no harm done. The corporal dominating them. No need to throw his weight about, make a scene, have them shifted. Saw the turban, creased and clean. It stood out in the light, the sun playing on it.

273

He turned toward the VIP suite past which the convoy would come.

The cars came fast down the straight line of the inner perimeter road, motor cycles in front, and all oncoming traffic blocked far ahead. Sokarev saw the arrowed signs to the right marking the route to the VIP suite.

Jimmy said, 'Just about there now, sir. No farewells out on the tarmac. The car goes right up to the steps and you're to be straight on to them. Don't stop. Don't hesitate. Just go straight on up. Inside don't look out of the windows, just get into the seat. They're not going to hang about, you'll be straight off.'

Sokarev did not reply. Jimmy could see the nerves on his ageing face, wrinkles accentuated, eyes wide open staring but at nothing, and the lips clamped fractionally apart, breathing coming in irregular sucked heaves. Poor sod, not taking it well. Ten to bloody nothing his legs will freeze half-way and we'll have to carry him on.

The convoy swept past the low-built lounge with its decoration of hot-house plants. Marigolds and snapdragons and embryo rhododendrons. In front was the Jumbo.

'Goodbye, Elkin,' Jimmy leaned across Sokarev, hand outstretched. It was not taken. The Israeli's attention was outside his window, fingers clamped on his sub-machine-gun.

The cars spattered through the gap in the fencing and raced toward the jet. Jones found himself reflecting at the vulgarity of it all. Big men, hunched and crammed together on the seats. All so difficult to take seriously, just a game for grown-ups. Only Sokarev playing, though. We're all in with the spectators, thought Jones, it's only the old man who goes out on to the field. No dignity in the moment, nothing of the third floor at the Department, and Jimmy lording it over everybody. Intolerable, really, and he'd have to be spoken to. The plane was huge now in its silver closeness, dwarfing them, a fortress in its own right. And the steps were there, in position, waiting for them.

The stiffening of the soldiers, the way their hands quickly changed the grip on their rifles, fingers to the trigger guard, telegraphed to Famy the imminence of the arrival.

His right hand ferreted down inside the overalls for the safety mechanism of the M1. Already cocked, already a bullet nestled in the breach of the firing chamber. A hundred yards to the steps of the plane. Take him twelve to thirteen seconds. The problems were fading, over everything a devastating simplicity. When the cars came into sight that was when to start running. Fast, but weaving, ducking low, and the shot when the man was at the base of the steps. Bank on chaos. However much they have prepared for you, they will never quite have expected the presence, that was what the men had told him in the camp. There will always be confusion; it is the greatest weapon in your hand, they had said.

Three cars in the convoy, snouting round the corner, braking because of the angle they were negotiating. Famy was on his feet.

Without hesitation, a continuous rippling movement, he pulled the zip fastener down the length of his chest. The Guardsman was barely aware of his action that produced the rifle before the bullet hit him low in the muscle wall of his stomach, throwing him back and clear from the path of Famy's sprint.

In front of him, as if in slow motion, the doors of the car were opening, the men in their suits jumping out. Unaware, they don't realize. The insane exhilaration that he had achieved surprise. Run, weave, duck, maintain the rhythm, give no one a clear sight. When do the bullets come? How long? The bundle in grey, half out of the car, helped by the darker suits, reluctant to come, slowing them down, impeding them. The first bullet spat into the ground close to his feet. Fools, idiots, crazy men, firing low. Half-way there. Sokarev in sight, his head clear, the body half-shielded by the men round him. The orange groves, upright, regimented, before the spring brings the sun of Palestine to make fertile their leaves and their fruit; merging together the fantasy of the trees and the sharpness of the men as he pounded his way forward.

More bullets now edging closer, the little puffs of nothing in the concrete, and the hostile, honed whine of the ricochets off the concrete. And the ranging blast, wide but creeping, of the big machine-gun. Sokarev near the steps, wrestling with the men round him. They taking him toward the plane. Doesn't want to go, the little bastard, wants to crawl and hide and bury himself. The moment to shoot.

In full stride Famy flung himself, arching forward in a swallow

275

dive, with a strange grace, on to the tarmac. His knees and elbows took the impact, ripping at the cloth that covered his body. The gun was at his eye, down the barrel, down the needle sight. Eyes smarting with the pain from the fall, blinking the moisture out. The man in the grey still struggling. He fired, finger released the trigger. Knew with that deadening instinct that he was wide, high as well, knew it even as he felt the jolt in his shoulder heard the empty clatter of the discarded shell case. A moment, breathtaking of silence, then again the machine-gun.

No more to see of Sokarev, so still everything in front of him, no man standing. Gone, all of them, at a stroke. Disappeared, vanished. At the steps no target.

Four in a burst they teach the soldiers to fire when they feed the belt into the machine-gun. More than that and the barrel waves too greatly for the accuracy to be maintained. One in the right foot, two in the calf, fourth in his hip. As if a man with a pickaxe was striking him. Not aiming at a rock face but a muscle, vulnerable tissue, and the delicacy of his flesh. There was nothing in his hands, only the flat oil-smeared concrete for his fingers to grasp at. The rifle was far to the front, pitched clear, beyond reach, beyond his chances of hope and salvation. In the distance, and to his ears the words echoed and had a strange quality, came the ordered shout, voice of command.

'Stop firing.'

Between them Jones and Elkin carried Sokarev up the flight of steps to the plane. The strength he'd summoned earlier to resist them had gone. Elkin at his shoulders, Jones at his thighs. Both men panting, and the narrowness of the steps preventing further aid.

Jimmy rose from his knees where he had taken cover in front of the scientist between the steps and the door of the car, and began to walk toward Famy. Slow paces, all the time in the world now, the end of the stampede. Around him soldiers were lifting themselves from their firing positions, uncertain what to do, and uneasy in the sudden silence. So many of them, and so many rifles and revolvers, and only this one enemy in contention.

He saw the eyes of the prone man still locked on his rifle, tantalizing, out of range, far from the capability of heroics. Jimmy swung his foot, lazily and without care, and kicked it

276

noisily into the middle distance.

'Good try, boy,' Jimmy said, quietly spoken, a private remark. Famy watched him, awkward from the ground, neck stretched back, face unmarked. 'Good try. Just not good enough.'

Jimmy raised his voice so the Arab could hear him.

'McCoy told us you'd be here. Told us this morning. We didn't think you'd get this far. But it wasn't far enough, boy. One shot you got off, just one. Way off target. Looked good, looked dramatic, but set yourself too much. Should have been an aimed shot. Never works, all the running around, not with a pop gun like that, anyway.'

He saw Famy smile, overcoming the pain, mouth moving but no sound.

'That was what they gave you, the M1? Not very generous, not very suitable. Would have liked something with a bit more guts, right, boy?'

Famy nodded, slight movement, agreement. As far round as his eyes could see the men were now advancing on him, soldiers and police, their guns no longer aimed. Pointed at the ground and the sky.

Jimmy put his hand in his pocket, under the cover of the cloth, and when it emerged the PPK was there. He saw Famy begin to squirm away, trying to move, but pinioned by the damage to his legs and his hip. Whimpering, like a dog that expects a beating but is too trained to run from the threat.

'Don't make it difficult, boy. You knew what it was all about when you came on the joy-ride. And you did well, considering.'

Jimmy fired into the centre of the pale brown forehead, below the clear white rim of the turban. Even with a moving target he was usually accurate.

The noise of the shot was drowned by the four fan jet engines of the taxiing 747.

From beside the car, still stationary, still with the engine ticking quietly over and with the front and rear doors open, Jones had watched it all. There had been words that he'd tried to say, some sort of call, helpless and faint, for Jimmy to come back, but the roar of the engines prevented his being heard by any other than those immediately beside him.

He had seen the pistol in Jimmy's hand, small and blurred in the distance but silhouetted as a recognizable shape against the great emptiness of the tarmac. He hadn't looked after that. The plane was turning toward the runway, its power rising into deafening, ear-blasting crescendo as it eased its way clear of the group of men with their dark suits and hardened eyes.

'Bloody good job and all,' muttered the Branch man, whose eyes had never wavered from Jimmy and who now stared over Jones's shoulder.

Jones swung back. Jimmy walking toward him now, the one he knew just by the name of Famy abandoned and unmoving behind the erect and brisk figure that was soon close enough for him to see the almost boyish grin of satisfaction that wreathed the mouth. Cat with the cream, thought Jones, as if he's scored a bloody try at Twickenham.

'Bloody good job, the way it should be every time,' the Branch man said again, and Jones bit on his lip, unable to speak his mind, out of step with the mood.

Well, they'd had their money's worth out of Jimmy-boy this time. Earned his retainer, hadn't he? There'd be a mass of paperwork to be getting on with, the predictable escape mechanism, and Jones went in search of a car heading for Central London. Knifing through his mind the continuous thought . . . it was what they'd wanted, it was what they'd asked for, those bloody politicians with their directives from on high, and they'd been gratified.

In the first-class cabin, occupying two seats at the rear, were Sokarev and Elkin. The pilot had swung the plane hard round and lined himself on to the 3600-metre-long Runway 5, given precedence over all other flights. Clearance from the control tower was immediate, and the aircraft hammered its way into the slight wind down 28L.

Just before the moment of lift off Sokarev whispered, straining to Elkin's ear, that he felt sick.

'Don't worry,' Elkin said. 'It's all over. It's finished now. We are going home. There is nothing more to fear.'

They were all going home. Mackowicz in the tin box on the freight deck beneath them, Elkin who had been his friend, Sokarev who had been his charge. The security man noted the pallor of the scientist, and the perspiration on his balding head and the way that he struggled to reach upward to direct the cold air nozzles toward his face. When they were airborne it would be easier. He told himself that, and settled back, deep, into the comfort of his seat.

At first the pains were slight and concentrated in the centre of his chest, but the nausea and desire to vomit were uppermost. As Elkin slept beside him Sokarev was able to worm a path over the legs of his bodyguard and into the aisle towards the lavatories. He'd had little food and his retching was painful and hard. By the time they were flying over the Mediterranean the pain was spreading in area and intensity, and still Elkin's eyes were closed, insensible to the outer world. When at last a stewardess noticed Sokarev's distress he was doubled up in his seat, his hands across his body. Over the loudspeaker system of the aircraft the chief steward called for a doctor.

Elkin stood out in the aisle now, for once helpless, unable to offer aid to the man he had been ordered to protect. The doctor reached low over the heaving form of Sokarev, whom they had stretched across the two seats, centre arm rest pulled out.

When he stood up the doctor, young and in a T-shirt displaying the name of Hamburg where he had been holidaying before joining the flight, asked if anyone were accompanying the passenger. 'He is subject to severe coronary attack?'

Elkin nodded, unable to speak, stunned at the revelation. Now of all moments . . .

'Has he been under strain?' The doctor's voice carried the hush of concern.

'He is David Sokarev.'

'I don't know the name, I have not been in Israel some weeks.'

'He is the one the Arabs tried to kill. At the airport and before that last night.'

'The reason for the troops? The passenger on the far side of the airfield?'

'Yes.'

'He has been under severe strain?'

'Total strain. They were trying to assassinate him.' Enough of the talk. There must be action that can be taken.

'He needs morphine,' said the doctor.

'And . . .'

'And I do not have morphine. I do not carry it with me.'

Elkin looked away from the doctor, down to the pain on the professor's cheeks. 'Call the Captain,' he said. 'Get him off the deck and here.'

The pilot, mid-forties, shirt sleeves, grey hair, a decision-maker, offered no options. 'We go for Ben Gurion. Lebanon and Cyprus are nearer, but are out. Beirut, obviously, Larnaca is too short for the plane. Athens might save a few minutes, but it's marginal and the facilities at home are superior. We have a little less than an hour till we are down. The necessary people will be waiting.'

The doctor said aloud as he bent once again over Sokarev, 'He is an old man to have gone through all this. Overweight, not equipped to take such turmoil. The bastards always hit when they are not expected.'

Elkin could not reason why he spoke. There was no need, no requirement, but he replied. 'We have known for some days that an attack was planned. The Professor has known too.'

'And you took him, and you exposed him? Knowingly you brought him to Europe? At his age, in his condition?'

'A decision had been taken.'

'There is no wound on him. Remember that. You and your people will have to make their own decision if he dies. You will have to know who killed him.'

There was darkness round the jet as it whispered on its way, ten miles every minute toward the coastline of Israel and the landfall.

On the intercom the Personal Assistant announced that the Prime Minister was calling from Downing Street. With resignation the Director General cleared the papers that obscured his note-pad, took in his hand a sharpened pencil, and raised the receiver of the telephone. He heard the Prime Minister being informed that the link was now through, that the other party was waiting. There was quiet in the room, fitting for the moment before the verbal

280

assault that he had anticipated and predicted to himself. It was an understatement that the Prime Minister was furious. Voice raised. The head of the Security Services held the telephone a clear inch from his ear.

'It was turned into a clear fiasco by your man.'

'In what way, sir?' Don't give the blighters an inch, don't get into the apology situation, don't make it easy for the inquiry.

'In what way? Because of what your fellow did on the tarmac. Right out there in the middle, with half the bloody world looking on.'

'You'll have to explain, sir.' Stall the inevitable. Let the heat cool, then counter-attack.

'Don't play the fool with me. Your man has executed – only word for it – this Palestinian, or whatever he was, right out there, in public . . .'

'Your instruction was quite clear, sir. You did not expect the Arab to survive our contact with him.' They'd be taping at Downing Street, nice to get that on the magnetic ribbon.

'Not like that. I didn't expect him killed like that, not . . .'

'He had grenades on him. Live and primed. He was still capable of using them. His hands were moving. He could have used the grenades.'

'You're justifying your man?'

'His target was still armed and dangerous. My operative made a quick and correct decision. More lives could have been lost if he had hesitated. He acted quite correctly.'

'It makes our position fearfully difficult.' Always the same with these politicians. Can't take it on the chin, can't ride a right hand, weakening already. The Director General had the telephone close again, against the lobe of his ear. 'The shooting of this fellow could have very grave repercussions.'

'I think our man would have felt that faced with the circumstances that confronted him the actual danger to life was of paramount importance when compared with the possible diplomatic repercussions.'

Abruptly and without further comment the Prime Minister rang off. The Director General waited for his line to clear then dialled the extension to Jones's office.

Long into the evening Jones sat in his office, alone at his desk.

The coffee in the beaker remained undrunk and sealed with a skin surface. Helen had gone now, eyes reddened and aware of the conversation he had had with Jimmy.

Sod it. Cock Robin kicked the fucking bucket. Bloody waste, a man like that going, getting the chop. Still full of sap, years more of it. Awkward bastard, couldn't deny that, but then Jones had always fancied he alone could handle him. Bloody-minded when he wanted to be, but not just now. Had gone with his own dignity, hadn't made a fuss, just let the blade run through the timber, and keeled over gracefully and without protest. Hadn't argued, just accepted it, made his excuses and disappeared out of the door toward the basement to check his gun in. Jones had seen him from the upper window walk out into the street and stride away toward the Underground Station. Could have had a car home, but not his style to ask for one, not when he'd just had the push. Typical of the way the bloody Department exists. DG couldn't do it himself, had to get a minion to scrub the dirty pants, rinse the unmentionable stains. Told him what to do, told him what the PM wanted, and he'd carried it out. To the letter, careful and in copperplate, he'd done it . . . and that was why Jimmy was walking home. On the scrap yard and the best man they had.

Didn't any of the stupid bastards understand the new warfare? Gone past, the Queensberry Days. No rules that governed this combat. Have to fight the McCoys and Famys with their own kind . . . Would they have left Sokarev half dead for an ambulance team to cart away? Would they, shit? He thought he'd never see Jimmy again. Wouldn't be the way of the Department for him to have further contact with a man he'd fired. Went back a long way, lot of years, lot of late nights and talk and togetherness. Now all screwed up because of a little swine from God knows where in a place called Palestine that doesn't exist.

When he telephoned home his elder son answered. Wife out at the Women's Institute Committee. They'd had their food before she went. Didn't think anything had been left for him. No reason why it should. It was a clear week since he'd last phoned and said he might not be home that night. It had been the best bloody week in his time at the Department and it had ended all loused up. And he scratched and worried at the irritation of his scars.

*

The detective had to screw his legs under the wooden chair to leave room for the nurses who worked round McCoy's bed. They fussed and pecked at their patient and then went in crocodile line out through the door. There was light from the car park outside and shadows thrown against the wall. For what seemed an age, frighteningly long to the policeman, the Irishman lay still, unmoving, unblinking on the crisp white of the bed clothes.

When eventually he spoke it was too dark in the room for the detective to see his face.

'What happened to him?' The words were slow in coming, spoken so faintly that the other man had to lean forward, cursing in his mind the murmur of the distant traffic.

'Did he make it?'

The detective was uncertain what he was allowed to say, and kept silent.

'Did he get the bastard?'

Conscientiously the words were written down.

'Did he get him? For Christ's sake, tell me.'

'He tried and he didn't make it. Shot a soldier, fired on the Israeli. Missed. He's dead now, they shot him on the tarmac.' From the bed there was a deep, heaved sigh, then only the regular, drug-controlled breathing. McCoy said nothing more.

Through the haze of images there was a certain hard-won precision. Of how the news would spread from Cullyhanna to Crossmaglen, what the talk would be in Forkhill and Mulaghbane, what the men would say in the hills round Slieve Gullion and Lislea as they nestled in the bracken and grass and watched and waited with their binoculars and their Armalites. And he felt against the clamminess of his arms the white tiles of the cell walls that would be his. There would be bars and heavy doors, and iron-shod feet, and uniforms, and he would slowly rot away, praying and hoping each night for the mercy of sleep.

Behind the barman and hidden by the inverted spirits bottles the radio played music from the BBC Northern Dance orchestra. Jolly and conventional and designed to cheer the customers of the pub. There was much noise in the 'Public', and the swill of beer before closing would soon be under way. There was talk of the day's affairs, not of the economy, not of inflation, not of sport, not of the boobs on the inside pages of the tabloids. Attention was gripped to the events of the airport. To be expected . . . the picture of the Agency man with his telephoto lens had made the final editions of the London evenings. Not much detail, but the figure on the ground, and the man above him with the gun were recognizable enough. The art department had helped with the gun. The photograph justified the headlines – 'Execution' and 'High Noon at Heathrow'.

Jimmy sat in the far corner, near the door, solitary, uncommunicative and now on his fifth double whisky. He was slumped low with his head close to the glass and his eyes deep in the amber, watching the stillness of the liquid, following its reflections, amused by the shapeless patterns of the bubbles that rose from the diminishing ice cubes. No bitterness. Just a sense of regret. Passing of time. Ending of an institution.

The barman rang the big ship's bell hanging above the polished counter.

'Last orders, gentlemen. Last orders. One more gulp for the road.'

Compulsive for Jimmy. Never could resist the last one. Had to have it, rain or shine, success or cock-up. He was on his feet, pushing with the throng, thrusting forward his glass with the rest of them. The signature tune of the news headlines rose and faded above the shouting and demanding. First words indistinct, drowned by the big man wanting the big round. Fatuous face, filled out with beer and distended sub-skin veins. Heard the word 'Sokarev'. Heard the words 'Heart Attack'.

'Shut up,' Jimmy yelled. 'Shut your bloody faces.'

A score of faces were turned on him, saw the power of his eyes, of his chin, of his shoulders.

'. . . an hour after Professor Sokarev had been admitted to the intensive care wing of a Tel Aviv hospital it was announced by the Foreign Ministry in Jerusalem that the efforts of doctors to save his life had failed. The Professor, who was aged 53, was one of the country's principal scientists working at the nuclear centre at Dimona in the Negev desert.

'In London, Scotland Yard have still not given any details on the unnamed security man who shot dead an already wounded Arab terrorist on the tarmac at Heathrow after the unsuccessful attempt on Professor Sokarev's life this afternoon. But our political editor reports that Government ministers are demanding disciplinary action against . . .'

284

His deep, raucous, baying laughter shook the bar. Head well back, face taking on the crimson of exertion, body shaking. And all around the faces of hostility and reaction.

'What's so funny about that?'

'Nothing to bloody-well laugh about.'

'Warped little bastard.'

'What's the matter with him? Half pissed.'

He ignored them with grand contempt. So bloody funny. Hilarious. Laughed till it hurt in his guts, till the pain came to his chest and was laughing as he stumped out into the coldness of the street. Cheated them all, you little bugger. Denied the bloody satisfaction to Famy and McCoy. Fucked the triumph of our side. What price now, Mr bloody Elkin, or Jonesey. How much champagne already downed, and what now? . . . A fair old belch there'd be back at the Department. And you, Jimmy boy. He screwed you, too, and after all that. All the bloody heartache, all the bloody pain. You screwed everyone, Dr Sokarev, sir. The whole lot of us. Both sides. Didn't know you had it in you, you crafty little sod.

The flat would be empty. There was no hurry to approach its loneliness, its vacuum. Slowly Jimmy made his way down the pavement, and the hiccups were intermingled with the laughing, and that soon faded to little more than a giggle.

Failure had been a familiar bedfellow. So many missions launched with high expectation, and rarely the wounding blow that they sought. Barely a fortnight without the young men departing for their objectives, erect in their confidence, and then hard on their heels the devastation of disappointment. Undisturbed beds, unused mess tins, shortened ranks on the morning parade. And when does frequency become inevitability? When does the dimness phase into darkness? When is there no longer hope of success? The leader of the General Command had been brought the transcript of the World Service news from London and had read without comment of the death of Famy, the survival of Sokarev, the flight of the El Al jet from Heathrow. He had walked into the sands seeking solitude and absence from the new recruits. It had been a good plan, he reflected, and he had sent good men, but it had been insufficient. He stood more than an hour as the dusk came down over the desert, so still that an earth-coated

285

mouse ran close to his feet as it meandered a path to the ambush of the adder. And the killing was quick; startled eyes, frozen movement, and the job completed. The land where the soft, and the gentle and the harmless did not survive. He yearned for the snake's speed and resolution, remembered the cold, unfeeling and mechanical strike of the reptile and craved the ability to impart the simplicity of that minute brain into the minds of the men who would leave the camp before midnight and drive in the jeep to the frontier and walk forward toward the minefields and the wire and the enemy.

When the night had advanced and the stars risen he made his way back to the camp and went and sat with the four who were eating together with their friends, perhaps for the last time. He hid his depression behind humour and quiet exhortation, and made no mention of the news from Europe. When the time came for them to leave he walked with them to the jeep and hugged them deep and kissed each on both cheeks, and watched the tail lights till they were too distant and had gone among the shallow hills. Afterwards, in his tent, he lay on the canvas bed and read again the operational plan on which they had been briefed. He was close to sleep when the old man pulled aside the tent flap and illuminated by a storm lamp came across the floor to him.

'They have been monitoring the Israeli broadcasts. Sokarev is dead. He died tonight in Tel Aviv . . .'

'From what?' The confusion of the leader showed. Half-sitting up in the disarray of his blankets he said, 'The reports made no mention of his being injured.'

'The Israelis say he was unhurt in the attack, but that he suffered a heart seizure on the plane.'

'So it was not us, not by our hand?' He sank back on to his roughened pillow, the momentary excitement extinguished.

'But he is dead.'

'But not at our hand.'

'We sought to kill him, and he is dead, and . . .'

'Listen, old man.' Weariness crept tantalizingly and irrevocably through him. It was not the time for discussion. 'Listen. His death is unimportant if it was not at our hand. We had to show we had the power to strike successfully at him. Instead we showed we were not capable. That is no victory.'

'We could say . . .' and the old man, mindful that he had been interrupted before and aware of the leader's failing attention,

286

let his words tail away.

'We could say nothing. To make people of whatever country, wherever in the world, aware of the mushroom clouds that can rise over our men and women and children then we had to be triumphant in our attack. We were not. The mission is over and completed. Sleep well, old man.'

When the light had gone and the tent flap had been folded back into place the leader turned toward the canvas side that was close to his face. And before he slept he thought of the lights of the jeep and the bright furnace eyes of the men he would not see again.